No.1 bestseller Mark Billingham has twice won the Theakston's Old Peculier Award for Best Crime Novel, and has also won a Sherlock Award for the Best Detective created by a British writer. Each of the novels featuring Detective Inspector Tom Thorne has been a *Sunday Times* bestseller, and *Sleepyhead* and *Scaredy Cat* were made into a hit TV series on Sky 1 starring David Morrissey as Thorne. Mark lives in North London with his wife and two children.

Also by Mark Billingham

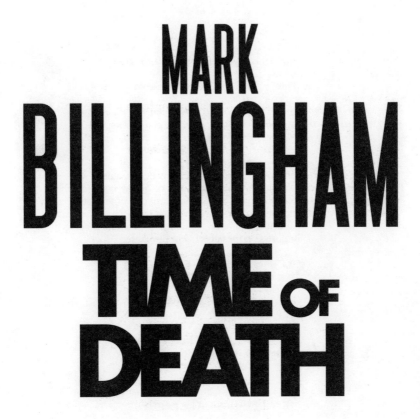

# MARK BILLINGHAM

# TIME OF DEATH

Little, Brown

LITTLE BROWN

First published in Great Britain in 2015 by Little, Brown

Copyright © Mark Billingham Ltd 2015

The moral right of the author has been asserted.

A CIP catalogue record for this book
is available from the British Library.

Hardback ISBN 978-1-4087-0481-3
Trade Paperback ISBN 978-1-4087-0482-0

Typeset in Plantin by M Rules
Printed and bound in Great Britain by
Clays Ltd, St Ives plc

Papers used by Little, Brown are from well-managed forests
and other responsible sources.

MIX
Paper from
responsible sources
FSC
www.fsc.org  FSC® C104740

Little, Brown
An imprint of
Little, Brown Book Group
100 Victoria Embankment
London EC4Y 0DY

An Hachette UK Company
www.hachette.co.uk

www.littlebrown.co.uk

For Caroline Braid. She knows why.

# PROLOGUE

# EVERYONE, EVERYBODY

He's sitting in the only half-decent café there is, drinking tea and picking at a muffin, when he sees the car slow down and pull over to the kerb on the opposite side of the road, and watches a girl, just like the one he's been thinking about, walk up to it, smiling, as the passenger window glides down.

Of course she's smiling, she knows the driver.

Why wouldn't she smile?

Now, she's leaning down towards the open window. She tosses her hair and grins at something the driver says; pushes her shoulders back, her chest out. She nods, listening.

He finishes the muffin, closes his eyes for a second or two, enjoying the sugar rush. The rush upon the rush. When he opens them again, the waitress is hovering, asking if she can take the empty plate away, if he needs another tea.

He tells her he's fine and says, 'Thank you.'

She knows his name of course and he knows hers. It's that kind of place. She starts to talk, high-pitched and fast, something about the river that has burst its banks again a dozen or so miles away, how terrible it must be for those poor people living nearby. All that filthy water running into their living rooms. The stink and the insurance, the price of new carpets.

He nods at the right moments and says something in return, one eye on the car and the girl, then looks at the waitress until she takes the hint and wanders away with his empty plate.

The girl stands up and steps back on to the pavement, casts a glance each way along the street as the driver leans across and opens the passenger door. Even though she knows him, trusts him, she knows equally well that she shouldn't get into his car, not really. She's not worried about anything bad happening, nothing like that would ever happen here. She probably just doesn't want to be seen doing it, that's all, doesn't fancy the dressing-down she'll more than likely get from the 'rents later on.

Cradling his mug, he inches his chair a little closer to the window and watches without blinking. He's enjoying her few seconds of caution, and the fact that it *is* only a few seconds, that there's not really any good reason to be cautious, makes him think about what it's like to live here, just how long it's been since he moved out of the city.

The reasons he came to this place.

A jolt to begin with, no question about that. A city boy all his life, then waking up to the whiff of cowshit. Birds he couldn't name and bells singing from fields away and several weeks until he realised that the sound he *wasn't* hearing was the blare of car horns from drivers every bit as stressed out and pissed off as he used to be.

The feel of the place though, that was the main thing. The community spirit, whatever you wanted to call it. It was what he supposed you'd describe as tight-knit ... well, relative to what he'd been used to anyway. The people here weren't living in each other's pockets, not exactly, but they were aware of one another, at least. The size of the place has a lot to do with it, obviously. With that closeness and sense of concern. With the whispered tittle-tattle and the perceived absence of threat.

There was still trouble, still drunks around on a Friday night, of course. There was no shortage of idiots, same as anywhere else, and he knew that one or two of them could easily have a knife in his pocket or might fancy taking a swing because they took a dislike to someone's face. But it hadn't taken very long before he knew most of their names, who their friends or their parents were.

The girl pulls the passenger door closed.

Her head goes back and he can see that now she's laughing at something as the driver flicks the indicator on and checks his mirror. She reaches for the seatbelt like the good girl she is. Like the good girl all her friends, her teachers up the road at St Mary's, her mum and dad and brother know her to be.

She knows the driver and he knows the driver and the driver knows the waitress and the waitress knows the girl.

That's how it is here. It's why he likes it.

He drains his mug and turns at the door to wave and say goodbye to the waitress, before stepping out into the cold and standing beneath the awning, buttoning his jacket as he watches the car disappear around the corner.

It's the sort of place where everyone knows everybody else's business.

But they don't know his.

# PART ONE

# ALL LOVELY AND SCREAMING

# ONE

'So, a big Sunday roast?' Thorne had asked. 'That kind of thing?'

'And a cream tea on the Saturday with a bit of luck.'

'No mooching around in antiques shops.'

'No mooching.'

They stopped, holding their breath as they listened to Alfie coughing in the next room. Thankfully, he stayed asleep.

Thorne adjusted his pillow. Sniffed. 'A decent pub with a toasty fire.'

'I bloody well hope so.'

'And definitely no walking?'

'Only as far as the pub.'

Thorne had grunted cautiously and pulled Helen closer to him, thinking about it. 'Just the weekend though, right . . . ?'

Now, on their first night away, a month after those tentative and delicate bedtime negotiations, walking back to their hotel after dinner in a more than decent pub, Tom Thorne decided that he'd got off reasonably lightly. It had taken a good deal of organisation, not to mention the calling in of several favours from sympathetic colleagues, to co-ordinate the holidays they were both due and he knew that Helen had been angling to spend at least a week of it holed up in the Cotswolds.

'It was nice food, wasn't it?' Helen asked.

'Yeah, it was all right.'

She shook her head. 'You miserable old git.'

Thorne could see the sly smile, but had no way of knowing that Helen Weeks too thought she'd had a result. Thorne was not the most adventurous of souls. He was still uncomfortable spending time south of the Thames, so she knew that, given the choice, he would rather stick needles in his eyes than spend precious free time in the countryside. Just hearing the theme tune to *The Archers* was normally enough to give him the heebie-jeebies.

'Home-made chutney and bloody am-dram,' he'd said once. 'I couldn't care less.'

All things considered, she had decided that a weekend – a *long* Valentine's Day weekend – was a fair return for the time spent trying to persuade him that it would be good to get out of the city for a few days. A few days on their own, before they'd head off somewhere good and hot for a week; a nice resort with a toddlers' club, where they could really kick back and do sweet FA until they were due back on the Job. The 'no walking' agreement had been a sacrifice she was prepared to make and the somewhat contentious 'mooching' issue had been worth giving ground on. That said, she had her walking boots stashed in the boot of the car and there *was* a nice-looking antiques shop on the main road. Helen took a gloved hand out of her pocket and put her arm through Thorne's. She felt quietly confident that the four-poster bed that was waiting for them back at the hotel might lead to the re-opening of discussions.

'I'll accept the *miserable*,' Thorne said. 'But less of the *old*.'

They turned on to the cobbled side street that led to their hotel. Halfway along, a middle-aged woman passed by with a spaniel that appeared to be feeling the cold every bit as much as

Thorne and Helen were. Thorne smiled at the woman and she immediately looked away.

'See that?' Thorne shook his head. 'I thought they were supposed to be friendlier in the countryside. I've met serial killers who were friendlier than that. Sour-faced old bag.'

'You probably scared her,' Helen said. 'You've got a scary face.'

'What?'

'If someone doesn't know you, that's all I'm saying.'

'Great,' Thorne said. 'So, that's miserable, old and scary.'

Helen was grinning as Thorne stepped ahead of her and shouldered the front door of the hotel open. 'Those are your good qualities.'

Inside, Thorne smiled at the teenage girl behind the reception desk, but did not get a great deal more in return than he'd got from the old woman with the dog. He shrugged and nodded towards the small lounge bar. 'Quick one before bed?'

'I think we should head up,' Helen said. 'Maybe have a quick one *in* bed.'

'Oh . . .'

'Or a slow one.'

Thorne's hand moved instinctively to his gut. He was suddenly regretting the decision to eat dessert. 'You might need to give me twenty minutes.'

'Lightweight.'

'Fifteen, then. But you'll have to do all the work.'

Helen walked towards the stairs and, as Thorne turned to follow her, he caught the eye of the girl behind the desk. He guessed that she had overheard, as she had suddenly managed to find a smile from somewhere.

Thorne was in the bathroom when Helen called him. He was brushing his teeth, smiling at the orderly way in which Helen had

11

laid out the contents of her washbag, replacing the range of complimentary toiletries that had already been secreted in her suitcase.

'Tom . . . '

He walked back into the bedroom, still brushing. He spattered his Hank Williams T-shirt with toothpaste as he managed a muffled 'What?'

Helen was sitting on a padded trunk at the end of the bed. She nodded towards the TV. 'They've made an arrest.'

They had been following the story for the past three weeks, since the first girl had gone missing. It had all but slipped from the front pages, had no longer been the lead item on the TV news, until the previous day when a second girl had disappeared. This time the missing teenager had been seen getting into a car and suddenly the media were interested again.

Thorne walked quickly back into the bathroom, rinsed and spat. He rejoined Helen, sat next to her as she pointed the remote and turned the volume up.

'It was always on the cards,' Thorne said.

Helen would have been keenly monitoring such an investigation anyway, of course. As a police officer who worked on a child abuse investigation team. As someone all too aware of the suffering that missing persons cases wrought among those left waiting and hoping.

As a parent.

This one was different though.

On the screen, a young reporter in a smart coat and thick scarf talked directly to camera. She spoke, suitably grim-faced, yet evidently excited at breaking the news about this latest 'significant development'. Behind her, almost certainly gathered together by the film crew for effect, a small group of locals jostled for position in a market square that Helen Weeks knew well.

This was the town in which she had grown up.

The reporter continued, talking over the same video package that had run the night before: a ragged line of officers in high-vis jackets moving slowly across a dark field; a distraught-looking couple being comforted by relatives; a different but equally distressed couple being bundled through a scrum of journalists brandishing cameras and microphones. The reporter said that, according to sources close to the investigation, a local man in his thirties had been identified as the suspect currently in custody. She gave the man's name. She said it again, nice and slowly. 'Police,' she said, 'have refused to confirm or deny that Stephen Bates is the man they are holding.'

'Ouch,' Thorne said. 'Right now there's a senior investigating officer ripping some gobshite a new arsehole.'

'Leak could have come from anywhere,' Helen said.

'Not good though, is it?'

'Not a lot anyone can do, not *there*. Somebody knows somebody who saw him taken to the station, whatever.' Her eyes had not left the screen. 'It's not an easy place to keep secrets.'

Thorne was about to say something else, but Helen shushed him. A photograph filled the screen and the reporter proudly announced that this picture of the man now being questioned had been acquired exclusively from a source close to the family.

'Another "source",' Thorne said. 'Right.'

Helen shushed him again. She stood up slowly and stepped towards the screen.

It was a wedding photograph, a relatively recent one by the look of it, the happy couple posing outside a register office. The groom – a circle superimposed around his head – in a simple blue suit, grinning, a cigarette between his fingers. The bride in a dress that seemed a little over-the-top by comparison.

Thorne said, 'Looks like a charmer—'

'Shit!'

'What?'

13

'I know her.' Helen jabbed a finger towards the screen. 'I was at school with her. With the suspect's wife.'

Thorne stood up and moved next to her. 'Bloody hell.'

'Linda Jackson. Well, she was Jackson back then, anyway.'

'Are you sure?'

Helen nodded, stared at the screen. 'We were in the same class ...'

They watched for a few minutes more, but there was nothing beyond the same news regurgitated and once they had run out of horrified locals to interview and began running the same footage for a third time, Helen wandered into the bathroom.

Thorne turned the sound down on the TV and began to get undressed. He shouted, 'She looks seriously pleased with herself, that reporter. Obviously reckons she's got a promotion coming.'

Helen did not respond and, a few minutes later, as Thorne was climbing into bed, she came out of the bathroom. 'I want to go up there,' she said.

'You what?'

'I want to go home.'

Thorne sat on the edge of the bed. 'Why?'

'Think about what she's going through. She's got kids.' She waved a hand towards the television. 'They said.'

'Hang on, how long's it been since you've seen her?'

'So?'

'Near enough twenty years, right?'

'I know what that place is like, Tom.'

'Well, I can't stop you, I suppose, but I think it's stupid.'

They said nothing for a few long seconds. Helen opened the wardrobe and took out her suitcase.

'Hang on, you're not thinking of going *tonight*?'

'Dad's expecting us to be away all weekend,' Helen said. She opened a drawer, took out a handful of socks and underwear and

14

carried them across to the case. 'So there's no problem looking after Alfie.'

'I know, but still.'

'We can be there in an hour and a half . . . *less*.' She went back for more clothes. 'There's not going to be any traffic now.'

Thorne got off the bed and grabbed one of the two towelling dressing gowns that had been hanging inside the wardrobe. It was too small, but he pulled it on anyway. He placed himself strategically between Helen and her suitcase. 'You've got no family up there any more, right? Where do you think you're going to stay?'

'I'll sort something out.'

'The place is teeming with coppers and reporters. You wouldn't find anywhere tonight even if you went.' He waited, relieved that she seemed to be thinking it over. 'Why don't we do this tomorrow?'

She nodded, reluctantly. 'I'm going though.'

'If that's what you want.'

Helen took another look at the TV. There still appeared to be nothing new to report. She walked back towards the bathroom, stopped at the door.

'You don't have to come with me, you know.'

'I know I don't, but what am I going to do here on my own?'

'You could go home,' Helen said. 'Hang out with Phil for a few days.'

'Let's talk about this in the morning,' Thorne said.

'You mean talk me out of it?'

'Well, I *do* think it's a stupid idea.'

'I don't care.' Helen was about to say something else when her mobile rang. She stabbed at the handset and answered in a way that Thorne had become used to; the voice tightening a little. Helen's sister, Jenny. Thorne was not her favourite person and the antipathy was entirely mutual. Much of the time, Helen could

15

not bear her sister either, impatient at being patronised by a sibling two years younger than she was.

'Yes,' Helen said. 'I saw it. I know . . .' She rolled her eyes at Thorne and walked into the bathroom, closing the door behind her.

Thorne lay on the bed, nudged the volume on the TV back up. The reporter was talking to the studio again.

'It's hard to describe the atmosphere here tonight,' she said. 'There's certainly a lot of anger.'

Thorne could hear Helen talking in the bathroom, but could not make out what she was saying.

The reporter was winding up, the crowd behind her larger now than it had been minutes before, the wind whipping at the ends of her scarf. Her voice was measured, nicely dramatic. 'With two girls still missing and one of their own being questioned in connection with their abduction, the tension round here is palpable.' She threw a look over her shoulder. 'This is a community in shock.'

Thorne watched as the woman attempted to sign off, struggling to make herself heard above raised voices from nearby. Something about 'our girls' and 'justice being done'. Something about stringing the bastard up.

He reached behind him, punched up the pillow.

It was not the holiday he'd had in mind.

# TWO

They drove towards the M40, north through Oxfordshire on small roads crowded with mud-caked Chelsea Tractors, negotiating Saturday morning shoppers as they skirted Banbury. The bad weather had not let up since they'd set off. It was certainly looking like they would be on the road for rather more than the hour and a half it might have taken the night before.

'A week in the sun's sounding better than ever,' Thorne said. He turned from the curtain of rain draping itself across the bonnet of the BMW and glanced across at Helen in the passenger seat. 'What about Portugal? Or Tenerife, maybe?' Another look. 'Dave Holland's always banging on about Tenerife.'

Helen just nodded, her gaze fixed on the shops and houses, the rain-lashed walls and hedges that drifted past. Since checking out of the hotel, after a disappointing breakfast and a tetchy exchange with the hotel manager, she had said very little. She had spent half an hour on the phone before breakfast making arrangements, but since then had seemed preoccupied. As determined as ever to make the trip, but clearly apprehensive about what awaited them when they reached their destination.

On the radio, the news led with the latest from Polesford.

Police were still refusing to confirm the identity of the man they had taken into custody but were, they said, continuing to question him. A senior officer made a short statement. He said that further information would be released, but only when the time was right. Echoing the reporter from the previous night's television news, the correspondent talked at some length about the atmosphere in the town.

Anger, fear, profound shock.

Above all, she said, there was an overwhelming sense from the residents that theirs was not the sort of town where things like this happened.

Back in the studio, they began to talk about the latest unemployment figures and Thorne turned the sound down. 'So, come on then, which is it?' he asked. 'A small town or a large village? You always talk like it's a tiny place.'

After a few seconds, Helen turned to look at him as though she had failed to hear the question. Thorne shook his head to let her know it wasn't important. He switched from the radio to the iPod connection and cued up some Lucinda Williams. He nudged the wiper speed up, spoke as much to himself as to Helen.

Said, 'Yeah, bit of sun sounds good.'

Ten minutes later, making slow progress on the crowded motorway, Helen turned and said, 'It's actually a small market town. We lived in one of the villages just outside. There's a couple of them a mile or two in each direction.'

'Sounds nice,' Thorne said.

'It's not like where we were yesterday.'

'No antiques shops to mooch around in?'

She barked out a laugh. 'Hardly. It's like the Cotswolds, only without men in garish corduroy trousers, and a few more branches of Chicken Cottage.'

18

'So, not all bad then.'

Thorne indicated, took the car past a van that was hogging the middle lane. He gave the driver a good hard stare as he pulled alongside.

'I thought it was exciting when I was fifteen,' Helen said. 'Polesford was where we used to go on a Friday or Saturday night.'

'Bit of clubbing?'

She shook her head. 'As much snakebite as we could afford, a bit of dope in the bus shelter.'

'Never had you pegged as a wild child.'

Helen smiled for the first time since they'd set off. 'Just a crafty Woodbine in your day, was it? Or were cigarettes still rationed?'

Thorne returned the smile.

The fact that he was closer to fifty than Helen was to forty was something they joked about now and again. He would pretend to be outraged that she could not remember the Sex Pistols. She would ask him what it had been like to see Bill Haley and the Comets. Based on a few things Helen had said, Thorne guessed that the sort of comments her sister and several of her friends made about the age gap were rather more cutting.

'It used to be nice,' Helen said. 'There's *still* some nice bits. There's an abbey.'

Thorne adopted his best countryside accent. 'Ah ... too many incomers, was it? City folks coming in and ruining the place?'

'It's not in *Cornwall*,' Helen said.

'Only rural accent I can do.'

'Well, promise me you won't do it again.' She turned towards the window. 'It's Warwickshire, for God's sake. It's more like the accent on *The Archers*, if anything.'

'Oh, God help us,' Thorne said.

An hour later they turned off the motorway and within ten minutes were driving slowly along the main street in Dorbrook, two miles south of Polesford. The village in which Helen had spent her childhood. Thorne could see what she had meant earlier. There was rather more stone cladding on display than thatch and Thorne doubted that, come the summer, there would be too many roses growing over the doorways.

They turned off the main street, slowed as they drove past a terrace of cottages that looked to be from the twenties or thirties. Cars were parked within a few feet of most front doors, their wheels on the pavement to allow heavy vehicles to get past. There was a convenience store opposite, a Chinese takeaway, a small area of asphalt adjacent, with a swing-set and roundabout.

Helen pointed, said, 'There.' Thorne slowed still further. 'That was our house.' She pushed the button and her window slid halfway down. 'Front door was red when we lived there. There wasn't double-glazing.'

Thorne stopped the car, checked to see there was nothing behind him. 'You want to get out and have a look?'

'It's pissing down.'

'There's an umbrella in the back,' Thorne said. 'Go on, knock on the door, see who's living there.'

Helen shook her head. She was still staring. 'No, I don't think so.'

'Only take five minutes.'

'Who the hell wants a stranger banging on their door?' She put the window back up. 'Poking around.'

'I just thought you'd be interested.'

'I want to go and see Linda,' Helen said, a little sharply. She turned and looked at Thorne, blinked slowly and found a half-smile. 'What's the point, anyway?'

The rain was easing as they drove the few miles further on, along snaking lanes with high hedges or skeletal trees pressing in on either side. It had more or less stopped completely by the time they reached the river, drove across the bridge into Polesford and Thorne saw the sign for the Market Square.

It might have been a Saturday, but Thorne guessed that the place was still somewhat busier than it would usually have been. Not that too many of the residents appeared to be there in search of second-hand paperbacks or knock-off perfume or whatever else was on offer. Though a handful of traders had braved the bad weather in the hope of brisk business, they hardly looked to be beating away customers with sticks. Most were sat nattering and drinking from flasks, beneath striped plastic awnings that snapped and danced in the strong wind.

Hard-faced, disappointed.

Instead, the people milling around the fringes or gathered together between the stalls in threes and fours, seemed more intent on animated conversation. Thorne watched them as he drove slowly around the square. He saw men huddled, smoking in doorways. A trio of young women, each nudging a pushchair back and forth on the spot. He saw the nodding and shaking of heads, the pointing fingers, and, even from a distance, it felt as if the entire place was humming with the jibber-jabber, the feverish speculation.

'Paula said we should try and park behind the supermarket.' Helen pointed to a turning and Thorne followed her instructions. 'We can walk from there.'

Paula. The woman in whose house they would apparently be spending the night, though Thorne had still not found out very much about her, or about her relationship to Helen.

'You were right,' Helen had said that morning, packing quickly after a spate of calls. 'Can't even find a hotel room in Tamworth, never mind in town. But I think I've managed to sort something out . . .'

Approaching the supermarket, they saw a patch of fenced-off waste ground next to the small petrol station opposite. A man in a dripping green cagoule, the hood tight around his face, stood at the entrance. He nodded towards the sign that had been taped to a makeshift barrier. ALL DAY PARKING £7.50.

'Jesus,' Helen said. 'Making money out of it.'

They stared as they drove slowly past. Plenty had already coughed up.

'He won't be the only one,' Thorne said.

Driving into the legitimate car park behind the supermarket, they saw that half the available space had been coned off and was taken up by a large number of emergency vehicles. Vans, squad cars, an ambulance they knew would be there on permanent stand-by. Helen got out and shifted a cone or two, allowing Thorne to park up next to a pair of police motorbikes. While Helen was grabbing an overcoat and umbrella from the back seat, Thorne moved the cones back into position and laid a printed card on the dashboard.

METROPOLITAN POLICE BUSINESS.

They walked for a few minutes in silence, past a school and a small parade of shops. The streets were less busy, but there were still one or two people standing outside their houses, chatter spilling from the open doorway of a crowded pub.

The house where Linda Bates – who used to be Linda Jackson – lived was in a terrace not unlike the one Thorne and Helen had stopped to look at in Dorbrook. There were a few photographers outside, but the majority of journalists were elsewhere, knowing very well that the family of Stephen Bates was no longer in residence.

The circus had moved on.

To all intents and purposes, the property now belonged to Warwickshire Police, and would continue to do so until the painstaking process of forensication was complete. Thorne and Helen walked by on the other side of the road, weaving between the handful of smartphone-wielding onlookers. Crime tape ran around the house, which was obscured from view at the front by

22

a phalanx of police and forensic service vehicles. A uniformed officer stood at each corner of the muddy front garden, two more in the middle of the road to ensure that nobody unauthorised got too close. The coppers looked thoroughly bored, though Thorne noticed that at least one had the good grace to try to disguise the fact when a camera began flashing a few feet away.

An old man with a wire-haired terrier said, 'Aye aye, there's PC Plod on the front of the *Daily Mail.*'

Helen nodded, but she and Thorne both knew that when it came to the media, the big boys would be where the action was.

The house Thorne and Helen were on their way to.

It was the kind of estate that had probably caused outrage among more long-standing residents, when it had been built twenty or thirty years earlier. A bulb-shaped collection of identical properties, most already old before their time. Ugly garages and red-tiled roofs that bristled with satellite dishes.

As well as the predictably large gathering of reporters, there were a good few members of the public huddled close together on the pavement opposite number six. Mums, dads, young kids perched on shoulders. Thorne could hear the muttering increase in volume as he marched up to the cordon and showed the uniformed officer his warrant card. Camera shutters began to click behind them as Helen produced her ID and the pair of them ducked beneath the tape and walked towards the front door.

It was open by the time they reached it.

The female detective was in her late twenties. Tall and skinny; ash-blonde hair pulled back hard, dark trousers and jacket. Thorne guessed that she was a family liaison officer, that there would probably be more inside, uniform and CID.

She looked at Thorne and Helen, faces and warrant cards, then waved them inside.

As soon as the front door was shut, she turned and introduced

23

herself as DC Sophie Carson. Her manner was not especially collegiate and if she had taken in the details on the warrant cards, she did not seem overly concerned that she was talking to two officers of senior rank. She waited for Thorne and Helen to say something and, after a few seconds of awkward silence, she stepped away from the door.

'Should I know about this?'

'Nothing to know about,' Thorne said, thinking that if the woman *was* a family liaison officer, she might want to ratchet up the warmth a notch or three. He introduced himself quickly and when Helen had done the same he said, 'Detective Sergeant Weeks is an old friend of Linda's.'

'Right,' Carson said. She nodded, but looked uncertain and as she moved towards them, her hand drifted automatically to the Airwave radio clipped to her belt.

The hallway was narrow and Thorne and Helen had to press themselves against the stairs to allow the DC to get past. She knocked on a door and pushed it open. After a cursory glance into the room, she leaned in and mumbled a few words that neither Thorne nor Helen could make out, then nodded again to indicate that they could enter. She followed them inside and closed the door behind her.

A woman wearing jeans and a baggy sweatshirt sat leaning forward on a battered black-leather sofa, a teenage girl close to her. Two uniformed officers, a man and a woman, sat on hard chairs on the other side of the room. The remains of tea things were scattered on a low table between them: mugs, a carton of milk, an open packet of biscuits. It looked as if they had been watching television, though the sound was turned down.

Thorne and Helen stood side by side, waited. The room was overheated and stuffy and the curtains were drawn. Thorne could hear voices from somewhere above him; a radio or another television.

Carson nodded towards Helen. 'Says she's an old friend of yours.'

The woman on the sofa stared at Helen for a few seconds, then stood up slowly, her face creasing as confusion gave way to recognition.

'Helen?'

'I'll leave you to it then,' Carson said. She waved the uniforms out and one by one they stood up and trooped past her into the hallway. Thorne kept one eye on Carson as she followed them. He watched her key the radio and could hear that she was already reporting events to Operational HQ as the door hissed across the thick carpet and finally snicked shut.

A few seconds before Linda Bates rushed, sobbing, into Helen's arms.

# THREE

She tries to sleep, but not because she is tired.

Awake, it's cold, despite the thick coat that he let her keep, and there is not so much as a pinhole of light. The tape is still tight around her mouth and having lost the battle to control her bladder, she is starting to feel sore. It had warmed her a little at first, but quickly became clammy and cold. The floor is rough and wet beneath her backside and the pipe that she is chained to is ridged with bolts that press against her spine, even through her coat. It's been a long time since she was brought here. A day or two at least, she thinks. It's hard to tell when it's so dark, when there's no sound save for the drip and trickle of the water that's coming in. She knows she's below ground, she's certain about that much at least. He had given her enough of whatever was in that bottle to be sure that she would not fight back, but she hadn't quite been unconscious. She remembers being taken down out of the rain into the quiet and the stink. She remembers the strangest feeling that this was a place she knew, that it was somewhere she'd been when she was younger.

Awake, she is weak with hunger and her throat burns when she tries to swallow and though she knows there are things moving in her hair when she's asleep, running across her legs, anything is better than the pain that screams in her belly, the desperation for food that even the rank smell of the place cannot keep at bay for very long.

Awake, she suffers through every second of every minute alone and uncertain as to when the man who brought her here will be coming back. At first it was terror that he would come back, the thought of what he would do to her when he did. Now it is all about his absence. The thought of being abandoned in this place.

Awake, she tries to tell herself that it's some kind of attempt to break her spirit or whatever. That there *will* be food, but it will probably be offered in return for those things she's been so terrified about. But the offer won't be made until she's been sufficiently starved. Until she cannot possibly refuse it. Each time she hears something skitter and splash in the darkness, one of the rats she knows are down here with her, she wonders if the man is coming back. If somehow they can hear his footsteps far above them, feel them through the water up above, the damp, rotten fabric of the place. It never happens though. He never comes.

Awake, there is nothing to do but sit and listen and hum and weep and try to tell herself that there will be people trying desperately to find her. Nothing to do but imagine the hell her parents are going through. She moves, tries to get a little more comfortable. The chain is just long enough so that she can lie down. That's me being nice, he'd said. Last thing he'd said. No, that's not right, not quite the last thing. Apologies for the whiff, he'd said, climbing back up the steps.

The whiff . . .

Awake, she holds her breath and fights the constant urge to gag at the rank, meaty stench of it. She imagines that she can feel

27

particles of it moving against her face, that she is breathing them in through her nose.

She lies down, one arm beneath her head to keep her face dry.

There is so much she doesn't know or understand. So much she can only guess at and try to make sense of. But she knows she is not alone, not strictly speaking, anyway.

Awake, she knows there's a body down here with her, in the wet and the dark.

# FOUR

Thorne stayed at the house for another few minutes, but he felt awkward, and more than a little voyeuristic. He was starting to wonder why he had bothered coming at all. He had thought Helen would want the company, but it was quickly becoming clear that she did not really need it. That he was surplus to requirements. He told Helen that she should call when she was ready to leave and he would come back to collect her. She said that she would probably be there a while and would catch up with him later.

'It's a small place,' she told him. 'I'll find you.'

He did not speak to anyone else in the house on his way out. Sophie Carson was still on the radio.

The cameras went into overdrive as he walked out and several journalists shouted predictable questions at him as he ducked back beneath the crime tape and picked up his pace. He said nothing, kept his eyes forward. He doubted that he would stay anonymous for very long. Some eagle-eyed journo on a crime desk would almost certainly recognise him eventually. He had made the papers often enough himself, had been plastered all over them just a few months before.

When a prisoner he had been escorting had escaped. When four people had died. When Thorne had almost lost his closest friend.

He walked back to the centre of town and saw that most of the market traders had all but given up and were packing their things away for the day. It was starting to rain again. Walking along the high street, he could see that Helen had been right to say how little the place had in common with the middle-England market town they had left that morning. There seemed to be a proliferation of nail bars and hairdressers. There was an internet café and a small games arcade and Thorne counted four fast food outlets within fifty yards of each other. Not an antiques shop to be seen.

He stopped at a newsagent for a local paper and carried it across the street to a café called Cupz. He ordered coffee and a sausage sandwich and began to read. The first four pages of the newspaper were dominated by the latest on the missing girl and carried the now widely circulated picture of Stephen and Linda Bates on their wedding day. The headline was typically crass and undeniably powerful:

LOVE, HONOUR AND ABDUCT?

Several pages were devoted to the flooding in villages on lower ground to the north. There were pictures of the swollen River Anker, of dirty water lapping at front doors, of a family going to the shops in a small dinghy. The misery was only set to worsen, one story said, with more bad weather forecast and resources stretched to breaking point.

Thorne glanced out through the window, watched people hurrying to find shelter, the rain dancing off multicoloured umbrellas.

A young girl brought his food to the table. She nodded down at the newspaper in front of him. 'It's terrible, isn't it?'

'Which?' Thorne asked. 'The missing girls or the flooding?'

The waitress looked a little uncertain. 'Well, both,' she said. 'I mean, I'm obviously not trying to compare them. God knows what those families must be going through.' She reddened slightly. 'The families of those poor girls, I mean.'

Thorne took a sip of coffee which was not as hot as he, or anyone else would have liked. 'Did you know them?'

'I'd seen them both in here a few times,' she said. 'After school, groups of friends, you know?'

Thorne turned back to the front page of the newspaper and pointed at the picture from the Bates' wedding. 'What about him?'

The waitress pulled a face and shook her head. 'Thank God.'

'He hasn't been charged with anything,' Thorne said.

'He will be.'

Thorne took a bite of his sandwich and waited.

'Well, there were witnesses, weren't there? A couple of Poppy's mates saw her get into his car.'

Poppy Johnston. The most recent girl to have gone missing. Her name was still mentioned rather more often in the newspaper reports than the girl who had vanished three weeks earlier. Just 'Poppy' though now, even to those who had not known her personally.

'Doesn't prove he abducted her though.' Thorne looked at the girl, but she had clearly made up her mind.

'I meant to ask, do you want ketchup?'

'Brown sauce,' Thorne said.


When he had finished his lunch, Thorne walked back through the market square and followed the signs that led to the single-storey Memorial Hall just behind it. The building, adjacent to a small community library and health centre, had been commandeered and was now functioning as the Police Control Unit. Signs were prominently displayed near the entrance showing the

31

phone number for the incident room and there were uniformed officers talking to members of the public just outside. It was from the PCU that the search teams would be co-ordinated; volunteers organised, or more likely dissuaded, since their usefulness was often outweighed by their capacity to unwittingly destroy evidence. It was where locals would come to pass on information or share tittle-tattle, helping themselves to free tea and biscuits while they did so, and it was usually where the media gathered for any official press briefings.

Thorne wandered inside.

He had often heard stories about journalists who had returned from war zones, only to find themselves unable to handle the ordinariness of normal life and desperate to go back. There was, it seemed, a powerful craving for the rush that went with danger. It was a drug, pure and simple. Thorne would not describe his own feelings in quite those terms, but just sensing the excitement, the urgency around a major investigation such as this one, had already got those endorphins kicking in.

Driving from that twee hotel, he had told himself that he was doing no more than keeping Helen company, that this was nothing to do with him. It wasn't just a matter of jurisdiction either. He was supposed to be on holiday; a much-needed one since the events on Bardsey Island a few months before. He was rather better at kidding others than he was himself. That slow drive around the market square had been enough, and now the chatter in this place, the smell of stewed tea and damp uniforms, had got his blood pumping a little faster. It was a long way from a Major Incident Room back at home, but that buzz was universal. The urge to poke around and to get a taste of it all was as strong as a drowning man's impulse to push himself towards the surface.

Thorne simply could not help himself.

A uniformed officer, stocky and red-faced, stepped in front of him and asked if he needed any help.

'Can you tell me where they're holding Stephen Bates?'
Thorne asked.

The young PC sighed. 'Move along, would you, sir?'

It was Thorne's turn to sigh as he took out his warrant card.

'Oh. Sorry, sir.' An altogether different 'sir'. He stepped a little
closer and lowered his voice. 'He's at Nuneaton, far as I know.'

'Thank you.'

Thorne was about to walk away, when it suddenly dawned on
the PC that any detective involved in the investigation would
surely have known the answer to the question Thorne had asked.

'Can I see your warrant card again, sir?'

Thorne fished for it, held it close to the officer's face.

'Since when were the Met involved with this?'

'I'm just here to advise,' Thorne said.

'Right.' The PC looked dubious.

'Look, I know the guv'nor, all right?'

'And he would be . . . ?'

Thorne tried his best to look merely exasperated, while he
racked his brains trying to remember the name of the senior
detective he had heard talking on the radio. It came to him. 'I'm
a mate of Tim Cornish's.'

'Fair enough.'

'Happy?' The copper nodded and stepped away. 'Good lad,'
Thorne said. 'Now go and help some old people across the road
or something . . . '

Walking back to his car, Thorne began to feel guilty about the
way he had spoken to the young constable. He had long ago
resigned himself to the person the Job could so easily turn him
into; the side-effects of that buzz. The impatience, the intoler-
ance, the capacity to behave like a major-league arsehole.

He pulled out of the car park, turned the music up good and
loud and tried to forget about it.

# FIVE

Linda's daughter was sixteen and called Charli. 'That's how she prefers to spell it,' Linda had explained, shrugging: a powerless parent. The girl was taller than her mother and a little heavier, and unlike Linda, her hair was cut short and she wore a lot of make-up. She had not spoken, other than to murmur a small 'hello' when Linda had introduced her and, after several minutes staring into space, she got up and walked out of the room without a word. Helen could hear one of the officers in the hallway asking the girl if she was all right, but there was no response. Just the noise of heavy footsteps trudging upstairs.

'Danny's up there,' Linda said. 'Her brother. He's barely been down since we got here. Just to grab a drink or something to eat then he's away again. An officer brought them over a computer they could use, which was nice of him. Didn't have to do that, did he?' She looked at Helen. 'They took both the kids' laptops.' She shook her head, brushed something from her skirt that wasn't there. 'They took everything.'

'I know,' Helen said.

'You wouldn't believe the stuff they took. CDs, DVDs, the lot. Bags and bags.'

'I know,' Helen said again. 'I'm a police officer.'

Linda stared at her, opened her mouth a little, then closed it again.

'I'm not here because of that, though. I'm not working. I came because I saw your picture on the news and I thought you might need a friend.'

'Oh, you did?'

Helen saw how what she had said must have sounded. 'I mean, I'm sure you've got loads of friends, but . . . I thought I might be able to help.'

Linda nodded and leaned across to the table. She picked up a biscuit then put it back. 'I didn't know we were friends,' she said. 'How long is it since you left?'

'Twenty years,' Helen said. 'Good as.'

'And you've not been back?'

Helen shook her head.

'We had a school reunion. You could have come to that.'

'I wanted to . . .'

Linda looked as though she was trying to decide whether to believe Helen or not. Either she did, or she decided that it didn't much matter. 'It was a laugh, as it happens.'

'Maybe there'll be another one.'

Linda ran fingers through hair that was thick and frizzy, with a good deal of grey at the roots. Her face was drawn, the lines pronounced around her eyes and mouth. Her lips were cracked. Helen knew she had changed a good deal herself in twenty years, but the woman sitting next to her was barely recognisable as the smiling bride in the recent wedding photograph.

'Can't see either of us going now,' Linda said. 'Can you?'

They said nothing for a minute or more. Outside the officers were talking and suddenly music began to play upstairs.

Something with no words and a repetitive beat, like a racing pulse.

'God, I must sound like such an ungrateful bitch,' Linda said.

'It's fine.'

'No, really, I appreciate you coming. You didn't have to.'

'I wanted to.'

There was a knock on the door and a uniformed officer poked his head around it. He asked if anyone wanted more tea and they both said they did.

When the door had closed, Linda rolled her eyes. 'Bloody tea,' she said. 'I'm swimming in it. They teach you that, do they?'

'What?'

'At cadet school or whatever it is? If in doubt, make the poor buggers some more tea.'

Helen smiled. 'I know it must seem like they're just trying to pretend everything's fine, but it's not that. Sometimes it's just about being nice, but mostly it's because you don't know what else to do.'

'Yeah, fair enough.' Linda leaned forward again, took the biscuit this time.

Helen looked around the room. Like the sofa on which she was sitting, most of the furniture was modern, but well worn. There were colour prints in clip-frames on one of the walls; pictures of motorbikes and drag-racers. The carpet was light green and the curtains a darker shade with prints of leaves. There was a brownish, mock-marble fireplace containing a gas fire and the TV next to it, though certainly big enough, was not a make Helen had ever heard of.

'So, whose place is this, anyway?' she asked.

'Nobody's.' Linda popped the last of the biscuit into her mouth. 'Well, it was, but I don't know who they were. It was repossessed.' She shrugged. 'Whoever they were, they didn't have a lot of luck.' She puffed out her cheeks, clearly aware of the irony in what she'd said. 'I don't think we're doing a fat lot to change things.' Before Helen could respond, Linda looked up, brighter suddenly, as if fearful of bringing the mood down; of slipping back into a darker place she had been trying to avoid. 'How's your dad?' she asked. 'I always liked him.'

'He's fine,' Helen said. 'Awkward and ridiculous a lot of the time, but that's how they get, isn't it?'

'What about your younger sister? Jenny, was it?'

'Yeah, she's good. Married with a couple of kids.'

'You?'

'I'm good, too.'

'Any kids, I mean.'

'I've got a two-year-old.'

'Bloody hell, you left it a bit late, didn't you?'

'The job,' Helen said. 'Well, not just that, if I'm honest.' She grinned, thinking about her son, the rings he'd be running round her father by now. 'He's great, though. Keeps me on my toes, anyway.'

'And what about him?' Linda nodded towards the door. The last place Thorne had been standing. 'He your old man?'

'Well, we're not married,' Helen said. 'And he's not Alfie's dad.'

Linda waited, but Helen did not want to say any more. She could not be sure that Paul – the man with whom she had been living and who died while she was pregnant – was the father of her child. There had been an affair. A painful mistake that had not been fully rectified before Paul was killed, though it had been more than paid for since in shame and guilt.

And there was always Alfie.

'He's good with him though, is he?'

'Tom? Yeah, he's great. I mean we haven't been together very long, so it's still early days.'

'He a copper as well, is he?'

37

Helen said that he was.

'Yeah, he's got the look.'

'And obviously I haven't?'

Linda cocked her head, studied Helen, as though trying to make up her mind. 'Maybe,' she said. 'Going that way.' She saw Helen's expression tighten a little. 'I'm only kidding.'

'I shouldn't really be surprised anyway,' Helen said.

'So ... London then, is it? Must be bloody rough down there.'

It seemed odd to Helen, that she was the one answering all the questions, talking about her life. She guessed that Linda was finding that easier than saying too much about her own. Perhaps she thought that quite enough speculation about how her family lived was going on already. Either way, whatever put Linda most at ease was fine with Helen.

'It's not too bad,' she said. 'Actually, it's no worse than anywhere else. I work with kids, so—' She stopped, aware that she was venturing into territory that might make Linda uncomfortable. If that was the case, the woman showed no sign of it.

'Got to be worse than here though, surely, the crime.' Another shake of the head, another biscuit. 'Well, up to now, anyway.'

'What about you?' Helen asked. 'How long have you been married to Stephen?'

Helen saw Linda stiffen momentarily at the first mention of her husband's name. Linda cleared her throat. 'Oh, only five years,' she said. 'He's not from round here. Charli and Danny aren't his kids.'

Helen held herself back from asking how he was with them, but Linda clearly understood the cause of the silence. 'And yeah, he's great with them. Like they're his own, since it's pretty bloody obvious what you were thinking.'

'Sorry,' Helen said. 'I haven't come back here so I can put my foot in my big fat gob and make you feel awkward, honestly. I'm just here to keep you company. If that's what you want.'

Linda's expression softened. 'That'd be good.' She nodded towards the door. 'That lot aren't exactly a bundle of laughs.' She raised a hand before Helen could say anything. 'I know, I know, they're just doing their job. Did they really have to go through the bins though, take the rubbish away? Did they really need to take my dirty washing?'

'It's about being thorough,' Helen said. 'The smallest thing can make a difference, you know? Can help get to the truth.' She took a moment, as she really wanted Linda Bates to fully appreciate what she was going to say next. 'Right now, they're as interested in proving your husband's innocence as his guilt. You need to remember that, OK?'

Linda thought for a few moments, then sat back as though she was finally ready to discuss the thing that everyone else in town was talking about. 'He didn't do it, you know?' She took Helen's hand and looked hard at her. Her fingers dug in. 'He didn't take those girls.'

There was a knock, and a cheery voice announced the arrival of tea.

Helen nodded, because there was not a lot else she could do.

# SIX

Once Bates and his solicitor were seated again, DI Tim Cornish closed the door and joined them at the table. Pulling back a chair, he began removing photographs from a green, cardboard folder. He took a last drag on his e-cigarette – the tip glowing blue – then slipped it back into his top pocket.

He said, 'So, are you done? We ready to get back to it?'

The duty solicitor was a young woman called Tasmina Khan. She had never had any dealings with Cornish before; had never been involved in anything with as high a profile as this investigation already had. If she was daunted by the new-found notoriety of the man sitting next to her, she did not show it.

She sat back in her chair. 'My client has every right to consult with me privately whenever either of us chooses.'

'Goes without saying,' Cornish said. 'Just keen to crack on, that's all. Sooner we can get this done, the sooner Mr Bates can get back to his family.' He smiled at Stephen Bates. 'To Linda and the kids.'

Khan said nothing. A look was enough. She knew as well as

Cornish did that Bates was unlikely to be seeing his wife and kids any time soon. The twenty-four hours after which Cornish would have to charge or release would be up quickly enough, but she knew that he would apply for a custody extension. She knew that he would get it.

Cornish pressed the red button on the twin CD recorders built into the wall of the interview room. He glanced up at the camera in the corner, then across at the two-way mirror, through which he knew that a small crowd of colleagues and senior officers would be watching.

'Interview with Stephen Oliver Bates, recommencing at one thirty-seven pm on Saturday, February 14th.' He identified himself and Khan, his fingers fluttering at his top pocket. 'So, this was the first time you had given Poppy Johnston a lift? The day before yesterday. You'd never seen her before?'

Bates hesitated, glanced at his solicitor.

'It's a simple enough question, Mr Bates.'

Stephen Bates was forty-three years old and had described himself to the police as a self-employed painter and decorator. He was pale-skinned, with dark hair that was shorter than it had been in his wedding photograph and a scruffy, gingerish beard. He was skinny; his jeans baggy on him, as was the paint-flecked polo shirt he had been wearing when police arrived to arrest him at his home the previous afternoon.

'Seen her, yeah,' Bates said. His voice was quiet and flat. A Midlands accent. 'Said hello or whatever. That's all though.'

Khan turned to look at him, and Cornish understood that after more than half an hour together, solicitor and client discussing the options available, the issue of whether it was in Bates' best interests to say anything at all had still not been resolved.

It was good to know.

'And she was in your car for what, fifteen minutes, you said?'

'Less than that. Ten minutes or something. I told her I couldn't take her all the way, but I was happy to run her as far as the bus stop on the Tamworth Road.'

'Good of you.'

'It was on my way. It looked like it was about to piss down.'

'What did you talk about?'

'I can't remember.'

'School? Boyfriends?'

'I can't remember. Maybe.'

'And you didn't stop anywhere on the way?'

'I took her to the bus stop, I told you. Straight there.'

'Because you thought it might rain,' Cornish said.

'Hasn't bloody stopped raining, has it?'

Cornish grunted, looked down at his notes. 'Tell us again what you did after you dropped Poppy off.'

Bates sighed, but his answer sounded confident enough. 'Went to check out a job in Atherstone. Woman over there wants the outside of her house painting, so I drove across to have a look.'

'Half six at night? Pitch black by then.'

'I just needed to see the house, that's all. Get a rough idea of what I'd be dealing with.'

'And after that?'

'I told you, I went for a pint at a pub up the road from there. You can check all this with Linda.'

'We did and that's certainly what you *told* her you were doing when you rang her.' Another glance at the notes. 'At about six thirty, she says.'

Bates looked pleased, as if that should be enough. 'There you are.'

'She told us that you didn't get home until after nine.'

'I had a couple of pints and something to eat. Truth is I wasn't in a rush to get back. Me and Linda had a row that morning, so ...'

'A row about what?'

'Can't even remember now. Sod all, probably.'

'Problem is, Mr Bates, we can't find anyone in the pub who can verify that you were there.' Cornish leaned back. 'Landlord doesn't remember you.'

'Why should he?' Bates said. 'Place was rammed. There was a big game on the TV.'

That much Cornish had been able to verify. Chelsea had beaten Arsenal at Stamford Bridge. There had indeed been a bigger than average crowd in the pub that night.

Cornish took three photographs of Poppy Johnston and lined them up. In two of them, she was posing with friends in a local pub. The most striking of the group; blonde and blue-eyed, made-up and dressed for a night out. The newspapers had chosen to use the slightly more demure photograph of the girl in her nicest party dress. Fresh-faced with a smile that was rather more tentative.

Cornish tapped at a photograph. 'She was all dressed up on Thursday night, wasn't she? Glittery top and a short skirt. "Too short", her dad says.'

'I don't remember what she had on,' Bates said. 'She was wearing a coat anyway. One of those padded ones.'

'So that wasn't why you stopped and offered her a lift then? It wasn't because you liked the look of her? Because she looked nice?'

Bates shook his head.

'Just out of the kindness of your heart.'

'I've told you,' Khan said to Bates. 'You do not have to answer these questions if you don't want to.'

Bates was looking at Cornish. 'You want me to say I don't think she was pretty, that it? Jesus, I'm not blind, am I?' He stabbed at the picture. 'Course she's pretty. That what you wanted to hear?'

Cornish let it hang for a few moments, then produced another photograph and slid it across the scarred black tabletop. 'Could you please look at this photograph?'

After a second or two, Bates looked down, but not for very long. 'Have another look,' Cornish said. When Bates looked again, Cornish leaned towards the CD recorder. 'Mr Bates is looking at a photograph of Jessica Toms.'

'That's the first girl who went missing.'

'You knew her?'

'Only to say hello to.'

'You say hello to a lot of fifteen-year-old girls, do you, Mr Bates?'

'I would advise you to ignore that,' Khan said.

'You see people around, don't you?' Bates said. 'In the pub, in the street or whatever.'

'Did you give Jessica Toms a lift on January 23rd of this year?'

Bates shook his head. 'I did not.'

'Was Jessica Toms ever in your car?'

'No.'

'You quite sure about that?'

'She was never in my car.'

'You know we've got your car, obviously.'

'If you damage it, you'll pay me for that, right?'

'You know we'll be taking it apart and that if she *was* in your car, we're going to know about it? She'll have left a trace behind, everybody does. These days, somebody so much as kisses you on the cheek, we can get DNA from it. Just saying, in case you want to think about your answer a bit more.'

'I never gave her a lift.'

'You remember where you were on January 23rd?'

'Do you?'

'I'm not the one under arrest,' Cornish said.

'No, I can't remember,' Bates said. 'Working.'

Cornish nodded, happy enough to leave the question, though

44

not for very long. He glanced towards the two-way mirror, then picked up the photograph of Jessica Toms. He looked at it himself for a few seconds, then laid it down again. 'So, you think *she's* pretty?'

'Do *you*?' Bates gave the first hint of a smile, pleased with himself.

'Really? You think you're helping yourself, just throwing questions back at me like that?'

Bates scratched at his beard, the smile gone, uncertain.

Khan leaned forward. 'OK, I'd like some more time to confer with my client in private.'

'Again?' Cornish asked.

Bates turned to the solicitor. 'Thing is, if I say nothing, they think it's because I've got something to hide.'

'It's your right to refuse to answer questions.'

Bates wasn't listening. He nodded at Cornish. 'That's right, isn't it?'

Cornish held up his hands.

'If I don't answer you, just say "no comment" or whatever, you think it's because I must have done it.'

'That's not how it works,' Khan said.

'Miss Khan is spot on,' Cornish said. 'You can sit there all day long and say bugger all if you want, but we are allowed to draw what's called an *adverse influence* from that.' He waited, to be sure that Bates understood what he meant. 'You remember what was said to you when you were arrested?'

'I've been through all that with him,' Khan snapped. 'I have done this before.'

Cornish leaned closer to Bates. 'About you failing to mention something which you later come to rely on in court? About how that can harm your defence?' He sat back, folded his arms. 'But it's entirely up to you, obviously.'

Bates looked at the table.

Khan turned towards him again. 'When we were talking earlier, Mr Bates. Remember those three options?' She spoke with an emphasis that bordered on the patronising. Cornish was happy to see that she had clearly decided her client did not know decent advice when he was given it. Or else was simply not the sharpest tool in the box. 'You can answer questions if you wish, or you can say nothing. The third option is to provide the police with a written statement and then refuse to answer any more questions after that.'

'Yeah, I remember,' Bates said. 'You think I should do that? The last one you said?'

'As of this moment, that would be my best advice.'

Cornish had to stifle a smile. *Because you're worried about looking guilty, but you can't keep your big gob shut . . .*

Bates thought for another few seconds, then nodded and looked across at Cornish. 'I'll go for that one.'

The DI looked up at the mirror again. 'Your call,' he said.

Cornish terminated the interview for the record and began gathering up the photographs. He picked up the picture of Jessica Toms and looked at it again. He said, 'She's really pretty. Any idiot can see that.' He reached for his e-cigarette. 'To be honest, Stephen, I would have been a damn sight more suspicious if you'd said she wasn't.'

# SEVEN

Thorne had been waiting in the incident room at Nuneaton station for half an hour or so when Cornish finally appeared. Thorne didn't mind. He had passed the time talking to as many of those working on the investigation as possible, and, even if he had not learned anything that he did not already know, the coffee was an awful lot better than the stuff that got dished out back at Becke House.

It became quickly obvious to him that the whole place was rather better equipped than the incident room he was used to at home. The computers seemed newer, the whiteboards somehow whiter.

The place did not feel quite as tired.

It was probably just a question of funding, of a more efficient distribution of available funds. Or perhaps the place just saw a lot less action. Waiting for Cornish to arrive though, Thorne could not help asking himself how much of it was down to the drive and energy of the people working here. Were some of those he worked with at home just burned out, or going through the motions these days? He wondered if the day would come when he would be guilty of 'phoning it in' and if it did, would anyone tell him. Holland? Probably not. Hendricks . . . ?

Yeah, he thought that Phil Hendricks would.

Cornish was easy enough to spot. The one being collared by a member of his team the moment he walked in, staring across while the man who was waiting to see him was helpfully pointed out.

Thorne stood up and Cornish beckoned him over; waved him into an office.

'You had coffee? I'm always gasping after a couple of hours in the bin . . . '

Cornish was a few years younger than Thorne and if there was any grey in his hair he had covered it up skilfully. He was compact and wiry, like a flyweight. In his smart suit and rimless glasses, Thorne thought that he looked like an accountant, albeit one who might knock you out if you questioned his calculations.

As soon as he had sat down behind a cluttered desk, Cornish said, 'What took you so long?'

Thorne took the chair that had been offered. 'Sorry?'

'I've been expecting you, Mr Bond!' Cornish took an e-cigarette from his pocket and puffed on it theatrically.

Sophie Carson had clearly given her boss a complete report on the visitors from London.

'No big deal,' Cornish said. 'We've got a few like you round here. Can't take a day off.'

'I'm just killing time,' Thorne said.

'Course you are.'

'Don't know what else to tell you.' Thorne laughed, but the remarks had hit home. Was that what he had become? 'Job-pissed' was what they called the type Cornish was talking about, what Thorne called them too. It was usually aimed at those who played everything by the book, who would rather die than deviate

48

from procedure. Thorne knew that wasn't him, but he was clearly finding it hard to leave the job behind. Perhaps being 'job-pissed' wasn't the issue. Maybe it was just a question of what your tipple was.

Some people could only get pissed on the hard stuff.

Thorne pointed to the e-cigarette as Cornish took another hit. 'What are those things like?'

'Bloody gorgeous when you're not allowed the real ones.' Cornish leaned across and passed it over for Thorne to examine.

'It's heavy,' Thorne said.

'The Federation's trying to get them banned in police buildings.' He leaned forward again to take it back. 'But right now . . .' he took another drag, blew out the smoke or steam or whatever it was, 'it's absolute bliss, mate. You a smoker?'

'Was.'

'You should try one of these.'

'Can't risk it,' Thorne said. 'A few days on those, I'll be in the garden first thing in the morning with a packet of Silk Cut.'

'Addictive personality.'

'Probably,' Thorne said. He glanced around. Even the office was nicer than the one he shared most of the time. There was a window, for a start. He sniffed, caught a hint of aftershave that he guessed had not been purchased at the market. 'So, how's the search going?'

'It's a bloody nightmare, mate,' Cornish said. 'The flooding means we can't search as thoroughly as we'd like in some areas. Can't search at all in a few. River's so fast, it's hard for the divers. We've got the fire brigade helping us out with specialist equipment, but we're still stretched when it comes to manpower. This weather makes it all more of a pain in the arse than usual.'

'Haven't you got the army helping out as well?' Thorne had read about it in the paper. 'In the flooded areas, I mean.'

'Yeah, but they can't handle some of the extra crime that we've got to sort out.' He saw the confusion on Thorne's face. 'Not the girls ... we've got looting from some of the abandoned properties. Scumbags driving down from Ashby and Burton-on-Trent in four-by-fours. Obviously the missing girls are our main concern, but somebody's got to deal with that.'

'You think that's where they are?' Thorne asked. 'In the river?' There was no need to go around the houses. Both men had dealt with enough cases like this one. Whatever might be said publicly, both presumed that Poppy Johnston and Jessica Toms were already dead.

'Be the obvious thing,' Cornish said. 'It's flowing so fast in some places, they'd be gone like that.' He clicked his fingers and sat back. 'In terms of getting rid of bodies, weather like this is pretty useful.'

'You would have thought one of them might have turned up by now though,' Thorne said. 'Even if it's fifty miles away.'

Cornish looked at him, rolled his e-cig between thumb and first finger. 'You would have thought.'

'So, what's Bates saying?' Interesting as it was to learn about e-cigarettes and the logistic headaches that went with searching in bad weather, this was what Thorne had come to find out.

Cornish would have known that too, but appeared to have little problem with it. 'He's given us a written statement,' he said.

'Saying?'

'Saying he picked Poppy up when she was heading to Tamworth on a night out and took her as far as the bus stop three miles out of town. About half past six, he reckons, though he can't be sure. We've checked and the bus she would have been waiting for stopped there at six forty-seven. She wasn't there to get on it. So, he doesn't deny picking her up ... well, he can't really, there were too many people saw him do it. He wasn't exactly hard to find.'

50

'Why was she going to Tamworth?'

'She was going to a bar. Meeting a boy.'

'Really?' Husbands, wives, lovers; always people worth looking at.

'It wasn't a serious thing, not according to any of her mates. Just someone she'd got off with a couple of times.'

'He's in the clear, I take it.'

Cornish nodded. 'He waited for her, then went to the bar anyway. Plenty of people can verify he was there all night. So, that leaves Mr Bates, right at the top of a list of one.'

'What about the first girl?'

'Says he never picked her up, so we're obviously keen on finding something in his crappy little car. A spot of blood, a strand of the girl's hair, whatever. They're pulling out the stops, top priority, all that, so I'm hoping to get some good news later tonight or first thing in the morning.' He hit the e-cig again. 'I get that, I'm charging him.'

'If not?'

'I'm probably charging him anyway. We've got enough.'

'Sounds about right.' Thorne saw Cornish glance at his watch. 'Listen, I'll get out of your way . . . '

'Bloody nasty,' Cornish said. He puffed out his cheeks. 'That business on the island.'

Thorne took a second or two to respond, tried not to look quite as taken unaware as he was. 'Oh, yeah.'

'Seriously. You OK?'

The physical injuries Thorne had sustained on Bardsey Island were not life-threatening. A patch-up at a local hospital and a couple of sessions in the dentist's chair had been all that was needed. He knew Cornish was not talking about that.

He stood up, blinked away an unwelcome image. 'I'm fine,' he said.

'Glad to hear it.' Cornish stood up too.

'I like your suit,' Thorne said, keen to take the conversation elsewhere.

Cornish glanced down, as if he'd been unaware he was wearing it. He nodded and pointed at Thorne, the e-cigarette still held between his fingers. 'Well, clearly you flash boys in the Met can get away with not making quite as much effort.'

Thorne shrugged. He was wearing jeans and Timberlands, a brown leather jacket over a thick sweater, that dirty Hank Williams T-shirt underneath. 'I'm on holiday.'

'Oh yeah, course you are. I forgot.' Cornish smiled. 'You and your girlfriend. Detective Sergeant Weeks works on a child abuse investigation team, that right?'

Thorne blinked again, said nothing. Cornish had not got that information from the newspapers.

'You should make the most of your free time,' Cornish said. 'I mean, obviously the weather's a bit grim, but there's still plenty to see around here.' His eyes widened at an idea. 'Actually, there's a fantastic model village in Shuttington if you're interested.'

'Not sure that's my thing,' Thorne said.

Cornish laughed. 'Yeah, well it's under a foot of water at the moment anyway. Like a real village has been hit by a giant tidal wave or something. Bloody freaky, actually. Seriously though, head off from Polesford in any direction, get well away from the flooding obviously, there's some gorgeous countryside. Good as anywhere.'

'Maybe.' Thorne put his hands in his pockets and took a step towards the door.

Cornish came around his desk, his hand outstretched. 'Stay in touch though, whatever,' he said.

He looked as though he meant it.

# EIGHT

They thought it was all about sex, they always did.

The fact that both girls had been nice to look at was important of course, but not for the reason the police thought. Hard for your average copper to see that, he knew very well. To lift their head out of the gutter.

In the car, both of them had been talkative, happy to rabbit on about all sorts; at least they were up until that moment when he'd slowed down and turned off the main road. Quiet as mice once he'd pulled over and switched the engine off. The look on their faces right then, *that* was what it was really about. Right then, of course, the girls thought it was all about sex too. Bracing themselves for it, like there weren't any men around who could possibly have anything else in mind.

Men, obviously, always men.

That's who the police would have been looking for from the off and it made sense, statistically if for no other reason. There was always the odd one of these when a woman was involved, or sometimes a woman helping a man, but they could be fairly confident they were after a bloke. The father was usually the first one they cast a beady eye over. Course it was. Too many times in the past when dads had blubbed away for the cameras, voices breaking as they stared out and begged for the safe return of their precious darlings, knowing full well they were safely tucked away in the loft or pushing up daisies on the allotment. Had to be sure that wasn't likely to happen, didn't they? So, the dad would have to be eliminated before anyone else was looked at.

It was probably how this one had gone, he reckoned. At least until the second girl, when witnesses had come forward, the ones who'd seen Poppy getting into the car. All change then, of course, once they had a description, a few letters from a registration plate. Just coppering by numbers from that point. Then it would be about the tech stuff: the search for fingerprints and DNA, the trawling through computer files, all of that.

Sex would come up again then, more than likely. The things they discovered. Skeletons more likely to be found on a hard drive than in a cupboard these days.

He wasn't going to deny that it was there in the mix.

He'd certainly felt *something*, turning to look at those girls, as they'd tried to shift back towards the passenger door. Coming down the steps to the first one, pushing the food towards her, whispering in the dark. The worst thing about what was happening now was having to leave the second girl; being unable to visit. How would she be feeling, stuck there on her own?

What would she think of him?

He sits and works everything through and wonders how much Cornish has actually got already. He thinks back, imagining what it would be like to be one of the coppers on the case. He takes each of those steps through the investigation since that first, frantic call from Jessica Toms' parents.

House to house, alibis checked, that nice close look at mum and dad.

Then there are the questions; the suggestions and the setting of traps. The words of wisdom from the duty solicitor.

Last of all, he asks himself if there's enough to bring a charge if those boys in the lab come up empty-handed for some reason. All hypothetical of course, but he would never have done any of this without a good deal of thought.

He's not worried.

He knows what they'll find in the car.

# NINE

Linda had been upstairs with her kids for fifteen minutes. Charli had not returned, Danny had not shown his face at all, and finally, the music that had been the soundtrack to conversation downstairs for the last couple of hours had been turned off. Helen guessed that Linda was trying to catch up on some much-needed sleep.

Helen stood, drinking tea in the kitchen with Sophie Carson and one of the uniformed officers, a much shorter woman whose name was Gallagher. With little else to do, the second PC had stayed in the living room to watch *Countdown*.

'I reckon she's dead to the world up there by now,' Carson said. 'I saw some tranquillisers.'

'You can hardly blame her,' Gallagher said. A harsh Scottish accent belied the woman's round, soft face, the smattering of freckles.

Helen nodded, thinking: Saw them or *found* them?

It didn't much matter. Helen knew that Carson and the other family liaison officers were doing a job that went far beyond the dispensing of tea and sympathy. That stuff was important, obviously, but primarily they were there as investigators. They were in the house to observe the way the family worked, in the hope that something they saw might indirectly help the inquiry. On a basic level, they were looking for signs of disharmony, anything which might suggest that the crimes under investigation had their root in something that was happening at home. It was established practice. It was crucial to establish anything his wife might know, or suspect, and studying the family would help them draw a clearer picture of the kind of man Stephen Bates was.

The same went for the children.

As someone whose job it was to catch those who abused children, Helen knew very well what else Carson and the others were on the lookout for. In a case of this nature, where the victims were children, it was important to keep a watchful eye on Bates' own; for any indication that the crimes for which he had been arrested might not be the first he had committed.

It was delicate and complex work. The immediate family of anyone arrested in these circumstances was unlikely to be behaving normally. Charli and Danny Bates would be traumatised, and that could manifest itself in moods or actions similar to those displayed by the victims of physical and sexual abuse.

It took training and experience to see the difference.

'I wonder if she was on them before,' Carson said.

Helen said, 'What?'

'The tablets.'

Gallagher nodded, as though this might be significant.

Though it would all have changed once the second girl had gone missing, Helen knew equally well that for the first few days after Poppy Johnston had disappeared, the police would have been watching *her* parents equally closely. That was the way it worked. You watched and you asked yourself simple questions.

How were things at home? Had the girl any reason to go missing and was it something she had done before?

Was she from a 'good family'?

Helen knew that, though they might use the excuse of statistics or simple experience, there were some coppers for whom it came down to prejudice, pure and simple. If they were looking for the missing child of Surrey stockbrokers with nice cars in the drive, those investigating would usually be more concerned than if the child's parents had blue-collar jobs or claimed benefits.

It was a largely unspoken protocol and one which always made Helen uncomfortable.

'What if she was?' Helen asked. 'I know plenty of people who need a happy pill or three to get through the day.'

Carson said, 'True,' and sipped her tea. 'More than a few coppers, that's for sure.'

'I think I'll stick with a large gin and tonic,' Gallagher said.

Helen laughed along, thinking about the bottle of Diazepam at the back of the cupboard next to her bed, the few tablets that were still left. She had taken the drug twice: once in the months after Alfie had been born and Paul buried, and later, for a few weeks following the armed siege during which she had been held hostage. An incident which had left her with a repeat prescription and a new partner in Tom Thorne.

She sometimes thought the two things complemented one another pretty well.

'You come back here a lot then?' Carson asked.

Helen shook her head. 'First time in a while.'

'No family left?'

'Not here.'

They all looked up automatically at a creaking from above them; the noise of someone turning over in bed.

'Must be weird,' Gallagher said. 'Seeing Linda again after so long.'

'I suppose,' Helen said. 'Circumstances don't exactly help.'

'What was she like at school?'

'I don't know . . . we were all a bit wild, I suppose. Growing up in a place like this, there's not a fat lot to do except drink as much as possible and chase lads. I seem to remember she did plenty of that.'

'And you didn't?' Carson asked.

'More than Linda did, probably.' Helen wrapped fingers around her mug, remembering. 'Listening to grunge in somebody's bedroom. Sneaking into some pub or other, dressed like a tramp with a bottle of cider in my pocket.'

Gallagher looked at Carson. 'What's grunge?'

Carson was younger than Helen, but even she looked askance at Gallagher's question. 'Bloody hell, maybe you should be upstairs with Charli, chilling to a bit of trance or whatever the hell that was.' She rolled her eyes at Helen, said, 'So, what's your mate doing? Thorne.'

It sounded an innocent enough question and Helen decided it was probably best not to let Carson know that Thorne was more than just a mate. 'No idea,' she said. Helen was not sure where Thorne was, but she was pretty sure he wasn't sightseeing.

There was another noise from upstairs. If Linda was asleep, it did not sound as if it was remotely peaceful.

'How long should we let her sleep for?' Gallagher asked.

The question was aimed at Carson, but Helen took it upon herself to answer. 'Long as possible,' she said.

'There's a statement at five o'clock. She'll want to be up for that.'

'I'll wake her just before then,' Helen said.

Carson leaned back against one of the worktops. 'Nothing earth-shattering, I don't suppose. Not heard anything that makes me think her old man's copping to anything.'

'You're presuming there's something to cop to.'

'Well, we haven't had forensics back yet, but I wouldn't bet against it.' She looked at Helen, saw something she didn't appear to like. 'You weren't here when we nicked him.'

'Go on then.'

'You get a sense, don't you? Somebody's innocent, they react like they are.'

Helen pretended to consider the theory for a moment or two. 'I've nicked people who've been abusing kids for donkey's years. Aggressive, predatory paedophiles. Then you turn up on their doorsteps and it's like you're arresting Mother Teresa.'

Carson wasn't having it. 'Bates didn't exactly look shocked, that's all I'm saying.' She glanced at the ceiling. 'Neither did *she*, come to that.'

'Well, we know he had the girl in his car, and he must know he'd been seen, so maybe he was expecting the knock.'

'Looked like more than that to me,' Carson said.

Helen carried her mug across to the sink and rinsed it out. She let the water run longer than was necessary and stared out through the back window. The heavy rain had petered out into drizzle. The beds were bare, but neatly enough laid out; the lawn overgrown and muddy in patches, but more or less squared away. The weather wasn't doing the garden any favours, but whoever had lived here, though they had clearly been unable to keep up their mortgage payments, had taken care of it.

'Do they ever cop to it?' Gallagher asked. 'Straight away, I mean, before there's a lot of evidence.'

'God, yeah,' Carson said. She was clearly someone who enjoyed bestowing the benefit of her experience on others. 'Some of them are proud as punch. Can't wait to spill their guts.'

Gallagher nodded slowly. 'Oh yeah, I suppose. The ones who enjoy it.'

'You worked on anything like this before?' Helen asked the PC.

Carson stared at her. 'You want to see her CV?'

'Only asking,' Helen said.

'Look, you might have rank on both of us, but as far as I understand it you're only here as a friend of Linda's, right?'

Helen nodded.

'Right. It's just that I'm not quite sure why you're suddenly quizzing officers about their job experience.' Carson smiled, quick and thin, her point made. 'That's all.'

'I'm just making conversation,' Helen said.

Gallagher shrugged, the freckles disappearing as she reddened slightly. 'I'm usually with the victims,' she said. 'Family that have lost someone or whatever. It's different being with the suspect's family, isn't it? I mean, you're not dealing with grief.'

Helen remembered the look on Linda's face when she had said that her husband was innocent. Helen did not know if it was true and she suspected that Linda didn't either. She could still feel those fingers digging in, nails bitten down to the quick.

Helen looked at Carson, then at Gallagher. 'Yeah,' she said. 'You are.'

# TEN

Thorne was not sightseeing exactly, but he wanted to see what the police had to say at the daily press statement and, with half an hour to kill before then, he decided to take another look around the centre of town. There were streets he hadn't got to yet. He wanted to get the feel of the place and see if he could locate any of those nice bits Helen had mentioned.

'Make the most of your free time,' Cornish had said.

Thorne fully intended to.

The high street branched off in two directions. Following one, he came to another parade of shops much like those he had seen already. He walked past a bookmaker's and a curry house, a pub called the Star with blacked-out windows, and, sandwiched between vacant premises, a milkshake bar that appeared to knock out tacky, reproduction Americana on the side. Cadillac-shaped mirrors; Stars and Stripes bunting; neon bar signs. Thorne stared in through the door and saw that, save for a young woman sitting behind the counter painting her nails, the place was empty. He wondered how either of the lines on sale kept the place in business.

A little further on, he stopped in front of a party shop called
Celebrations. The unlit window display was festooned with
heart-shaped balloons, cards, bows and teddy bears. Thorne
could only suppose that the place was closed as a mark of
respect; that even on what would otherwise be one of their
busiest days of the year, the owners had realised that people in
the town would have little to celebrate.

Gestures were important, Thorne thought. When there was
nothing else you could do.

He doubled back and turned on to the other branch of the
high street. It was immediately obvious that this was the older
part of town, or at least, the part that had yet to be developed. He
passed a tall and imposing building, looked up at the inscription
on the ornate brickwork and saw that it had once been a school.
The huge windows were boarded up and there had been some
half-hearted work with a spray-can on the ground-floor boards.
He wasn't altogether certain that gang-style graffiti had reached
Polesford yet, but if it had, TRACY IS A SLAG was a piss-poor
attempt at tagging.

On the other side of the street was a line of even older buildings; the walls uneven and criss-crossed with black or brown
timbers. Elizabethan, was it? Jacobean? Thorne was not even
sure which one of those came first, but he didn't need a history
degree to see that, with one exception, they were empty and had
fallen into serious disrepair. The property on the end had been
converted into a pub and, judging by the sign on the pavement
outside, the Magpie's Nest had a great deal to offer its customers.

*Quiz Night with GREAT prizes. Karaoke. LIVE Premiership
football and an EXTENSIVE menu.*

A glance inside was enough to confirm that these were the
things that the punters of Polesford wanted. The place was certainly doing a lot better than its rival just up the road. Thorne
wondered about nipping in for a quick half, but decided to wait.

A minute further on, a grand archway that was clearly even older than the buildings he had just been looking at led to the abbey that Helen had mentioned. Thorne looked up at the gargoyles above the abbey entrance, higher still to the flag of St George, snapping in the wind above the turrets. A noticeboard told him that parts of the building were from the thirteenth century, that the gatehouse itself was four hundred years older still. There were pictures of the famous stained glass windows in the baptistry, of tapestries, carved screens and memorial tablets. A notice explained that a full guide to the abbey's historic interior and the 'sensory garden' adjacent to it could be found in the visitors' centre.

Thorne did not bother going inside.

A long, straight track, no more than three feet wide and with spiked railings on either side, led Thorne to the river and he stopped on the bridge across which he and Helen had driven only a few hours before. He remembered Helen's silence as they had approached the place, the atmosphere in the car. She seemed determined, yet apprehensive. Like someone who knows they need to get rid of the pain, but still dreads the hospital visit. No, it wasn't quite that, Thorne thought. The truth was, he could only guess at what had been going on in Helen's head, because he was still not familiar enough with her moods.

He could almost hear Hendricks laughing. *Yeah, plus you're an insensitive bastard at the best of times ...*

It was probably just down to coming home, going back to your roots, whatever. There would always be mixed feelings, Thorne supposed. Only supposed, because he had never left home as Helen had done, never moved away from London. There had been many occasions when he'd wondered if he should have done.

Looking over the edge of the bridge, the green-brown water was spattered with drizzle, the odd plastic bag or bottle trapped in its currents moving quickly beneath him. The banks seemed solid enough, but not very far away, the Anker had joined with rising groundwater in low-lying areas and water every bit as uninviting as this was now sloshing about in people's living rooms. Thorne had seen a little of how the people of Polesford were handling a man-made tragedy, but he wondered how they would cope with the worst that nature could throw at them. He had a sense that, for all the talk of a town united in shock or outrage, it was not a place that took a great deal of pride in itself. He thought about those historic buildings, now derelict or ringing with the sounds of karaoke on a Friday night. He guessed that anyone trying to galvanise the locals for a 'Polesford in Bloom' bid would have their work cut out.

A community coming together in the wake of a terrible crime was a story that always played well. But Thorne had been rather more struck by those who seemed only to be thinking about themselves.

He looked at his watch.

He still had ten minutes before the press statement was scheduled.

Thorne walked across the bridge, away from the town centre, until he came to St Mary's. The school that both Poppy Johnston and Jessica Toms attended. It was very different from the building on the other side of the bridge, its honey-coloured brickwork now decorated with chipboard and sixth-form graffiti.

Grey breezeblock and glass. A desolate playground, dotted with puddles.

The gates were padlocked, and adorned with small bunches of flowers and soggy cards; a collection of sodden cuddly toys fastened to the metalwork or wedged between the railings. Thorne had expected no less. The shrine was always the first thing to appear these days, the most obvious manifestation of that 'community united in grief'.

Easy, knee-jerk . . .

He looked at the water running down the cellophane, dripping from the ears of a smiling, stuffed rabbit. Thorne tried to suppress his cynicism, if only for a while, and remind himself how important these gestures could be to people. The simple fact that for most, they were sincere and heartfelt.

There were more flowers, piled together at the bottom of the gates, most – other than those freshly laid – wilted or flattened. Petrol station arrangements.

Thorne crouched down to read some of the messages.

# ELEVEN

The curtains in the bedroom were drawn, but they were thin and badly fitted, and what was left of the day was bleeding through the fabric or creeping around the edges. Helen nudged one back and peeked to see what was happening outside. Almost immediately, a camera flashed and she quickly drew her head back. The fading light and poor weather had driven all but the most determined of the locals away and now, thankfully, the journalists were outnumbered by police officers, the more experienced among them having left to secure prime positions for the forthcoming press statement.

Helen saw a woman pointing up at the window, so she let the curtain fall back and stepped away. She walked across to the bed and bent to lay a hand on Linda's arm.

'Linda.' She waited a few seconds, then said it again, rubbing gently at skin that felt rough and cold. If Linda had pulled the duvet up to cover herself, it had fallen from her as she'd moved in her sleep. She was wearing a grey T-shirt and knickers. The rest of her clothes – shoes, jeans, sweatshirt – lay in a heap by the side of the bed. A black bra strap was visible, twisted across her pale shoulder.

Linda turned over slowly. Her eyes flickered for a few seconds then opened suddenly and she shifted away towards the wall. She closed her eyes again and groaned.

'Sorry. Forgot where I was for a minute.' Her voice was quiet and cracked.

'Don't worry,' Helen said.

'What was happening.'

Helen put a hand on her arm again. 'You want me to get you some water or something?'

'Jesus.' Linda leaned to turn on a lamp next to the bed. She raised herself up and looked around the room. A plain white wardrobe and matching chest of drawers. Linda's suitcases and several bin-bags stuffed full of clothes lay next to the door. 'And I thought *we* lived in a shithole.'

Helen laughed and when she stopped she became aware of voices in the next room. Charli and Danny. The conversation was just audible, a word or two, so Helen spoke quickly, suddenly worried that it might not be something she or Linda would want to hear.

'They're making a statement in five minutes. Thought you'd want to come down for it.'

'Is there much point?'

'I honestly don't know.'

'What do you think the chances are they'll say, "Sorry, we cocked this one up and we've arrested the wrong man"?' Mercifully for Helen, Linda did not let the silence that followed become too awkward. 'No chance, right?'

'They'll probably spend ten minutes saying precisely sod all,' Helen said. 'Enquiries are ongoing, grateful for the co-operation of the public, blah blah blah. Basically, they've got to give the press something.'

'The press have got *us*,' Linda said. She pointed at the window, at those she knew were gathered outside the house. 'We're the fresh meat.'

'I know it feels like that.' Helen was not sure if by 'us', Linda was including her husband or not. 'It's not for ever, trust me.'

Linda looked at her, and Helen could see how much the woman wanted to believe it, but ultimately could not. 'Christ, I'm tired. I'd happily knock myself out, try and sleep through all of it.'

Helen glanced at the bedside table but could see no sign of the tablets Carson had mentioned.

'I can't though, can I? I need to keep everything together for them two.' She nodded at the wall. 'God only knows what it's like for them.'

'Not easy.'

'What they're thinking.'

'They'll be worried about you, course they will.'

'They'll be worried about their dad,' Linda said quickly. 'That's how they both think of him and they'll be wanting to know when he's coming home.'

It was obvious that Charli and Danny were able to hear that their mother was awake, because the music began again. A low drone, then something that hissed like an amplified aerosol; a few angry squirts before the drums kicked in.

'All that teenage stuff,' Linda said. 'Tantrums and drugs and the rest of it. I can deal with that, but *this* shit . . . '

Helen laughed again and so did Linda, and, just for a moment or two, Helen saw the teenage girl she had known twenty years before: badgering her to pass the cider bottle; nodding out to Pearl Jam and Nirvana. 'Thank God I've got a while before all that starts.'

'It'll come quicker than you think.'

'Don't.'

Linda swung her legs off the bed. She rubbed some warmth

69

into her thighs, then leaned down to pick her jeans up. Helen bent to help her, got to them first and passed them over.

'You do cases like this, right?' Linda looked at her. 'Murders and rapes, I mean. Serious stuff.'

'I have done,' Helen said.

'They get it wrong, don't they? Sometimes, they just make a mistake and I mean we probably don't get to hear about most of them because nobody likes to look bad, do they? It happens though, right? Somebody just gets something wrong. Not their fault, they just get some duff information, whatever. All I'm saying, they make mistakes, don't they?'

Helen was not surprised at straws such as this being so desperately clutched at. Even with what little she had heard about the case against Stephen Bates, it was all they could realistically be.

She took a breath. 'Linda—'

Linda stood up quickly and stepped into her jeans. The volume of the music had gone up a notch and, without saying anything, she snatched up her sweatshirt and marched out of the room. Helen heard her open the door to the bedroom her kids were in and ask them to turn the music down. She didn't shout. She said 'please'.

A few seconds later, Linda appeared in the doorway shaking her head. She cranked up a smile that faltered a little at first, then set itself. The effort necessary to keep it in place, to hold the tears or the scream at bay, was obvious enough.

'Yes, we make mistakes,' Helen said. It was a simple truth. It did not change her belief that this time they had almost certainly got it right. 'We make lots of mistakes.'

# TWELVE

Everyone had gathered in the small car park that served the health centre and library as well as the Memorial Hall. It was also, according to a handwritten sign, the venue for a car-boot sale the following weekend. There were perhaps a dozen print journalists and half that number again working with cameras from the BBC, ITN, Sky and Channel Five. The day was dimming quickly and several technicians wielded hand-held lamps, ready to go.

Thorne stood behind the media line; just another interested observer, alongside those locals who had braved the cold weather instead of simply watching it at home on one of the rolling news channels.

'Bloody daft, all this. All these people . . . '

Thorne had found himself standing next to the same old man with the terrier who had spoken to Helen outside the Bates house. 'So, why are you here?' he asked.

The old man looked at him as though the question were ridiculous. 'Got to walk the dog.'

Thorne turned side on to the old man and took out his phone.

'Bit ghoulish though, wouldn't you say?'

With no way of knowing that he was a police officer, Thorne had to presume that the old man had him marked down as one of the ghouls. He heard him hawk spit up into his mouth.

'Won't hear anything we don't already know, I don't suppose. They won't be answering any questions.'

The expert opinion, casually rendered, suggested that it was not the first such event the old man had attended in the past few weeks. Clearly, his dog needed a lot of walking. 'So, what is it you think you know?' Thorne asked him. The dog was sniffing at his shin.

'He took those girls, didn't he? Bates.' He spat the name out, pulling the dog back towards him. 'They're still looking for them, because he won't tell anyone where they are. That sort never do though, do they?' He pointed, his hand shaking slightly, towards the cameras ahead of him. 'They want all this carry-on, don't they? They want to be famous.'

Thorne said nothing, though he could not deny that he'd come across a few of that sort. One man, especially. He held his breath as the roar of waves crashing against rocks rose suddenly above the low chatter of those around him. The scream of seabirds and the feel of something obscene between his fingers.

'We get a few visitors here.' The old man appeared not to care that the conversation had become a monologue. 'To see the abbey and what have you ... they'll be coming because of all this, now. Guided tours, I shouldn't wonder, to see where it happened. Not that some of the shopkeepers will be complaining. The restaurants.'

Thorne moved away. Dialling Helen's number, he walked back out on to the pavement.

'It's me,' he said, when Helen answered. 'Everything OK?'

Helen said that everything was fine.

Thorne told her where he was, stepped back as a white van

rounded the corner quickly and tore through a large puddle in the road.

'Yeah, we're about to watch it,' Helen said.

'How's it going?'

'Yeah . . . '

Thorne understood that Helen could not speak freely, so he didn't push it. He asked when she wanted him to come and pick her up.

'About half an hour?' She sounded tired, ready to call it a day.

The lamps were coming on behind him, so Thorne walked back into the car park. 'I'll see you in a bit,' he said.

Flanked by several officers and civilian staff, the Assistant Chief Constable for Warwickshire walked briskly out through the doors to the Memorial Hall. He was around the same age as Cornish; younger than Thorne. He was tall and skinny, an imposing and authoritative figure in his best dress uniform, though the cap was perhaps a little large for his head. As he took a notebook from his pocket, a smartly dressed young woman stepped ahead of him.

'Assistant Chief Constable Harris will now make a short statement, after which I'm afraid there will not be time to take any questions.' There were immediate grumblings, but the media liaison officer simply raised a well-practised hand. 'In an investigation of this nature, I'm sure you will appreciate that time is of the essence. So, thanks for your understanding.'

She smiled and stepped back, nodded to the ACC.

Harris glanced down at his notebook, then addressed the gathering without needing to look at it again.

'We are continuing to question a forty-three-year-old local man, in connection with the abduction of Poppy Johnston and the disappearance of Jessica Toms. As far as that investigation goes, all possible efforts are being made to ascertain their whereabouts and we remain hopeful of a positive outcome. Further information will be made available as and when it becomes appropriate to do so, but until then I can assure you that we are doing everything we can. We are giving this case the highest priority. Once again, I'm grateful to the residents of Polesford for their continued support and their co-operation in this matter. Thank you ...'

Short and sweet. The media liaison officer looked pleased.

The instant the ACC stepped back, the questions that he would not have time to answer began to be asked; shouted.

'Can you confirm that the man you've arrested is Stephen Bates?'

'Do you think the girls are still alive?'

'What's Bates saying to you ...?'

They were still shouting as the ACC and his entourage disappeared back inside the Memorial Hall, and they were still filming. Footage of the police refusing to answer questions was always nice to have.

Thorne watched the crowd begin to disperse as soon as the doors had closed. The lamps were switched off. Journalists and cameramen climbed into vans or headed away quickly in search of the nearest pub.

The old man and his dog walked past him. 'Told you,' the old man said. 'Bloody waste of time.'

Thorne turned and moved off in the other direction and found himself walking alongside one of the reporters who had been firing questions at him earlier, when he had left the house in which Linda and her family were holed up. The man had a recorder slung over his shoulder. He detached the microphone as he walked, wound the lead around it and shoved it into a rucksack.

He nodded to Thorne. 'What did you make of that?'

Thorne could not be certain that he had been recognised. The reporter did not seem to be paying a great deal of attention to him, professional or otherwise, and to all intents and purposes he was simply making conversation.

Thorne had nothing to say, one way or the other.

'Like the man said, you've got to stay hopeful, right?' The reporter heaved his rucksack on to his shoulder. 'That's the line most of tomorrow's papers are going to be taking, anyway. That's the big headline.' He raised a hand as if to write it in the air. '*Keep hoping . . .*'

Thorne jogged across the road and away in the other direction.

Walking towards the supermarket, where he'd left the car, he was thinking about those flowers propped against the gates of St Mary's school, some of the messages he'd seen.

Words that had faded, or run in the rain.

PRAYING FOR YOU.

ALL OUR THOUGHTS WHEREVER YOU ARE.

OUR LITTLE ANGELS.

The implication was clear enough, and sobering.

Hope was all well and good.

# THIRTEEN

Helen said, 'We didn't exactly have a lot of choice.'

Thorne grimaced. 'I'm starting to miss that hotel. Will we have our own bathroom?'

'You're welcome to sleep in the bloody car.'

With help from her sister, Helen had arranged to stay with a woman called Paula Hitchman, who lived on the outskirts of town, close to where housing gave way to farm and field. Paula had gone to the same school as Helen and Linda, but was two years younger, and though Helen vaguely remembered her, it was Jenny that she had been friends with. On the phone that morning, an enthusiastic Paula had said that she and her boyfriend would be working late, but that Helen and Thorne were welcome to get there whenever they fancied and make themselves at home. She told Helen that she would leave a key for them.

'Good of her,' Helen said. 'Considering it was Jenny she was mates with.'

'Your sister had friends?' Thorne asked.

'She was nicer when she was a kid.'

'I should hope so.'

'We were close, believe it or not.'

'So what happened?'

'You get older, don't you?' Helen looked at her feet. 'You grow apart.'

They had decided to get something to eat first. Helen didn't much like the look of the Punjab Palace, so with little other choice they had parked near the abbey and were walking back towards the Magpie's Nest to check out the 'extensive' menu it seemed so proud of.

'Still sounds like it might be a bit awkward, though,' Thorne said. 'If you don't really know this woman.'

'It'll be fine.' Helen stopped at the entrance to the abbey, stared through the archway.

'You want to go in?' Thorne asked.

It was almost six o'clock and bar a distant light near the visitors' centre, the building and surrounding grounds were in darkness. Helen shook her head and carried on towards the pub.

'Does she know you're a copper? Paula?'

'I'm not sure,' Helen said. 'Probably.' She stopped outside the pub and looked at the same chalkboard Thorne had seen earlier. 'Why?'

'Maybe she thinks she's going to get all the gossip.'

'Maybe she's just being nice.'

Thorne pushed the door open, let Helen go past, then followed her into the pub. 'Yeah, maybe,' he said.

The fabric of the building might well have been centuries old, but the interior had been gutted and the refit was far from sympathetic. A bar clad in polished pine and bog-standard pub furniture; the small dining room and snug brightly lit. One whitewashed wall was home to an arrangement of stuffed fish with engraved plaques beneath, the collection sandwiched between a hand-drawn sign advertising various pub events and a poster listing televised Premiership fixtures.

Thorne and Helen weaved their way through the crowd of drinkers to the dining area and sat at one of the four melamine-topped tables. The room smelled faintly of bleach and a Simply Red track was drifting from a speaker high up on the opposite wall.

'You sure about that Indian?' Thorne whispered.

The only other people eating were a family of four: mum, dad and two young children, who began bickering loudly as soon as Thorne and Helen sat down.

'I'm too hungry to care,' Helen said.

Thorne wasn't arguing. There was a top note of cooking fat just discernible above the smell of bleach and the music could usefully have been employed in a Dignitas waiting room, but he had eaten nothing but a few biscuits since breakfast.

One of the children at the next table let out a piercing scream. The mother caught Thorne's eye and mouthed a 'sorry'. The father turned and glared until Thorne looked away.

Thorne snatched up a menu; images of hearts and flowers at the top. With only a lone, semi-deflated balloon hovering halfway up the wall in the far corner, he guessed that the landlord was displaying a degree of sensitivity similar to that shown by the owner of the party shop; that he had scaled back the celebratory paraphernalia. It had clearly been too late to do anything about the special 'Menu for Lovers'. One quick look told Thorne that the pictures of hearts and flowers were the only things about it that were in any way special.

They each ordered steak and chips, a pint of Guinness.

The food was delivered with merciful speed and, as Simply Red gave way to Adele and then Mumford and Sons, Thorne and Helen put it all away in fifteen minutes, without a great deal in the way of conversation. The couple, whose kids were now both screaming, looked relieved when Thorne and Helen took what was left of their drinks and walked back towards the relative conviviality of the small bar.

'Told you we should have gone to the curry house,' Helen said.

'What?'

She grinned at Thorne's outraged expression and pushed him into the crowd.

They were lucky enough to bag a small table in the corner, but within a few minutes of sitting down, they were joined by a man in jeans and a denim shirt, who had clearly been drinking a little longer than they had. He stood with his thighs pressed against the edge of their table until they finally looked up.

'Helen . . . ?' The man grinned and raised his glass.

Helen stared for a few seconds, then her eyes widened in recognition. 'Pete?'

'Pete' immediately sat down without being invited, squeezing in next to Thorne. After a few awkward exchanges, it became clear that this was yet another person Helen had been at school with.

'First girl I kissed,' he said, looking pleased with himself. He turned to Thorne. 'No offence, mate.'

Thorne raised his hands: none taken. He sat, listening for a few minutes with a fixed smile, until they began talking about old teachers, at which point he necked what was left of his pint and announced that he was going to the bar. 'Before you two start talking about whatever it was you got up to behind the bike sheds.' He asked if anyone wanted a drink, but neither took him up on his offer, which was lucky as he had no intention of coming straight back. Standing up, he caught a look from Helen that suggested she was not altogether thrilled at being left alone with her first love. Thorne looked back, making it clear that it was a bit late. He could hardly just sit down again, could he? His glass empty . . .

Making his way towards the bar, Thorne took a closer look at the arrangement of stuffed fish proudly displayed on the wall. The various plaques told him that there were carp, perch and rainbow trout, all of them caught within the last fifteen years, with the most recent caught just a few weeks before. Thorne had never seen the allure of fishing and was even less convinced about stuffing them. Wasn't a photograph enough? Looking at the poster further along, he was rather more interested to see that the pub would be showing the Spurs v Manchester City game in a couple of nights. He wondered if he and Helen would still be here then. He sincerely hoped not.

He found a vacant stool at one end of the bar and waved his empty glass.

The man behind the bar poured him a fresh pint of Guinness. He took Thorne's money, brought him his change, but seemed happy enough to hang around. As Thorne took a sip, the barman stuck out a damp hand and introduced himself as Trevor Hare. 'It's my name above the door,' he said as Thorne shook his hand. He nodded at a woman with bleached-blonde hair who was busy pouring wine at the other end of the bar. 'And that's my wife, Jacqui.'

He was mid-to-late fifties, with glasses and grey hair cropped close to the scalp. There was a little fat on him, but he still looked like he wouldn't have too much trouble ejecting difficult customers, if it came to it.

Hare leaned into his bar and lowered his voice. 'You a copper, then?'

There seemed little point in asking the landlord where he had got his information from. What had Helen said about this being a difficult place to keep secrets?

Thorne nodded. Said, 'And you *used* to be.'

'Bloody hell,' Hare said. 'Is it that easy to spot?'

Thorne had made an educated guess, but he was right about these things more often than he was wrong. It was a certain ... watchfulness he could usually pick up on, though of course pub landlords tended to have much the same look.

'What is it with ex-coppers running pubs?'

Hare laughed. 'I reckon I'm in a minority these days. Most of them end up in private security, or else they're technical advisers for films and TV shows.'

'If they are,' Thorne said, 'they're doing a terrible job.'

'Anyway, I'll give you "pub".' Hare stood up straight, mock-offended. 'The Magpie's Nest is actually a hotel, strictly speaking. Well ... we've got four rooms upstairs.'

'Must be hard work,' Thorne said.

'You're telling me, but every one of them's occupied at the moment, so we're not complaining.'

Thorne grunted, drank. Someone else doing well out of what had happened. Counting the takings, while two sets of parents cried themselves to sleep.

'Coppers in most of them, as it goes. Not enough room in town for them all.'

'Yeah, we had trouble,' Thorne said. He turned to look across at the corner table. Helen's old boyfriend was laughing at something and Helen seemed happy enough about it.

A man a few feet away had clearly been eavesdropping on the conversation with Hare. He leaned forward and spoke along the bar. 'I heard a whisper about tents.'

Hare took an empty glass from a customer and began to pull a pint. 'Tents?'

The man nodded. 'Well, it's all right for the ones that live local, or in Tamworth maybe, but plenty of us live a fair old distance away.'

81

*Us.* One of those coppers putting money in Trevor Hare's pocket.

'I mean, all the man-hours we're losing bussing bodies in every shift, some bright spark came up with the idea of putting everybody up in tents. Dozens of them, I heard. Those big flash ones.'

'Be like bloody Glastonbury,' Hare said.

'It's the weather worries me.'

Hare handed over the customer's beer, went to the till and back. 'Never going to happen,' he said.

As Hare leaned across to speak to Thorne again, a small cheer went up and Thorne turned to see a man in a shapeless tweed trilby and muddy Barbour jacket coming through the door. He was thin-faced, the veins visible on his nose and cheeks. Watching him talk softly to the collie at his side, Thorne thought that he could be anywhere between fifty and seventy.

'Here we go,' Hare said.

As the man got closer to the bar, the dog snaking slowly between people's legs, several of those nearby began grunting and squealing like pigs. There was a good deal of laughter, but the man looked less than amused. When he got to the bar he quietly said, 'Very bloody funny.' Then, 'Pint of best.'

Hare said, 'Evening, Bob,' and began pulling the beer. He winked at Thorne. 'Bob was in here a few weeks back, shouting about how someone had come on to his farm in the middle of the night and nicked one of his piglets.' There was another burst of comedy grunting from a few of those near the bar. 'Accusing all and bloody sundry, weren't you, Bob?'

The farmer took his beer, handed over an assortment of coins. 'Well, some bastard took it, didn't they?'

'Gave *me* the third degree for a start,' Hare said to Thorne. 'Checking to see if I had spare ribs on the menu.'

'Yeah, and I'm still watching you.' The laughter started up

82

again, a few more grunts and snuffles, as the farmer took his dog and his drink to a table in the corner.

'Local character,' Hare said. 'No harm in him really.'

'Every pub's got one,' Thorne said.

'Oh, we've got more than one.' Hare wiped down the bar, tossed a few empty bottles into a plastic bin, then came back to Thorne. 'So, you up from London then?' He nodded towards the table where Helen was still talking to Pete. 'You and your wife?' He added a question mark to the final word. He saw Thorne hesitate. 'Partner?'

'That'll do,' Thorne said. 'She grew up here. I'm just a spare part really.'

'Not sure I believe that,' Hare said.

From his table, the farmer suddenly shouted out, raising his glass in mock salute. 'Plenty of pigs in here, mind you . . .'

There were a few jeers and sarcastic whistles as Hare came around his bar, shouting, 'Oi, keep it shut, if you want another drink.' He shook his head and rolled his eyes at Thorne, before pushing his way through the crowd of drinkers and starting to gather up empties from several of the tables.

Thorne could see what the farmer meant.

If retired police officers were easy to spot, those still on the Job might just as well have been wearing badges. There were five or maybe six he would have bet a week's wages on. Some were almost certainly staying in bedrooms upstairs, but the place felt like it was a regular haunt for the local coppers too, who would always gravitate to a boozer run by one of their own.

Thorne looked towards Helen's table but couldn't see it clearly. He craned his head and saw that Hare had stopped off at the farmer's table to make a fuss of the dog. The animal was wagging its tail and lifting its head towards the landlord's hand. Looking around, he fancied that he'd spotted three or four journalists too. He took a drink, then turned back to the bar, exchanging an

83

innocuous nod with one of those he had seen at the press briefing.

Reporters with big ears and coppers with pints in their hands.

They might just as well have added INFORMATION to that chalkboard outside.

As Hare moved past him and walked back behind the bar, Thorne said, 'So, what do you reckon then? Bates ... '

Hare thought about it, looking pleased to be asked his opinion. 'Always nice enough with me,' he said. 'Drinks in here a couple of nights a week, has something to eat, whatever. Never any problem.'

Thorne watched him lift up the bar gun and squirt what looked like lemonade into a glass.

'Nice enough family too. Nothing out of the ordinary.'

'Rarely is, though,' Thorne said. 'People who do this don't tend to advertise the fact.'

'Fair point.'

'Always the nicest person in the pub, right?'

'Tell you what I *do* think.' Hare leaned a little closer, as well aware of who some of his customers were as Thorne was. 'I don't believe they've got enough to hold him.'

'How come?'

'So, that girl was in his car, nobody's arguing with that. Let's say the first one was in his car as well. Let's say they find DNA from both of them.' He shrugged. 'Doesn't prove a fat lot, not when you weigh it all up. We've had Poppy and Jessica in *our* car.' He nodded towards his wife. 'Our boy goes to St Mary's and you're forever giving somebody a lift somewhere. Same goes for lots of people round here if you ask me.'

'Different if they find blood though,' Thorne said.

'Yeah, obviously, but what if they don't? I went to the police and said all this, told them we'd had both those kids in our car. I had a good chat with Tim Cornish. Well, you've got to do your bit, haven't you.'

Thorne wondered how Cornish had reacted to being told that his evidence was not going to mean a great deal. 'I suppose,' he said.

'Just saying.' Hare downed his drink and smacked his lips. 'Unless they've got something else we don't know about, I wouldn't be surprised to see Steve Bates back in here tomorrow night, with a pint in his hand.'

Thorne was suddenly aware that Helen was standing next to him. He looked past her and saw that her old schoolfriend was now standing with a group of his mates. He was leaning close to say something and they were all staring at Helen.

'Ready when you are,' she said.

'Oh.' Thorne raised his glass to show her that he still had a third of a pint left. 'You OK?'

Before Helen could answer, Hare was leaning towards her. 'Sorry about this bloody weather.' He reached to give his wife a squeeze as she passed behind him. 'Probably spoiled your homecoming a bit.'

'It's fine,' Helen said. 'We didn't really come here for that.'

'We've been luckier than some, mind you.' He turned to his wife. 'Haven't we, love?' She nodded and Hare smacked his hand down on to the bar. 'Touch wood.'

'Never gets flooded here though,' Helen said. 'I don't remember it, anyway.'

'No, we'll be all right, but you've got to feel for those poor buggers lower down, haven't you?'

'Must be horrible,' Helen said.

'Irony of it is, there used to be a pumping station round here. Derelict now though ... ten or fifteen miles south?' He looked to his wife for confirmation as she moved back to the other end of the bar. She said something about one of the barrels. Hare sighed, long-suffering. 'No rest for the wicked ...'

Helen leaned closer to Thorne. 'Can we go?' She blinked slowly. She looked pale, suddenly.

Thorne put what was left of his drink on the bar and stood up at the same moment as the farmer pushed between them and laid his own glass down, demanding the same again.

'You'll have to wait a few minutes,' Hare said. 'Barrel needs changing.'

One of the other drinkers at the bar said, 'You want a packet of pork scratchings with that, Bob?'

'Piss off,' the farmer said.

# FOURTEEN

It was killing him that he couldn't see her, that he couldn't just jump in the car and go down there.

He felt like someone who was on the wagon or trying to get off the fags or something. He would forget. Just for a second or two he would think about going, start looking forward to it. His heart would lift, only to plummet when he remembered what was happening; that it was just not possible at the moment. Difference was, you wanted a drink there was always one around and it was easy enough to go and buy a packet of fags when you were gagging for one.

It had been the thing that got him through the tedious, everyday crap. The shitty jobs and the social niceties, such as they were. It had been the bright spot on his horizon.

Bright, and dark.

Now, thinking about her, about all the things he was missing, was making every minute of every hour almost unbearable. He had always known it might come to this, of course, but it didn't make it any less painful. He could vividly recall that last image of her down there; yanking at the chain that he knew would never give; kicking her Doc Marten boots through the shallow puddles and screaming at him; calling him every name under the sun. A foul mouth she had on her, but he supposed it was understandable, all things considered.

She'd be cold down there, and hungry. She'd be trying to block out that smell which was only going to get worse, and she'd be trying not to think of the things he might do when he came back. That he *would* do, given half a chance.

'Don't panic,' he had said. 'I'll be back.'

Worst of all though, he reckoned, would be the loneliness. Hard to put up with that. He'd been on his own plenty of times over the years and it wasn't something he'd recommend. He was lucky, he knew that, having someone to share his life with, someone who loved him. He appreciated that every day, but the simple truth was that it would never be enough. Whatever your set-up was, marriage or boyfriend and girlfriend or whatever it was the homosexual contingent got themselves into, a man needed something for himself. Something that was his. A woman as well, probably, but he could never claim to be any kind of expert when it came to that.

Some space, some time, something to get the blood jumping a bit.

He was never cut out for trains or stamps or any of that nonsense. A shed full of gardening tools and tat was never going to do the job. This had been his thing. Yes, a release . . . he'd heard it called that. Something he'd seen on television.

Now though it was just frustration, and sometimes it felt as though he could hardly breathe. It was sitting there, twenty minutes' drive away. Just waiting for him, her all lovely and screaming in the dark and nothing he could do about it.

Not for the time being, at least.

# FIFTEEN

'So, come on then,' Paula Hitchman said. 'What's the latest?'

Thorne looked at Helen, but she refused to meet his eye. She just said, 'We know about as much as you do. Less, probably.'

'I don't believe that for a minute,' Paula said. She worked as a nurse at a hospital in Nuneaton and had only been home for half an hour or so when Thorne and Helen arrived. She had answered the door wearing a dressing gown and tracksuit bottoms; teddy bear slippers with ears on them.

'Out of my uniform, quick shower to get rid of the smell of the place and into my jammies,' she told them.

Thorne and Helen dropped their bags at the bottom of the stairs and followed her into the kitchen. They told her how grateful they were for her offer to put them up and she told them not to be so daft; that there was no point having a spare room if you weren't going to use it and that old schoolfriends should stick together. They stood and watched her make toast, turning down her offer to stick a couple more slices under the grill for them. Helen said that they'd already eaten and when Thorne told her where, Paula laughed and told them where the bathroom was. Said that there was every chance they might need it in a hurry.

Paula put her toast on to a plate and said, 'Come on, let's go and sit down and you can fill me in.'

Following her into the living room, Thorne gave Helen another 'told you so' look, but got no response.

'So, how's she doing? Linda.'

Helen hesitated, said, 'She's OK.'

'Really?'

'As well as can be expected, I suppose.'

'Yeah, right,' Paula said. She bit into a piece of toast and chewed enthusiastically. 'That's what we tell people at hospital, when a relative's about to snuff it.'

They were sitting in a living room almost as sparse as the one Thorne had seen at the house where Linda Bates was staying. The furnishings were a lot newer and more expensive though. Leather, chrome and glass, with shelves of neatly organised CDs and DVDs. Thorne could just make out some of the titles sitting beneath an enormous flat-screen TV. *The Expendables*. *Iron Man*. A box set of Adam Sandler comedies.

The house was on a nicely kept estate with good-sized front gardens and a view across fields at the back. There was a new Mini and a four-by-four parked on the drive. Thorne had no idea what Paula's partner did for a living and knew that a nurse's salary was far from lavish, but with no kids to support, he guessed that they were doing all right for themselves.

'You stayed in touch with Linda then?' Helen asked. 'Since school.'

'Well, obviously she wasn't in my year, but I see her now and again. The supermarket or the pub. We're not what you'd call friends exactly, but still, horrible what's going on.' She polished off her slice of toast. 'Horrible for everyone.'

'What about her husband?' Thorne asked.

'Sorry?'

'You know him?'

'About the same, really. Just to say hello to or whatever. The four of us had a drink a few months ago, but it wasn't planned or anything. Jason and me just ran into them in the Harvester in Tamworth ... would have been a bit awkward not to sit together, that's all it was. Jason knows Steve better than I do, so you should ask him really.'

On cue, they heard a car pull up outside. They waited silently until the front door was opened and, a few seconds later, Paula's boyfriend breezed into the room. As soon as the introductions had been made, Jason Sweeney tossed his leather jacket on to the back of a chair and quickly disappeared into the kitchen, returning half a minute later with cans of lager for everyone.

Thorne and Helen tried to refuse, but their protestations were ignored. Thorne was exhausted and Helen looked even more ready for bed than he was, but both knew it would be rude not to stay up and have a drink with the people who were putting a roof over their heads.

Sweeney opened his can, sucked the froth off then leaned across to touch it to Thorne's.

'Cheers, mate.'

He was good-looking, if a little florid. Somewhere near forty, Thorne guessed, wearing stonewashed jeans and a T-shirt that showed off his nicely developed gut and budding man-boobs. His dark hair was curly, slicked back into something approaching a mullet.

He sat down next to Paula, held her hand.

'How was it, love?' she asked him.

'Haven't bloody stopped since lunchtime.' Sweeney took a long swig of lager. 'One fare after another.' He clicked his fingers. 'Bang, bang, bang.'

'That's good.'

'Tamworth, Burton, up to Derby ... '

'What is it you do?' Helen asked.

'Jason's a taxi driver,' Paula said.

'Get it right, love.' Sweeney beamed. 'I'm *the* taxi driver. Only game in town, mate.'

'You must be busy all the time then,' Thorne said.

'Yeah, but it's mental at the moment. Well, you've been in town, so you know.'

Thorne nodded. Another local business on the up.

'I've got all my usual customers, plus everyone who's here because of what's happened. Getting a lot of journalists in the back of the car, I can tell you that much.' He smiled. 'Charging *them* double, obviously.'

Thorne laughed. He had no problem at all with that.

'It's crazy, mate, swear to God.'

'Like a normal Saturday night in Leicester,' Paula explained. 'Wanted somewhere a bit quieter, didn't you, love?'

'I wanted the work,' Sweeney said, 'don't get me wrong. Driving a cab in a big city though ... it's one arsehole after another, isn't it? Pissing in the back of the car, throwing up, doing runners. Did my head in.'

'So, you thought you'd move somewhere a bit nicer,' Thorne said. 'Where nothing ever happens.'

'Yeah, right.' Sweeney squeezed the can gently, denting the metal with a *pop*.

'You hungry?' Paula asked. 'Want me to do some more toast?'

Sweeney emptied his can and handed it to her with obvious expectations of a replacement. 'Actually, I could murder a sarnie.'

'Ham and cheese?'

'Good girl ... '

When Paula had gone, Thorne nodded towards the street. 'That your Land Rover out front?'

Sweeney said that it was.

'It's his bloody pride and joy, that's what it is,' Paula shouted from the kitchen. 'Spends more time messing about in that thing than he does with me.'

Sweeney looked at Thorne and shook his head, looking in vain for a little male solidarity. 'Actually, it's been a bloody lifesaver recently,' he said. '*Literally*. I've been doing a few runs down to some of the villages that are flooded, seeing what I can do to help.'

'That's good of you,' Thorne said.

'Nice to put it to some use. Not made for going shopping in, are they?'

'Not round here, maybe.' Thorne took a mouthful of beer. 'In London, people seem to think a dirty big four-by-four is the perfect thing for doing the school run or going to get your nails done.'

When Paula had come back with a sandwich and a fresh can of lager for Sweeney, she put a CD on. Paolo Nutini. 'I love him,' she said. Sweeney ate half his sandwich in two bites, made approving noises as he chewed.

Thorne exchanged a look with Helen. It didn't seem as though their hosts would be ready to call it a night any time soon.

'It's funny really, when you think about it.' Paula had taken Sweeney's hand and was staring at Helen, half smiling. 'You sitting here.'

'Why's that?' Helen asked.

'Well, you weren't exactly very nice to me at school.'

Helen blinked. 'Sorry?'

'You and Linda.' The half-smile was still there, but was not reflected in the tone of voice. 'I suppose it was because we were a couple of years younger . . . me and Jenny, but the pair of you never wanted us hanging around.'

'I don't remember that.'

'Always trying to get rid of us.' Paula sniffed, thought for a few seconds. The smile was a little thinner. 'Used to bully us quite a bit, actually.'

Helen had reddened, aware that Thorne and Sweeney were both looking at her. The taxi driver was drumming his fingers against his knee in time to the music. 'I wouldn't really call it bullying,' she said.

Paula laughed, dry. 'So, you obviously remember it a *bit.*'

'Well ... I'll take your word for it,' Helen said. 'I mean ... If that's what you thought, I'm sorry.'

Paula nodded, and her smile broadened suddenly. 'Oh, don't be daft, it was a long time ago.'

Sweeney broke what was threatening to become an uncomfortable silence. 'So, what's happening, then? They going to charge him, or what?'

Paula slapped his leg playfully. 'Leave them alone. They're only here because Helen's a mate of Linda's and anyway, they wouldn't be allowed to talk about the case, even if they knew anything. Right?' She looked at Helen and shook her head, as though she herself had not been digging for dirt only five minutes earlier.

'Paula was saying you knew him quite well,' Thorne said. 'Stephen Bates.'

Sweeney looked at Paula, then shook his head, chewing. 'Pint and a game of cards in the Magpie, that's about it. We both like rock music, so we talked about that now and again, bands we'd seen, you know. Went to see Metallica with him in Birmingham a few months ago.'

'Really?'

'Yeah, they were good, actually.'

Thorne was aware of Helen tensing next to him. Aside from the awkward exchange with Paula, she hadn't spoken a great deal and had not touched her drink.

94

'Pretty good bloke,' Sweeney said. 'I mean, obviously he *isn't*, is he? Not if he did what everyone reckons he did.' He turned to look at Paula, took her hand again. 'Just goes to show, you can't ever really know people, can you?'

'Except when they're seriously ill,' she said. 'No point pretending then, is there? You can really see what a person's made of when they're scared to death.'

'I knew the girls as well, a bit.' Sweeney looked at Thorne, then down to his plate. 'I mean, I'd had both of them in the cab a few times, Poppy and Jess. When you're the only taxi there is, you pick up everybody eventually, don't you?'

'Where did you take them? Can you remember?'

Sweeney thought about it. 'I suppose Tamworth was pretty regular for all those girls. A Friday or Saturday night to some club or to one of the bars. There was usually three or four of them, all dolled up and gassing on the back seat, always asking if they could smoke out of the window and moaning at me when I said no. They split the fare, you know, so it was probably just as cheap as getting the bus. Not the same when they were on their own though.' He raised the can to his lips. 'Maybe if they'd had a couple more quid in their pockets, Poppy and Jess might still be alive.'

Paula looked at him. 'Hang on, we don't know they *aren't* still alive.'

'Yeah,' Sweeney said. 'All right.'

'Top of the stairs?' Helen stood up suddenly. 'The bathroom?'

Paula nodded. 'Lock's a bit iffy though,' she said.

Thorne turned to watch Helen leave the room, while Sweeney belched softly behind him.

# SIXTEEN

Danny slammed the lid of the laptop computer down hard. 'Fucking wankers!' He leaned back and pushed the machine away, across the top of the small table that one of the coppers had carried up from downstairs for them. 'Cheap piece of shit, anyway. When are we going to get our own computers back? It's not fair.'

Charli was lying on the bed. 'I told you not to look.'

'I want to know,' Danny said. 'I want to know what people are saying about him.'

'Facebook's just full of retards,' Charli said. 'They're just trying to get a reaction. That's the whole point of it.'

Danny pushed his chair back, walked across and dropped on to the end of the bed. 'They know nothing,' he said. 'They're going to look really stupid when this is all over.' His jaw was set and Charli could see the muscles working in the side of his face, but there were tears brimming at the corners of his eyes too.

'Do you want to see what's on TV?' she asked. She nodded

towards the portable TV on a chest of drawers in the corner of the room. Something else the coppers had brought up for them.

'Trying to get on our good side,' Danny had said. 'Make up for the fact that they've fucked our lives up.' Now, he shook his head. 'It's going to be on TV too.'

'I'm not suggesting we should watch the news.'

'I don't care.'

'Might be a film on or something.'

'Can't be arsed,' Danny said.

Charli put down her book, folded over the page she had been staring at for the last twenty minutes. She leaned across and pressed PLAY on the portable CD player. They didn't have a lot of good music on disc; just a couple of albums that her mum or Steve had bought them, thinking they knew what kids were into, not realising that they'd much rather have vouchers and download stuff for themselves. All the decent stuff was on their phones, but those had been taken away too.

She thought it was probably a good thing. She didn't even want to think about some of the moronic messages her friends and schoolmates would have sent. Some abuse and stuff, that was only natural, but the sympathetic ones, with the sad-face emoticons, they'd have been far worse.

When the music kicked in she turned the sound down. She didn't want to wake her mother. She said, 'You snore, by the way.'

'Yeah, jokes,' Danny said.

'Last night you were snoring like a pig. I had to put my hand over your nose.' She laughed, hoping that her brother might join in, but he didn't. It was the first time they had shared a room in years. There were only three bedrooms in the house. Their mother was in the big one and the box room had been taken by whichever copper was sleeping over tonight. Last night it had been the male one which was fine by Charli as she thought he was quite fit. She guessed that it might be that bitch Carson tonight. She always had a face on her like someone had just shat in her dinner and was probably a lesbian and Charli had seen her looking at their mother like she *knew* something.

Like she was so much better than they were.

'How long, do you think?' Danny asked.

'I've got no idea.'

'Until Steve comes back.'

'I told you.'

'Until we can go home then. Days or weeks?'

Charli shrugged and watched Danny pick up a pillow and throw it at the far wall. She could not help but laugh as it flopped harmlessly down on to the carpet, but once again, she failed to elicit anything but an angry glare.

'How can you laugh?' He pushed at her feet. 'Have you been smoking weed or something?'

'I wish.' She wondered if the police had found the small stash at home in her bedside table. She wondered if they would do anything about it.

'You're just sick in the head then.' He turned away in disgust. 'You don't hear me or Mum laughing, do you?'

Charli turned her head away and tried to lose herself in the music. She wondered if she would ever go back to school. The same school, anyway. The coppers had said she was allowed to bring her books after Linda had told them she had important exams coming up. How stupid was that? Like she could just sit and do revision when all this was going on. The Russian Revolution and *The Merchant of* fucking *Venice*.

She lay there and wondered if the people who marked the exams would take it into account, what had happened. Like when kids were really ill or one of their parents died or something. Would she get better grades, maybe?

She was a bit ashamed just thinking about it and felt her face redden.

She thought about that woman who had turned up out of the blue to keep her mother company; her and her boyfriend. Yeah, she was an old friend and all that, but they were both coppers, so maybe she was there for some other reason. Some kind of under-cover thing, like maybe her mum would say something to her she would never say to one of the other coppers. They'd talked a lot, her mum and that woman Helen, but Charli hadn't really been able to hear it. Her mum had told her to keep an eye on Danny, so it was hard to keep up with everything else that was going on.

She'd heard the coppers talking though, Carson and the Scottish woman in uniform. Something about how long they could keep Steve at the police station. Something about a magis-trate and 'further detention'. She wasn't going to say any of that to Danny.

He stood up and said, 'I need a piss.'

On his way out, he picked up the pillow and threw it at her. There was a half-smile there, finally, but he still looked pale; dif-ferent.

As soon as Charli heard the bathroom door close, she got up and went to the laptop. She opened it and logged quickly on to her Facebook page.

There were more messages than she would have time to read before Danny came back. She scrolled through them, the con-versations that had sprung up beneath each comment.

perv dad = perv kids! lol!!
u r so ignorant
least i'm not a perv
no, just a moron
if he did stuff to those girls he probably did it to his own kids as well . . .

When she heard the flush, she logged off and closed the lid of the laptop. She was back on the bed by the time Danny came back in. He looked excited.

'We can sue them, yeah? You see it on the news and stuff. When people are arrested or accused of something and then it's proved they didn't do anything, they get tons of money. Compensation or whatever.' He nodded. 'Those twats on Facebook won't be laughing when we're the ones in a mansion with a couple of sports cars parked outside.' He flicked his fingers, as 'gangsta' as it was possible for any white fourteen-year-old from Polesford to be. 'Safe.'

'Sounds all right,' Charli said. Looking at her brother and wondering if the time would ever be right to ask him the question. Wondering if it had ever occurred to him, to ask her.

If he touched those girls . . .

They both froze as the track ended and the sound of their mother crying softly next door began to leak through the thin wall. Charli looked at Danny, but he dropped his head and stared down at the carpet. As soon as the next song started, he walked quickly to the CD player and turned the sound up, just enough.

# SEVENTEEN

Helen was already in bed by the time Thorne came back from the bathroom. She lay with a pillow propped up behind her, wiping off her make-up and dropping the used cotton-wool balls on the floor beside the bed. Thorne began to get undressed.

'Bit bloody nippy in here.' He rubbed his arms and bent to press a hand to the radiator. It was only lukewarm. 'Well, no chocolate on the pillow was bad enough, but this has definitely cost them their five-star rating,' he said. 'If it's not the full works for breakfast, I'm inclined not to come back.' He looked to Helen for a reaction and she glanced up. 'I might even write something snotty in the visitors' book.'

She gave him a thin smile and carried on wiping.

They had managed another half an hour or so downstairs, before Paula had finally noticed Thorne stifling his third or fourth yawn in as many minutes and told them there was no need to be polite. Thorne could still hear music playing. It was possible of course that they had made an effort to be sociable simply because they had visitors, and had been every bit as desperate to turn in as Thorne and Helen, but Thorne had them marked down as regular night owls.

He could empathise with a nurse's need to kick back a little after a day at the sharp end in a major hospital; to decompress. No matter what time he or Helen got in after a late shift, even if Alfie was asleep, it was rare for either of them to go straight to bed. It always took a while for the buzz to settle or the disgust to dissipate. A drink would often be taken to help the process along. TV might be watched in silence or, very occasionally, whoever was in bed woken gently and some of the day's darker moments shared.

Helen's were almost always the toughest to talk about, and to hear.

It was possible of course that taxi drivers felt that same need to wind down at the end of a long day, but Thorne strongly suspected that Jason Sweeney just enjoyed drinking.

Though still not exactly thrilled that they were here at all, he was glad that he had listened to Helen and packed pyjamas. He put them on quickly and swapped his dirty T-shirt for a clean one. Helen was wearing one of his T-shirts too. He could see the top half of it above the duvet: Johnny Cash giving the world the finger.

As he walked towards the bed, Thorne heard the music stop suddenly, then, half a minute later, the sound of their hosts coming upstairs; whispering and laughing. He climbed quickly into bed, not really sure why he did not want the two of them to hear him moving around. He lay still and listened. The boards on the landing creaked as each of them used the bathroom and then, finally, the door to their bedroom closed.

Helen put her make-up remover on the bedside table. She adjusted her pillow and shuffled down beneath the duvet.

'You can keep your bloody feet away as well,' Thorne said. 'Like blocks of ice.'

'I've got socks on,' she said. She reached to turn her light off, then rolled back and lay there, staring at the ceiling.

They lay in silence for a while.

'So, what was all that about downstairs?'

'All what?'

Thorne tut-tutted, shook his head. 'I'd never have had you down as the school bully.'

'I *wasn't*,' Helen said.

'I'm kidding.'

'Yeah, I'm sure me and Linda didn't want her and Jenny following us around, but it's ridiculous to say we bullied her. And why would she be happy for us to stay and then bring all that up?'

'Maybe it's *why* she wanted you to stay,' Thorne said. 'We should probably lock the door.'

Helen showed no sign of thinking Thorne's remark was funny and clearly had nothing else to say about it.

'So, how's she holding up?' Thorne kept his voice low. 'Linda.'

Helen took a few seconds to answer. 'What I said to Paula, really.'

'Really?' Thorne had presumed that downstairs, Helen had simply been trying to avoid any kind of in-depth conversation about what had gone on between her and Linda Bates. Now he wondered if she was trying to avoid one with him.

'She's tough.'

'That's good,' Thorne said. He tried to sound as though he meant it. He was hoping that having seen how 'tough' her old schoolfriend was, Helen might now decide that there was no real reason for them to stay.

'I mean she's hardly dancing a jig or anything.'

'Was she glad you came?'

Helen shrugged and pulled the duvet up a little. 'Yeah, I suppose.'

'Well, I don't think DC Carson was that thrilled about it. She was on the phone to her boss before anybody put the bloody kettle on.' The truth was that Thorne had expected as much. If *he* had been SIO on the case, he'd have been furious if she hadn't called; two coppers from a different force turning up on the doorstep. 'Cornish wasn't as chippy as he might have been, matter of fact. Could be he's just trying very hard, but he seemed pretty decent.' That look of concern right at the end might have been laid on a little thick though, Thorne thought. 'He knew about Bardsey.'

Helen said, 'Yeah?'

'What about you?'

Helen did not answer and Thorne was not even sure that she'd heard him. She wore that same expression – blank, distant – that he had seen in the car driving towards Polesford and in the Magpie's Nest just before they'd left. She was very still, as though she was holding her breath. Then she suddenly became aware of him studying her, and turned.

'What?'

'Are *you* glad you came?'

'It was the right thing to do.'

'That wasn't what I asked.'

Helen sighed. Said, 'Look, I'm tired, OK?'

Thorne moved towards her just as she turned on to her side. He slid an arm around her waist and across. 'Happy Valentine's Day, by the way.'

'Funny one,' Helen said.

Thorne pushed his groin into her backside. 'It's not over yet.'

'We can't.' Helen took Thorne's hand and pressed it against her belly, as if to stop it creeping any lower. 'Not in someone else's house.'

'We don't have to make any noise,' Thorne whispered.

104

'I usually sleep through it anyway.'

Thorne laughed, pushed again.

'No.' Helen's voice was louder suddenly and her body stiffened against his. 'I'm not . . .'

'OK,' Thorne said. 'Sorry.' He turned away and reached across to turn his own light off.

'Knackered,' Helen mumbled. 'That's all.'

Thorne was asleep before she was.

# EIGHTEEN

Polesford had gone to pot, there was no question about it.

The last ten, fifteen years, the old man had watched the town he loved turn into somewhere he barely recognised any more. Full of shops he didn't feel welcome in, takeaways serving food he wouldn't be caught dead eating, and people who didn't seem to care that the place had become a shithole.

Back when his wife was still alive, there had been a proper butcher and an ironmonger, and the people who came to see the abbey and enjoy the countryside seemed to genuinely care about the town, to relish the time they spent there.

It was the people who had come from somewhere else, they were the problem, the start of it all. They were the rot that had set in. People who just wanted a bit of green around them, a reason to buy wellies, but buggered off every morning to work in Burton or Birmingham. They weren't *invested*, that was the trouble. Yes, that was a good word for it, they didn't have a stake in the place, not emotionally at any rate.

Now this terrible business with those girls.

That kind of thing would never have happened back when he

was their age, or when his own children were teenagers, come to that.

He bent to let his terrier off the lead, watched him scamper into the trees.

However bad it got though, he still had the woods that backed on to his house to enjoy every day. That was the clincher, back when he and his wife had first bought the place. They'd both loved walking, and now, every time he took the dog out, he felt that small ache down in his stomach because she wasn't at his side. These were *their* woods, always would be, however many noisy teenagers were tearing about on motorbikes or starting fires at night.

First thing every morning and last thing at night, ever since the dog was a puppy; him and her talking about their plans for the day. Then later on, looking back on how each of their days had gone. Now, it was mainly the dog he talked to.

He smiled, thinking that at least the dog never answered him back.

Said, 'Sorry, love, only joking,' to himself.

The dog came running out of the trees, panting. It sniffed the ground at the old man's feet, then raced back into the bushes. Poor old bugger was almost as old as he was now, in dog years at any rate, but he still had plenty of zip in him. Still gave the squirrels in his back garden a hard time and went mad if he caught a whiff of a fox or a rabbit.

He walked on, and it seemed as if the day was growing brighter with every few steps, the sun coming up fast above the lines of sycamore and silver birch. At least it looked like they might be getting a bit of good weather today, help out those poor souls up to their armpits in the Anker.

He turned, looking for the dog behind him. He whistled and felt for one of the little bone-shaped chews he always kept in his pocket.

He'd meant what he'd said to that miserable sod at the police press thing the night before. The place would only go downhill a damn sight faster now. Yobbos piling off coaches to take pictures of the street where the girl was taken. Chattering about how terrible it must have been for everyone, then queuing up for fried chicken and making it hard for the people who actually lived here to get to the bar at the end of the day.

She would have wanted to move, if she'd still been alive. He'd thought that more than once. Much as his wife had loved the town, she would not have been able to bear it now, the place it had become. The supermarket and the beauty salons. The yelling in the streets come chucking-out time and the scrabble at the post office to cash the benefits cheques.

He turned, but there was still no sign of the dog.

Maybe he'd write another letter to the local paper. Not that they'd bothered printing his last one. It was a disgrace, because he knew what he was talking about and he wasn't the only one who felt like this. He wanted his town back and what was wrong with that?

He could hear the dog yapping now, but it sounded a fair old distance away. He turned and walked back along the path, then cut into the trees. He gathered his overcoat a little tighter around him, pushed his scarf up to his throat. It was bright enough, but it was still bloody cold.

He whistled again, waited.

He shouted the dog's name, once, twice, then cursed under his breath and started walking towards the noise.

Bloody rabbits . . .

# NINETEEN

Thorne and Helen woke early, but, with no noise to indicate that anyone else was up and about, they stayed in their room, waiting for Paula or Jason to emerge from theirs.

Helen called her father to see how Alfie was, confident that her son would have woken long before they had and would already be giving him the runaround. Her father assured her that all was well and that he was loving every minute of looking after his grandson. She talked to Alfie briefly. She told him to be good and that she would see him soon.

She said 'love you' and he said it back.

When her father came back on the line, Helen reminded him to call if there was any problem. He told her not to be silly. He urged her to make the most of the break and to enjoy herself. Listening in, Thorne was interested to see that Helen took care to give no hint that they were anywhere other than where they were supposed to be; that they were, in fact, in the town where her father had lived for so many years. When Helen finally hung up, she looked at him, as though well aware of what he was thinking. Thorne decided it was probably not a good idea to ask her why.

They lay in bed and read for a while, talking easily. Thorne was happy to see that Helen seemed a lot brighter than she had the previous evening. He hoped that one day in her home town would prove long enough for her to have come to terms with whatever mixed feelings she clearly had about coming back.

Helen flicked through a magazine, while Thorne made another attempt to get involved in a thriller he had picked up and put down again countless times. 'The copper in this is ridiculous,' he said.

'Don't tell me,' Helen said. 'He's got a drink problem and he's a bit of a maverick.'

'Have you ever met a copper like that?'

'I'm sorry about last night . . . '

The absence of a smile told Thorne that she was not talking about the Valentine's Day shag that never was. 'No need,' he said. 'I was a bit worried, that's all.'

'I think I'm just finding it hard, not being with Alfie.' She reached for Thorne's hand. He put his book down. 'This'll be the longest I've ever been away from him. Well, apart from . . . '

The armed siege.

Three days during which Helen had lived with the constant terror that she might never see her child again.

'I know,' Thorne said. 'It's understandable.' He was not convinced that this was the only reason why Helen had not been herself ever since they'd crossed the river into Polesford, but it was the only reason she seemed ready to give. 'Still, you heard what your dad said about making the most of it.'

She picked up her magazine again. 'Not exactly the right circumstances though, are they?'

'We don't need to stay,' Thorne said. 'We can drive back to the Cotswolds if you want.'

Helen shook her head. 'I need to be here.'

Thorne said, 'Well, it's your call,' and was surprised to find himself feeling relieved, and not just because of his aversion to the snootier parts of the English countryside. As far as the police operation in Polesford went, he was just an observer, of course he was, and he was under no pressure because he had no responsibility.

No part of this was down to him.

He was still excited though, knowing that a major investigation was taking place just five minutes up the road. That there was a suspect being held, officers putting a case together and, most importantly, victims still to be found. It had been the first thing he'd thought about when he'd opened his eyes.

*I'm on holiday.*

*He wasn't exactly hard to find.*

*I don't believe they've got enough ...*

That buzz had not gone away overnight.

As soon as they heard somebody heading downstairs, Thorne and Helen got up. Helen showered, dressed and went down. Thorne did the same and followed her fifteen minutes later.

It was not quite the 'full works' Thorne had joked about, but he was more than happy with a bacon sandwich on white, thick-sliced bread. He and Helen ate at a small table in the kitchen, while Paula stood at the cooker in her dressing gown, making another sandwich to take up to Sweeney who was clearly sleeping off the previous night's 'decompression'.

'Sorry about the pair of us putting you on the spot last night,' Paula said. 'Those questions about Linda.'

'Not a problem,' Helen said.

'Something like this happens, you can't help yourself, can you?'

'I'm sure I'd be exactly the same.'

'You like being a copper then?' Paula stepped back as the pan spat oil at her. 'I mean, you must do, right?'

'Most of the time, yeah.'

'Must be tough though. Some of the stuff that happens.'

'No tougher than being a nurse.'

Paula began buttering bread. 'Yeah, well you come back feeling pretty great some days, I'm not saying you don't. Others though . . . well, you know what they're like.'

Thorne remembered what Paula had said the night before, about getting home from hospital, and guessed it wasn't just the smell she felt the need to wash away.

'It's good of you to come back. I mean you've obviously got your own life in London, family and all that.' Paula turned and looked at Helen, pointed with the knife. 'Linda's lucky to have a friend like that.'

'She's got plenty of friends here, hasn't she?' Helen asked.

'She must do, but people tend to stay away when something like this happens, don't they? They think it's going to be awkward, that they won't know what to say.' She turned back to the cooker. 'Maybe some of them are wondering if Linda knows something about what happened. People always think that, don't they?'

'Is that what you think?' Thorne asked.

They waited, watched Paula cock her head.

'I'd be lying if I told you I hadn't ever considered it. I know that probably means I'm a horrible, suspicious person.'

Helen looked straight at Thorne. 'Like you said, it's what a lot of people think.'

'All I'm saying, she's bloody lucky to have you around. It's times like these you find out who your real friends are.'

'That's nice of you,' Helen said.

Paula turned round again. 'No, I mean it.'

Just for a moment or two, there was something in the woman's face – a sudden tightness, and something flat about the eyes – that Thorne thought he recognised. That he'd seen back before he'd joined the Murder Squad, on a few occasions he'd worked

112

rape or domestic abuse cases. Her job was hard enough, but he had begun to suspect that she spent most of the time when she wasn't working as an unpaid skivvy for her boyfriend. If he was right, he wondered just how controlling Jason Sweeney could be. How many friends Paula Hitchman was allowed to have.

Paula's mobile began to ring out in the hall, so she took the frying pan off the heat and went out to answer it.

'You going to see Linda today?' Thorne asked.

'I said I would.'

'She was right.' Thorne nodded out towards the hall, where Paula was talking on the phone. 'About Linda being lucky that you're here.'

'I'm not a real friend,' Helen said.

Out in the hall, they could hear Paula say, 'Are you serious?'

'What are you on about?' Thorne asked.

Helen shook her head. 'If I was, I wouldn't have waited for something like this to happen, would I? A real friend would have come back a long time ago.' She turned to stare out of the window, across a brown field that swept down towards scattered farm buildings, lines of sodden stubble.

'What was that look before?' Thorne asked.

'What look?'

'When she was talking about wondering how much Linda knows? You gave me a look.'

'I didn't.'

'Like, was I wondering the same thing.'

'Come on,' Helen said. 'I know very well it crossed your mind.'

'And it didn't cross *yours*?'

Paula came back in, phone in hand. She pointed at what was left of Thorne's and Helen's sandwiches. 'Come on, bring them through. I think we might want to put the telly on.'

'What?' Helen asked. Thorne was already standing up.

Paula waved her phone. 'That was a woman I know from step

class, who runs a coffee shop on the high street. Cupz? Anyway, the place was full of coppers first thing this morning and she overheard them talking.' She shook her head. 'Trust me, if she knows something, she'll have told *everyone* by now.'

'Told them what?'

'She reckons they've found a body.'

PART TWO

# MORE COPPERS
# THAN POETS

# TWENTY

Poppy is delighted when the car stops.

That's one more drink she can buy with the money she's going to save on the bus fare. Callum has a part-time job and she knows he'll be happy enough putting his hand in his pocket, but she can't let him pay for everything. She knows there are plenty of girls willing to do that, sit there all night downing free rum and cokes, but there are lads who take that the wrong way. Who think it means they're owed something at the end of the night.

It's cold too, and it looks like there's rain coming, so getting a lift is a double bonus.

'Where you off to, Pops?' he asks.

'Tamworth,' she says. 'The All Bar One near the station?'

He thinks about it for a few seconds, like he's trying to get his bearings, then tells her he can probably take her all the way, that he's got to meet someone to talk about some business thing.

'You're in luck,' he says as he leans across to open the door for her.

It's warm in his car, and he tells her she can change the station on the radio, find something she likes. He's been listening to some rubbish with endless guitar solos, so she starts searching through the stations.

'You look nice,' he tells her. 'I like your boots.'

'They're new,' she says. She looks down at her shiny red DMs, wiggles her feet around. 'Birthday present.'

'You on a date?'

She laughs, tells him that nobody says 'date' any more, that he sounds like he's a hundred years old or something. He doesn't seem to mind her taking the piss, says he feels that old sometimes, that he's used to teenagers reminding him that he's out of touch. 'What's the right word then?' he asks.

The road crosses the M42 and she looks down at the traffic, the necklace of red lights in one direction, white in the other. 'I don't know,' she says, laughing. 'I'm just meeting a friend, that's all.'

'Probably have a few drinks though,' he says.

'Probably have more than a few,' she says.

She finally finds something decent on the radio and he laughs when he glances across, sees her nodding her head in time.

'I don't get this stuff,' he tells her.

'You're not supposed to, are you?' she says.

'I know, I'm too old.' Keeping one eye on the road, he stretches an arm into the back and drags a plastic bag across. 'Here you go,' he says. 'Take this with you, put it in your bag or something.'

She reaches in and takes half a bottle of vodka from the bag. It looks like it's been opened already, but it's more or less full. 'Serious?' she asks.

'Prices they charge in these bars,' he says. 'Bloody extortionate, it is.'

'You sure?'

'Just buy some cranberry juice or whatever, then you can mix it.'

'Thanks,' she says. She leans down to get her handbag from the footwell.

'Have a drink now if you like,' he says. 'There's plenty.'

The road narrows on the outskirts of Glascote and begins to twist where the streetlights get further apart. He flicks the headlights to full beam.

'You want some?' She holds the bottle towards him.

'I'm driving,' he says. 'Besides, I can't turn up to my meeting pissed.'

She takes the top off the bottle and has a swig. It tastes a bit funny, warm because it's probably been sitting in the back of the car for a while, but she enjoys the burn at the back of her throat. She takes another, then screws the top back on.

'Don't worry about me,' he says. 'I'm not going to tell anyone.'

'I'll have some more in a minute,' she says.

A car comes up fast behind them. It flashes its lights and overtakes. He switches off the full beam until it has disappeared around a corner. There are a few houses just beyond the trees on her side of the car, windows lit, but suddenly they're gone.

'How long until we're there?' she asks.

'Ten minutes?'

She looks at the time on her phone. 'Great, thanks.'

'I'm sure your boyfriend won't mind if you're a bit late,' he says. 'Treat 'em mean and all that . . . '

Poppy closes her eyes, just for a second or two, enjoying the music. The bottle is wedged between her legs and she thinks she can hear the vodka inside, sloshing around in time to the drumbeat, like the sea on a shingle beach.

She feels herself lean to the left as the car turns suddenly and she opens her eyes.

'This isn't the right way,' she says. She knows it's not, she's taken the bus loads of times and it never turns off, not until it gets into the town centre, the one-way system.

'Traffic can get bad at the big roundabout,' he says. 'There's temporary lights.' He's turned on to a narrow lane and she can't see anything but bushes on either side; darkness beyond and mud and stones creeping beneath the headlights. 'This is a good short cut, trust me.'

He looks at her and smiles and tells her not to worry. He tells her to help herself to another drink if she wants.

He says, 'Don't worry, I'll get you there.'

# TWENTY-ONE

The news confirmed what Paula's friend had told her, but there was not a great deal in the way of detail. That did not stop both reporter and studio anchor passing on what little they did know as if it had come to them etched on stone tablets. There had been a major development in the investigation into the disappearance of Poppy Johnston and Jessica Toms; a break in the case. The words slid by on a rolling caption every thirty seconds. The body – believed to be that of a teenage girl – had been discovered in nearby woodland.

Believed to be ...

Thorne knew that could mean one of two things. Either the body had been found out in the open and been clearly seen, or else a grave site had been located and the media were jumping to what was probably a reasonable conclusion.

Sweeney had appeared shortly after they had begun watching. He skulked into the living room, looking every bit as rough as he clearly felt, and complaining about the non-appearance of his bacon sandwich. Seeing what they were all watching, he quickly settled down next to Paula and leaned towards the screen.

'No great surprise though, is it?' He sat with his knees apart, a ratty towelling dressing gown just about protecting his modesty, presuming that he had any.

'Think about those two sets of parents,' Paula said. 'Each of them praying that it's not their daughter. That it's the other one.' She turned to Helen. 'God, can you imagine that?'

'Yes, I think I can,' Helen said.

'It'll be the first one,' Sweeney said. He reached beneath his dressing gown to scratch. 'Jessica.'

Paula nodded. 'Yeah, course.'

'Why?' Thorne asked.

'Because she's been missing the longest.'

'Doesn't necessarily follow.'

'Has to be.'

'There's no reason why you shouldn't find a more recent victim first,' Thorne said. 'Sometimes it's a sign that a killer's getting careless, or it might be because they're trying to muddy the waters. Sometimes, it's just how it happens.'

Sweeney looked like he was thinking about it, that he *might* concede that the homicide detective sitting on his sofa knew a little more about such things than he did. 'Yeah, I suppose you can't assume anything. Makes an ass out of you and me, right?'

'What?'

'*Ass-u-me.*' Sweeney helpfully broke the word up into three parts.

'Ass' was not the word Thorne had in mind, but he nodded politely. On the screen, a shot from a helicopter showed a clearing in the woods. Figures in bodysuits milling around a white forensic tent, stark against the surrounding trees.

Sweeney said, 'Well, we'll just have to wait for the ID, I suppose,' and when he started talking about something he'd seen on an episode of *CSI* Thorne stopped listening.

Now, half an hour later, Paula was upstairs in the shower and

Thorne and Helen stood in the kitchen. That view across the fields was marred slightly by the figure of Jason Sweeney, the wind blowing the flaps of his dressing gown around, as he stood smoking in the back garden.

'He's not what you'd call a catch, is he?' Thorne said.

Helen looked at him. 'They've been together a few years, I think, so Paula must think he is.' Thorne had never been very good at disguising the way he felt about someone, at keeping those feelings from showing in his face. She read his expression, said, 'There's plenty of people reckon *I* can do a lot better than you.'

'Your sister, you mean?'

'One of many.'

'Since when did you listen to her?'

Helen leaned against him. 'I'd be a damn sight more worried if she liked you.'

'Does that mean I can stop trying to be nice to her?' Thorne asked.

Outside, Sweeney was trying to light another cigarette, shielding it from the wind with his dressing gown. When he had succeeded, he took his phone from the pocket and began tapping away at it.

'So, you want me to drop you at Linda's?'

'I want to stop off somewhere on the way.'

'Right ... '

Helen stepped away and let out a long breath. Her lips stayed together when she smiled. 'I want to go and see my mum.'

The wind tore at the cellophane around the small bouquet as Helen laid it at the foot of the grave. Petrol station flowers; the best she could get hold of on a Sunday morning. She stepped back and reached for Thorne's hand.

He studied the weathered headstone, the dates beneath Sandra Weeks' name. Helen saved him the few seconds of maths.

'She was forty-nine,' Helen said. 'Only twelve years older than I am now.'

There wasn't too much to say and Thorne could not think of anything anyway. He knew that it had been breast cancer, but had not known quite how young Helen's mother had been when she died. He squeezed Helen's hand.

'It was six years after I left.'

'So, you were . . . what?'

'Twenty-four,' Helen said. 'A year after I joined the Met.'

'Were you . . . had you been expecting it?'

'Kind of. She'd been diagnosed in my last year at college.'

'Must have been horrible.'

'At least I had an excuse for doing so badly.' There was a laugh in her voice. An attempt at one. 'I mean, I probably would have messed up my exams anyway, but I used to tell myself that was why. What I told other people too.'

'It's understandable,' Thorne said.

Helen nodded slowly. She bent to straighten the flowers and re-scatter grit that had been blown on to the path. 'She'd actually been in remission for a couple of years, but once it came back it was quick, you know?'

'That's something, I suppose.' Thorne shuffled his feet and felt a familiar tightening in his gut. That same clench of uselessness and embarrassment he had felt many dozens of times; trotting out platitudes for those who had lost loved ones. The parents of a teenage boy knifed to death for the latest Samsung; a woman whose husband had been shot trying to fight off a carjacker; a man whose wife had been on the wrong tube train on 7/7.

*I'm sorry for your loss . . .*

'Less than six months, once they'd told her the cancer was back,' Helen said.

'Right.' Thorne hadn't quite said, 'That's a mercy,' but it was close enough.

'Jenny was still living here then. I think that's the reason she's the way she is with me sometimes. Still pissed off that I wasn't here when Mum died, pissed off that I'd got away. One of the reasons, at least.'

Thorne stared at the inscription, afraid to turn his head and see the pain he knew would be etched across Helen's face.

Pain and perhaps guilt.

'So, when did she get away?'

'A year or so later, somewhere round there. Straight from being here with Dad, working in pubs or whatever, to a life of wedded bliss with Tedious Tim.'

Thorne laughed. Each conversation with Jenny's husband about car maintenance or Formula One was etched in his memory.

'Dad stayed for a few years after that, then bought the place in Sydenham.' She took her hand from Thorne's and tightened her scarf. It was cold enough already and the wind was getting stronger. 'I can't remember if he'd met Andrea by then.' She put her hand in her pocket. 'I'm not even sure I know *where* he met her.'

Robert Weeks' second marriage had only lasted eighteen months and neither Helen nor her sister knew exactly what had gone wrong. 'I think Dad just wanted her to be Mum,' Helen had said once. 'And she got fed up trying to be.'

They both looked up at the crunch of footsteps on gravel and watched an elderly couple walking slowly past. The man wore a brown anorak and hat and was carrying a large arrangement of flowers. Thorne smiled at the woman who was half a step behind. She smiled back and, for no reason that he could identify, Thorne knew that they were visiting their child's grave.

'Come on then,' Helen said.

'Sure?'

'I'm freezing.'

She turned and began walking away and Thorne followed happily. A cemetery would never be a pleasant place to visit, however charming or historic the setting. How could it be if you were stricken with grief or guilt or overwhelmed by bad memories? Not even if you were simply tongue-tied and certainly not when it only served to remind you how long it had been since you had visited your father's grave. Since you had laid down so much as a tatty bunch of daffs from Tesco.

As they walked back beneath the ancient archway towards the main road, Helen's phone rang. It was a brief and terse conversation. Thorne saw Helen's expression darken, heard her say, 'right', 'when?' and 'fine'.

'What?' he asked, as soon as she had hung up.

'That was Carson. I gave her my number.'

'Everything all right?'

'Looks like I won't be seeing Linda until later on.'

'She OK?'

'I doubt it,' Helen said. She started walking again. 'Carson's driving her to the station at Nuneaton. They want to question her.'

# TWENTY-TWO

Cornish reminded Linda that the interview was being recorded, that she would be presented with a copy afterwards, that she was being questioned under caution as a witness and that she had waived her right to have a solicitor present.

'I don't need one, do I?' Linda asked.

'You have the right to one. We need to make sure you're fully informed of the fact, that's all.'

Linda nodded and smiled nervously across the table at Sophie Carson, who was sitting next to Cornish. Carson did not smile back.

'You're probably aware that a body was discovered early this morning in woodland to the west of town.'

Linda nodded. Even if she had not seen the news, the rapid expansion of the crowd outside the house would have told her something significant had happened. She had watched the TV report with a growing sense of dread; a sick feeling spreading from her stomach, prickling on her arms and legs. She had fought to keep it from showing on her face, all too aware that

Carson, Gallagher and the other cops in the living room were looking for any reaction; watching her watching.

'Which one is it?' she asked Cornish. 'Poppy or Jess?'

'There's been no formal identification as yet,' Cornish said. There was a good reason why not, but he did not want to get into that for the time being. He was holding that back until it was needed. 'But I can tell you with certainty that it was the body of Jessica Toms.'

'God . . .'

Cornish and Carson waited a few seconds, watched Linda's shoulders slump, her head shake slowly.

'Did you know her?' Cornish asked.

'I knew who she was. But I didn't know her.'

'What about Steve?'

'Same.'

'She'd never been in his car?'

'Not as far as I know.'

'Right,' Cornish said. 'That's what he told us.'

Linda had been staring at a spot on the other side of the table, at Sophie Carson's hand lying across a manila folder. The nicely kept fingernails, pillar-box red. Now, she looked at the woman's face and at Cornish's. Neither told her anything. She said, 'I've already answered questions like this.'

'Your husband told us that Jessica Toms had never been in his car,' Cornish said. 'But I'm afraid to say he wasn't telling the truth. The forensic tests prove beyond any doubt that she had been.'

'So there must be a mistake.'

'DNA doesn't lie,' Cornish said.

'But people make mistakes. The police make mistakes.'

Cornish looked away for a few moments. 'Steve smokes Marlboro Lights, doesn't he?'

Linda did not answer immediately. It was starting to feel as if every question they asked, however simple it sounded, was nudging her a little further into a minefield. 'Yeah, so?'

'We found a cigarette end with the body. Caught in the plastic.'

'What plastic?'

'Jessica's body was wrapped in bin-bags,' Carson said.

'So?'

'It was a Marlboro Light.' Cornish steepled his fingers. 'We'll have the DNA results on that later today. By this afternoon with a bit of luck. And I know it's going to have your old man's DNA on it.'

'No way,' Linda said, without missing a beat. 'That's not possible.'

'You don't have to do this,' Carson said.

'Do what?'

'Say the things you think you should say to cover up for him.'

'I'm not.'

'He's not the one you should be worrying about, all right?'

Linda looked at Carson. The officer had leaned a little closer to her, but her expression was blank.

'*Me*, you mean? You think I know something?'

'If you know anything at all that might help us, now's the time to speak up. That's all I'm saying.'

'I've told you what I know and what I don't know. How could you think I'm trying to hide anything? Why the hell would I?' She shook her head at Carson, raised her hands. 'Come on, Sophie, you've spent time with me, with my kids.'

The officer said nothing, showed nothing. 'Sophie' when she was making tea, laying a supportive hand on Linda's shoulder. 'DC Carson' in the interview room.

Cornish opened a file and studied it. 'You're aware that we took your husband's computer from your house.'

'I'm aware that you took all sorts of things.'

129

'We found certain material on his hard drive which we believe to be significant.'

Linda stared. She did not need to be told what the copper was talking about. Once or twice, she had walked into the room and seen her husband scrabble to close a screen. She shrugged. 'Blokes look at that stuff, so what? I bet you look at it, don't you?' She waited for a response but did not get one. 'What you're talking about, what you found on the computer. You mean like porn, right?'

'*Like* porn.' Cornish emphasised the first word.

'What does that mean?'

'I don't really think you want me to go into details, Linda. Let's just say it was specialised.'

Linda shifted in her seat. Those prickles were creeping along her arms again. Her belly was starting to cramp.

'Take a minute,' Carson said.

Linda closed her eyes for a few seconds, unable to focus on anything but those details they were so thoughtfully sparing her. The vile images she could not help but imagine. 'I don't know what you're expecting me to say.'

Cornish nodded. 'OK, let's talk about the night Poppy Johnston went missing.' There was a tone Linda recognised in the copper's voice, suddenly; something like concern, like sympathy. It reminded her of the doctor who had told her that her dad was dying. 'Last Thursday.'

'Right.'

'Steve told you he was in the pub.'

'Because he was in the pub.'

'Well, let's not argue about that. Why would he go to a pub all the way out in Atherstone, sit there drinking on his own?'

'Because that's where the job was. He'd gone over to take a look at a house.'

'Easy enough to drive back, get a pint here. Magpie's Nest, that's his local, isn't it?'

'He drinks in a few places.'

'So, why not go to one of them?'

'You'll have to ask him.'

'I did ask him.'

'What did he say?'

'Same thing you just did.' Cornish pulled a face, as though pained slightly by whatever he was about to say. 'Only problem is, Linda, it's a pack of lies, because I don't think he was in the pub at all. I don't think he went to look at any job in Atherstone or anywhere else and there's no record on your home phone or on his mobile of any call from anyone asking him to come and quote for a job. I think that, whatever he told you, he picked up Poppy Johnston that night and took her somewhere in his car.' He left a second or two. 'You're bright enough to know exactly what we think he did after that.'

Carson let out a long breath. Said, 'Had you got any reason to suspect he might be lying to you last Thursday?'

Linda shook her head.

'Any occasion in the past when you thought he'd lied to you?'

'What? Are you married?'

'You know what I'm talking about.'

Linda shook her head again. Carson nodded towards the recorder. Linda said, 'No,' but it sounded as though there was something stuck in her throat.

'Like I said, Linda, I know you're bright.' Cornish was leaning forward now. As he spoke, he began removing photographs from the folder in front of him, though Linda could not quite see what they were of. 'Whatever happens, there's still you, and there's still Charli and Danny, and you've still got a life together to think about.' He removed the last picture, began to arrange them. 'That's what you need to concentrate on, and I know you would never do anything ... I know you would never not tell us any-thing ... that might endanger that.'

131

'You and your family are victims too,' Carson said. 'You need to remember that.'

Suddenly, all Linda could remember was the face of that lovely Indian doctor. Bright eyes and so many lines on her cheeks, around her mouth. A small woman with thick glasses and grey hair tied back and that small red dot on her forehead, whatever it was called. A whisper of a voice when she spoke, and Linda's arsehole of a father being horribly rude to her, right up until the end.

# TWENTY-THREE

They drove north out of town, towards the flooding.

'I know a pub that does a decent lunch,' Helen had said.

'Where?'

She had told him there was a place a few miles north, towards Burton-on-Trent. The kind of food he liked, she assured him. Decent portions and a good selection of beers.

'It means we'll have to go around the area that's flooded.' Thorne had said.

'That's OK.'

They had been talking across the BMW's dirty roof, one on either side of the car. 'There'll be diversions or whatever. It'll take ages.'

'What else are we going to do?'

'You don't fancy somewhere in town?'

'Not really.'

'What about Dorbrook, then?' Thorne had asked. 'Must be one of your old haunts we could try.' He had considered asking her who had told her about this pub she seemed so keen on, and when. He thought about pointing out that if it was somewhere she'd known about twenty years before, there was no guarantee it would even be there any more. Instead, he shrugged and got into the car, suddenly aware that whether or not the pub was decent, Helen was keen to get away for a while.

Now, Thorne took the car through the villages of Bramsworth and Warmwood, slowing down each time, as the road signs instructed him to do, though there seemed no real reason for it. Little to see beyond Greggs the bakers and very few pedestrians around. The road soon began to bend and roughen, narrowing as the housing gave way to dark fields; distant industrial estates, grey beyond the overgrown hedgerows and stretches of crumbling dry-stone wall.

Within fifteen minutes, with no sign of water anywhere, they reached the first diversion. A battered triangular sign reading DANGER OF FLOODING and a makeshift barrier allowing access to emergency vehicles only. A hard-faced copper in a high-visibility jacket, one hand raised, the other imperiously pointing the BMW in a different direction.

'Nice to see people enjoying their job,' Thorne said. He glanced in the mirror as he accelerated away, raised two fingers.

'Right, like you always enjoy it.'

'Most of the time.'

Helen smirked.

'What?'

'You should try letting your face know about it.'

As they followed the diversion signs that would take them around the perimeter of the flood zone, Thorne told Helen what Cornish had said about having to police the area to keep looters away. The difficulties in allotting manpower.

'Ridiculous,' Helen said.

'You can see his problem though.'

'Not really.' Helen stared out of the passenger window.

'Getting it in the neck if he doesn't do anything, I mean.'

'What's more important?'

'I know—'

'Extra hands pitching in to find a missing girl or nicking a few arseholes in four-by-fours? Is that really a priority?'

'Not a priority, no.'

'Making sure people don't come back to discover that some toe-rag in waders has had it away with their widescreen? Jesus ...'

'People get upset, don't they? Bad enough having to leave your home.'

'It's only stuff, isn't it?' Helen turned to look at him. 'They get it all back on insurance anyway, so what's the big deal? What are Poppy and Jessica's mum and dad going to get back?'

'I'm not arguing with you,' Thorne said.

Turning a corner, he was forced to slow down as he drew close to a lorry, sand or cement dust spilling from the back and drifting into the BMW's windscreen. He inched out, muttering, looking for a stretch that would allow him to overtake. 'Hard to get insurance at all though, I would have thought. Near enough impossible if you're somewhere that's likely to flood every couple of years.' He glanced at Helen, but it appeared that she had said her piece or was thinking about something else. He waited another few minutes, then lost patience and accelerated hard past the lorry when it was not altogether safe to do so. He waited for the dressing-down he would normally have expected, but it never came.

Despite Thorne's concerns, the diversions only put forty minutes or so on their journey. The route took them a dozen miles to the west and, after turning north again and passing through Bagford-on-the-Hill, they were able to look left and see the flood-zone spread out below them.

Thorne pulled the car over.

It looked somewhat less dramatic than he had been expecting. Water lay across the fields, tea-coloured against the stark outlines of surrounding trees, but walls and hedges were still visible. There were no farms or houses cut off completely, none of those 'islands' that had featured so prominently in newspapers and on TV when the Somerset levels had flooded the year before. He remembered the picture he had seen of the family shopping in the dinghy and wondered if the local paper had used an old photo, or even one from somewhere else altogether. He would not have been hugely surprised.

'It's not as bad as I thought,' Thorne said.

'Apparently it's a damn sight better than it was a couple of weeks ago,' Helen said. 'No thanks to the powers that be.'

'Not a big shock,' Thorne said.

'People around here have had to sort it out for themselves. Muck in or whatever. Do what they could.'

'All hands to the pump, sort of thing.' Thorne left a few seconds. If Helen appreciated his feeble pun, she showed no sign of it. 'Like Paula's boyfriend.'

'Right,' Helen said. 'It's pretty bloody obvious that the government doesn't give a toss. It's all just talk, until it's the Thames that's flooding. Until it's them and their mates' big houses in the Home Counties on the receiving end.'

Thorne raised a clenched fist. 'Right on, Comrade!'

'Not funny.'

Thorne considered a remark about someone getting out of the wrong side of the bed that morning, but thought better of it. It was not just because he feared it might sound obtuse or insensitive, when Helen had so recently been standing at her mother's grave. Thorne could see that her mood was not one she would be easily shaken out of or questioned about. He realised that he had been second-guessing her reaction to things ever since they'd arrived in Polesford.

136

He started the car again and asked how far away the pub was.

A few miles later, they were back on the road they would normally have reached within fifteen minutes of leaving Polesford. A mile or so further on, Thorne glanced at a sign by a narrow turning and slowed.

'What?' Helen asked.

Thorne backed the car up and pointed to the sign.

PRETTY PIGS POOL.

'Where have I seen that before?'

'No idea,' Helen said.

Thorne stared at the words, black paint against a flaking white board, but could not remember why the name was familiar. 'What's with the whole pig thing, anyway?' They had already passed a pub called the Three Pigs. He had seen a variety of pig-related paraphernalia for sale on market stalls in town, there was a collection of ceramic pigs behind the bar in the Magpie's Nest and pig-shaped condiments in the café.

'Area's famous for it,' Helen said. 'There's loads of pig farms around here. Polesford sausages are a speciality.'

Thorne remembered the farmer who had come into the pub the night before, the story about his stolen piglet, and now he remembered where he had seen the name on the sign. It was on one of the plaques on the wall of the Magpie's Nest, inscribed below some stuffed fish or other. He said as much to Helen, and she said, 'OK.'

He looked through the gate to the water beyond: a group of large ponds bordered by grassland with woods along one side and stretching away into the far distance. The land around the pool nearest him appeared to be under water, but not by a great deal. Water was running down on to the road, sloshing into a drain by the side of the car, but it was no more than an inch or so deep on the flat.

'They fishing pools, then?' There was no sign of any anglers, but Thorne seriously doubted that conditions made it possible.

Helen nodded. 'Loads of birds and whatever as well. Formed by mining subsidence after the war ...'

Thorne tried not to stare at her. Her voice was flat. She looked pale and uncomfortable and he wondered again if she was coming down with something. 'Do you fancy a walk?'

She looked at him as though he had suggested they strip naked and go for a swim. 'I'm fine,' she said.

'Oh, come on.' Thorne opened the car door. 'Work up an appetite for these decent portions you've been promising me. Maybe a few of those famous sausages.'

'I don't really feel like it.'

'There's wellies in the boot.'

'Let's just go to the pub.' There was a half-smile when she looked at him, but it might just as well have been plastered on to the face of one of Trevor Hare's stuffed fish.

'Fair enough.' Thorne closed the door. He had no desire whatsoever to go tramping across waterlogged fields, but had thought it might do Helen some good. She was the one forever banging on about how much she enjoyed walking, that she would like to do more of it. He knew she had secretly packed walking boots, despite their agreement.

'Maybe later on,' she said.

Thorne grunted and put the car into gear. Yes, he was growing increasingly concerned about her, about the moods and reactions that were so out of character, but holding his tongue and walking on eggshells did not come easily to him. The truth was that he was irritated at having his attempt to cheer her up thrown back in his face.

'I should probably just have gone back to London,' he said.

'When?'

'When you told me you wanted to come back here. I said I

138

thought it was a stupid idea and you said I didn't have to come, remember? That I should just go home, hang around with Phil for a while.' His hands were tight around the steering wheel. 'Starting to think I should have bloody well listened.'

As he pulled away, Helen said, 'You never listen.'

Thorne swore under his breath and reached for the radio.

At the same time, an unmarked car driven by DC Sophie Carson was on the road to Polesford. Linda Bates sat staring straight ahead, a uniformed officer next to her on the back seat. Linda started slightly, sucked in a breath when the officer's radio crackled into life.

Carson glanced at her rear-view mirror. 'You all right?'

Linda nodded. 'Couldn't be better.'

Next to her, the officer murmured into his radio. He told the Police Control Unit at Polesford that he, DC Carson and the witness were about ten minutes away. He smiled when the woman at the other end let him know that she would have the kettle on.

'I know that was hard on you,' Carson said. 'In the interview room.'

'Because you and your boss made it hard.'

'We've got a job to do.'

'Right.'

Carson took a mint from a packet on the front seat, then lifted it up and offered it to Linda. Linda shook her head then watched the uniformed cop reach forward quickly to take one.

'You trying to be nice again, now?'

'I'm not trying to be anything,' Carson said.

'You certainly didn't have to try being a bitch in that interview room,' Linda said. 'All came very naturally.'

'Sorry that's what you think.'

'Now it's back to being all touchy-feely, I suppose. Nice

139

copper and nasty copper all wrapped up in one.' She was aware of the uniformed copper's eyes on her. She did not want to turn to look at him, but felt certain there was a smirk there, or close to it. 'Keeping me on my toes, right? Hoping I might let my guard down or some shit.'

Carson looked in the mirror again. 'What is it you want, Linda?'

Linda closed her eyes. She said, 'Right now, I want you to get me home to my kids.'

# TWENTY-FOUR

There is barely a breath of wind and the boat moves easily through the water. It's brand new, red with yellow sails. A clipper, is that what it's called? She watches it for a few minutes, then gets distracted by a pair of dragonflies dancing together a few feet away. She watches them swoop then rise up and drift towards her brother. He doesn't pay them any attention, eyes fixed firmly on the toggles of his remote control; tip of his tongue protruding, deep in concentration. Each time he looks up to watch his boat, his face cracks into a grin, matching the one their dad is wearing, standing next to him. Her father has a hand on her brother's shoulder, muttering instructions, shouting encouragement. Somewhere nearby, Mum is taking sandwiches from Tupperware containers, pouring orange squash into paper cups. Her mother had been sitting under a tree, but suddenly she seems to have vanished.

She calls her mother's name as her father gives more instructions and the small clipper artfully navigates a tangle of weed.

She has no idea why she has woken thinking about dragonflies and toy boats. A memory, distorted. Perhaps she had been dreaming and it has taken a while for the images to resurface. On waking a few minutes before, she had been able to think about little besides the weight she could feel on her legs. Something shifting, sopping; the rat that scuttled away through the water as soon as she started to sit up.

Her eyes are stinging and she struggles to swallow.

The tape around her mouth has come away a little at one side and she lowers her face to the floor to slurp at the shallow puddle.

The water tastes rusty, rank.

She thinks it's daytime, but it's no more than a guess. Impossible to tell, in darkness. Sometimes she drifts off and it's hard to know how long she's been asleep for, but stretching out her legs she feels as though she's had a good few hours this time. The third day, is it? She wishes she wore a watch instead of relying on her stupid phone.

Her phone . . .

She makes a noise behind the tape, excited. Surely her phone could help. They can trace people through them, can't they? The signal they give off or whatever it is. The satellite. Then she remembers that he had taken her bag before he'd left, shining a torch inside, rifling through it as he'd climbed back up the stone stairs. He'll have found her phone and got rid of it, won't he? He's clearly not stupid.

Or maybe he is. Maybe people like him aren't like the killers you see on TV, the weird-looking ones in those programmes her nan likes so much. They're always so clever in films and TV shows, always one step ahead, taunting the police or whatever.

Is that what he's doing?

Is that why she's still alive and he hasn't come back?

Maybe he's told the police that he's holding her somewhere, that he wants something in return for telling them where. Money or something.

She sucks in a breath through her nose, the meaty smell along with it, and she knows that if that's what he's up to, then it didn't work last time. They didn't pay up and he let the last one die.

She'll do whatever he wants, she knows that now. If he has just been staying away because he's waiting for the fight to go out of her then he's waited long enough.

He's won, she wants so much to tell him that.

She screams, the noise deadened by the tape slick with her spit.

She thrashes the chain against the metal pipe until there is no strength left in her arm.

She has no strength left anywhere and she starts to think that's what real hunger actually is. Not like when you fancy a bacon sandwich or a bag of chips. Hunger that feels as if you're all but dead. So weak that you can't think straight. As good as empty, like the needle in the red on the dashboard of her dad's car.

She remembers that there was an energy bar in her bag, too, and chewing gum.

She leans back against the ridged pipe and contorts her face, pushing at the tape with her tongue. She tries to remember all the words to the songs on the last Arctic Monkeys album, but she quickly gets muddled, struggles to get even halfway through the first track.

She closes her eyes and tries hard to think about nothing. Not food or her soft bed. Not the dead thing that's floating nearby. Not tails like worms, claws and teeth.

It was blue, she remembers, not red.

Her brother's model boat.

Blue with yellow sails.

# TWENTY-FIVE

'They showed me these photographs,' Linda said. 'Of the body. Jess's body. Why on earth would they do that?'

'I don't know,' Helen said, lied . . .

They were in Linda's bedroom, side by side on the edge of the bed. The curtains were still drawn, noise from the crowd on the street below leaking in from outside; chat and clamour, the occasional shout.

'They were disgusting,' Linda said. 'Made me feel ill.'

'I know.'

'Why though?'

Helen did not know what to say. That it was a stunt, a trick? That they were trying to get a reaction? That they wanted to make her feel disgusted enough to give up her husband? She did not know what to say because she had done the same thing herself many times. Pictures of battered children passed across the table in an interview room as though they were holiday snaps. A bruise big enough to cover a baby's face, a tiny body dotted with cigarette burns. Fresh, scabbed . . .

Pictures designed to elicit horror, guilt, a confession.

'It's their job,' Helen said.

'I'm getting sick of hearing that.' Linda looked ready to spit. 'It's what that cow downstairs said. Her excuse for talking to me like I'm a piece of dirt. Like I'm trying to hide something.'

'They're just trying to find out if you know something you don't know you know. Does that make any sense?'

'None of this makes any sense.'

'Sometimes people don't think a bit of information's important when actually it can be crucial, you know? Something they heard somebody say. Something they saw that they'd almost forgotten about.'

Linda shook her head. 'It's not that.' She kicked off her shoes then moved to lean back against the headboard; stretched to rub her feet. 'Look, I know they think Steve took those girls. Killed that girl. I'm not daft.'

'I know you're not—'

Linda grunted a laugh. 'They kept on telling me that, telling me how clever they thought I was. Like only someone who was thick as shit could possibly believe he hadn't done it.' She grimaced, as though there was a bad taste in her mouth. '"We know you're very *bright*, Linda".' She looked at Helen. 'I don't need a copper to tell me that.'

Helen said, 'Course you don't.' She had done that, too. Flattered when necessary, even if the individual on the receiving end was barely one notch above pond-life. Anything to strengthen a case, to secure a prosecution, to make a child safe.

'They told me all sorts of things,' Linda said. 'About DNA results, stuff they'd found on Steve's computer.' She swallowed hard and cleared her throat. She leaned forward and gripped her toes through her tights, pulled them back.

'Do you want to tell me . . . ?'

'DNA in Steve's car, from the girl.'

'Right.' Happy enough to talk about that part, at least.

'Which apparently proves he's a liar, because he told them she'd never been in his car. And obviously if he's a liar then he's a murderer as well, right? What kind of bollocks is that?'

'They won't make a case based just on that,' Helen said. 'Not on a single lie. It gives them a good reason to take a closer look at everything, that's all.'

'That's what I'm saying though.' Linda sat up a little straighter. 'They base everything around that and ignore the fact that there's so many ways those results could be wrong.'

'The DNA?'

Linda held out a thumb, counting. 'Simple cock-up, for a start. Some idiot gets the wrong . . . I don't know, test tube, right? Labels it wrong.' A finger. 'Or . . . say it *did* come from the girl, but it doesn't mean what they think it means.'

Helen waited.

'Her DNA could have been in the car even if she wasn't. What if her DNA was from something on one of her friends? A hair or something.'

'Did they say it was a hair?'

'They didn't tell me, but that's what it usually is, right?'

Helen moved her head; not a nod, but close enough. A hair, only one of many possibilities. Sweat, spit, skin . . .

Blood, the obvious one.

'A hair stuck to a jacket on a mate of hers, say. Caught on a zip or a button. You know what it's like, hair gets bloody everywhere.'

'I suppose.'

'These teenage girls going around arm in arm, always hugging each other, you know, like we used to?'

Helen nodded, struggled to remember. Drunken embraces at the end of a night, cheap wine on their breaths; tears from one or the other over some boy, comfort cuddles . . .

'I can see that happening. That could so easily happen. A friend of hers, a relative or something.'

146

'Feasibly,' Helen said.

'I bet I've got Charli's DNA all over me.' Linda held out her arms, stared at them as though her daughter's cells might somehow make themselves visible for her; glitter like diamond dust among the freckles and soft hairs. 'Danny's, an' all.'

'It's possible.'

'Yeah, right?'

Helen stood up and walked across to the window.

'They just don't even consider that,' Linda said. 'Whatever fits in with their theories, that's all they're interested in. That's how innocent people get banged up.' She watched as Helen pulled at the edge of a curtain and looked out. 'How many?'

'Twenty-five or thirty,' Helen said. 'Maybe a few more.'

'Journalists?'

'Yeah, a few.' Alongside the predictable crop of mobile phones, raised and pointed, a couple of more expensive cameras brandished or slung around necks.

'How many pictures of a front door can anyone need?'

Helen turned. 'You want me to get you anything?'

'I think I might have a lie-down for ten minutes.'

'OK.'

Before Helen had reached the door, Linda said, 'You think I'm in denial or something, don't you?'

'What?'

'You think I'm stupid and I'm kidding myself about Steve. Ignoring what's staring me and everyone else in the face, right?'

'Please don't get upset.' Helen walked back to the bed and sat down again.

'You need to believe me, Hel. There's no way on God's earth he did what they're saying. Everything they reckon they've got on him, there's good reasons for all of it, and if those coppers do their jobs properly they'll work that out eventually. They've got

147

to, right?' She leaned back again, blew out a breath that wheezed in her chest. 'No way. There is just no way . . .'

'You should sleep,' Helen said. 'Like you said.'

'Hel?' Linda looked at her, reached for her hand. No need to ask the question.

Outside, somebody shouted, 'They should nick the lot of you,' already convinced, desperate for a police van to bang on. Downstairs, Helen could hear the tinny report of a radio from the kitchen.

'I don't know Steve,' she said. She had decided that was probably a very good thing. She squeezed Linda's hand and stared towards the curtained window.

Thinking, *I don't know* you.

As Helen closed the bedroom door behind her, Charli stepped out of the bathroom. The girl stuck her hands into the back pockets of her jeans. Helen stared at the patterns embroidered on the legs. A peace symbol, a marijuana leaf.

'All right?' Helen asked.

Charli let her shoulders drop and smiled at the stupidity of the question.

Helen felt the blood move to her face. 'You and your brother want anything?'

The girl looked up and stared past her, the cistern filling noisily behind the bathroom door. 'What are we having for tea?'

'I don't know.' Helen guessed that food was being brought in regularly but was unsure about the arrangements. She had not seen it happen the day before. 'Want me to find out?'

'Can we get chips?'

'I'll ask,' Helen said.

Charli spun a multicoloured bracelet around her wrist for a few seconds, then walked past Helen, keeping close to the wall.

Helen turned to watch Linda's daughter open the door of the second bedroom, just wide enough to squeeze through the gap.

Walking into the kitchen, Helen had the distinct impression that she had interrupted something; the rise and fall of a muttered exchange, audible as she had come down the stairs. An Airwave radio unit lay on the worktop next to the sink. Carson and Gallagher watched her as she hooked her bag on the back of a chair and flicked on the kettle for want of anything else to do.

'How's she doing?' Carson asked.

Helen did not want tea. What she really needed was a large glass of wine, but she thought better of it, having put a couple away over lunch with Thorne an hour before.

'Not great.'

The pub, which Paula had told her about, had turned out to be no better than average, but Thorne had seen off a plate of shepherd's pie happily enough, a pint and a half of Guinness. She guessed that even if he had been disappointed, he would not have said anything. She could tell that he was being ... careful around her, still smarting from the argument by the fishing pool and, though she felt bad about it, she did not want to risk bringing the subject up. Getting into anything. She knew that his suggestion that they go for a walk had been purely for her benefit; that fresh air and exercise were right up there with heavy metal and sticking needles in his eyes. She could see how much she had pissed him off.

Eating lunch, they had talked about Alfie and about her father, an unspoken agreement to leave what was happening in Polesford behind them for a few hours. They talked about Hendricks, Helen's sister, the holiday in Portugal or Tenerife that they both knew now was unlikely to happen.

Helen had said the right things, laughed when she might have been expected to and tried to be nice. Normal.

'Wasn't easy for her,' Carson said now.

'Sorry?'

'This morning, at the station. A lot of things she didn't want to hear.'

'She told me.'

'She tell you anything else?'

'Such as?'

'Anything. I don't know.'

Helen looked at her. 'What, like how she knows where the other girl's body is, you mean? How the pair of them were in it together, some weird sexual thing. The two of them shagging each other's brains out afterwards?'

'Come on.'

'Seriously, what do you think she's going to tell me?'

'Well, I'm sorry,' Gallagher said. Helen and Carson turned to look at the PC. 'But I've spent the morning with Jessica Toms' parents, so you know . . . ' She nodded up at the ceiling. 'I'm a bit short on sympathy.'

'So, she deserves to feel like shit?' Helen stepped towards her. 'That what you're saying?'

'Not "deserves".'

'She deserves what she's getting from those idiots outside?' Helen pointed back towards the front of the house. 'You *can* hear some of the things they're shouting, can't you? You're not deaf as well as stupid?'

'Haven't we been through this before?' Carson waited until Helen turned to look at her. 'Professionally speaking, this isn't really any of your business.'

'Aye, right,' Gallagher said. 'I mean that's the whole point, isn't it? You're her mate.'

'*What?*'

150

The PC's face had reddened, those freckles subsumed by blood again, but she was trying hard to stand her ground. 'All I'm saying, you're maybe not the best judge, that's all.'

Helen fought to keep her voice down, its tone as even as possible. She had no desire for Sophie Carson to see her lose it. 'Listen, whatever the twat she's married to has done, and that still remains to be seen, you know, as far as the *law's* concerned ... *she* has done nothing. All right? Nothing.'

Gallagher sniffed, looked away.

'So, until you've got the faintest idea what you're talking about, *constable*, I suggest you keep your mouth shut and we won't fall out.' She turned away, walked back to where the kettle had just turned itself off. She needed that wine more than ever, but went through the motions anyway. She opened a cupboard, reached for a mug and set it down nice and carefully on the worktop. She opened the fridge and looked inside for milk.

'They charged him with murder half an hour ago,' Carson said.

Helen turned, one hand on the open fridge door.

'The twat she's married to.' Carson stared, nothing in her face. Gallagher spread her legs and straightened a cuff of her crisp white shirt. 'Thought you might want to tell her.'

# TWENTY-SIX

It took no more than a single, short conversation with the woman at the café to find out where the woods were. A fifteen-minute walk away, that was all. Had they known where to look, he and Helen would have seen them from the car as they had driven out of town a few hours before.

Thorne was still getting used to the speed at which word got around in this place.

News spread quickly enough through a station, Thorne was well aware of that, quicker still within a squad. News, rumour, gossip; serious, malicious or simply because there was nothing else to do.

There were not too many days like that, but coppers got bored easily.

*Chief Superintendent so-and-so has got the Rubberheelers on his case.*

*Sergeant Whatsherface is on the sauce again.*

*Detective Inspector You-Know-Who is having problems in the bedroom . . .*

Thorne knew how it went, had been on the receiving end of it himself often enough. He had come to recognise the look on faces, a moment before they turned away; the subtle change in the atmosphere when he walked into an incident room. Months now since the events on Bardsey Island and the jungle drums were still being beaten. A rumour that Thorne had let a prison officer die rather than risk the life of a friend. Waking from dreams of blackened bones and a stream of blood running over clifftops, he had thought about simply announcing that the rumours were true and that he would make the same choice again, if he had to. In the end he had decided to say nothing, well aware that those with a mind to bad-mouth him would quickly find some other reason to do so and happier that this story, at least, was one about which he was not ashamed. Truth or tittle-tattle, gospel or garbage; he had learned to live with it.

This place though.

Jesus . . .

Thorne guessed that there would always have been something to talk about. Who someone was sleeping with or who had money troubles. Usual stuff. Gossip was currency in a town like this one, and suddenly everybody had struck gold. When it came to a station or a squad room, it was usually the same couple of people at the centre of everything. The ones getting those drums out. It was Thorne's bad luck that the gobby DS who could always be relied upon to have the latest gen had been with him on Bardsey Island.

He wondered who the movers and shakers were in Polesford when it came to spreading the word.

The woman who ran the café – had Paula said she was a friend? – was certainly a contender. Hare, the landlord of the Magpie's Nest, clearly liked to talk, and with a bar full of cop-pers he was getting his info from very reliable sources. It was interesting to speculate, but Thorne knew that it was easy enough to find out. He would just need to see who the media were talking to. Who those reporters were thrusting micro-phones or cash at.

He walked towards the woods thinking about the subtle dif-ference between the smell of the truth and the stink of a lie. The people who were trusted to sniff them both out.

Thinking about wolves, and people waving fresh meat around.

If finding the woods had been straightforward, locating the spot where the body had been discovered was even less taxing. Though there was still an hour or so of good daylight left, the arc lamps had already been switched on around the crime scene. From the edge of the woods, Thorne could see a semi-circle of them burning, the light milky against trunks and bare branches a hundred yards into the trees; the glow of activity.

Halfway there, Thorne stopped at a line of crime-scene tape. It snaked away on either side of him, tied to trunks and saplings; circling the grave site. He waited as a uniformed officer trudged across, showed his warrant card and ducked beneath the tape.

That moment again . . .

Wherever, whenever, hillside or housing estate. Just that move-ment, that simple act of lifting then ducking down and under, the tape brushing his shoulder, his iffy knee cracking; enough to get the blood ticking a little quicker.

*Like you always enjoy it,*
*Most of the time . . .*

Though the body was long gone, there were still four or five scene of crime officers hard at work. Those ubiquitous plastic bodysuits, the familiar rustle as they moved. Watching them from Paula Hitchman's front room, shot from the news helicopter, they had looked like aliens wandering in the woods. Some Spielberg movie. Gathering samples or waiting for a ship to col-lect them.

A white forensic tent covered the area six feet or so around the grave. Thorne watched one SOCO walk in, another walk out.

Plastic trays and evidence bags were piling up on a table in the centre of the clearing, though most seemed to contain only soil. The gravecut.

Thorne walked across to where a SOCO was working with a sieve; singing quietly to himself, poking at clumps of sticky black earth with a nitrile-gloved finger. He looked up for a second at Thorne, went back to poking.

'Anything interesting?' Thorne asked.

The SOCO looked up again. He barely glanced at the warrant card Thorne was once again brandishing. 'Interesting stuff's already gone to the lab,' he said. The man wore glasses and had a dark moustache. There wasn't too much else to be seen under the blue plastic hood. Might just as well have been an alien, albeit one with a Geordie accent. 'We're just tidying up, really. Belt and braces, you know how it goes.'

'What stuff?'

The SOCO laid down his sieve, scratched at his chest through the plastic suit. 'There was a fag-end they were all getting very excited about.' He nodded back towards the tent. 'In with the body.'

'You find that?'

'Somebody else.'

'Who found the body?'

'Old man out with his dog. Usual story.'

If he found it at all odd that a detective working the case would not know the answer to such basic questions, the SOCO showed no sign of it. Often the scene of crime team would be brought in from well outside the area. They might have no direct connection with the murder squad assigned to the investigation, would not necessarily even know their names.

'Dog had done most of the digging for us,' the SOCO said. 'It wasn't very deep.'

'What kind of state was she in?' Thorne asked.

155

The SOCO stared for a few seconds, then laughed. 'Sorry, I thought you were talking about the dog there for a minute. Not actually sure if it was a boy or a girl.'

'The body,' Thorne said.

'She'd certainly been here for a while.' The man stuck out his bottom lip and blew air up on to his face. The weather had improved considerably since the morning and though it was not what anyone would call balmy, Thorne knew how hot it could get inside those bodysuits. 'Well, dead for a while, at any rate.'

'Any clothing?'

The SOCO shook his head. 'Not much of anything, like I said.'

'Weeks, then?'

'God, yeah ... she'd burst, pretty much. Plenty of creepy-crawlies in there helping themselves.'

'Right.'

'Burned as well, by the look of it. Seriously stinky.'

Thorne looked towards the tent and sniffed, convinced for a second or two that there was a trace of the smell lingering. Not barbecue weather, so probably no more than simple association. Like fighting the urge to scratch when somebody talked about head lice.

He knew what burned flesh smelled like.

'So, there goes your killer's DNA.'

'Probably why he did it,' Thorne said.

'Must be a pain in the arse for you guys.'

'What?'

'Trying to catch the smart ones.'

'Sometimes they think they're smarter than they are.'

The SOCO smiled and picked up his sieve again. 'Unfortunately, the same goes for some coppers too.'

'Plenty of coppers,' Thorne said.

The SOCO nodded, looking at Thorne as though trying to

decide if he was one of them. Thorne thanked the man for his time and left him to his soil and his singing; trying and failing to place the song as he walked away. By the time he reached the crime scene tape on the far side, he was desperate for a piss. He ducked beneath the tape and walked deeper into the woods, in search of somewhere suitable.

Five minutes later, job done, Thorne emerged from behind a clump of bushes into the path of a man walking a large black dog. The dog immediately began barking and pulling at his leash; straining towards the bush behind which Thorne had just 'marked his territory'.

The man stared at Thorne, pulling the dog back.

'Nice dog,' Thorne said. The dog did not look particularly nice, but it was socially a little more acceptable than explaining what he had been doing in the bushes. The man kept staring and Thorne wondered if he should show his warrant card. 'What kind is it?'

'Labradoodle,' the man said.

Thorne wondered if this might be the dog responsible for discovering the body, then remembered that the SOCO had described the man as being old. This dog's owner was mid-forties, if that. Though he was neither old nor decrepit, as far as Thorne could tell, he was carrying a walking stick. Thorne could only presume it was an affectation of some sort. 'Labrador and poodle, right?'

The dog was still pulling hard. 'I'd normally let him off,' the man said. 'Give him a run. They've told us not to though, because of what's happening over there.' He nodded back towards the area of the woods Thorne had come from.

'Probably be gone by tomorrow,' Thorne said.

'One of those girls, is it?'

'I think so,' Thorne said.

The man looked away, stared off in another direction for a few

157

moments. 'Doesn't bear thinking about, does it.' He pulled at his dog. 'I've got a daughter the same age, near enough.'

'Right.'

'Sounds like they've got the bloke though, so I suppose that's something.'

The dog began barking again, and Thorne and the man turned to see another dog-walker – a young woman with a sausage dog – approaching. She stopped when she reached them and the two owners exchanged nods and watched their pets greet one another. The usual canine pleasantries.

I sniff your arse, you sniff mine.

Clearly acquainted with one another, the man and the woman began to talk. About the weather looking better which was a blessing, you know, considering the flooding. About having to keep their animals on leads which was a real shame, but understandable obviously, given the terrible circumstances. The woman glanced at Thorne once or twice, but didn't speak directly to him. Perhaps she was wondering where his dog was.

When the woman was walking away, Thorne said, 'You walk your dog here a lot?'

'Every day usually,' the man said.

'Quite a few other dogs around as well by the look of it.'

'Yeah, like I said, it's a good place to let them run.'

Thorne nodded, shifted his weight from one foot to the other. 'I'd better let you get on.' He nodded towards the labradoodle. 'Looks like he's bored with me now.'

'You a copper?'

'What makes you think that?'

'You look like one,' the man said.

# TWENTY-SEVEN

Charli said, 'That woman gives me the fucking creeps.'

Danny was lying on the bed, headphones plugged in, staring into space. He shook his head, irritated, then yanked one earbud out. 'What?'

'Her,' Charli said. 'That copper. The new one.'

Danny shrugged. 'She's a fed, what do you expect? They're all wankers.'

'Yeah, well you would say that.'

Danny pulled a face.

'Public enemy number one.' She pulled a face back. 'Gangsta boy.'

Danny gave her the finger, plugged his earbud back in.

A few months before, a police officer had arrived at the door to talk to their mother. Danny and a few of his friends had been making nuisances of themselves, there had been a complaint. There was some talk about strong drink and weed being smoked. It was a warning, that was all; the copper was local and their mother knew him. She promised to have a serious word and that was the end of it. There had been several extremely serious words, a clout or two and Danny had lost his computer for a fortnight which had really been hitting him where it hurt. Later on, Charli had asked her brother about the weed and he had said that one of his mates had been smoking it. He'd been lying, obviously. She always knew when he was lying and she suspected he'd been helping himself to some of her weed, so she just made sure he knew she was on to him and moved her stash somewhere else.

She'd stopped worrying about the police finding it when they searched the house. Even if they had, they surely had bigger things to worry about and they were hardly going to come after her for a twenty bag of weed, were they? She wondered if she could have a quiet word with that copper, Weeks. If she really was a mate of her mum's, she might be able to pull some strings, whatever.

Could we have chips? Can you put in a good word for Steve? And maybe you could try and get my stash back . . .

She dropped on to the bed thinking how much she would love to skin up right then and there and get out of it for a while. She wouldn't even mind sharing some with Danny.

She stared at her brother until he sighed heavily and turned his music off again. He yanked out his earbuds.

'What?'

'Nothing.'

'You got that face on.'

'What face?'

'Like when you're about to ask if you can squeeze one of my spots or do something stupid to my hair.'

'You seen how many there are outside?' Charli asked.

'Bunch of twats.'

'Seen how many though.'

'Yeah, so what.'

There had been enough of them standing out there in the

morning and once Charli had checked her Facebook page it became pretty obvious why. There was all sorts of stuff about the police finding a body; which girl it was and what had been done to her. It was all over the TV apparently. She could understand why maybe the coppers downstairs had decided not to invite her and her brother down to have a look at the news, but it was a bit silly when stuff was on the internet long before you found out about it on the radio or TV. Her and Danny probably knew what had happened before the coppers in their living room did.

'Now, I mean. There's loads more turned up.'

She had been checking every few minutes for the last hour or so. Ever since they'd heard the noise from the room next door. Something going on between her mum and Weeks. A conversation, then raised voices and her mum screaming. Charli didn't know what all the shouting had been about, but something kept taking her to the window, telling her that whatever had been going on in the house was the reason why the crowd outside was getting bigger.

'It's like what happens with a car crash on the motorway,' Danny said. 'That's all. What do you call it?'

'Rubbernecking,' Charli said.

'Yeah, when people slow down to look because there's police cars or fire engines.' He shrugged. 'Doesn't mean there's actually anything to see, does it? Doesn't always mean anyone's been killed or whatever.' He nodded. 'Same if a couple of people stop in the middle of the street and start looking up at something or pointing. You know, even when there's nothing to see. People always stop to look, just in case they're missing something.' He nodded towards the window. 'Let's face it, there's nothing else to do round here, is there?'

Danny was wrong, Charli could sense it, but he had a point. She remembered a conversation with her mum about what it

161

was like when she was the same age as Charli. It had been the same night that policeman had come round about Danny. After her mum had screamed at him, when she'd calmed down a bit, she and Charli sat in the front room and her mum had a bottle open. She poured a glass for Charli and started to talk.

'I can't really blame him,' her mum had said. 'Not a lot for kids to do round here, is there? Just drink and get into trouble. I wasn't a whole lot better, if I'm honest.'

She'd sounded serious, but suddenly there had been a smile. Charli had sat there and drunk her wine and listened. Enjoying it.

'We'd buy the cheapest booze we could get our hands on. Four bottles you could get for what one of these cost. Maybe a bit of dope too, if there was any around.' She had looked at Charli then. 'Yeah, I know . . . but it's different when it's your own kids. You'll know what I'm talking about one day.' Charli had watched her drain the glass, reach for a refill. 'It was just about getting out of the house really, getting off your face on whatever was handy.'

Sitting on the bed now, Charli wondered if Helen Weeks had been part of that same group. That copper and her mum. Necking cheap wine in the bus shelter, same as the kids did today. Talking bollocks . . .

'All we talked about back then was getting away,' her mum had said. 'Going somewhere less boring. I knew even then that this place had a way of pulling you in if you weren't careful. Sucking the life out of you. It was all talk, obviously. I mean, I'm still here, aren't I? I'd love to say it was because I never had the chance, but it was more like not being brave enough, really. Taking the easy option.' She had laid down her glass and reached across for Charli's hand. 'You need to be braver than I was, all right? You and your brother. Promise me that, all right, chick?'

Now, Charli sat and listened to herself breathing; to the hubbub rising up from the street below. She leaned across and

162

pushed gently at Danny's leg. 'That time when the copper came round, said you'd been smoking weed. You had been, right?'

Danny hesitated, gave himself a few seconds' thinking time, same as he always did when there was a lie coming. 'No. I told you, it wasn't mine.'

'No, because it was mine.'

'My mate brought it, I swear.'

'Don't lie to me, Dan.' She put a hand on his leg. 'You and me need to be honest with each other from now on, all right? It's important. You tell me the truth and I swear I'll do the same. No bullshit any more, OK? Not now.'

They both looked up at the sound of the door to the next room opening. A few seconds later there was a gentle knock, and their mother walked in.

'I need to tell you what's happened with Steve.'

As soon as she saw the look on her mum's face, Charli was off the bed and being pulled into her mum's arms as Linda's voice began to crack.

'It's going to be all right, I promise. It's all going to get sorted out . . .'

Charli turned her head against her mum's shoulder to look at her brother. She watched him swallow; saw the muscles working in his jaw and the tears blooming at the corners of his eyes.

She couldn't remember the last time she'd seen him cry.

# TWENTY-EIGHT

In the main bar of the Magpie's Nest, Thorne was nursing the half he'd been eking out for the last twenty minutes, looking at the stuffed fish that had been caught at Pretty Pigs Pool. It was – so the small plaque told him – a twelve-pound carp; plump and greenish-brown, the whiskered mouth open, which made it look a little surprised. Thorne supposed it had been.

'Not another bloody fisherman ...'

Thorne turned to see the landlord's wife smiling at him from behind the bar. He could not remember if Trevor Hare had told him her name. If so, Thorne had forgotten it. 'No, just looking.'

'Tell your wife she can count her blessings,' the woman said. 'Bane of my life, being a widow to that. I wouldn't mind if he ever caught anything we could cook. If he didn't come home stinking of fish.'

'I'm not married,' Thorne said.

'And you won't be, not if you ever take up bloody fishing.'

Hare emerged, grinning, from the room behind the bar. 'I can hear you, you know ...'

His wife shook her head. Said, 'Put a sock in it and make yourself useful.'

The pub was getting busier. It had been almost empty when Thorne – unable to think of a better way to pass the time – had wandered in half an hour before, but had been filling up slowly as the regulars arrived to occupy their usual tables or seats at the bar.

When Thorne had finished his drink he slotted into a gap at the bar and ordered another half. He guessed that it might be a few hours yet before Helen was ready to be picked up.

'Driving,' he said, as Hare handed the glass across.

'Want me to stick a bit of lemonade in?'

They talked about cars for a few minutes, then football, when Hare let slip that he was a West Ham fan. The conversation ran its course and Thorne could sense that the landlord was keen to talk about more important things.

He didn't have to wait long.

'Looks like I was wrong about Bates,' Hare said. 'Them having nothing on him, I mean.'

'Looks like it.' Helen had called Thorne while he was walking back from the woods, told him that Stephen Bates had been charged. 'I'll need to keep Linda company for a while, is that OK?' Thorne had told her that he was happy to amuse himself and to call when she needed picking up.

'Once they'd found Jessica, it was just a matter of time, I suppose,' Hare said.

As far as Thorne knew, the body had yet to be formally identified and the police had not made any official announcement. The word in town, however, was that it had been Jessica Toms' body that had been discovered in the woods. Thorne had no reason to doubt it. He was learning that those spreading the word were remarkably well informed. 'You said you knew her.'

Hare nodded. 'Smashing kid. Nice family. Not wild like some

of them are. Well, you know ... a few drinks, what have you, a stupid tattoo ... but that's like being a goody-two-shoes round here.' He snatched an empty bottle from the bar, lobbed it into a large plastic bin. 'He was probably just hoping they wouldn't find her. Bates. Waiting it out, like.'

'Par for the course.' Thorne sipped at his beer.

'Yeah. I suppose his brief will have told him to say bugger all.'

'I can count on one hand the number of times a killer's sat there and coughed to it.'

'Hard to get a conviction without a body though.'

'Not impossible,' Thorne said.

'He must know the game's up now, surely.' Hare turned to see his wife glaring at him. There were people waiting to be served. 'Talking of which.'

'No rest for the wicked.'

Hare laughed, leaned close. 'Trust me. You're better off *not* married.'

Thorne asked quickly if he could order some food and Hare handed him a menu before moving along to start serving other customers. Thorne ordered at the bar and drank slowly while he was waiting, one eye on the TV mounted high in the corner. The sound was turned down, but the captions and rolling headlines were every bit as good as subtitles. They were talking to the old man whose dog had discovered the body and Thorne recognised the pair from the press briefing he had attended outside the Memorial Hall the previous evening. A headline said that a forty-three-year-old Polesford man had been charged with murder. Over the umpteenth close-up of the dog, another said that a second victim was still missing.

A man standing next to Thorne at the bar said, 'Bastard deserves everything he's going to get ...'

Thorne carried a plate of ham, egg and chips across to an

unoccupied table and got stuck in. Looking up after a few minutes, he realised that the stocky young man in jeans and sweatshirt at the next table was the red-faced PC he had met outside the Police Control Unit the day before. He was drinking with a friend and Thorne was not even sure that the PC had recognised him, but when the friend got up to go to the bar, Thorne left his unfinished meal and moved across.

'I just wanted to say sorry for being a twat yesterday. Pulling rank.'

The PC didn't look at him, shrugged. He had clearly clocked Thorne immediately. 'No worries,' he said. 'I've had worse.'

'Be your turn one day.'

'I can't wait.'

Thorne lifted his glass. The PC did the same. They drank.

'Everyone must be pretty chuffed this morning,' Thorne said.

The PC looked at him for the first time. 'I don't know about that.'

Thorne knew the PC was thinking about the parents of the dead girl. That Thorne was an even bigger twat than he'd thought he was. 'Cornish and the Homicide boys, I mean.'

'Yeah, I suppose.'

'You know anything about this fag-end they found?'

'No more than you.'

Perhaps the young officer had been asking around, but the half-smile said he clearly knew now that Thorne had no official role in the investigation. Both off duty for the time being, they were simply two blokes talking in the pub, which suited Thorne fine. 'I know bugger all,' he said. 'Just making conversation.'

The PC took a few seconds, swilled around what little beer he had left in the bottom of his glass. 'They've got plenty already,' he said. 'They found that stuff on his computer almost straight away.'

'What stuff?'

'What do you think? Teenage girls.'

Bad as that was, the way the PC had said it, Thorne had been thinking it might be something a lot worse. 'When you say teenage . . .'

'Young girls.'

'Thirteen, fourteen? Seventeen? What?'

'I've not seen it, have I?'

'A lot of blokes look at teenage porn.'

'They don't all abduct teenage girls though, do they?'

'Some of the girls on these sites are pretending to be younger than they are. Dressing up as schoolgirls.'

'I don't think too many of them bother showing their passports or whatever though, do they?'

'No . . .'

'Anyway, the men looking don't care how old they are.'

'I'm just saying.'

'You seem to know a fair bit about it.'

Thorne stiffened. He had felt guilty for pulling rank on the PC the day before. He wondered how guilty he would feel about smacking him in the face. 'You said they found it straight away.'

'What I heard.'

'So he can't have tried very hard to hide it, can he?' Thorne knew that those really seeking to keep their predilections secret took rather more trouble. The most disturbing sites were usually hidden somewhere on the so-called Dark Web and images buried there could only be retrieved with the help of forensic computer specialists. 'If they were really dodgy, it would have taken a lot longer.'

'I don't get it,' the PC said.

'What?'

'Why you're rubbishing the evidence.'

'Doesn't sound like it *is* evidence.'

'Like you're defending him.'

'I'm not.'

Thorne looked up as the PC's mate arrived back at the table. He deposited two fresh pints and sat down. He nodded to Thorne and Thorne nodded back. The three of them sat in silence for half a minute until Thorne said something about needing to get back to his dinner and moved away.

Fifteen minutes later, Thorne took his empty plate back to the bar and ordered another drink. The girl who served him was probably eighteen or so, but she might have been younger. She could certainly have looked younger if she chose to, just as easily as some fourteen-year-olds could look a lot older. Wasn't that the most common explanation given for their actions by those who slept with underage girls?

He wondered why he was so bothered about it. Why he was conjuring explanations. Excuses. Perhaps because a liking for teenage girls, however unacceptable, did not make you a murderer.

Thorne paid a visit to the Gents and, on the way back, he stepped outside into the small pub garden and play area. There were lights switched on outside, a couple of tables with benches attached on the patio and a pair of outdoor heaters. On the small patch of grass was a see-saw and swing-set and a grubby-looking plastic playhouse shaped like a large shoe. Thorne tried to remember the nursery rhyme. The old woman who had so many children . . .

A man with his back to Thorne sat smoking at one of the benches. He had long, curly hair tied back into a ponytail and he wore a black apron over a white T-shirt.

'Ham, egg and chips was a triumph,' Thorne said.

The man looked round and raised a thumb. He was a little younger than Thorne was expecting, no more than mid-twenties, with a straggly beard and glasses. 'That's the idea,' he said. 'We like a happy customer.' He was well spoken, with the kind of resonant voice you heard on the radio.

Thorne stepped towards the table. 'Had the steak and chips yesterday.'

'My signature dish.'

'That was pretty good too.'

'Well, feel free to pass on your praise to the magpie-in-chief. He might feel inclined to give me a raise. Pigs will have to take to the air first of course, but one can but live in hope.'

The sarcasm was relished and topped off with a wolfish, if slightly wonky grin. Thorne could not smell anything, but wondered if there might be something other than tobacco in the chef's skinny roll-up. He sat down, happy enough to be out of the bar, to breathe in some of the cigarette smoke.

'Tom Thorne.'

'Shelley.' The bracelets rattled on the man's wrists as he shook Thorne's hand. Silver, leather, beaded.

'First name or second?'

'People just call me Shelley.' He picked up a book from the table in front of him and held it up. English romantic verse. 'Not too many people reading poetry round here.'

Thorne reached for the book. He turned it over and looked at the back. Blake, Coleridge, Byron. A picture of a horse. He thought that the man had sounded rather pleased with his nickname and could not help wondering if it was one he had actually given himself.

'Not something I know a lot about,' Thorne said. The only poet he had ever seen in the flesh was Pam Ayres. His mum and dad had loved her; that poem about looking after her teeth. They had gone to see her show at some arts centre when Thorne was at school. He decided against mentioning it now.

'I write a bit too.'

'A chef who writes poetry?'

'Other way round, really.'

'Must be a reality TV show in there somewhere.'

Shelley flashed a quick smile. 'Just doing this to earn some cash,' he said. 'Getting the money together to go back to uni.' He took a final drag on his roll-up. 'Didn't really suit me first time round.' He flicked what was left of the cigarette into the bushes. 'Actually, I didn't suit *them*.'

'I didn't go at all,' Thorne said. Something he regretted now and again and was often made to feel bad about by senior officers a lot younger than he was. Fast-tracked with impressive-sounding degrees. 'So . . . '

'University of life.'

'Something like that.'

'Nothing wrong with it.' The young man smiled again; like he was saying something amusing that nobody else was quite bright enough to get.

'You got a place in town, then?'

The chef shook his head and pointed towards a pair of single-storey outhouses at the rear of the play area. In the spill from the garden lights, they were black against the charcoal sky. Thorne could see rubbish bins lined up in front of them, a pair of bicycles. 'Lord and Lady Magpie generously provide accommodation for some of their staff. Means they can pay us a bit less.' He shrugged. 'It's basically a shed with a sink, but it does the job.' He reached for his book again, patted it gently. 'As long as I've got these, I'll be fine. You know what they say. Books do furnish a room.'

Thorne thought that furniture furnished a room, but said nothing.

Shelley sat back and took out a tin from the pocket of his apron. He removed tobacco and papers and set about rolling himself another cigarette. 'So, what's your game then?' There was a trace of a mockney accent as he asked the question.

'I'm a copper,' Thorne said.

'Ah.' The chef nodded, knowingly. 'Well, there's a lot more coppers than poets round here at the moment, that's for sure.'

'I'm not working,' Thorne said. 'I'm just here with a friend.'

Shelley seemed to find that funny. 'Bit of a busman's holiday.'

'Not my idea, I promise you.'

Shelley licked the edge of a rolling paper. 'So, just an interested party, then?'

A couple came out on to the patio, noise leaking from the bar until the door closed behind them. They carried drinks across to one of the other tables and sat down. They held hands and began talking quietly.

Shelley watched them. 'Young love,' he said. 'Sweet.'

Thorne was starting to get a little cold.

'So, what do you think about evil?'

'Sorry?' Thorne had heard well enough, but was taken aback by the grinding gear-change. The casual manner of the question.

'Just wondering if you believed in it? What's going on here for a start. You believe the man responsible is evil?'

It took Thorne a good few seconds. 'Well, I think you can describe what he's *done* as evil … but I think the people that do this stuff are just greedy or twisted or sick in the head. Not sure "evil" is the right word. Not sure it does us any favours. If it helps, I don't really believe people are naturally *good* either.'

'Interesting,' Shelley said.

'Is it?'

The chef popped the completed roll-up in the tin and put it back in his apron pocket. 'I was thinking I might write about what's happening, you know? Missing girls and bodies in the woods. I think somebody *should* write about it.'

Thorne stared at him.

'Poets have always written about good and evil, life and death. It's what we do. I mean, it's basic, isn't it? Primal.'

172

Thorne nodded, thinking about Pam Ayres not looking after her teeth.

'Walter Raleigh said, "All men are evil and will declare themselves to be so when occasion is offered."'

'The potato bloke.'

'He was also a poet.'

'I didn't know that.'

Shelley smiled, like he hadn't expected him to. 'He's saying it's in all of us, somewhere.' He held out his arms, waiting for the profundity to sink in. '"Murder is an act quite easy to be contemplated."'

'Who said that?' Thorne asked.

'Emerson.'

'What did Lake and Palmer think about it?' Thorne waited, enjoying the fact that it was the chef's turn to look confused.

'Right then.' Shelley got to his feet and stretched. 'Better go and clean up, I suppose. Chief cook and bottle-washer.' He nodded back towards the pub. 'They certainly like to get their money's worth.'

Thorne followed Shelley back inside. As they stepped into the hallway outside the toilets, the young girl who had served Thorne earlier came out of the Ladies. She smiled at him, then blushed slightly when she saw Shelley. The chef arched an eyebrow at Thorne, then carried on towards the kitchen, clutching his precious poetry book.

Thorne walked back into the main bar. It was a little less busy than it had been, those who had stopped in for a quick one after work having left to eat at home. There was still no word from Helen, so Thorne decided there was probably time for another drink. He took a ten-pound note from his wallet and waved to attract the attention of the young girl who was back serving again.

*Just an interested party, then?*

And getting more so all the time.

The girl behind the bar nodded, to let Thorne know he'd be next.

He waited, asking himself why he had felt the need to explain his lack of involvement in the case; if it had sounded as feeble to the poetry-reading chef as it had coming out of Thorne's mouth. Why he had talked to that PC and why the man's accusations about questioning the evidence against Stephen Bates had hit home as they had.

He was thinking about the woods.

Those dog-walkers . . .

# TWENTY-NINE

He still enjoyed the music he'd loved when he was fourteen or fifteen; had never really grown out of it. He supported the same football team he'd shouted for back then too, and liked the same food.

Nothing strange about any of that, was there?

He'd started fancying girls like Jessica and Poppy around the same time, earlier even, back when he was twelve or thirteen. The girls a year or two above him at school. Most of the time they knocked about with older lads, wouldn't give him the time of day, but he would watch them gathered together; whispering in the playground or exchanging gossip in the dinner hall. He would watch and find that he wasn't breathing quite so easily and imagine what it would be like to do it with them. At night, fumbling beneath the duvet in the dark, he would construct each detail of it nice and carefully; what they would say to him, when and where it would happen. The very best part, *always*, was imagining that they found it every bit as exciting as he did, as much of an adventure.

Showing a younger boy like him the ropes.

Wasn't that absolutely normal? Wasn't that what kids his age thought about? He knew it was, knew very well that most of the boys his age felt exactly the same way, because they told him. Hormones kicking in and going mental all over the place. Doing the same thing he was, *thinking* the same things every night.

So, why should it be so normal to grow out of it? To stop thinking about girls that age when you got older. You fancied who you fancied, surely, and who the hell defined these things, anyway? He knew some men, older than he was, who liked to think about doing it with middle-aged women; who specifically looked for those sorts of women online. MILFs or what have you. *GILFs*, even. He remembered one bloke telling him about some granny-porn website he'd been looking at and saying it was more of a turn-on because it was a bit more realistic. It was far more exciting, he said, because it was more . . . achievable.

*That* was just stupid. *That* was not normal. Surely the whole point of a fantasy was that it was *un*achievable.

Usually . . .

When fantasy had not been enough, he had found ways to get closer to those girls, that was all. Different whens and hows. The Jessicas and the Poppys, the girls who would not give him the time of day.

Old songs, favourite foods, the team you'd followed since you were a kid. None of that was a worry to anyone or a problem to sort out. Other things though were a little trickier to arrange.

Tricky, but not impossible.

# THIRTY

Collecting Helen from the house that Linda Bates and her kids were staying in was far from straightforward, but Thorne had known it would be. There was no rear exit from the house; not unless you fancied scrabbling over a garden fence and clambering across waste ground. Helen had told him on the phone that she was happy to leave on her own and meet him somewhere nearby, but Thorne had insisted on picking her up. They had already braved the crowd outside the house once, he told her. They had already been photographed together several times.

The genie was well and truly out of the bottle.

The crowd was bigger now of course, angrier. The photographers and journalists that much more determined.

*Is Linda going to stand by him?*

*How are the kids holding up?*

*You think she knew?*

They moved towards the car as quickly as they were able, saying nothing. They kept their eyes on the tarmac. Thorne's hand drifted automatically towards Helen's, but he held back. There seemed little point giving the pack anything else to feast on.

Neither of them spoke until they were on the road to Paula Hitchman's house. Until there was nobody left to be seen when Thorne checked his rear-view mirror.

'How much longer are we staying?'

'I don't know.'

'A few days? Longer?'

Helen looked at him. 'I can't go back just yet. Linda's in a really bad way.'

'Right.'

'I told her I'd stay for a while.'

'What about Alfie?'

'I called my dad,' Helen said. 'Told him we were staying on a bit longer in the Cotswolds. He's fine about looking after Alfie. He's enjoying himself.'

'Really?'

'What he said.'

'I bet the poor old bugger's knackered.'

'Exercise'll do him good.'

He saw Helen smile; the expression that settled afterwards. He knew she hated being away from her son, how much she missed him. Thorne was missing the boy badly enough himself.

'So, is that OK?'

'What?'

'Staying here.'

'Whatever you think,' Thorne said.

'A pain for you though.'

'Don't worry, I'll cope.' Thorne thought about telling her what he'd seen in the woods, his disquiet about what the PC had told him. He decided to keep his concerns to himself for the time being, at least until after the conversation he planned to have the following morning. 'I'll find something to keep me busy.'

They were driving along a stretch of road without lighting, so

Thorne flicked the headlights to main beam. 'Bloody hell, when it gets dark round here it really gets dark.' He glanced at Helen and did not need telling what she was thinking.

Things were seriously dark.

Thorne had made his feelings about the countryside plain often enough. A nice enough place to visit – briefly – but you wouldn't want to live there. Now though, he was rethinking his attitude, at least towards those things people were capable of doing to one another in largely rural areas like this. Not the kind of place you would want to be a copper, that's what he had always thought. Not if you didn't want to spend your life dealing with underage drinking and pulling over tractors with out-of-date tax discs.

Here, now, it sounded like a cheap stand-up routine.

What had that chef said to him? Something about murder being easy enough to contemplate.

Just as easy for people living here and every bit as hard to cope with for the friends and relatives of the victims. Harder, probably, if you weren't in a big city; when you didn't live with the expectation of it. The grim acceptance that it was part and parcel of daily life, like overpriced housing and urban foxes.

Turning a corner, the headlights swept across the body of a badger; twisted and dusty-grey, hard against the kerb.

'You know why so many badgers die on the roads?' Thorne asked.

'Because they don't know the Green Cross Code?'

'Because they always go the same way. It's hard-wired in them or whatever. They're following ancient tracks and it doesn't matter if those tracks happen to cross the M42. They just can't go a different way.'

'Creatures of habit.'

'It's what kills them.'

Helen nodded. '*You're* a badger,' she said.

Thorne glanced across and laughed and his hand moved to his hair. 'Any more grey I'll certainly look like a badger.'

'Might not have been run over anyway,' Helen said. 'Farmers round here shoot them, then leave them in the road. Or lampers.'

Thorne looked at her.

'Twats who go out at night with these huge lamps mounted up on their four-by-fours, across the fields, you know? Shoot anything they find. Rabbits, badgers, deer sometimes. Pissed-up farmers' boys ... local lads, trying to impress the girls. Idiots ...'

'Didn't impress you then?'

'I went once, when I was about fourteen.' She shuddered theatrically at the memory. 'Linda used to go out lamping though. I remember we had a big row about it. I told her they were all wankers and she told me to mind my own business.' She turned away and looked out into the blackness. 'This place is full of wankers.'

'Is that why you hate it?'

She turned quickly to stare at him. 'What?'

'Look, I just thought ...'

'That's stupid.'

'With the way you've been acting—'

'And how's that, exactly?'

Thorne came close to telling her how moody and irritable he thought she'd been ever since they'd got here. Instead he just took his hands off the wheel for a few seconds. Held them up. Surrendered.

'I don't hate it,' Helen said.

They drove the rest of the way in silence, Thorne thinking about the case that was building against Stephen Bates and the one piece of evidence that was the most important.

The body of Jessica Toms.

Remembering what he had said to Jason Sweeney about killers muddying the waters.

180

# THIRTY-ONE

'That's an even nicer suit than you were wearing last time I was here.'

Once again, DI Tim Cornish glanced down at his jacket. He ran a thumb and finger down his shiny tie. 'I'm going to court this morning.'

'It's only the remand hearing.'

Cornish pulled on his e-cigarette. 'You should see what I've got lined up for the trial,' he said.

Thorne returned the DI's smile. It was only the latest of many he had seen since he'd walked into Nuneaton station. Outside in the main incident room, the atmosphere was very different to the one he might have expected on a cold Monday morning. It felt like being at school on the last day before the holidays. 'Nice way to start the week,' he said.

'You brought a cake?'

'Sorry?'

'Well, a card then, at least. Seeing as you're here to congratulate us.'

'I'll put one in the post after you've got your conviction,' Thorne said.

'See as you do.' Cornish was on his feet, busying himself. He was putting papers into a briefcase, taking others out. He checked his phone every minute or so.

'I've just got one stupid question,' Thorne said.

Cornish glanced at his phone again. 'They're my favourite.'

'I was just wondering when the last time was that the woods were searched. Where you found the body.'

'You mean last time they were searched *before* we found the body, obviously.'

'Right.'

Cornish thought for a few moments, looked distracted. 'Well, I'd need to check to be absolutely sure. Like I said before, the whole search procedure has been a nightmare because of the flooding.'

'Those woods weren't flooded though.'

'No, course not. I just meant the organisational side of it.' His phone pinged. He checked the text, put it back on his desk. 'It would definitely have been a couple of days earlier, maybe even the day before.'

'With cadaver dogs?'

'That I couldn't tell you. Like I said, I'd need to check.' He looked at Thorne. 'Why?'

'I was up there yesterday.'

'Oh yeah? Just out for a stroll?'

'Place is crawling with dog-walkers.'

'Good job, or we might never have found her.'

'Why wasn't she found before though?'

'I couldn't tell you.'

'There's people out there with dogs every day,' Thorne said. 'Morning and night. So why did it take until yesterday for one of those dogs to find the body?'

Cornish just looked at him. He drew on his e-cig, the tip glowing blue. He raised his arms.

'Sorry,' Thorne said. 'I told you it was a stupid question ... but it's not like the grave site was in the middle of nowhere. If it hadn't been cordoned off yesterday, there'd have been dogs all over the place, same as there normally is.'

'I'm honestly not trying to sound funny,' Cornish said, 'but you'll have to take that up with those dogs. One of them found her and that's all we need.'

'How can she have been there that long though?'

'Well, other than being certain she was buried some time before we nicked Bates, we can't really be sure how long she was there, can we?'

'That's what I'm talking about,' Thorne said.

Cornish talked across him. 'We can be a bit more confident about how long she'd been dead for.'

Cornish's demeanour was still cheerful enough, but Thorne could sense an irritation being held in check, over and above the fact that the DI was busy, or trying hard to appear so. It was understandable. Thorne had yet to make his suspicions clear, but his questions implied a scepticism that would have been unwelcome at almost any stage of the investigation into Stephen Bates. Today of all days, he was well and truly spoiling the party.

He decided to rein himself in a little. 'Yeah, I gather it was in a bit of a state.'

Cornish nodded. *You know what it's like, we've both seen them.* 'Jessica, right?'

Cornish nodded again. 'We couldn't have a formal ID because there was no way I was going to let her parents see her like that. There was a bracelet they were able to identify. Rest is down to dental records, which we should have back later today.'

'I was told she was burned too.'

Cornish did not seem overly concerned about who might have

done the telling. He had clearly become as used to the leaking and the jungle drums as Thorne had. 'Not completely, but enough to get rid of his DNA. Bates knew what he was doing.'

Thorne nodded, thinking that you'd have to be fairly dim not to know that burning would be a handy way to destroy evidence. 'Left a fag-end behind though, right?'

'Right. Caught in the plastic.' There was a little curiosity now, a narrowing of the eyes, but Cornish kept it in check. 'We got a ninety-five per cent match on that before close of play yesterday. Be a hundred by the time the lab boys have finished.'

'Can't argue with that.'

'They always do something stupid, right?'

'Like the porn on his hard drive,' Thorne said.

Cornish grunted and moved behind his desk to look for something in one of the drawers. Busy, busy, busy. There was a burst of laughter from the incident room. A cheer.

'Nasty stuff?'

'It's all nasty.'

'You know what I mean,' Thorne said.

'Bates likes teenage girls.'

'Or women who look like teenage girls.'

Cornish stopped and smiled, took another drag. 'Listen, the man himself is due in court in an hour, so some of us need to get a shift on.'

'Sorry,' Thorne said. He stepped back towards the door, giving Cornish space to go about his business.

'No worries. Any other time, you know ...'

'What you were saying before. About the time of death?'

Cornish took a second to focus. 'The entomologist is still working on his report, but there was no shortage of bugs and beetles.' Another beep and he snatched up his phone again; a few swipes and stabs at the screen. 'We're talking weeks.'

'Killed her just after he took her then.'

'Looks like it.'

'*Looks?*'

'I'm not an idiot,' Cornish said. 'I mean I do realise she was dead well before she went into that bag or the bag went into that hole in the woods. Blowflies don't burrow through two feet of soil to infest a body, do they? They're flies, not moles ... there's a clue in the name. There weren't holes in the bin-liner.'

'So what did he do with her after he killed her?'

Cornish looked up. 'Well, eventually, he buried her.'

Thorne cocked his head, said nothing.

Cornish stared just long enough to make it clear that a line was being drawn. He dropped his e-cig into the top pocket of his jacket and said, 'Right then.' He picked up his case and fastened it as he moved towards the door. 'Look, it's all *extra*. Stuff like his dodgy browsing history. It's icing on the cake, right? We've got a body, we've got his DNA, we know he lied about the girls being in his car. A jury is not going to take very long, put it that way.'

'So, he's stuffed.'

'Comprehensively.'

'You've done a good job,' Thorne said. 'Wish they were all that easy.'

'Well, I wouldn't have said it was "easy", but it's definitely not a case we need any help with. See what I'm saying?' Cornish opened the door and waited for Thorne to leave ahead of him. 'How's your other half doing with Bates' wife?'

Thorne looked at him. At that moment, Helen was on her way to the magistrates' court too, with Linda Bates. She and Thorne had arranged to meet for lunch in the centre of Nuneaton as soon as they were both free.

'She's doing OK.'

'That's good.'

'A shoulder to cry on, you know?'

'Poor cow.' Cornish blinked at Thorne. 'Linda Bates.'

'Listen, would you mind if I had a quick look at the file?'

Cornish pulled the door to his office closed and studied Thorne for a second or two. He patted his top pocket. 'Like I said, we don't really need any ... input, so is there a good reason why you'd want to do that?'

Thorne watched a young woman walking towards them. 'Not really.'

'Just as a professional courtesy, kind of thing, right?' Cornish spoke calmly enough, but made it obvious that he believed both 'professional' and 'courtesy' to be words that Thorne was, at best, no more than dimly acquainted with.

The woman, who was wearing jeans and a tailored leather jacket touched Cornish on the shoulder and said, 'Have fun, boss.'

'Holiday reading,' Thorne said.

He dragged the contents of two thick manila folders out and laid them on the empty desk Cornish had pointed him towards. As he organised them, Thorne was aware that he was being watched by several of Cornish's team, who made no attempt to disguise the fact.

He looked up and caught the eye of the woman he had seen ten minutes earlier outside Cornish's office. He smiled at her. An older man at a desk opposite was staring; nose like an old spud, twisting an elastic band around his fingers. Thorne gave him a smile too. He said, 'Don't suppose there's any chance of some tea?' and the man slowly turned back to whatever it was he should have been doing.

Any information pertaining to the Bates investigation would have been entered immediately it had been gathered on to HOLMES – the home office large computer system – but Thorne still preferred hard copy. The feel of documents, a picture you

186

could hold up to the light. You could miss things, scrolling through pages on a screen.

A creature of habit, like Helen had suggested.

His eyes were drawn immediately to the photographs of Jessica Toms' body.

Mush in a bin-bag . . .

Cornish had been right; the body had only been partially burned, was not blackened except where it had putrefied. The heat had been enough to open the skin, but had left enough muscle and fat to attract the insects. Thorne had seen all this before: the remains more liquid by now than solid; tissue all but gone from the head and around the natural orifices; the creamy strips of bone beginning to show through the sludge.

A couple of weeks at least.

He set the photographs aside to read through the initial reports following the abductions of Jessica Toms and Poppy Johnston. The bald facts: dates, times last seen, witness statements.

He studied the results of the search at Bates' house and garage. The analysis of data on his mobile phone and computer, including the times he had visited websites such as *Barely Legal* and *Teasing Teens*. He looked at the report confirming a DNA match between material found in Stephen Bates' Vauxhall Nova and samples provided by the parents of both missing girls.

He read through the statements given by Stephen Bates. The transcripts of several interviews. The lies, signed to. Then he looked over the interview that Bates' wife had given the day before.

Looking at their questions, he could sense the frustration of Cornish and Sophie Carson.

It was impossible to tell if Linda Bates was covering for her husband. If she was, it was equally difficult to tell if that was because she believed him to be wholly innocent. Thorne had watched the partners of plenty of men and women they knew to be guilty as sin, lying through their teeth for no other reason than they loved them.

He would ask Helen what she thought.

Thorne stuffed the papers and printouts back into their folders and stacked them one on top of the other. He looked up and saw that once again he had the undivided attention of the man with the elastic band.

Thorne blanked him, because he didn't feel much like smiling any more.

Then he picked up the photographs of Jessica Toms' body again. He laid them in a line and stared at them until it began to feel indecent.

# THIRTY-TWO

*Stephen Bates* was trending on Twitter.

Normally, Charli would have been on it like a shot. She always checked out those topics, the ones everyone was talking about; it was how she got news. Which celeb was sleeping with which other celeb. Who had done or said something stupid. Who had died.

Not this time, obviously, because she knew what it would be like. Why was she even looking? Hadn't she told Danny not to go anywhere near this stuff?

She checked to see what people who knew her were saying instead, and immediately wished she hadn't. There were a couple of nice messages, a *#staystrong* hashtag, but the rest were all about Steve. Making disgusting suggestions, asking questions she did not want to think about. Maybe there were fewer messages from those girls she had really thought of as friends because they'd been told to steer well clear by their parents. At school, there were girls who would be treated like they had the plague if they wore stupid shoes or said something to the wrong boy.

189

Not really much of a surprise that Charli was being treated like she was a paedo or something.

Danny came in with a bottle of Coke and a large bag of crisps. He took one look at the computer and even though Charli was at the mirror on the other side of the room, he knew that she had been on it. He was the same at home. One glance at his laptop or his phone and he knew if someone had been messing with them. He changed his password every five minutes to stop their mum looking at his messages. Charli had seen him change it once and remembered the code; logged in when he was in the toilet. There was nothing much to see, just the usual teenage boy shit. Such and such a girl was well fit and some boy was gay. School was gay. Everything was fucking gay . . .

She had told him he needed to stop using that word, that it was offensive. What if one of his friends turned out to be gay? What if *he* was gay? He had taken the piss, obviously. Told her she was gay.

'What you been looking at?' he asked.

'I just wanted to see what people were saying.'

'You said to ignore it.'

'I'm just bored.'

'Yeah, when are they going to let us go out?'

Charli turned from the mirror, carried on teasing at her hair. 'You want to go out?'

Danny shrugged. 'See my mates.'

'Everyone's going to give you such a hard time.'

'Let them try it.'

Charli wanted to run across and hug him right then, but knew that he wouldn't let her. 'Whatever happens, we might have to move, you know that, right?'

'That's not fair,' Danny said. 'I'm not moving anywhere.'

'We might not have any choice. It's what's safest for us.'

'I can look after myself.'

'For Mum, too.'

'What do you mean, "whatever happens"?'

'Nothing.'

'What do you think is going to happen?'

'Just saying. Either way.'

'Is Steve going to prison?'

'How should I know?'

Danny looked at her for a while, then flopped down on to the bed. He opened his crisps. 'Remember that time you threw up after you'd been on that rollercoaster?'

'What?'

'Yeah, you do.'

'When?'

'When he took us to Alton Towers? Remember? When Steve took us.'

Charli shrugged. 'So?'

'It was your birthday and Steve said you could go anywhere you wanted, do whatever, and you said you wanted to try that new rollercoaster.' He shoved a handful of crisps into his mouth, nodded. 'Steve bought us massive burgers and Cokes before, remember, and then you chucked your lumps when we'd been on it and Steve and me were just pissing ourselves.' He nodded again, stared up at the ceiling. 'Yeah, that was ace, that was. That was an ace day ...'

Charli said, 'Yeah.' Went back to teasing her hair.

'There's only one fed left downstairs.' Danny twisted the cap off the bottle. 'The one in uniform, you know?'

'He's all right,' Charli said.

'He's a dick.' Danny sat up and took a swig. 'Kept calling me "mate" and asking me what kind of music I like.'

'He's just trying to be nice.'

Danny glared at her. 'He doesn't give a shit.'

Charli remembered her brother on his first day at school.

Standing in the playground in a blazer that was too big and shoes that he'd somehow managed to scuff within moments of walking through the gates. Their mum had asked her to keep an eye on him, and Charli had promised that she would, but she'd forgotten about it after the first few days. She'd been too busy with her friends, partying and playing up to the sixth-form boys and, before she knew it, Danny had been strutting up and down the corridors; a group of them with their ties undone and hands round their bollocks like a gang of toy-town drug dealers.

He never even acknowledged her if they passed.

So stupid, when she knew him better than anyone. How soft and easily swayed he was. She knew that he just wanted to play computer games with his mates all day, that he loved nothing more than curling up in his onesie to watch *Monsters Inc* or *Frozen* with a bag of chocolate éclairs.

No bad thing, she thought, that they'd never be going back to that school again.

She walked across to the window and peered out.

'A lot less of them today.'

'I told you,' Danny said.

'What?'

'Said they'd lose interest after a while.'

Charli let the curtain fall back, straightened it. She knew that those who had left would not be away very long. She knew that they had simply gone where the action was.

There were photographers of course, but not as many at the entrance to the public gallery as Linda had expected. Helen explained that a good number would be at the other side of the building, looking for that all-important shot of the police van that was carrying Steve. They would be hoping for a gaggle of angry onlookers and plenty of shouting, and someone might even throw something at the van, which was always a result.

Helen had known reporters to hand out eggs.

These days, it was not so much of a dilemma; the need to be in two places at once. Most of the papers would pay for any half-decent shot taken on a camera-phone. Wasn't that always the first thing members of the public reached for? In a bombed-out tube train or at the site of a house fire. The smartphones would be aloft well before anyone thought about helping the injured or calling the emergency services.

They waited in silence while visitors produced ID, then walked in; slow and calm.

Helen had already given Linda instructions. 'Don't react,' she had told her. 'It's exactly what they want. Don't smile, because they'll say "she looked smug" or that "she didn't seem to care". Don't hide your face and whatever happens, try not to get pissed off. They'd love to see you getting angry.'

Linda had said, 'They want to see me looking guilty.'

There were no empty chairs in the small public gallery. Members of the press were already busy with their phones and a line of court officials stood at the back, ready to step in should anyone shout or try to stand up. Helen sat to one side of Linda and a pair of uniformed police officers sat together on the other, to ensure separation between the accused's wife and the families of Jessica Toms and Poppy Johnston.

Helen turned to look at them. The two sets of parents were easy enough to spot; hands held, breathing deeply. Based on pictures she had seen of the girls, Helen thought she could tell which set of parents was which. The woman she guessed was Jessica's mother had the same round face as her daughter, the same colouring. Poppy's father was tall and skinny, same as she was. The four were sitting together in a line at the front and Helen wondered if they had known each other before, if they had been friends. She wondered how the parents of the dead girl felt about those whose daughter was still only missing.

*Only ...*

Sympathy? Envy? Resentment?

Helen could sense that the two couples knew she was looking at them and that they were choosing not to look back. It felt like a refusal.

For the first time since she had taken the decision to come back, she felt conflicted. Now, a few seats away from the parents of a dead girl, she could well understand the looks she was getting from Polesford residents seated nearby.

She told herself she was here for good reasons, for the right reasons.

She was reminding herself what those reasons were, when the judge entered and the court was told to rise.

It did not take long.


Once the judge was in position, the order was given to bring the defendant in. Bates was led into the dock. Linda watched him the whole time, but his eyes were fixed straight ahead.

The clerk of the court asked Bates to confirm his name and address.

Bates did so and was asked to sit down.

The prosecution counsel announced that the accused was charged with one count of murder and two counts of kidnapping. She asked for a preliminary hearing to be fixed at Warwick crown court in two weeks.

The defence counsel said that there would be no application for bail.

The judge made a note of it.

The defence counsel said that this was out of concern for her client's safety.

The judge ordered Bates to stand. He announced that the case had been duly listed for a date two weeks from today and told Bates that he was to be remanded in custody until that time.

Then Bates was being led away. He nodded as the officer with him took hold of his arm and walked him out of the dock. Linda said his name, but not loud enough for anyone other than Helen to hear. The police officers stood to escort Linda from the gallery, making sure that she was on her way before the parents or anyone else.

The reporters were busily texting or tweeting as Linda climbed the steps towards the door. A voice hissed behind her.

'Bitch ...'

Linda and Helen turned together. There were several faces turned towards them. Expressions of scorn, disgust, naked hatred.

It could have been any one of them.

# THIRTY-THREE

Thorne called from the car park at Nuneaton station.

'How were the Cotswolds, then?'

'We didn't stay long.'

'Buy yourself a nice pair of pink corduroy trousers?'

'You got a minute, Phil?'

'Well, I've got an appointment with a banker, but seeing as he chucked himself off a building at Canary Wharf yesterday afternoon, I don't think he's going anywhere.'

Thorne was well used to black humour from those who spent their working lives dealing with the dead, but his friend's jokes were usually blacker and funnier than most. Phil Hendricks was the finest pathologist Thorne had ever worked with, despite an appearance that would frighten people coming out of a Slipknot concert. Thorne was always pleased to hear Hendricks in a good mood, even more so since the terrible events on Bardsey Island.

The price for their friendship, paid in blood and skin.

Thorne told Hendricks where he was calling from, and why. Like anyone else who read the newspapers or watched TV,

Hendricks knew all about what was happening in Polesford, but was shocked to hear that Helen was so personally involved.

'She's not been herself since we got here.'

'Never easy going home,' Hendricks said.

Thorne understood. Hendricks had come out early and, though he had never said too much about it, Thorne guessed that life for a gay working-class teenager at a tough northern school had not been altogether easy. Hendricks was proud enough of where he came from, but did not go back to Manchester very often.

'You know the body they found?'

'The first girl, right?'

'Jessica . . . '

Watching police vehicles come and go, the lightest of drizzles settling like mist on the windscreen, Thorne explained his concerns. He went over the same ground he'd covered with Cornish an hour before, but without the niceties.

'I'm not sure there's very much to get worked up about,' Hendricks said, when Thorne had finished. 'With all the other evidence.'

'Yeah, I know how it sounds.' It was much the same thing that Cornish had said. What anyone would say.

'Dogs aren't always that reliable anyway, mate.'

'They're usually pretty good at finding bodies.'

'Mental, a lot of them are. My mate's golden retriever sits there all day barking at clouds. Eats cat-shit like it's tapas.'

'All right, I know it's not much.'

'It's bugger all, is what it is, Tom. They've got DNA, witnesses and we already know he lied about the girls.'

'It's just the body.'

'You said.'

'Doesn't smell right.'

Hendricks laughed. 'If it's half as bad as you say it was, I'm not surprised.'

'Come on, Phil ...'

Not very deep, the SOCO had said. Not very hard to find. Thorne imagined that yapping terrier scampering back to its master with the dead teenager's liquefied flesh smeared around its muzzle.

'All right.' Hendricks let out a long-suffering sigh Thorne had heard plenty of times before. 'Let me get this banker pancake out of the way and I'll have a think about it.'

'Cheers, mate.'

'And listen, I hope Helen's doing a bit better.'

Thorne said, 'Thanks,' and started the car.

'Give her my love, all right?'


They met at a small Italian place on a square near the main shopping centre. Shoppers moved between the predictable selection of chain bakeries, charity shops and fast food outlets, eating their lunch on the move or squeezed on to benches. Teenagers stood around smoking, talking on the phone; a few leaning against the plinth of a large statue at the centre of the square. A seated woman, eyes cast down, pensive-looking.

'George Eliot,' Helen said, as they waited for drinks. 'She was born here.'

Thorne lowered his menu and looked across at the statue.

'Not a bloke,' Helen said.

'Yeah, I thought the skirt was a bit of a giveaway.'

'Did you know that?'

'Yeah.'

'Liar,' Helen said. She seemed in a good mood; certainly by comparison with the night before. Thorne had arrived at the restaurant ten minutes before her and been happy to see the look on her face when she walked in and spotted him at a table in the corner.

When bottles of Peroni had been delivered and food ordered,

Thorne said, 'All right, smartarse, did you know Walter Raleigh was a poet?'

'He the one that stuck his cloak over a puddle?'

'I'll take that as a no then.'

'So, how the hell did *you* know?'

Thorne laughed and told her about his encounter with Polesford's resident poet.

'Sounds like a bit of a knob,' Helen said. She told Thorne that there were always characters like Shelley in a small town, that she remembered a couple from when she was a teenager. 'Like to make out they're a bit brighter than everyone else, a bit mysterious or something. Swanning around with books under their arm and trying to cop off with stupid girls who think it's exotic.'

'Like Ian Brady,' Thorne said. He remembered reading that the moors murderer had swept Myra Hindley off her feet in much the same way. A long, dark coat and his nose in a book.

'You should watch what you order next time you're in that pub,' Helen said. 'He might be a poisoner.'

Thorne added Tabasco to the spiciest pizza the restaurant had to offer and Helen had linguini with clams. Halfway through, they ordered more beer.

'Bates didn't even look at her,' Helen said. 'In court. Linda stared at him all the way through, but he didn't look across. Not once.'

'Ashamed?'

'Best I can come up with.'

'How was she?'

'Well, she was all right on the way there, you know, because she was going to see him. She wasn't quite so chirpy afterwards.'

'Did she say much?'

Helen shook her head. 'I told her I'd see her back at the house.' She lifted her beer. 'I needed a bit of a break, to be honest.'

Thorne had made the mistake of adding the hot sauce without

tasting the pizza first. The peppers were a little more potent than he had been expecting. Helen rolled her eyes as he quickly poured water from the jug on the table.

'You think she believes him?' he asked.

Helen shrugged. 'I can only go on what she's told me.'

'I know what she *says*, but she's got to put on a brave face, hasn't she? For you and all the other coppers swarming all over the place. For her kids.'

'She talked about being in denial.'

Thorne nodded, chewed.

'Only because it's what she thought I was thinking.'

'So, is she?'

'Look, she's not stupid. She knows he lied about having the girls in the car, but right now, if I had to put money on it, I'd say she genuinely doesn't think he killed anyone.'

Thorne wiped his hands and drank some more water. He said, 'I read the transcript of her interview with Cornish.'

Helen opened her mouth, closed it again. 'You read the file?'

He had told her he was going back to the station that morning, but Helen had not asked him why. She had been distracted, getting ready to go and collect Linda for the trip to the magistrates' court and Thorne had not been altogether sure that she had even taken it in. 'What did you think I was going there for?'

Helen still looked shocked and confused. 'I don't know. I thought you were probably just making a nuisance of yourself because you hadn't got anything better to do. Sounds like I was bang on. Jesus, Tom . . . '

'I saw the pictures of the body,' Thorne said. 'I saw everything. I've been talking to people.'

'Do you not think this is hard enough?'

'Sorry?'

'You can never let it go, can you?' She folded her arms,

200

furious. 'Poking around in all the misery. Like you know better all the time, while some of us are trying to do the right thing.'

'Helen—'

'You can be such a wanker sometimes—'

'Just let me tell you.'

Helen shook her head, pushed her plate away. Listened.

Thorne went over it again, much the same way as he had for Phil Hendricks. The body and the state of it. The dogs. The timings.

When Thorne had said his piece, Helen thought about it, or pretended to. 'What about everything else? The *evidence* they've got.'

'I can't explain it.'

'That's a shame.'

'But this is something, isn't it?'

'It's pissing in the wind, that's what it is.'

'I thought you'd be pleased.'

Helen laughed, just once and narrowed her eyes. 'Please don't say you're doing this for me.'

'I didn't mean it like that.'

'Because if this is some sort of belated Valentine's Day present, I'd rather have had some shitty chocolates—'

'*Listen.*' Thorne had not meant to raise his voice, but he was aware of people on the next table turning to look. 'No, I haven't got an explanation for a lot of it. For most of it ... but even if something's only a *little* bit wrong, it's still wrong, isn't it? If it doesn't add up, you do the sums again. That's all.' He leaned towards her, lowered his voice still further. 'Linda Bates believes that her husband didn't take those girls, didn't kill Jessica Toms, OK?'

Helen waited, her face showing nothing.

'Well, I happen to think she's right.'

\*

Walking back towards the car, Thorne said, 'Phil says hello, by the way.'

'When did you speak to him?'

'After I left the station. I was running all this by him. The body.'

'I bet he said the same thing I did.'

'More or less.'

The teenagers at the statue had moved on and been replaced by a small gathering of Nuneaton Goths eating pasties. George Eliot did not seem overly concerned.

'Best not say anything to Linda. Not just yet, anyway.'

Helen stopped and turned to him. 'What exactly do you think I'm likely to say to her?'

'Just in case you were.'

'"No need to worry, because my smartarse boyfriend thinks there's something a bit iffy about that body they've found. Oh, I know your old man's DNA was found in the grave and the girl's DNA was found all over his car, but trust me, it's all going to be fine". Come on, *seriously* . . . '

Thorne had stopped listening. 'Shit . . . '

Helen turned and followed Thorne's eyeline to the rack of newspapers on display outside the newsagent behind her.

The most prominent tabloid. Stephen Bates in his wedding suit. A banner headline: CHARGED.

And a sidebar with a photograph above it.

Thorne and Helen.

# THIRTY-FOUR

She dreams about her brother's boat, and she knows it's a dream, because this time she's aboard it.

The water is rough, drenching her; cascading over the brightly coloured bow as the boat tries to avoid weeds and logs, empty cans and plastic bags. She can see her brother on the bank, but he can't hear her when she shouts, urging him to bring the boat back to shore. She sees a huge wave approaching and tries desperately to steady herself, but the chain makes it impossible. She closes her eyes, but the water rises up like a fist and punches her over the side.

She is falling for a long time.

Her eyes are open as she sinks fast and takes in the first mouthful of water. She can see the man who took her, his face getting smaller, shimmering at the surface. He calls and stretches out a hand, but she is already too deep to reach, already swallowing again. Something cold brushes against her leg and she knows other things are coming for her.

When she opens her eyes, the side of her face is in the water, pressed against the rough concrete. It is an effort to raise her head, the weight of it, but when she finally manages to sit up, she feels the icy water running down her neck, the trickle inside her shirt. She thinks about what's in it, this water she sips and pisses; the rotting pieces, dissolved now and drying on her skin.

She stares into the blackness.

She shivers, she screams, and the time passes.

Sometimes, she imagines she can see things in the dark, ragged shapes that loom and then retreat, but she knows they aren't really there, so she is not scared of them. It's the stink, and the sound from what's stinking that frightens her. The buzz, the scratch-scrabble, the snick and flutter of teeth and wings. She knows the flies that tickle her face and the beetles and the rats are only there because there is food and somewhere to lay eggs. Because something has died and because something else will be dead very soon.

She imagines she's already stinking of death too.

# THIRTY-FIVE

Linda switched the television off as soon as she got back to the house. She checked to see how Charli and Danny were, wept for a while in the bathroom, then went back downstairs. She moved from room to room, unable to settle, then began rooting aimlessly through the cupboards. In a plastic bag she found a few CDs that the previous occupants had left behind and smiled when she came across a nineties compilation. She put the CD on and stood listening to the first song. She was happy that she could remember the lyrics. In the kitchen, she exchanged a few words with Gallagher and the other uniformed PC, then brought a bottle of wine back into the living room.

She was halfway through it when Helen arrived.

'Want me to get you one?' Linda held up her glass.

'I'm fine,' Helen said. She sat down in one of the armchairs. 'I had a couple with lunch.'

'Nice?'

'Not bad. Some Italian place Tom found.'

'He all right?'

'Yeah, he's good,' Helen said. She was still thinking about what

Thorne had told her in the restaurant. Bodies lying undiscovered for too long. Sums that needed doing again.

Linda nodded towards the stereo. 'Remember this?'

'Course,' Helen said. She listened for a while. R.E.M.: 'Man On The Moon'. 'I think it was playing when Colin Sharples tried to feel me up at a school disco.'

Linda laughed. 'I *let* him feel me up. It was Whitney Houston, though, if I remember.' She sang along quietly with a couple of lines from the R.E.M. track, hummed when the words were indistinct.

'I never knew what that bit was either,' Helen said. 'Somebody wrestling?'

Linda took a mouthful of wine, then let her head fall back. 'Steve's lost weight,' she said.

'Really? It's only been a couple of days.'

'That suit was hanging off him.'

Helen knew that Bates' clothes would have been seized immediately after his arrest, that any suit he owned would have been bagged up for forensics. 'They'll have given him that to wear,' she said. 'There's always a box of clothes knocking about in the station.'

'Must have belonged to a darts player,' Linda said. 'He looked pale as well.'

'He won't have been getting a lot of sleep.'

'Probably because they've not let him, right?' Linda looked at Helen. 'That's what you lot do, isn't it? Drag them into interview rooms in the middle of the night, so they can't think straight.'

'Nobody gets dragged anywhere,' Helen said. 'And if a suspect was tired, their solicitor would be all over us. We do have rules.'

They said nothing for a few seconds as the R.E.M. track faded out. They both groaned when it was replaced by Right Said Fred singing 'Deeply Dippy'.

'Sorry.' Linda held up her glass. 'I wasn't having a go, honest. He just looked awful, that's all. It was hard ... seeing him.'

'I know.'

They both looked to the door when it opened suddenly. Sophie Carson put her head round.

'Everyone doing OK in here?'

'We're fine,' Helen said.

'What are you listening to?' Helen knew that the DS was doing her job, that ears were still being kept open, but for a moment or two Sophie Carson just looked like a woman who was miffed at being excluded from a girlie chat.

'What's happening outside?' Linda asked.

'Usual.' Carson stepped into the room, straightened her jacket. 'There's probably a dozen uniforms out there now, trying to keep it all under control.'

'Stupid,' Linda said.

'Yeah, well that's the thing,' Carson said. 'A lot of those officers would be a damn sight more use to everyone looking for Poppy Johnston.'

'Hey,' Helen said. Carson had been staring at Linda. 'It's not her fault.'

'I never said it was.'

'That's how it sounded.'

'I'm just saying ... if it gets any worse we might need to think about moving you.'

'I'm not going anywhere,' Linda said. 'I'm not under arrest, so you can't make me.' She turned to Helen. 'They can't, right?'

'It would be for your own safety,' Carson said. 'You and the kids.'

'Why are we not safe?' Linda looked towards the window. 'You're not thinking of inviting any of them in, are you?'

Helen was pleased to see Carson at a loss for a comeback. Suddenly a memory rose up from nowhere of an argument

Helen had witnessed between Linda and one of their teachers at school.

They would both have been twelve, thirteen maybe. They had been given the results of a comprehension test in English; a passage about a gypsy camp. One of the questions had been about the gypsies cooking hedgehogs and the question was about why they baked the animals in clay. Linda had demanded to know why her answer had been marked wrong. 'They bake them in clay so the spines get pulled out,' she had insisted. The teacher had shaken his head and handed Linda's exercise book back to her. 'But it doesn't say that anywhere in the passage, does it?' Linda had said that she *knew* that was the reason, that it didn't matter if it said so in the passage or not. The teacher would not listen and told her he was docking her another mark for arguing. Walking back to her desk, Linda had tossed her exercise book out of the window.

That was when Helen had decided that Linda was clever and liked a fight; that she would be fun to hang around with.

'Why wouldn't he look at me?' Linda asked when Carson had left. 'Steve.'

'I don't know,' Helen said.

'Yes you do. Or you *think* you do.'

'I've seen people in the dock do all sorts of strange things.'

'Guilty conscience, right?'

'Linda—'

'It's OK, really.' Linda smiled. 'Why should you think anything different from the rest of them? If I was at home watching all this on the telly, reading about it in the papers every day, I'm sure I'd think exactly the same thing.' She leaned forward for the bottle and poured what was left into her glass. 'Funny how your attitude changes when you're on the other side of it. The way you judge people, I mean, all that "no smoke without fire" shit. Well, you know now, right?'

Helen looked at her.

Linda reached behind the cushion to the side of her and took out a folded-up copy of a tabloid. She unfolded it and smoothed it out on her lap, stared down at the front page; the picture of Thorne and Helen. 'They were reading this in the kitchen,' she said. 'Carson and the rest.'

'I bet they were,' Helen said.

'It says all sorts of things in here about your boyfriend.'

'I read it.'

'Stuff he's been accused of in the past.'

'Look which paper you're reading,' Helen said.

'Says he might have been responsible for a man's death, on some island.'

'He wasn't.'

'Well, you're bound to say that, aren't you?'

'Listen, I know him, all right?' Helen kept her tone good and even. 'Whatever it says in that rag, I don't believe Tom did anything wrong.'

Linda nodded. She folded up the paper and slid it back behind the cushion. She said, 'Well, now you know how I feel.'

# THIRTY-SIX

The Police Control Unit was even busier than the last time Thorne had been there. A press conference was scheduled for six o'clock and with the parents of Poppy Johnston due to make a direct television appeal for the first time, there was a good deal of activity. While camera positions were being chosen, seats laid out and a small stage prepared, very different arrangements were being made at the other end of the Memorial Hall.

With not much more than an hour's light left, the last search team of the day had been assembled and would shortly be sent out to look for Poppy Johnston. Twenty or more locals were being briefed, along with twice that many uniformed officers. While maps were consulted and instructions given, Thorne noticed that several officers had dogs with them. He still found it impossible to believe that no similarly equipped search team had scoured those woods many days before Jessica Toms' body was eventually discovered. Despite Hendricks' misgivings, Thorne knew what cadaver dogs were capable of; how unlikely they would be to miss a stinking corpse less than two feet below ground.

'You coming with us then, detective?' Thorne turned to see the

PC he had spoken to in the pub the night before; the one he had been so rude to on his first day. The officer was wearing walking boots and wet-weather gear together with an expression that suggested he was rather pleased with himself. 'Fancy getting your hands dirty?'

'I'd be happy to,' Thorne said.

'Really?'

'But I need to be at the press conference.'

'Yeah, that's probably a good idea.'

Thorne studied him. 'You got something to say to me?'

'Just thinking you might want to hear what Poppy Johnston's mum and dad have got to say.'

'Because ... ?'

'Because it might make you rethink some of that sympathy for the bastard that took their daughter.'

'I've got no sympathy for whoever took their daughter.'

The search team began to head out. The PC stood his ground, while colleagues and members of the public pushed past him, funnelling through the main doors and out on to the street.

'That's good to hear,' the PC said. 'I mean, sympathy's not what you expect, is it?'

'Depends who it's for.'

'Not from someone on the job.'

Thorne started to see where this was going.

'I mean, you wouldn't have sympathy, I don't know ... for someone who'd cost a prison officer his life. You know, just as an example. I'm damn sure I wouldn't.'

Thorne stared down at the officer's walking boots, well-worn brown leather, red laces. He was very hot suddenly as he struggled to think of something to say. By the time he'd managed to string enough invective together, the PC was moving away; falling in with his colleagues and leaving the hall without a backward glance.

211

Thorne muttered the words anyway.

He walked slowly to the far end of the hall, weaving between the men and women who were putting out the chairs in nice, neat rows. He stood and watched as two officers at the back of the platform carefully erected the banner bearing the logo of the Warwickshire police: a bear and a ragged staff.

*You know, just as an example . . .*

Thorne had not been particularly surprised at the PC's reaction. He had clocked the looks he was getting from the moment he set foot in the hall. He could easily imagine the laugh that Cornish and his cronies were enjoying at Nuneaton station.

A major result and to top it all, just look at that know-it-all wanker from the Met splashed all over the front page. All those skeletons rattling out of his closet. Icing on the cake.

When Thorne's phone rang a few minutes later and he saw the caller's name, he wondered simply what had taken him so long.

He was not given the chance to ask the question.

'Well done!' DCI Russell Brigstocke got straight to the point, as usual. 'What's next? You going to get your tits out on page three?'

'Thought you read the grown-up papers,' Thorne said.

'Couldn't bloody avoid it, could I?'

'I suppose not.'

'It's up on the noticeboard, for Pete's sake.'

'Before you kick off, none of this is my doing, all right?'

'It never is, is it?'

'I'm just here keeping Helen company.'

'I know exactly what you're doing. I read it in the paper, remember.'

'What could I do?'

'You could avoid sodding journalists for a start.'

'You want me to start punching photographers, like some arsey film star?'

212

'I want you to be doing what you told me you'd be doing. Eating cream cakes or looking at castles or something.'

'This wasn't what I had in mind either.'

'You should have known they'd go digging,' Brigstocke said. 'Snuffling for dirt like pigs looking for truffles. Where you're concerned, the dirt isn't very hard to find, is it?'

'There's nothing in there I can't defend,' Thorne said. 'Nothing you can't defend either.' He stood aside as two officers carried a table past. 'Right, Russell?'

Brigstocke took a few seconds. Said, 'Look, I'm not getting into that now.' His voice was indistinct suddenly and Thorne guessed that he was eating. 'I've been talking to Warwickshire.'

'What, the whole county?'

'Can you hear me laughing, Tom?'

Thorne said nothing.

'I suppose that wasn't your fault either, marching in there like the big "I am" and pissing everybody off.'

It gave Thorne some small degree of satisfaction to learn that his instincts about Tim 'keep in touch' Cornish had been right. The sort of copper he was. A flash suit and a winning smile; unwilling to call you a twat to your face then picking the phone up to bitch to his superiors the minute you've gone. 'He said I could look at the file. What's the big deal?'

'Why would you even ask?'

'There's not exactly a lot to do round here.'

'You need to shut up now, and stop being a smartarse, OK?'

Thorne listened.

'I mean . . . for God's sake, you're telling me you're just there to keep Helen company, so why are you sticking your nose in where it isn't wanted—?'

'What's the harm?'

'Where someone's very likely to cut it off, and you know what, I don't think I'd blame them.'

'This Bates thing isn't solid,' Thorne said.

'Oh, I know.' There was more chewing. 'Some crap about dogs and bodies, and to tell you the truth, I really don't care.'

'Not even if they've got the wrong man in custody.'

'Not even then.'

'So you don't want me to tell you?'

'I couldn't give a toss if you think Jack the Ripper killed that girl,' Brigstocke said, 'and Shergar helped him bury the body. Not when I'm the mug getting it in the neck from the Chief Superintendent of Warwickshire Constabulary because I can't control my officers.'

'Come on.'

'I'm serious, Tom.' And Brigstocke's voice, low suddenly and heavy with threat, left Thorne in little doubt that he meant it.

'All right.'

'This is the kind of thing people lose jobs over. Especially people like you.' There was a pause. 'Tom?'

'What?'

'Stay out of the local boys' way, got it?'

Thorne grunted a 'yes'.

'And if you can persuade Helen, I'd suggest the pair of you piss off back to the Cotswolds at the first opportunity.'

Thorne looked up at the banner, now fully erected behind a long table; the logo a foot high against the white canvas. He pictured the bear in an expensive suit, puffing on an e-cigarette, turning to show its teeth before snapping.

Thorne remembered reading somewhere that if you were attacked by a particular sort of bear, the best thing to do was run. There was another sort, however, where that was exactly the wrong thing to do; when the best strategy was to play dead.

He could never remember which was which.

# THIRTY-SEVEN

'I just don't understand why you lied, that's all.'

'I know.'

'Why didn't you want to tell me where you were?'

'I'm sorry, Dad.' The truth was that Helen did not understand either. Not completely.

She was alone in the living room. Linda had gone upstairs to spend some time with the kids and Carson and the rest of them were gossiping in the kitchen. She said 'sorry' again to fill the silence. She had known this conversation with her father was coming from the moment she had seen the front page of the newspaper.

'I probably wouldn't have known you were there at all, but one of the neighbours came round with the paper.'

Helen gritted her teeth. 'Good of them.'

'They thought I'd want to know, you know.'

'I was going to call.'

'I mean I've been following it on the news, obviously.'

'Course.'

'We talked about it before you went, didn't we? When the first girl went missing.'

'Yeah . . . ' Helen remembered several conversations about the events in Polesford. Each time her father had insisted that 'nothing like that' would have happened back when he was living there. She wondered if rose-tinted spectacles got handed out to people on the same day they qualified for a free bus pass.

'Nasty business.'

'Can I talk to Alfie?'

'He's asleep, love.'

'Oh.'

'I thought I'd worn him out in the park, but he was still full of beans when we got back. Hang on, let me turn the telly down a bit . . . '

There was a clatter as the phone was laid down. Helen moved to the window, looked out through a gap in the curtains at the crowd outside. A man was shouting something at one of the officers.

'Right then. Maybe you can call back later, before he goes to bed.'

'Yeah, I will,' Helen said. 'Thanks again for having him.'

'Don't be daft.'

'I feel bad though.'

'I'm just a bit thrown by this business of you being in Polesford, that's all. Polesford of all places, and not telling me.'

'I know,' Helen said. She flopped down on the sofa. 'I went to see Mum.' She listened to her father breathing. 'Tom came with me. It was nice.'

'That's good.'

Helen felt a rush of guilt at changing the subject, the way she'd changed it. 'We took some flowers.'

'See, I'd never have known that, would I? You not telling me you were there.'

'I would have said eventually.'

'I must be going senile, because I still don't understand.'

The shouting outside was getting louder.

'Everything that's going on here,' Helen said. 'I just didn't want you to worry.'

'That's ridiculous.'

'Why?'

'What you do. I worry every day, love.'

There was a loud banging on the front door and Helen heard footsteps moving quickly down the hall from the kitchen. Her father asked what the noise was and she told him that she would need to call him back.

She hung up, relieved.

Helen saw Linda coming a little nervously down the stairs and got to the front door just as Carson was opening it to an equally nervous-looking PC. Behind him, Helen could see two of his colleagues at the end of the front garden, fighting to restrain a well-built man who was shouting about his rights and knowing them.

'What?' Carson snapped.

'This bloke,' the officer said. He pointed, just as one of the struggling PCs took a firmer hold of the man and asked him if he was trying to get nicked. 'He reckons he's Linda Bates' ex-husband.'

# THIRTY-EIGHT

There seemed little reason for the handwritten name cards that had been placed in front of Michael and Annette Johnston. It was not hard to work out who they were. Though they were as smartly dressed as the two police officers and the press liaison officer with whom they shared the platform, they were the only ones staring down at the table. The two whose hands were joined. They were the ones that everyone else in the room was looking at, as Assistant Chief Constable Harris spoke words almost certainly written for him by the woman standing at the side of the platform.

'As most of you will know already, Stephen Bates, the man we believe to be responsible for the murder of Jessica Toms, is now on remand awaiting trial. While I commend Detective Inspector Cornish and his team for their excellent work on this tragic case, we must not lose sight of the fact that there is an inquiry still ongoing that continues to demand our full attention . . .'

Thorne was sitting towards the back of the hall. He had been at plenty of these things before and seen similar speeches made countless times. The words may have been different on each occasion, but the rhythms were much the same. The same pauses, the moments when the officer looked up, towards the cameras. Thorne remained convinced that Cornish and his team had done a job that was anything but excellent, but he couldn't fault Harris' performance. Serious, sincere; nothing inappropriately upbeat, despite having cleared up a murder so quickly. Thorne still thought the man's hat was a little too big for him.

'Our sympathies are with Jessica's family of course, but all our efforts must now be concentrated on finding Poppy Johnston, who remains missing.' Harris looked along the table. Poppy Johnston's father glanced up briefly. 'So ... Poppy's parents, Michael and Annette, are going to make a short statement, after which I will be happy to take a few questions.' The ACC cleared his throat, straightened his papers.

Tim Cornish leaned towards Poppy Johnston's mother and whispered something. She nodded and Cornish laid a hand on her arm.

Michael Johnston unfolded a piece of paper. He took out a pair of glasses, looked down and read. 'Stephen Bates has persistently refused to tell police where our daughter is.' His voice cracked a little. Cornish pushed a glass of water towards him, but he didn't take it. 'So ... today we're appealing to anyone who might know anything that might help us find Poppy to please come forward. Anything at all. If anyone saw anything or has heard anything, please call the incident room, night or day. It doesn't matter what it is, just call. You don't have to give your name.' He folded the piece of paper again. 'We just want to find her.' Now, he reached for the water.

'Please,' Annette Johnston said. She had no piece of paper to read from, and something about the way she spoke up suddenly made Thorne wonder if she had come intending to speak at all. 'Somebody must know *something*.' She leaned forward, found a camera. 'If by any chance you're watching this, Pops, we're trying our best to bring you home.' She tensed, and it was hard to tell if she was squeezing her husband's hand or he was squeezing hers. 'We love you so much ... '

Cornish said, 'OK,' and laid a hand on the woman's arm again. Chairs scraped noisily against the floor as they stood, one by one, and Cornish helped the couple to the edge of the platform. From there, a uniformed officer walked them towards a small door in the corner of the hall; cameras flashing as though they were walking a red carpet.

Assistant Chief Constable Harris waited for Cornish to return to his seat, then nodded out towards the phalanx of journalists.

'Do you believe that Poppy Johnston is still alive?'

Heads turned, all well aware that the Johnstons had not quite left the hall yet. Annette Johnston spun around and her mouth fell open. She scanned the room for the source of the question, but the man responsible had already lowered his hand. There was one more explosion of flashes before she turned away and was ushered through the door.

The following morning's front page.

'We are keeping an open mind,' Harris said, eventually. 'Our priority is to find her, but yes, until we learn otherwise, we remain hopeful.'

'Even though Bates must have killed Jessica Toms almost immediately?'

Clearly the press knew as much about the state of the body as they did about everything else. Based on that, the journalist's question was couched around the only explanation possible.

The very explanation that was troubling Thorne so much.

'As I said, we remain hopeful.'

A hand was raised within a few feet of where Thorne was sitting, and when the eyes of those on the platform were cast in his direction, Thorne imagined getting to his feet to ask a question of his own.

*If Stephen Bates is guilty of murdering Jessica Toms, are you not*

220

*concerned by the fact that her body was not discovered for* at least *two days? Despite having conducted extensive searches of an area that is usually crawling with dog-walkers?*

Harris answered the question that had actually been asked. Something about how Bates had behaved in custody. It prompted others.

'Poppy's father said that Bates has refused to say anything about where Poppy is.'

'That's correct.'

'But has he admitted taking her?'

'I can't comment on that.'

'Has he admitted killing Jessica Toms?'

'I'm afraid that, as of now, I can't comment on matters that may directly affect the prosecution.'

There were several more questions along the same lines and all were met with much the same response. Then proceedings were wrapped up fairly quickly. The press liaison officer gave the nod and Harris made a closing statement.

As before, he thanked the people of Polesford for their continued support. He said how grateful he and everyone else was to the media for showing sensitivity. He urged the journalists present to focus on the hunt for Poppy and not to dwell on matters that were unimportant, or at best 'peripheral to the case'. Thorne saw Cornish glance in his direction and could not help wondering if the comment had been aimed at him.

What else could Harris have been talking about?

He could imagine Helen telling him that he was being paranoid. There were plenty of other angles for the press to explore, after all, every bit as peripheral as the presence of a newsworthy Met officer. Thorne knew the kind of stories the papers would be shelling out cash for.

*I sat next to Stephen Bates at school.*

*Stephen Bates gave me a funny look at a bus stop once.*

221

*There was definitely something about him I never liked.*

Those were the stories that angered Thorne the most. The neighbours or old schoolfriends crawling out of the woodwork, queuing up to pocket a fee and point out that they always knew there was something dodgy about Killer X or Rapist Y.

No, they didn't. Simple as that.

That was why the people who did these things were able to get away with it for so long; precisely because they behaved every bit as normally as everyone else. You could appear just as kindly as the village vicar and be a sexual predator. You could look like a central casting serial killer and be as harmless as an infant.

Stephen Bates looked like . . . Stephen Bates. Not a killer, no, but probably not a choirboy either. Probably . . .

Thorne was suddenly struck by a possibility he had not considered.

What if Bates *had* been involved, but in league with somebody else? It would certainly explain the wealth of evidence against him. Perhaps he *had* taken the girls and his accomplice had disposed of the body. But that did not explain the cigarette butt with Bates' DNA that had been found in the grave. Perhaps Bates' partner was thinking on his feet and had been trying to stitch Bates up once he had been arrested.

Or Stephen Bates was being stitched up by someone else entirely.

Around him, the hall was emptying quickly, the majority of the audience needing to get their copy filed as fast as possible. Thorne stood and lifted his jacket from the back of his chair. Up on the platform, Tim Cornish was chatting to the press liaison officer; nodding and puffing away on his e-cig as the banner was being disassembled behind him.

Cornish turned and looked directly at Thorne. He smiled, showing plenty of teeth.

Thorne smiled back.

Play dead.

222

# THIRTY-NINE

Once Carson and her colleagues had established that nobody was in any physical danger, they retreated to the kitchen, but Helen was certain that they could hear the shouting. She guessed that the crowd still gathered outside could hear it.

'I want to see my kids. Where are they? I demand to see my fucking kids . . . '

Linda just sat there while her ex-husband ranted, as though she were well used to it. Looking on from just inside the door of the living room, Helen wondered if the man's prodigious temper might be one of the reasons he and Linda had split up in the first place. Watching him stomp around though, she thought the man's anger began to seem a little theatrical, as though he were playing the part of the furious father. Perhaps giving a perform-ance that could be easily overheard was exactly the point.

'You can't stop me seeing my own kids.'

'I know.'

'You got that?'

'Who's stopping you?' Linda said.

'Yeah, well you'd better not try.' Wayne Smart leaned against the wall, breathing heavily. He wore camouflage cargo pants and trainers; a green army jacket. Helen had no reason to believe he was ex-army, looking rather more like someone who fancied himself as a soldier. Someone who'd been turned down, perhaps. He was big enough, but a little bloated, with blond highlights and earrings in both ears. Helen had smelled booze on him as he'd pushed past her in the hallway.

Something he and Linda had in common.

Smart reached into the pocket of his jacket and took out cigarettes.

'Not in here,' Linda said. 'This isn't our place.'

'I couldn't give a monkey's.' Smart lit his cigarette and sucked in fast. He jerked a thumb towards the kitchen. 'Let one of your pet coppers come and arrest me if they want. There's enough of them.' He took another drag, then turned and stared at Helen. 'Who's this?'

'I'm another one,' Helen said.

'Yeah, well why don't you piss off and join your mates? Me and my ex-wife have got things to talk about.'

'She's a friend,' Linda said.

'She's *what*?'

'An old friend.'

Smart turned to look at Helen again.

'I'm not going anywhere,' Helen said.

Smart studied her for a few seconds, genuinely curious, then shrugged and marched across to the window. He pulled a curtain aside and looked out. Helen was aware of the movement as the crowd shifted to look, of cameras flashing.

'Shut that,' she said.

Smart did not move. 'You can't tell me what to do.'

'Shut it, or I'll nick you.'

'For what?'

'I don't know, for having shit hair?' Helen stepped further into the room. 'Or I'm sure I can make breach of the peace stick.'

224

Smart let the curtain fall back and turned round. He flicked cigarette ash on to the carpet. The anger had reappeared in his face, or been turned on again. 'Where are Charli and Danny?'

'Upstairs,' Linda said.

'Good.' He walked across and sat down in one of the armchairs. 'Go and get them.'

'Why now?'

'You what?'

'Why do you suddenly care so much now?' Linda leaned forward. 'How long since you've seen them, eighteen months? How long since you even bothered to call?'

'Yeah, well it's different now, isn't it?'

'What, you suddenly a model father, are you?'

Smart stabbed a finger at her. 'I'm a father who's found out who his kids have been living with.'

'You don't know anything,' Linda said.

The finger continued stabbing the air. 'So, don't come all high and mighty about who's a model this or model that, because you haven't got a leg to stand on.'

'Don't ...'

'Because I'm not the one who chose to marry a kiddie-fiddler, am I? A child murderer, for God's sake.' He glanced across to bring Helen into the conversation. 'Not that she was ever much of a mother to begin with. Not what you'd call "responsible".' He picked up the empty wine bottle from the table and dangled it between two fingers. 'Still caning it, I see.' He dropped his cigarette end into the bottle and banged it back down on to the table.

'You finished?' Helen asked.

Smart turned to her again. Said, 'Nowhere near.' He sat back in the chair, as if he had lived in the house for years. 'Who did you say you were?'

'She told you,' Helen said.

'Well, I've got no idea who you are and I've known *her* for the best part of twenty years, so you can't be that bloody close.' He seemed pleased that Helen did not have a quick response. 'I tell you this for nothing though. However much of an old friend you think you are, I know her a damn sight better than you do.'

'No,' Linda said. 'You don't.'

'She knows exactly what that pervert she married is like, and if she tells you any different, she's full of shit.'

'All right,' Helen said.

'And I'll tell you something else.' Smart leaned towards Linda and, for the first time, Helen sensed anger that was genuine; simmering and dangerous, barely contained. 'If I find out that bastard's touched my kids, you'll be the one I'm coming after.'

Linda's head dropped slowly.

'Now I can arrest you for threatening behaviour as well,' Helen said.

'It was a promise,' Smart said. He didn't take his eyes off his ex-wife. 'Not a threat.' He let out a long breath and reached for his cigarettes again. 'So, am I going to see my kids, or not?'

'How do you know they want to see you?' Helen asked.

'Why wouldn't they want to see me?' He tried to light his cigarette, shook the lighter. 'I'm their father, aren't I? I'm not the pervert.'

'Linda?'

'Yeah . . .'

Helen told Wayne Smart to wait, asked Linda if she'd be all right for a few minutes. Linda nodded.

'What do you think I'm going to do?' Smart asked.

Helen left without answering him, stepping out into the hall, careful to leave the living room door ajar. When she turned at the bottom of the stairs, she saw Charli and Danny looking down at her. They were sitting close together on the same stair, halfway up.

Like pyjama-clad toddlers who've crept down in the middle of the night.

# FORTY

It had been a good choice, those woods where he'd left Jessica in the night. The perfect place for that last hour or so they had been together. He was happy she had gone to sleep somewhere peaceful. He shook his head, adjusted the thought. Happy that it was where she had been *laid to rest*.

She had gone to sleep elsewhere, of course.

Places like that – natural, green, *quiet* – still felt a little strange, even after all this time. So different to where he had grown up, the places he had worked in before. He watched the local kids sneaking off into those woods sometimes, bags clinking with bottles, pockets full of condoms, and he was jealous because he couldn't help but wish that his first few times had been somewhere like that, under trees rather than flyovers. Birds and things that smelled nice. Moss on a girl's back instead of brick dust.

He remembered his first time, just like everyone else did. Forget that and you might as well cash in your chips. A week before his sixteenth birthday, a girl called Julia, who was a year younger than he was. They had been walking back to the bus from the cinema and it had been her idea to cut through a

227

narrow alleyway. She'd known exactly what she was doing, of course she had, but it had been more than OK with him.

In a stinking doorway, the clatter of heels on concrete somewhere nearby; the usual unzippings and fumblings. It had all been over pretty quickly, but the girl had been OK about it, he knew he was remembering that right.

She'd been putting her lipstick back on and he'd asked her. She'd said 'fine' or 'great' or something.

He remembered asking her.

Obviously there would be people who thought what he was doing was because he felt inadequate; hating these girls deep down, because of being laughed at in the past or something. They could not have been wider of the mark. In fact, all the girls he'd *ever been with* had made a point of saying how well he'd treated them, how nicely. He'd asked all of them, more than once, and every girl had seemed happy. They'd all made it pretty clear that he was no slouch in the bedroom department either.

He smiled. His hand dropped to his groin.

Bedroom, bathroom, back seat, whatever.

Obviously, he knew that girls like Jessica and Poppy were far more likely to be impressed with the things he could do, because most of them didn't have a lot to compare it to. No, if anything, it was the women his own age who tended to be more judgemental. Seen it all, done it all, blah blah. There hadn't been too many complaints, but surely there wasn't a bloke walking around who didn't recognise the occasional look of mild disappointment. Couldn't be too many who hadn't been told it didn't matter, when they knew very well that it did.

Younger girls were . . . kinder.

And he was kind to them in return, at the end. He was quick about it.

Poppy though. Sweet Pops . . .

It wasn't his fault, not entirely, he had miscalculated, that was

228

all. He hadn't thought things would get so hectic, and he probably should have done. No, he *definitely* should have done. The end, if it hadn't come already, would be anything but kind and he was living with the pain of that every day. Like an ulcer or something. Like cancer . . .

Cruelty did not sit easily.

It was not who he was.

# FORTY-ONE

Thorne guessed he was the only Spurs fan in the pub. He was certainly the only one watching the match who seemed upset about the fact that they were one down at home to Manchester City within fifteen minutes. He was starting to wish he hadn't bothered coming. Wasn't football supposed to be an escape from the stress and anguish of his job?

All that pain and grief.

Murder was a doddle in comparison . . .

'Not your boys' night by the look of it.' Trevor Hare was collecting empty glasses.

'Long way to go,' Thorne said.

They watched for half a minute. Thorne winced as his team's leaky defence almost gifted a second goal to the visitors.

'Steve Bates was sat where you are a week or two ago,' Hare said. 'Watching the match, same as you.'

Thorne looked at him. Was the landlord telling him in case he fancied moving to another table? Was he about to start another of those 'you think you know people' routines Thorne was getting so tired of?

'Won't be so relaxed now, will he?'

'I seriously doubt it,' Thorne said.

'Why not *tell* them though?' Hare shook his head. 'I don't get that at all. He's going down anyway, right? So why not put that poor girl's parents out of their misery and just say where she is?'

Thorne stared into his glass and decided against offering up his best guess.

*Because he doesn't know.*

Instead, he said, 'I'm amazed you haven't had the press on at you. Ex-copper running the killer's local, bang up their street.'

'Oh, don't worry, I have,' Hare said. 'And I told them where they could stick their blood money an' all.' He walked towards the bar, spoke over his shoulder. 'I never liked them when I was on the job ...'

Thorne turned his attention back to the game.

He ordered a cheese sandwich and chips at half time and had barely finished eating it when Spurs went two down five minutes after the restart. He swore and pushed his plate away. It wasn't hard to imagine what a passionate Arsenal fan would have to say.

He didn't have to.

'Only ever been one decent team in London, mate.'

Thorne looked up to see Phil Hendricks grinning at him.

'Whichever one of us supports a shit team gets the drinks in,' Hendricks said. 'Oh, wait, that's you.'

'What ... ?'

'Spit it out.'

'What the hell are you doing here?'

'Nice.' Hendricks seemed delighted to see his friend so lost for words. He told Thorne to shove up and squeezed in next to him. 'You're not the only one who needs a holiday, you know.'

'Yeah, but ... work?'

231

'I just got my squashy banker out of the way, switched things around with a couple of colleagues and jumped in the car. I'm pretty senior, you know, I can do that sort of stuff.'

'But you hate the countryside as much as I do,' Thorne said.

'Just one more in a long line of sacrifices I've made for you.' The smile faltered a little; the space between them suddenly charged by the memory of what had happened on Bardsey Island. Hendricks made the necessary effort to lift the mood. 'Listen, you don't *have* to say how pleased you are to see me, you know. I mean you're welcome to shed a tear if you want, I shan't be embarrassed.'

'Course I am. Just a bit gobsmacked at you showing up.'

'You said you wanted my help.'

'An email would have done it.'

'I work better on the ground, mate.' Hendricks smacked his lips theatrically. 'Actually, I work a damn sight better with a drink in front of me, but as your wallet's obviously welded shut, same as always, I'd better go and get them in.' He slid out and on to his feet.

'Where are you staying?' Thorne asked.

'Ah . . . haven't quite thought that far ahead.'

'How well do you work after a night on a park bench?'

'I'm sure you'll think of something.'

Thorne told Hendricks that he'd call Helen, see if her friend Paula was able to squeeze another guest in. 'Obviously, I'm not bothered either way, but Helen will be pleased to see you,' Thorne said. 'She's not been herself.'

Hendricks took off his jacket, tossed it at Thorne. 'Yeah, you said.'

'She's starting to get on my tits, frankly.'

'I thought that was my job.'

As Thorne took out his phone and dialled, he watched Hendricks find a space at the bar and immediately begin talking to a man with slicked back hair and a leather jacket. Hendricks turned to look at Thorne over the man's shoulder and widened his eyes. Thorne shook his head.

Mouthed: *Slag*.

Helen *did* sound pleased to hear that Hendricks had shown up out of the blue, but didn't say much beyond that. She told Thorne she would talk to Paula and volunteered to collect them both from the pub later on. 'I know you'll be making a night of it,' she said.

Hendricks laid drinks and crisps on the table and sat down. 'Might not need that bed at Helen's mate's after all,' he said. He slurped the foam from his pint. 'Is Leather Boy looking?'

'Are you kidding?' Thorne asked. '*Everybody's* looking.'

Hendricks' haircut was as brutal as usual. His scalp was the one part of his body (as far as Thorne was aware) that the pathologist had yet to tattoo, but it would certainly have been visible through the stubble. He was wearing a T-shirt with a diagram of human ribs on the front; cap-sleeved to emphasise the extravagant patterns of ink on his arms and tight enough to show the outlines of the nipple rings. There was plenty of other metal on show, through ears, nose and lips.

Thorne would not want to be stuck behind Hendricks in the queue at airport security, but, as always, he enjoyed the reaction to his friend's appearance.

'They don't like your sort round 'ere,' he whispered.

Hendricks was staring towards the bar. 'I think some of them do,' he said.

They watched the match for another ten minutes, but City seemed content to sit on their lead and Spurs seemed happy to let them.

'So, who burns half a body?' Hendricks asked. He might just as well have been asking Thorne to pass the cheese and onion.

'Sorry?'

'That's the only interesting bit in what you told me. The rest of it's not actually that exciting.'

'Exciting enough for you to come all the way here.'

'I've got a very dull life.'

'The body wasn't there long enough,' Thorne said. 'I think that's pretty bloody interesting.'

'Long enough for what? And don't give me all that crap about dogs again. It could have been there a few days, surely.'

'I seriously doubt it.'

'That's long enough for it to have been Bates who buried it.'

Thorne shook his head. 'The body was weeks old.'

'Doesn't mean Bates didn't kill her.' Hendricks looked round, suddenly aware that a couple on the next table were leaning a little closer. He lowered his voice. 'He kills her pretty soon after he's snatched her, then buries her much later. No big mystery.'

'Where's the body in the meantime?'

Hendricks shrugged. 'Maybe he liked having it around.'

'Right, because that's normal.'

'Nilsen did. Said he killed young men for company.'

'Yeah, but he didn't just sit there and watch them rot in his front room, did he? He chopped them up and flushed them down the drain.'

Hendricks nodded, conceding the point. 'Yeah, much more civilised.'

On screen, the post-match analysts were pulling every aspect of Spurs' performance apart. The young waitress came across to collect Thorne's plate and after chatting to her for a few minutes, Hendricks lifted up his shirt to show her his piercings. The pair on the next table were drinking in silence, as though waiting for Thorne and Hendricks to pick up their conversation again.

'The only way your worries would make any sense is if that body wasn't quite as old as it seemed.' Hendricks leaned to get a better view of the bar.

Thorne looked at him. 'Yeah?' He waited. '*Phil . . . ?*'

Hendricks straightened up and sighed. The man he'd been talking to at the bar earlier was nowhere to be seen. 'I tell you what, my gaydar's well off these days.'

'How do you mean, not as old?'

Hendricks grinned and held up his empty glass. The price of his further expertise. 'What I said before. Who the hell burns half a body?'

# FORTY-TWO

'What did he have to come here for?' Danny asked.

'He's our dad. He's got a right to be worried.'

'Shouting and swearing though.'

'He'd had a drink,' Charli said.

'He's always had a drink.' Danny was shouting himself, now; kicking out at the end of the bed. 'Mum's always had a drink. Why is our family so fucked up?'

Their dad had not stayed long, but Charli had been pleased to see him, and hated herself for it. All the usual hugs and kisses, like he couldn't bear to be parted from them, and crap about how much she and Danny had grown, how much he missed them both, but what did she expect? She wasn't under any illusions about him. She knew that her mum was better off without him, that she was happier with Steve.

Now her mum would have to get used to being without Steve. Something else Charli wasn't under any illusions about. She wondered how *she* would feel if Steve wasn't around. It would be different to when her dad had walked out. However much of a loser he was, however much he'd let them all down, he'd always be her dad. There would be feelings she could never get rid of, however deep she tried to bury them. Blood, or whatever. That was the difference.

Stupid really, but nothing you could do about it.

'I want to go into school,' Danny said. 'Pick up some stuff.'

'What stuff?'

'Books and shit. Might as well do some work if we're stuck here.'

Charli stared at her brother and tried not to laugh. He was hardly a model student and more than once he'd been pulled up for writing essays that he'd lifted wholesale off the internet.

He held out his arms, inviting her to say something sarcastic. 'What?'

He was bored, she knew that. They all were. 'They won't let you.'

'Can't stop me,' Danny said. 'What do you think would happen if I just went downstairs right now and walked straight out of the front door?'

'You'd get your picture in the paper.'

'That'd be all right.'

'Yeah. Mum would go mental, ground you anyway and take away your computer for a week.'

'What computer?' Danny walked across the bedroom and slapped his hand on top of the PC they'd been given by the police officers. 'I'm not counting this piece of crap.'

'Better than nothing.'

'When are we going to get our own computers back anyway? They must have finished with them by now.'

Charli thought that was probably true, but wondered how much longer they'd be working on Steve's. What they'd found already. 'So, what did they find on yours?' she asked. She grinned, but Danny wasn't looking at her. 'Stupid messages to your sad mates? Pictures of fit girls?'

237

Now he turned. 'Yeah, well what's on yours? Shit that's way more embarrassing, I bet.'

Charli couldn't bear to think of police officers looking at what was on her laptop; the photos, the conversations on Facebook and Instant Messenger. She felt a knot tighten in her stomach, remembering the last round of online chat between her and her best friend, Gabby. They'd fallen out over a party Charli had gone to. A boy Gabby had got with, who had subsequently bragged about it to everyone, had been there, so Gabby had refused to even think about it. She had accused Charli of wanting to get with the boy herself and being a terrible friend for going.

The knot got that bit tighter.

*thght we were mates*
*come on gabz just a party*
*friendship=over*

It wouldn't take much for Gabby and a whole lot of other girls to drop her now, Charli thought. Parties and misunderstood messages were nothing compared to this. Jessica Toms and Steve . . .

There was a soft knock at the door and her mum walked in. She carried her glass of wine across to the bed and sat down.

'You all right?' Charli sat down next to her and leaned in.

Linda nodded and smiled. 'Was it nice to see your dad?' She turned to see what Danny had to say. He was sitting at the desk, carefully studying one of the magazines that the cops had brought over. Something with a guitar on the front.

'Not sure it was nice,' Charli said. 'He was only here five minutes.'

'Good that he wanted to see you though.'

'Good?'

238

'You know.'

'What kind of dad wouldn't want to see his kids?'

'Yeah, you're right,' Linda said. 'He's a dick.' She grinned, giggly with the wine. 'Is that the right word? That what you two say? Dick?' She looked across at Danny again. 'Douchebag?'

Charli leaned away from her. 'We heard what he said, you know? When he was downstairs.'

Linda blinked slowly. 'Sorry.'

'We're not stupid, you know.' Danny tossed the magazine on the floor. Charli and her mother both turned to look at him. 'We know Steve's probably not coming back, right?'

'We don't know that,' Linda said.

'I said probably not, all right?' He stood up, thrust his hands into the pocket of his tracksuit bottoms. 'I mean obviously I'm hoping he will, right, but whether Steve comes back or not, I want you to swear that *he's* not coming back, not ever. I mean it, Mum. I want you to swear it, OK?'

'He's your dad.'

Danny's eyes were wet, hands balled into fists inside his pockets.

'*Swear.*'

# FORTY-THREE

The TV in the corner of the bar had thankfully been turned off, not that Thorne could have seen it anyway. There was standing room only, now that many of those who had been out searching for Poppy Johnston had returned from fields and woods and wasteland. They huddled together in small groups, warming up; keen to put a couple away before closing time and compare stories.

Thorne caught snippets here and there as he carefully carried drinks across to the table. Nothing much to tell, sadly, but the conversations were enough reason for Thorne and Hendricks to keep their own even more discreet than it had been.

'I mean, burning gets rid of DNA, obviously,' Hendricks said. He leaned forward and whispered, as though it were the punch-line to a dirty joke. 'Incriminating fluids.'

'Presuming there were any.'

'Even if there weren't, there's stray hairs, fibres, whatever. His fingerprints on her skin.'

'So, he knows what he's doing,' Thorne said.

'Bates?'

'Whoever.'

'Yeah, I reckon so.'

'But somehow he still manages to drop a cigarette butt in there when he's burying her.'

'We all make mistakes.'

'I'm not sure it was a mistake.'

Hendricks nodded, but it was clear he was thinking about something else. 'Still a bit strange though, don't you reckon, only doing half the job? So, maybe we should be asking ourselves ... is that the only reason?'

Thorne waited.

'For setting fire to the body.'

Thorne waited a little longer. 'So go on then, what's the other reason?'

'Well, I'm working on it ... '

Hendricks was into his fourth pint of Guinness without having eaten anything and was becoming a little vague. Still, Thorne knew he was sharper than most people, even when he was three parts pissed.

'You must have some idea.'

Hendricks grimaced and closed his eyes for a few seconds, fumbling to line up whatever his thoughts were in the right order. 'It's just weird, that's all I'm saying. You set fire to your body, pour on the petrol, whatever, out with the Swan Vestas ... and up she goes.' He threw up his hands. 'Then you rush over and put the fire out before the body's completely burned.' He cocked his head one way, then another. 'I don't know ... maybe I'm going nowhere with this and he just couldn't bear to see her completely burned. Maybe she was ... precious.'

'An hour ago you were saying he sat there watching her decompose.'

Hendricks nodded his head slowly, then shook it. He took a mouthful of beer and held it in his mouth for a few seconds before swallowing it. 'He burns the body just enough to destroy any forensics, but not enough to destroy *her*. See what I'm saying?'

'Not really.' Thorne was starting to think his friend didn't actually have anything to say that made any sense.

'Just enough for something else.'

'Such as?'

After a few seconds' frozen concentration, Hendricks sat back and shook his head. Whatever had been threatening to emerge into the light had drifted back into the murk; thick and black as the Guinness he was busily putting away. 'So, what do you think's going on with Helen, then?'

'Wish I bloody knew,' Thorne said.

Hendricks nodded, knowingly. 'Why do you think I prefer blokes?'

'Because they've got cocks?'

'Because they're much simpler creatures.'

'She was fine until we got here.'

'It was her idea to come, right?'

'Yeah, I tried to talk her out of it.'

'Like I said, it's strange, going home. Memories, whatever.'

'Nothing bad as far as I know.' Thorne stared at his glass. 'I mean, her mum died here, but I don't think it's anything to do with that.'

'Any people from her past she might not have wanted to see?'

'One ex-boyfriend so far,' Thorne said.

'Oh, I'm sorry I missed that.'

'In here, the first night.'

'Place is probably crawling with them,' Hendricks said. He gestured at Thorne with his glass. 'I mean she clearly has pretty low standards.'

'How long did you say you were staying?' But Thorne was smiling in spite of himself and, as far as his own relationship

242

with Helen went, he thought that Hendricks probably had a point.

He was definitely punching above his weight.

Thorne checked his phone to see if there were any messages from Helen, and, when he looked up again, Trevor Hare was standing at their table, with a drink of his own in his hand.

'Rushed off my bloody feet in here tonight,' he said.

Not so busy that he couldn't find time to wander across and check out the new face, Thorne thought. To enjoy a swift half. 'This is Trevor,' he told Hendricks. 'The governor.'

Hendricks stuck out a hand and introduced himself.

'You in a band or something?' Hare asked.

Hendricks laughed, put him right.

'Blimey,' Hare said, nodding. 'So, what, professional curiosity or something? Why you're here, I mean.'

Hendricks pointed at Thorne. 'Just here to keep him out of trouble.'

'I think you might have your work cut out,' Hare said.

'Oh, I know.'

'Not with me,' Thorne said. Hare had probably read the paper, he thought, or been talking to one of his customers.

'Only pathologists I ever knew wore suits and ties,' Hare said. 'Very straight, you know?'

Hendricks grinned. 'I'm a bit of a maverick.'

'Another round?' Hare looked at his watch. 'Last chance.'

'I think we're fine,' Thorne said.

Hendricks was about to demur, until he clocked the disapproving look on Thorne's face. He drained his glass then stared at it. 'Yeah . . . '

'Right, let's get this lot shifted,' Hare said. He pushed his way back to the bar and rang the bell.

'Do I smell bacon gone off?' Hendricks asked.

Hare shouted, announced that it was time for everyone to get

243

their drinks down their necks. He rang the bell again. People began doing as they were told.

'Ex Met,' Thorne said. 'Why this place is full of coppers. Fuller than usual, anyway.' He watched the landlord clearing glasses from the bar and turned in time to see Helen coming through the door. 'Here we go. Our ride's here.'

'Well yours might be,' Hendricks said. 'Mine left ages ago.' He grinned and waggled his eyebrows; like Groucho Marx, if he'd been born in Salford and had a thing for extreme body ornamentation.

'Look at you pair,' Helen said, when she reached the table. 'Having fun?'

They stood up, grabbed jackets and downed what was left of their drinks. Helen leaned in to kiss Thorne on the cheek and was then pulled into a prolonged hug from Hendricks.

'How you doing, gorgeous?' Hendricks drew Helen even tighter, looked at Thorne over her shoulder. 'You know it's you I've come to see and not him, don't you?'

Helen stepped back and said, 'Course I do,' and told Hendricks he was pissed.

'I'm . . . refreshed.'

'As a newt,' Thorne said.

'Come on then, Laurel and Hardy.'

'So, have I got a bed? Hendricks asked.

'You've got a sofa.'

At the door, Helen stopped and handed Thorne the car keys. 'Car's outside,' she said. 'I need to nip to the Ladies.'

Watching her go back in, Hendricks said, 'If she's gone to get condoms out of the machine, you know I always carry plenty, don't you?' He patted his jacket pocket, gave a clumsy boy-scout salute. 'Be prepared.'

'Don't think I'll need to trouble you,' Thorne said.

*

Helen came out of the toilets into the small hallway that led back towards the bar. It smelled only marginally better than the toilets themselves. Wiping damp hands on the back of her jeans, she looked out through the glass doors into the garden and saw two figures emerge from one of the buildings at the far end. They walked past a table where three teenagers sat smoking and as they passed beneath one of the overhead lights, she recognised a young girl she had seen serving behind the bar, straightening her shirt and leaning close to an older man with a ratty-looking beard and glasses. They opened the door and stepped into the hall. The girl did not look at her, but the man smiled as he passed, clearly pleased with himself. She watched them walk towards the bar, trying to remember the joke about ponytails always having arse-holes underneath . . .

She jumped as the door slammed behind her and turned to see that the three teenagers had come in from the garden.

'Blimey, look at this. It's Linda Bates' pet rug-muncher.' The biggest of the three stepped towards her. Dirty blond, with bad skin, the collar of his polo shirt turned up.

'Shit!' An Asian kid in a baggy American football shirt. 'She's got a nerve.'

The third one just stared, hands thrust into the pockets of his windbreaker.

Helen could smell the fags and the beer coming off them.

'How can you show your face in here?'

'Fucking *nerve*.'

'Where's your girlfriend then?'

'Waiting for you at home with her legs open?'

'Getting the strap-on oiled up.'

'All right, lads,' Helen said. A smile, but not in her voice. 'Just get yourselves off home, all right?'

The boy in the polo shirt spread his legs and stuck his neck out. 'Think you can tell us what to do?'

'Cheeky bitch.'

'You know I'm a copper, right?'

'Like I care,' the Asian kid said.

Helen glanced down to unzip her bag, rummaged for her warrant card.

'You're a disgrace . . . '

She heard the phlegm being hawked up and raised her head at the same time that the gobbet hit her in the face. She tried to lift her hand to wipe it away, but for a few seconds her body refused to do as it was told. She could only watch, and let the cold slug of spittle crawl down her cheek, as the three boys tore open the door to the garden and bolted, whooping, into the darkness.

# FORTY-FOUR

Paula Hitchman pronounced herself delighted to have another person staying and her other half sounded equally enthusiastic. Jason Sweeney seemed especially taken with their newest guest and, once he'd thanked them both for the use of their sofa, Hendricks was certainly not shy and retiring. Within ten minutes, with cans of beer opened and sandwiches on the go, he had responded to repeated invitations and shown his hosts more tattoos and piercings than the waitress in the Magpie's Nest had been privileged to see.

'You like metal?' Sweeney asked. 'The music, I mean.'

'I like stuff you can dance to,' Hendricks said.

'Seen a few people like you at gigs, that's all. Suppose it's more like dragons and stuff with them though. Eagles and skulls and that.'

Paula asked if there were any piercings in more 'intimate' regions. Hendricks winked and told her she might find out if she played her cards right.

Sweeney nodded, impressed. 'Seriously hardcore, mate. Seriously.'

'They reckon you can get addicted to it,' Paula said.

'I'm addicted to lots of things,' Hendricks said.

Sweeney nudged Thorne, who was next to him on the sofa. 'Not exactly Quincy, is he?'

Thorne said no and cradled his can and listened to the noises from the bathroom upstairs. Helen had announced that she was tired as soon as they had arrived, that she wanted a shower and an early night. It was the first thing she'd said since the three of them had set off from the pub. Walking to Paula's front door, Hendricks had caught Thorne's eye. A look that said, 'I see what you mean . . . '

'Still, at least your patients can't complain about what you look like,' Sweeney said. 'That what you call them, patients?'

'Stiffs,' Hendricks said. 'Various categories thereof.' He began to count off on his fingers. 'Crispy critters . . . floaters . . . pavement pizzas. Had one of them just before I came here, matter of fact. Banker who forgot he couldn't fly.'

'Cause of death not too tricky then,' Sweeney said.

'Oh, I can do all that stuff in my sleep.'

Hendricks was showing off, or rather the Guinness was; a character he slipped into if an audience demanded it. No more than booze and bullshit. The truth was that Thorne had never known a pathologist with so much empathy for the bodies he worked with; one as willing and able to hear whatever secrets the dead could pass on.

'I'm the corpse whisperer, me,' Hendricks said, winking at Thorne.

'I like that,' Paula said. 'That's a good one.'

Thorne knew the real reason Hendricks had come. They were both hoping that Jessica Toms might have something to say to him.

'Amazing though,' Sweeney said, 'the things you can do these days. The technology.'

'I think it's overrated,' Hendricks said. 'I still miss leeches, myself.'

Sweeney didn't get the joke. 'You can get results in minutes now, right?' He looked at his girlfriend. 'Did you know you can tell if a suspect's been in a room just by getting a sample of the air? Just from the air, for Christ's sake.'

Paula looked at Thorne. 'You lot'll be out of a job soon.'

'No complaints from me,' Thorne said.

'Let me guess,' Hendricks said. 'You're a big fan of *CSI.*'

'God, he watches all those shows,' Paula said. She nodded towards the drawer beneath the TV stand. 'We've got all the box sets under there, anything with a few bodies in it, and he's always got his nose in some gory book with dozens of murders. I like something a bit more literary myself.'

'So, I like crime stories.'

'Not so much fun when it happens on your doorstep though, is it.'

'No, I suppose not,' Sweeney said.

Thorne thought that the taxi driver looked a little crest-fallen. Disappointed by the terrible ordinariness of real murder.

He listened for a few minutes longer, then when the sand-wiches appeared and demands were issued for a few more blood-soaked war stories, Thorne excused himself. He'd heard the shower being turned off ten minutes before.

'Helen said anything about Linda Bates?' Paula asked. 'What she thinks about what her old man did?'

'She hasn't told me a thing,' Thorne said.

Thorne had to reach out a hand to steady himself and piss straight. He hadn't put away as much as Hendricks and he'd eaten before they'd really got stuck in, but he had never been the world's best at holding his drink.

He flushed and closed the lid. He washed his face, then sat for a minute or two to try and clear his head.

It was the very technology Jason Sweeney was so enamoured of that would put Stephen Bates away. The sort that actually existed, anyway.

His DNA on a fag-end in a shallow grave.

The victim's DNA all over his car.

Rock-solid evidence that showed Stephen Bates to be a liar, that proved a dead girl and a missing one had been where he insisted they had not.

Technology and good old-fashioned lies.

But technology didn't always tell the truth either, because facts were just facts at the end of the day and that wasn't gospel, was it? That wasn't the be-all and the bloody end-all. Sums that needed adding up again.

Thorne stood up slowly, groaning. He should have stopped drinking half an hour earlier.

When he emerged from the bathroom, Hendricks was waiting on the landing. He stepped close to Thorne. Said, 'It's all about the bugs.'

'What is?'

'This body business.' Hendricks nodded. 'How long it was buried in the woods and how long it had been ... a body. If there's a *difference*. Trust me, mate, it's *all* about the creepy-crawlies.' He was wiggling his fingers, making suitably creepy-crawly-ish gestures and grinning.

'Go to bed, Phil,' Thorne said.

Hendricks leaned even closer, conspiratorial. 'How can I?' He spoke like someone who had learned to whisper in a helicopter. 'Can't get me head down until they decide it's time for bed. I'm kipping in the front room, aren't I?'

'I'll see you in the morning,' Thorne said.

Hendricks pushed past him into the bathroom, singing; something that had been playing in the pub. Thorne stepped quietly across the landing and into the bedroom.

The lights were off and Helen was already asleep, or pretending to be.

# FORTY-FIVE

Helen had left early for Linda's, driving Hendricks back to pick his car up from the town centre on the way. Hendricks, with several strong coffees inside him, was heading to Nuneaton to see the pathologist who had performed the post-mortem on Jessica Toms. Sweeney had offered to drive Thorne into Polesford, but until he was dressed and ready to do so, Thorne had little choice but to wait and mooch around.

Sweeney finally came downstairs just after eleven. He made himself breakfast, sat around in the living room in his flappy dressing gown.

'What Paula was saying last night about not liking blood and gore?' He tore off half a slice of toast with one bite. 'Probably because she sees a fair bit of it at the hospital. All the messy stuff, you know? She can't even sit through an episode of *Casualty*.'

Thorne nodded. He didn't know too many coppers who came home and spent the evening watching box sets of *The Bill*.

'Other way round for me,' Sweeney said. 'Not a lot to get your pulse racing, driving for a living. Not round here. Someone throws up in the back of the cab occasionally, that's about as exciting as it gets.'

'Too exciting for me,' Thorne said. He quietly belched, tasted last night's beer. He knew where he was with the smell of blood, meaty and metallic, but just the suggestion of vomit was making him feel a little queasy.

All about what you were used to, he supposed.

'That's why people are so worked up about what's happened,' Sweeney said. 'This is not the most thrilling place normally.'

'Thought that was why you moved here.'

'Yeah, it was.' He thought for a few seconds. 'Swings and roundabouts though, isn't it?'

'It's definitely a bit conventional,' Thorne said.

'It's a bit . . . safe.'

'Really?'

Sweeney shook his head, acknowledging the unfortunate choice of word. He pushed the rest of his toast into his mouth. 'I was probably the funniest-looking bloke in the place until your mate showed up.'

'He certainly turned a few heads in the pub,' Thorne said.

'So come on then.' Sweeney brushed the crumbs from his lap, laid his plate on the floor. 'What's he really here for? He was being a bit mysterious last night.'

'Well, that's up to him.'

'Is he here as some sort of consultant on the Bates thing?'

Thorne shrugged. 'I think he just fancied a few days away.'

'Really?'

'Somewhere nice and conventional.'

'Come on, it's not like I'm going to tell anyone. Is he like an expert witness or something?'

'He just turned up,' Thorne said. 'That's it.'

Sweeney smiled and nodded, as though the lack of a convincing answer was just the answer he'd been expecting; as if he

253

knew Thorne was keeping something back and got a kick out of being party to the intrigue. He picked up the TV remote, jabbed at it and scrolled through the channels until he reached Sky News.

A sports round-up, the weather, then the latest from Polesford.

'Here we go.' Sweeney sat back, then groaned in disappointment when they cut to the reporter. 'God, this bloke's so bloody dull, don't you reckon? It's much better when that young girl's doing it.' He adjusted his dressing gown. 'I ran her back to her hotel the other night. She's even nicer in the flesh.'

The channel was running with a story they'd lifted from the daily papers. Piggybacking on somebody else's exclusive. They slowly zoomed in on the front page, describing it in detail, though it needed very little explanation. The banner headline was superimposed over the picture.

'Bloody hell,' Sweeney said. 'I wondered when he'd show his face.'

Thorne did not recognise the man on the front of the paper, but the words on the screen made it clear enough who he was.

Sweeney looked across at Thorne. 'Well at least it's knocked you and your other half off the front page.'

'He's a pig,' Linda said. 'He was always a pig. This though . . . '

Helen studied the picture. 'They probably offered him a lot of money.'

Sitting on the edge of the bed, Linda's knuckles were white as she gripped the edges of the newspaper. 'He's the one that did the offering,' she said. 'You can bet your life on it, and he'd have done it for fifty quid. Twenty . . . '

It was the second day running that Linda had been handed a copy of the newspaper by the police officers keeping her company. Today though, they had passed it across somewhat reluctantly; as though the pages themselves might have been coated in something toxic. There were none of the sly smiles she had seen the previous day, when Helen and her boyfriend had graced the front page.

'It's why he came,' Linda said. She handed the paper across to Helen. 'It was all set up, wasn't it? It was all just about this.'

Helen looked at the picture. Wayne Smart wrestling with a uniformed officer at the edge of the front garden. A more formal shot of him alongside; a teaser for the full story on a double-page spread inside. The headline: almost a direct quote from his conversation with Linda the day before.

IF HE'S TOUCHED MY KIDS, I'LL KILL HIM.

Linda was right, of course. The fracas outside had been as good as staged, the confrontation inside no more than material for the exclusive story of a traumatised father. Helen remembered Smart stomping around downstairs, shouting and issuing threats; the air of a performance about the whole thing. She found herself wondering if he might have been carrying some kind of recording device.

She turned to the story inside and scanned the text, her eyes quickly drawn to Smart's description of her. His ex-wife's 'so-called friend'. A serving police officer, he insisted, should know better than to comfort a woman who had allowed a child killer into her home. Into his children's home.

The tension in Helen's shoulders, the distaste that washed across her face, must have been obvious.

'Yeah, you get a good kicking too,' Linda said. 'Sorry.'

'Not your fault.' Helen was too tired to be overly concerned, and it was too late anyway. It did not make Linda's ex-husband any less of a sleazeball, but people had known who and what she was for at least twenty-four hours; had already marked her out.

Yesterday's front page had seen to that.

She remembered the look on the face of that boy outside the toilets the night before. Triumph, *amusement*, as he'd wiped the back of a hand across his lips and dabbed at the dribble on his

255

polo shirt, a second before he'd turned on his heels and led his friends away.

*You're a disgrace . . .*

'All that crap about our amicable split.' Linda leaned across to jab at the pages. 'His great relationship with the kids. You should hear what Danny said about him after he'd gone.'

Helen read on. *'I'd die for my kids', says frantic father Wayne. 'And I'll do whatever it takes to protect them!'*

There was a picture of Wayne Smart looking suitably frantic and, most shocking of all, a picture of the children themselves. It was several years old. Both were wearing Man United football shirts; Charli trying to smile and Danny trying not to.

'They can't do that, can they?' Linda asked. 'I mean, what about privacy or whatever it is.'

'They're his kids,' Helen said. 'His picture, I'm guessing. Both the kids are under eighteen, so he can give them permission to print it.'

'Doesn't mean he isn't a wanker for doing it.'

'No, it doesn't,' Helen said.

'Making out like he's whiter than white,' Linda said. Spat. 'I bet nobody's thought to check his criminal record, have they? Criminal damage, theft, assault. We had the police at the house every couple of months because of complaints from the neighbours.'

'Why did you marry him?' Helen asked.

Linda got up slowly. 'I settled, didn't I? Settled for him, settled for this place.' She walked across to the window, no more than a blade of dim light cutting in through a gap in the curtains. 'Settled for a series of shitty jobs . . . not that there's been any of them in a while.' She turned, panic-stricken suddenly. 'Will they stop my benefits?'

'Why would they?'

'All this.'

'You haven't done anything,' Helen said.

Linda nodded, then turned back to the window and calmly opened the curtains. She stood and stared down across the heads of the police officers on the pavement, towards the small crowd gathered on the opposite side of the road. She didn't move when people began to shout and point, when the phones and the cameras came out.

'You should come away from there,' Helen said.

'Sod 'em,' Linda said. 'Give them what they want, maybe they can find somebody else to crucify.'

'Or they can just keep on crucifying you.'

Linda turned and for a second it looked as though she might faint. 'I feel like I'm drowning,' she said. 'I need to get out.'

'I know,' Helen said.

'Not to a police station or a court. I need to get out of here, just for a few hours.' She heard voices from the next room. 'I should really go and talk to the kids about what it says in the paper. I mean I'm sure they know already ...'

'Do you want a drink?' Helen asked.

'Do you mean tea?'

'I mean, whatever you want.'

Walking down the stairs, Helen was thinking about that helpful neighbour who would almost certainly have brought a copy of today's paper for her father to see. She thought about him reading it and worrying about her.

She thought about Alfie, oblivious for now, but easily able to find that picture on the internet within a few years. No such thing as 'tomorrow's fish and chip paper' any more. She thought about that look on his face when he stopped walking halfway round the park and folded his arms and demanded to be carried. The way his lips pursed and he just got stroppier the more she laughed. She thought about the soft skin at the back of his neck, the smell of it.

The rattle in that shitbag's throat as he had hawked up phlegm. She was no disgrace to anyone or anybody.

Gallagher was sitting at the kitchen table with a male PC. Helen walked across to the fridge and took out the wine. She opened the cupboard and reached for glasses. She could hear Carson on the phone in the living room.

'I wanted to apologise.' Gallagher stood up, her propensity for blushing obvious yet again. 'For what I said to you the other day, about Linda. It was out of order.'

Helen closed the cupboard, set bottle and glasses on the worktop. She said, 'Do you want to make it up to me?'

# FORTY-SIX

They met at the edge of the woods and walked to the spot where Jessica Toms had been found. The evidential soil had been replaced and the forensic team had packed up and gone, but it was easy to see where they had been. The nearby undergrowth tramped down by dozens of plastic-covered boots, the marks on the ground where the forensic tent had been erected.

The shape of the grave still clear enough, if you knew where to look.

'It's not like we've got a secret handshake or anything,' Hendricks said.

'Still surprises me though.' Thorne shoved his hands into the pockets of his leather jacket. It was dry, but bitterly cold. 'The way you lot stick together, share information.' He thought about the smile on Tim Cornish's face the last time they had seen one another. 'Coppers aren't quite so good about that, even if they pretend they are.'

'What can I say? I'm a lot more charming than you are. That's not saying much, mind.'

'Nobody's arguing,' Thorne said.

'So, I took a look at the PM report, then I saw the body.'

They both stared down at the patch of ground from which the body in question had been removed. Lifted from the damp, black earth with rather more care than the man who put it there had taken.

Care for Jessica Toms, at any rate.

'Not a lot of her left,' Hendricks said. 'But you knew that.'

Thorne nodded, remembering the photographs he had seen.

'The skin had been burned away from the face and torso ... rather more left on her back and legs. A good deal of that was then removed by insect invasion.' Hendricks emphasised those final words, with a look on his face that Thorne had seen before; that told him Hendricks had finally managed to order his thoughts a little. That a suspicion had been confirmed.

'Tell me about the report.'

'Cause of death was impossible to ascertain due to the condition of the body.'

'Best guess?'

'Not even one of those,' Hendricks said. 'No sign of blunt trauma to the skull, but that's about it. I don't know, strangled, maybe? Suffocated?'

'What about time of death?'

'Yeah, well afterwards, I drove across to talk to the forensic entomologist. Believe it or not, he liked me even more than the pathologist.'

'Yeah, the charm thing, I know.'

'No, seriously.' Hendricks grinned. 'He *really* liked me.'

Thorne sighed. Said, 'So?'

'So, time's a bit easier, but still no more than an approximation. Four weeks, give or take, based on the insect activity. The types found within the remains, the order in which the different species arrive and get stuck in to their dinners. The blowflies first, then the clown and carrion beetles that follow to feed on the maggots in the active decay stage. You know all this stuff, right?'

'Yeah.' Thorne was thinking that this was all simply confirming what Cornish had told him. He could only hope there was some other reason Hendricks was so animated.

'I mean, it's not like you haven't seen a bug feast before.'

They turned at the sound of a dog barking, one of several they had seen or heard in the ten minutes since they had arrived at the woods. 'See what I mean?' Thorne asked.

'Plenty of them around, that's for sure.'

'And they can't all have no sense of smell.'

'My dog's got no nose,' Hendricks said.

Thorne had no time for old jokes. 'If Jessica was really dead that long, it means she was murdered almost as soon as the killer had taken her. That's the line Cornish and his team are taking.'

'But you don't think she was, do you?'

'No.' Thorne saw that look on Hendricks' face again. 'And now you don't either, do you?'

'Like I said, all about the bugs. The conclusions that get drawn from them.'

They turned again at a noise nearby and watched a dog come trotting out of the trees behind them. Thorne recognised the labradoodle, then its owner, who appeared a few seconds later, whistling for it.

The man ambled across, swishing at low-lying branches with his walking stick. He nodded at Thorne, took a rather longer look at Hendricks.

'Afternoon,' Thorne said.

'Last time I saw you, you were creeping out from behind some bushes.'

Thorne looked at Hendricks. 'I was caught short.'

Hendricks looked at the dog-owner and shook his head. 'Don't believe a word he says.'

The man stared, as though unsure how to respond, suspicious that he was being made the butt of a joke he didn't understand. Slowly, a smile appeared. 'It's what always happens on TV shows, isn't it?' he said. 'The cop coming back to the crime scene.' He looked at Hendricks. 'You a copper, as well?'

'No.' Hendricks bent to make a fuss of the dog, who was nuzzling around his legs.

'It's not like that,' Thorne said.

'The copper or the killer,' the man said. 'One of them always goes back to the scene of the crime. Both of them, sometimes.'

'Only if the TV show's run out of ideas,' Hendricks said.

'Can't happen though, can it?' The man snapped his fingers and the dog trotted back to him, jumped up to sniff at his pocket. 'Not the killer anyway. Not unless Steve Bates fancies breaking out of prison.' The dog barked at nothing in particular and the man told it to be quiet.

Thorne looked at Hendricks. 'We should be getting back.'

Goodbyes were quickly nodded or mumbled.

'Nice to have it back to normal though,' the man said. 'Nice that we can all walk our dogs again.'

Thorne and Hendricks trudged back the way they had come, the dog following them, until Thorne shooed it away, while its owner stepped forward and used his stick to prod tentatively at the ground beneath which Jessica Toms had been buried.

'It was the burning thing that was bothering me,' Hendricks said, once they were out of sight. 'The partial burning. Now I've read the report and seen the body, it doesn't bother me any more.'

'Now it's something else, though,' Thorne said.

'Let's assume you're right and that she wasn't dead four weeks, nothing *like* four weeks.' Hendricks moved ahead, then turned, stepping backwards a few feet ahead of Thorne. 'How do you make a body that's actually relatively fresh look like it's been rotting a fair while?'

'Never mind how,' Thorne said. 'What about why?'

'Well, I haven't got that far yet.' Hendricks waved his hands, impatient to get to his point. 'Anyway, that's your job, I would have thought.'

Thorne wasn't sure what his job was. Right now, all he could do was follow, and listen.

'We both know that once a body's been dead for more than a week or so, the normal signposts for time of death ... temperature, lividity, what have you, aren't really in play any more. Especially when you haven't got a lot of the body left to work with. We all know it's pretty much down to the entomologists after that, right? You ask me, almost anyone who's watched a cop show or two knows that much.'

'Why doesn't it bother you any more, Phil?' Thorne asked.

'What?'

'The fact that the body was only partially burned.'

Hendricks smiled, enjoying it. 'Because I know why he did it. He burned the body just enough to open it up, didn't he? To expose what was needed.'

'To open it up for what?'

Hendricks shrugged and answered as though it were blindingly obvious.

'To put the bugs in.'

Those watching the house reacted predictably quickly, despite the speed at which the people who came out of it moved down the front path, hurrying towards the waiting car.

The young male PC leading the woman with a blanket over her head.

The money shot ...

The officers stationed on the pavement opposite could not stop several people pushing past them and moving into the road; one or two getting to within a few feet of the woman, hurling abuse before the door of the squad car was opened and she was pushed down and into the back seat.

The male PC shouted, 'Go,' and 'Move.'

Though officers tried to clear a path for the vehicle, those few journalists who weren't pointing their cameras at the side window moved quickly to position themselves directly in front. They instantly began shooting through the windscreen, so that for ten or fifteen seconds, until they were pushed aside, the car could only nose forward slowly, while those still watching and shouting from the pavement walked quickly or jogged alongside, towards the end of the road. As the police car finally built up a little speed and switched on its blues and twos, people began to run to keep pace with it; motorbikes and scooters were fired up and a small convoy quickly formed to follow the car around the corner and away, their engines buzzing like angry wasps.

At the same time, the front door to the house opened again and Helen Weeks walked calmly out with Linda Bates towards a second, unmarked car. By this time, there was only a handful of people left outside the house, and nobody was paying a great deal of attention.

One woman looked up after stamping out a cigarette and tugged at the sleeve of the woman next to her. They both looked towards the corner around which the police car had gone, then back again. The confusion on their faces was clear enough from the other side of the road.

Linda smiled and climbed into the car.

She gave the women two fingers as Helen pulled quickly away.

# FORTY-SEVEN

Helen followed the same route she and Thorne had taken a couple of days before. There was still a good deal of chaos, but it was clear that the floodwater had subsided still further, as many of the roads that had been closed then were now just about passable. She stopped first at the pub she and Thorne had eaten in and left Linda in the car to check it out. Even though the food rush had finished, there were still too many customers taking extra-long lunch hours for her liking, so she drove twenty minutes further out, until she found somewhere a little less busy.

'Don't want a place that's deserted though, do we?' Linda had said. 'We'll stick out like the proverbial and it probably means it's a shithole.'

'As long as there's sandwiches and half-decent wine, I think we'll survive,' Helen said.

The pub provided both and Helen carried food and drink across to a table in the corner, out of sight of the door.

Linda got stuck in, talking more as she did so than at any time since Helen had arrived. Her spirits had visibly lifted the moment they'd left the house. She had cheered as they'd driven away, clearly relishing the subterfuge, laughing at the thought of Gallagher under that blanket and jabbering excitedly as though she and Helen were Thelma and Louise off on an adventure. Now, the first glass of wine safely put away, she continued talking about her relationship with Wayne Smart. She had known it was a mistake from the beginning, she told Helen, except for the kids who were the only decent thing to come out of it. She had made the best of a bad job once Danny and Charli had come along.

Helen nodded. 'What people do.'

'Stupid people,' Linda said.

'You're not stupid.'

'You can't make a silk purse out of a sow's arse.' Linda smiled as she said it. 'And that's what it was. What *he* was.'

'Still is, by the look of it,' Helen said. She thought about her father again, how upset he would be about the story Smart had given to the newspaper.

'That's what was so great about Steve,' Linda said. 'He was everything Wayne wasn't. He was great with the kids and he seemed to actually care about me, you know? Basically, he gave a toss and there haven't been too many people I could say that about over the years.'

'Counts for a lot,' Helen said.

'I'd always picked the wrong bloke until Steve came along.' She looked at Helen. 'Yeah, I'm well aware how that sounds under the circumstances.'

'It sounds fine.'

'Course it bloody doesn't,' Linda said. 'Sounds completely mental, but I still don't believe he's done the things they say he's done, so how can I not stand by him?' She laughed, poured more wine. 'God, I sound like that old song, don't I?'

She began to hum the tune to the Tammy Wynette classic. A

266

song Helen knew that Thorne liked. Helen looked around. There was a man working behind the bar, but he was not exactly being mobbed by customers. A couple sat at a table in the window and two men were drinking in the opposite corner. A woman sat at the bar, tapping busily at her phone.

'Would you stand by him if you thought he was guilty?' Helen asked.

Linda took a drink, thought about it. 'Yeah, I think I probably would. Better or worse, isn't it? I always thought women who did that were pathetic, but I'm just being honest.'

'Fair enough,' Helen said.

Linda sat back and grinned. 'You and me had a row about a boy once, remember? Because we both fancied him.'

'The one who went lamping?'

'Yeah.'

'I didn't fancy him.'

'Yeah, right,' Linda said.

'All right, maybe I did, a bit.' Helen smiled. 'Just not enough to want to go out shooting at things.'

'I think you just had higher standards than I did,' Linda said.

'They've dropped a lot over the years.' Helen tried to keep a straight face, but couldn't manage it.

When Linda had finished laughing, she said, 'Sorry you've been dragged into all this.'

'Dragged myself into it, didn't I?'

'Still.'

'I got spat at in the pub last night.'

Linda seemed genuinely appalled. 'Who by?'

'Gang of teenage gobshites by the toilets.' Helen looked at her drink. 'No big deal, really.'

'Couldn't you have arrested them?'

Helen had survived a three-day armed siege and faced down an assailant with a knife on more than one occasion. Last night

267

though, in that piss-stinking hallway, she had been confronted with no more than naked animosity, and she had frozen. Like most other coppers, she was well-used to the hatred that a uniform or a warrant card could breed, but this had been something purely personal, and it had shaken her. 'It wasn't worth it,' she said.

The woman at the bar ordered another drink, then got up and walked towards the toilets. She smiled at Helen as she passed the table and Helen smiled back.

'You'd do the same, right?' Linda asked. 'You'd stand by Tom, right?'

'What, if he did something, you mean?'

'Well, not something like this . . . but let's say he did something bad, turned out to be bent or whatever.'

The idea of Thorne being corrupt, at least in the way Linda was talking about, was not one Helen could ever entertain. But she knew there were things he had done which most people would find difficult to understand or condone. 'Yes,' she said, eventually. 'I'd stand by him.'

Linda looked pleased. She leaned closer. 'So, what's going on with you and him, anyway?'

'What do you mean?'

'Well, he's a bit older, isn't he?'

'He's not exactly a pensioner, you know.'

'Sorry. I was just saying.'

'I think I know what I'm doing.' It was something Helen had said to her sister more than once, with rather more edge than she was saying it now. 'I bloody hope so, anyway.'

Linda touched her glass to Helen's. 'I think we're both old enough and ugly enough.'

'Let's just go with old,' Helen said.

'Funny, but I don't feel that old with you back here. Talking, whatever. Feels like we're fifteen again.'

'I think we're both dressed a bit better.'

Linda smiled, emptied her glass. 'Why did you come back?'

'I told you on the first day.'

'Really, though.'

'I said. I thought you might need a friend.'

'I did,' Linda said. 'I just never thought it would be you. You've been away for such a long time and it wasn't like we kept in touch.'

'I felt guilty for leaving.' Helen felt the jitters in her belly. 'I still feel guilty.'

'Why?'

Now they were talking in whispers. 'Why do you think?'

Linda's hand drifted towards the bottle, but it was empty. 'That was like a lifetime ago.'

'I was a coward,' Helen said.

'That's crap.' Linda sounded angry, suddenly. 'You took the chance and you got out, and if I'd had a chance I would have done exactly the same. I'd've been gone like a shot.'

'I thought you'd hate me for it,' Helen said. 'Coming back here, I was scared to death. I thought you'd be the one to spit in my face—' Helen stopped, aware that someone was standing at their table. She looked up to see the woman who had been at the bar.

'Sorry to interrupt.' The woman was in her early fifties. Her grey hair was cut stylishly short and a pair of bright red glasses dangled from a chain around her neck. 'I just wanted to say that I know who you are and I understand what you're going through. Honestly. So, if you ever want to talk . . . ' She leaned forward and laid a business card on the table.

Helen moved to snatch it and recognised the logo of another huge-selling tabloid. 'She doesn't want to talk. Not to you, anyway.'

'That's a shame.'

'So you can put your cheque book away.'

'Can't she speak for herself?'

'Are you still here?'

The woman raised a perfectly manicured hand, evidently an experienced doorstepper. 'I just think she deserves a chance to tell her side of the story, that's all.'

Helen stood up fast. 'Are you deaf?' She saw the shock on the journalist's face, watched it become fear and enjoyed the rush. 'No, I thought not. Now, piss off and crawl back under your rock, before I come round this table and stick those stupid glasses up your bony arse.'

# FORTY-EIGHT

Donna Howland would never have described herself as nosy, because it was one of those words that made you sound bad. 'Curious' was a better word, she reckoned. *Interested.* Some people just had the sort of jobs which gave you a chance to talk to people and to listen. Like hairdressers or taxi drivers. You made conversation, nothing wrong with that, was there?

All sorts of people came into Cupz, so she heard all sorts of things. You didn't have to eavesdrop, because most of the time customers were happy to talk while you made their drinks or sandwiches and other times you couldn't help but catch a snippet or two as you served at a nearby table or cleared the plates away.

She'd known this pair would be interesting as soon as they'd walked in.

She recognised the copper of course, and from what Paula had told her when she'd been in that morning, the other one had to be his mate, the one who was sleeping on her settee. Some kind of CSI type, worked on bodies. Couldn't be two people in town who looked the same as him, could there?

Two teas, a chicken salad baguette and a toasted ham and cheese.

When the place was quiet, she liked to listen to music while she worked behind the counter. Cleaning up, restocking the fridge, whatever. A bit of Ed Sheeran, or maybe Rihanna if she fancied dancing. She didn't want to disturb the customers, obviously, so she always wore headphones. She thought she probably looked like a right nutcase, nodding along, *singing* along now and again, when she forgot there was anyone around. It was easy enough to slip an earbud out though and maybe turn the music right down, if it looked like there might be something more interesting to listen to.

Donna tidied the shelves, then began to wipe the counter down, on the side nearest the table where the copper and his mate were sitting. Where the one with all the tattoos was making short work of his sandwich.

She reached into the front pocket of her apron and turned the volume down. She tucked away an errant strand of hair and plucked out an earbud. After catching a word or two, she turned the music off completely and kept on wiping, long after the counter was spotless.

She'd definitely have a good story to tell Paula next time she came in.

'So, I'm him, right?'

'It would be a hell of a twist, but let's go with it for now,' Hendricks said.

'I burn the body just enough to open the skin, expose the muscles, organs, whatever.'

'That's the part they love best.' Hendricks bit into his baguette and chewed. 'Innards are like a slap-up dinner at the Ivy to your average beetle. Or a KFC bucket, if you happen to prefer something a bit more downmarket.'

'Do I need to keep the body warm?'

'Well, it's half-burned already, remember, but yeah, it would be a good idea to try and keep it warm for a while afterwards, while the invasion takes hold. They'll feed and lay eggs quicker.'

'The bin-bag would keep the heat in, right?'

'Yeah, that would be perfect. You burn the body, transfer your colony across, then wrap it all up in a bag. Job done.'

'Not forgetting to drop in the fag-end with Steve Bates' DNA all over it.'

'Wherever you've managed to get that from.'

'I followed him, I watched him drop one in the gutter, whatever. I'm not too worried about explaining that.'

'Fair enough.'

Thorne sipped his tea. 'So, I just ... pop them in, do I? All these insects.'

'More or less,' Hendricks said. 'Pretty messy job though I would have thought, because you'll need to dig well into what's left, get the bugs in good and deep.'

'I don't get the impression he's particularly squeamish,' Thorne said.

'You'd be surprised. It might be one thing doing ... whatever it is he did to Jessica when she was alive, but some people can get very funny about dealing with bodies. Other way round for some of us, of course.'

'So, where does he get them?' Thorne asked. 'All these flies and maggots. The different kinds of beetles.'

'Ordinary clothes moths as well, sometimes. Particularly fond of decomposing hair. That's usually only on bodies found in the home though.'

'Where did they come from, Phil?'

'Sixty-four-thousand-dollar question.'

'I can run to lunch.'

Hendricks put away his last mouthful, picked at the scraps of salad left on his plate. 'He's got to have bought them from somewhere.'

'What, he just nipped down the nearest pet shop?'

'You can laugh, mate, but some places keep a good stock of bugs. For people that have exotic pets . . . chameleons or iguanas.'

'Carrion beetles? Be serious.'

'Somewhere on the internet, then.'

'Really?'

'Come on, you really think there's anything you can't get if you know where to look or who to ask?'

'Still . . .'

'He could easily be getting them through a third party, on the dark web, if he's clever. Bitcoins, all that, and no questions asked. As good as untraceable.'

Thorne grunted. Since it had first been discovered a few years before, the Met had begun making inroads into the nefarious activities of the hidden, or dark web. The problem was that the better they got at uncovering the buying and selling of hard drugs, arms, hit men, *people*, the better those providing these services got at finding somewhere else to hide. If Hendricks was right and this was how the killer had sourced the insects he had needed to create a false time of death, Thorne might have rather more trouble proving it than he would have with an abandoned cigarette end.

'You finished with that?' Hendricks asked.

Thorne pushed his plate across. He had barely touched his sandwich, but still he was a lot less hungry than he had been when he sat down.

Driving back towards Polesford, Linda was even more geed up than she had been after escaping from the safe house, though the wine probably had more than a little to do with it. Helen slowed at a makeshift road sign and was waved through a foot of water by a uniformed officer in a high-vis jacket.

'Seriously, you were great back there.' It was the third time Linda had congratulated her. 'You really gave that hard-faced cow what for.'

'I shouldn't have lost my rag.'

'Don't be daft, it was fantastic.'

'It's what I said to you in court. You're only giving them what they want.'

'Who cares?' Linda drummed her palms against her legs, stared out of the window. 'I swear to God, I really thought you were going to deck her.'

Helen had thought so too.

She nodded her thanks to the officer and accelerated away.

She was not proud of losing control, but could not feel too much regret at telling the journalist exactly what she'd thought of her. The sick feeling in her stomach, which had begun as she and Linda had marched out of the pub, that continued to spread, was because of where the anger had sprung from so suddenly.

What she and Linda had been talking about. The past they had been about to dredge up.

*I know who you are and I know what you're going through . . .*

The fact that, just for a second or two, Helen had mistakenly thought the journalist was talking to her.

Linda continued to jabber, giggly and over-excited. She began raving about the countryside, pointing at skeletal trees or fields still brimming with brown water as though they were the most amazing things she'd ever seen. Steve, she told Helen, for all his faults, used to love getting out into countryside. It was one of the main reasons he'd moved to the area in the first place. Wayne on the other hand, the sow's arse, was a very different kettle of fish who, despite being a local lad, had hated every bush and blade of grass. Had thought it was 'boring'. Used to get ratty, she said, if

275

she as much as suggested a walk or maybe a drive out somewhere for a picnic when the weather was decent.

'Me and the kids left the miserable sod to it,' Linda said. 'Came on our own.'

Helen was about to mention similar conversations she'd had with Thorne, when her phone rang. She glanced across and touched the screen.

'Are you on speaker?' Sophie Carson asked.

'I'm driving.'

'Turn it off.'

Helen snatched the phone up from between the seats and disabled the speaker function. She slowed, though there was a line of traffic behind her, and began looking for somewhere to pull in.

'OK . . .'

'What?' Linda suddenly sounded rather more sober.

Helen listened. She said, 'Right' and 'Where?'

A horn sounded behind them. Linda said, 'Helen?'

Helen indicated and pulled in suddenly, hard against a wide, wooden gate. She ignored the mimed abuse from the van driver who accelerated past. She said, 'We'll get there as soon as we can,' and switched off the engine.

Linda said Helen's name again, fear in it.

'We need to get across to Bromsgrove,' Helen said. 'To the hospital.'

'Oh, Jesus, is it one of the kids?' Linda shook her head quickly. 'No, Bromsgrove would be stupid—'

'It's Steve,' Helen said. 'It's the nearest hospital to Hewell prison.' She was thinking quickly, trying to work out the fastest route. 'He tried to kill himself.'

276

# FORTY-NINE

Thorne received Helen's text as he was leaving Cupz, and, after a forty-mile journey, during which Hendricks bragged about several recent sexual conquests and repeatedly joked that the woman on Thorne's sat-nav had a promising career as a dominatrix, they got to Bromsgrove hospital half an hour after Helen and Linda.

They arrived to find Helen and Linda alone in a grim, overheated waiting room. Thorne introduced Hendricks, then, after exchanging a practised look, he and Helen stepped outside into the hospital corridor.

'He got hold of a ballpoint pen,' Helen said. She mimed repeated jabs to her wrist. 'Made quite a mess, by all accounts.'

'Is he all right?'

'Nobody seems keen to tell us very much, but I don't think he's in any danger.'

'Was he ever?'

'Not sure how quickly they found him.'

'Depends if he wanted to be found,' Thorne said. 'How serious he was.' He looked back through the waiting room's small window. Hendricks and Linda were sitting opposite one another in silence. 'How's she doing?'

'Well, she was frantic all the way here, but now she's just furious.'

'With Steve?'

Helen shook her head. 'With everyone *but* Steve.'

'And how are you doing?' Thorne asked.

'Me?' Helen saw Linda glance up at the door and raise a hand. She waved back. 'Come on, we should go back in.' She reached out to touch Thorne's arm. 'Go and rescue Phil . . . '

They walked back into the room and sat down to wait. Half a dozen mismatched armchairs were lined up against yellowing walls decorated with children's drawings. A coffee machine stood in one corner and several more chairs were dotted around a low plastic table covered with used plastic cups and magazines. Thorne carried extra chairs across, sat down and examined the reading material. It wasn't hard to work out why they had been donated.

*Practical Boat Owner. Home Building & Renovating. Investors Chronicle.*

'Anyone want a drink?' Thorne asked.

'How do they let him get hold of a pen?' Linda said. 'A fucking *pen*.' She gripped the arms of her chair and looked around for an answer nobody seemed eager to provide. 'I mean, don't they watch prisoners like Steve? Prisoners who are vulnerable?'

'They should,' Helen said. 'I don't know if he was actually on any kind of suicide watch though. If he'd given them any cause—'

'There must be a system in place, surely.'

Helen nodded because there was little else she could do. She looked at Thorne.

'Maybe it's exactly what they wanted,' Linda said. Thorne and the others could hear booze working in her voice, but her mood was very different to the one Helen had witnessed before taking

278

the call from Sophie Carson. 'It saves a lot of aggro, doesn't it? A shedload of paperwork and the cost of a trial. Lots more money to pay coppers overtime with.'

'I don't think so,' Helen said.

'No? Happens a lot, when you think about it though. Shipman topped himself inside, didn't he? Fred West, he was another one. You start to wonder if prison officers, coppers, whoever, are turning a blind eye.' Linda was leaning forward, spitting out the words. 'Here you go, mate, here's a handy length of bedsheet, there's a razor blade . . . you get on with it and we'll sit over here and look the other way.' She sat back, nodding. 'Yeah, would have done everybody a favour, Steve doing that. Fuckers . . .'

A minute or two passed. The reversing signal of a van or lorry sounded close to the window. There were voices outside the door, some laughter, then it was quiet again.

Linda closed her eyes. 'Sorry.'

'You've got every right to be angry,' Helen said.

'Why won't anybody tell us anything?' She looked at Helen, at Thorne. 'How long's it been?'

'Time always drags in places like this,' Thorne said.

'Right,' Hendricks said. 'A minute seems like ten.'

Linda nodded, summoned a smile. 'Listen, thanks for the support. Be bloody horrible if I was here on my own.' Her eyes widened. 'Shit, the kids. I should call them.'

'They'll be fine,' Helen said. 'I can call them if you want, but there's really no need.'

Linda looked at Thorne. 'She's been great, you know, your missus. You should have seen her earlier on.'

Thorne looked at Helen. 'What?'

'I'll tell you later,' Helen said.

'Stood up for me, she has.' Linda got up and walked across, wrapped an arm around Helen's shoulder. 'Been slagged off in the papers for it, an' all. Gobbed at.'

'*What?*' Now, Thorne was out of his chair.

'Gobbed at by who?' Hendricks asked.

Helen inched away from Linda. 'Just a few twats in the pub last night. When I went to the toilet.' She clocked the look on Thorne's face. 'Again, I'll tell you later.'

Thorne remembered how Helen had been, driving them back to Paula's the night before. The silence, and something he didn't recognise coming off her like a stink. He hoped, for their sake, that he never got hold of those responsible, but for once, at least, he had an explanation for Helen's behaviour.

'You look after her.' Linda pointed a finger. 'You've got a good one here.'

Thorne bought a round of weak teas from the machine and they all sat down again. Helen chatted quietly to Hendricks about work for a few minutes while Thorne tried talking to Linda about anything but the reason they were there.

The floods, the food in the local café, how her kids were doing at school.

It didn't last long.

'Why did he do it, d'you think?'

Once again, there was no answer anyone could give, but Thorne knew very well what most people would have said. He wondered if it was an answer that Linda was even considering.

'It just keeps going round in my head.'

'It wasn't your fault,' Helen said.

'I mean, there's always hope, isn't there? He must know me and the kids are there for him, whatever else happens.' She looked to Helen, got a nod which seemed to perk her up a little. 'I know prison's horrible, but Steve's a strong bloke, really he is.'

'I'm sure he knows,' Helen said. 'It won't have been that—'

Instinctively, they all stood up when the door opened, but it wasn't the nurse or doctor they were expecting.

'Everyone all right?' Tim Cornish asked the question as though they were guests waiting to go through for dinner. He took a good look at Thorne, and at Hendricks.

Linda stepped towards him. 'What's happening?'

'Well, you'll be pleased to hear that your husband's fine. All patched up.'

'Can I see him?'

'Well, not right now, but if he sends a visiting order, of course you can.'

Linda looked confused, but Thorne and Helen understood immediately.

'Are you winding us up?' Helen asked.

Cornish shrugged. 'Nothing I could do.'

'What's happening?' Linda asked. 'Why can't I see Steve?'

'They've already taken him back to prison,' Cornish said. 'The van left twenty minutes ago.'

'What?' Linda sounded on the verge of hysterics.

Cornish leaned back against the door. 'The cuts weren't much worse than superficial in the end,' he said. 'They stitched him up, gave him some painkillers and that was it.'

Helen shook her head. 'This is not on.'

'You know as well as I do that as soon as it's been established a prisoner's in no immediate danger, it's the responsibility of the prison service to have him returned to custody as soon as possible.'

'They told me to come.' Now Linda was shouting, looking to Helen for support. 'We've just been sat waiting here like idiots, for nothing.'

'It was the governor's decision.' Cornish held up his hands. 'Not mine.'

'You just got me here to take the piss. To make me suffer.'

'You're upset, Linda—'

'Bloody right, I'm upset.'

'Go back to your kids,' Cornish said. 'Just be grateful Steve's alive, eh?'

Helen could see that Linda was about as ready to take a swing as she herself had been a few hours earlier in the pub. She moved quickly to usher her from the room.

Thorne waited until the door had closed. 'There was no need for that.'

'For what?' Cornish was the picture of wounded innocence. 'I know you're on holiday, but you can't have forgotten the way things work *that* quickly.'

Thorne held himself in check, looked away. Just the partner of a woman who was here supporting a friend. No more than that.

Cornish looked at Hendricks. Hendricks moved to introduce himself, but Cornish held up a hand. 'I know who you are.'

Hendricks tried to look pleased. 'My fame is obviously spreading.'

'You can get famous very fast round here,' Thorne said.

Cornish smiled and loosened the top button of his shirt. He let out a long sigh, like he'd had a tough day. 'Ballpoint pen, eh?' He walked across to the coffee machine, digging into his trouser pockets for change. 'When I heard what happened, I thought he might have done us all a favour.'

Thorne stared at him. 'You what?'

Cornish jammed the first coin into the machine then turned. He looked at Hendricks, then at Thorne, as though unsure what he was being accused of. 'I hoped he'd written us a nice juicy confession.'

# FIFTY

Driving back, Hendricks seemed less amused than he had been by the strict tone of the woman giving them directions. 'She's got a point though,' he said.

'Who?'

'Bates' wife. Asking why he tried to top himself.'

'All sorts of reasons he might do it.'

'Yeah, maybe someone threatened him in the showers or his favourite football team lost again, but being guilty is pretty high on the list, I reckon.'

'What about being innocent when everyone *thinks* you're guilty?' Thorne glanced at his friend. 'What about knowing you're probably never going to see your family again?'

'Fair enough, but aren't you even going to consider the possibility that you might be wrong?'

'I thought you were on board with this.'

'OK, then, that *we* might be wrong?'

The ultra-stern sat-nav woman told Thorne to take the first exit off the next roundabout.

'No,' he said. Another glance at Hendricks. 'And that's to you, not her.'

A car coming in the other direction had its headlights on main beam. Thorne flashed and the driver dipped his lights, but Thorne swore at him anyway.

'What if he'd died?' Hendricks asked.

'I'm not with you.'

'If Bates had actually managed to kill himself. Would you have let it go?'

'He didn't though, did he?'

'Yeah, but if he had. Guilty or not, if he was dead you could just forget the whole thing and go back to your holiday. Get some sun on those pasty legs.'

For a few seconds, Thorne toyed with the kind of line that was trotted out in American cop shows. A serious look and a few desperately heartfelt words just before the ad break.

*The dead deserve justice every bit as much as the living.*

That kind of thing.

He knew that Hendricks would be the last person to buy it and the first to take the piss, so in the end he just settled for the truth.

'If I'm right, I want to damn well prove I'm right.'

Linda Bates had left the house like a schoolgirl on a spree, but she returned like a middle-aged woman with the weight of the world on her shoulders. With Helen close behind her, she walked as quickly as she was able along the path cleared for them by the ever-growing number of uniformed officers. Her eyes stayed fixed on the front door as the cameras flashed on either side; the comments and curses making it clear that many already knew where she had spent the last few hours, and why.

*He should have finished the job.*

*He obviously can't live with what he's done so how the hell can you?*

They could sense the atmosphere in the house straight away. Carson, Gallagher and two other officers in uniform stood silently in the kitchen, as though they had been waiting for them to get back, and Charli had begun calling for her mother from upstairs as soon as the front door had slammed shut.

'What's going on?' Helen asked.

Carson looked at Linda, who was standing in the doorway, seemingly afraid to cross the threshold. 'I didn't want to call you, while you had other things to worry about. I'm glad your husband's OK, by the way.'

'Call me about what?'

Charli shouted from upstairs again and Helen noticed that Gallagher was staring down at her nice shiny shoes.

'Danny was attacked.' Carson swallowed and carried on quickly. 'He's fine, honestly. It was nothing.'

'Attacked *where*?' Helen asked.

Carson turned and stared hard at Gallagher. 'Ask *her*.' She nodded towards the two PCs standing in the corner. 'Ask those idiots.'

Finally, Gallagher looked up, the colour flooding her cheeks. 'Poor kid was begging us to let him go up to the school. Said he wanted to pick up some books, kept saying how bored he was.'

'And you let him?'

'No, course I didn't . . . I mean, not on his own, but eventually I said we'd take him up there, if he was really that desperate to go. Myself and a couple of other officers.' She glanced towards the two PCs, statue-still with expressions like stunned fish. Both had clearly been on the receiving end of a major bollocking before Helen and Linda had got back.

'What about that lot out there?' Helen pointed towards the front of the house.

'I told him that,' Gallagher said. 'He said it didn't matter because him and his sister had been in the newspaper already.

Said he didn't care about them, he just wanted to go to the school for a few minutes to get his books.'

Linda was shaking her head. She murmured, 'This can't be happening.'

'I wasn't here,' Carson said. 'I want to make that clear. No way in hell would I have let this happen.'

Helen looked at the DC; an officer clearly well practised at making sure the buck got passed good and early. 'So, what happened?'

It took a few seconds before one of the PCs spoke up. 'We told the school we were coming,' he said. 'We made the call, then took him down there in one of the squad cars.' He looked to his left; his colleague's turn.

'Yeah ... so, we were both with him the whole time, there was no way we were going to leave him on his own. Then right at the end as we were walking back to the car ... I don't know ... maybe I looked away for a few seconds and this little twat came from nowhere, just started throwing punches.' He cleared his throat. 'It's not too bad, honestly. Just a split lip.' He rubbed a finger against his cheekbone. 'A bit of a bump.'

'Danny didn't seem that bothered about it, to be honest.'

The second PC nodded his agreement. 'We arrested him, obviously. The lad concerned.'

Helen looked at them. 'Congratulations.'

'What the hell have we done?' Linda spoke up suddenly, and everyone turned to look at her, visibly shocked at the agony in her voice. 'What the hell have me or my kids done?' She looked at Gallagher and Carson, at the two PCs. 'Anyone?

From upstairs, Charli called for her mother again and almost immediately, Danny shouted at his sister, told her to shut up.

'I'm going up to see him,' Linda said, walking out into the hallway.

Helen turned and pointed at Carson. She said, 'You were the

senior officer, so this comes back to you.' Then she walked out after Linda.

By the time Helen got to the foot of the stairs, Linda was already halfway up. She stopped and looked back. She might have felt fifteen years old a few hours before, but now she looked three times that, more. Her face was washed out and empty. She reached to steady herself against the banister.

She said, 'I can't do this any more,' then turned and carried on up.

Helen sat down on the bottom step. She took out her phone and texted Thorne. Told him she would be staying the night.

Thorne was relieved that Paula had decided on an early night. He was tired and not really in the mood for another late-night chinwag with Paula and her over-enthusiastic other half. She told Thorne and Hendricks that Jason would probably be out working until three or four o'clock and she had an early shift at the hospital, but they were more than welcome to stay up if they wanted, help themselves to drinks and some supper if they were hungry.

Thorne thanked her and said they might have a quick beer, if she was sure, perhaps a sandwich or whatever, if they could be bothered.

Hendricks had begun cooking sausages before Paula had taken her make-up off upstairs.

'Rough on Linda Bates,' Hendricks said.

'Yeah.' Thorne was sitting at the kitchen table, sending Helen a text.

sleep well. see you tomorrow. x

'She's certainly had one hell of a bad day.'

Thorne pressed *send* and laid his phone down. 'I still don't quite get what's happening with her and Helen though.' He picked up the phone again to check the message had gone. 'Why she's so keen to help her. It's like she feels obliged.'

Hendricks turned the sausages, spoke over the sizzle. 'They're old mates, you said. No big mystery.'

'They're not though,' Thorne said. 'That's the thing. Never heard Helen mention her name until all this. She's never talked about anybody from here.'

'Sometimes it's easier to do things for people you're not so close to. Helping total strangers. A bit less baggage.'

'Maybe.'

'I mean, it's only her time she's giving up, right? She isn't giving this woman a kidney or anything.'

'Not as far as I know.'

Hendricks turned to look at Thorne, his smile a little nervous. 'It's not like we're talking Bardsey here, is it?'

They still hadn't talked about it, not in any depth. What Thorne had done for Hendricks on that island, what had been taken from Hendricks because of him. Just jokes that weren't really funny, or the odd remark, much like this one. Thorne was still not sure if he was happy for things to stay that way.

He said, 'I suppose.'

'Helen's just being nice.' Hendricks turned back to the hob. 'She's a nice person ... who just happens to have awful taste in men.' He laid the sausages onto thickly buttered white sliced bread and carried the plates across.

Thorne was ravenous, having left most of his lunch. He took a bite, then got up to hunt for brown sauce in Paula's kitchen cupboards.

'These sausages are bloody gorgeous,' Hendricks said, mouth full.

'Local delicacy.' Thorne was opening and shutting doors. 'This place is the pork sausage capital of the western world, by all

288

accounts.' He found the sauce in the last cupboard. 'Pig farms all over the place, apparently.'

He sat down, lifted a slice of bread and squirted on the sauce. When he glanced up, he saw that Hendricks had stopped eating; mid-mouthful, sandwich in hand.

'What?'

'He wouldn't have needed to buy them.' Hendricks swallowed fast. 'Your killer wouldn't have needed to buy the bugs.' He dropped the sandwich on to his plate. 'I mean you're right, course you are, it's not like you can pop down to Tesco's and pick up a box of mixed beetles, is it? And yeah, there's the internet, *maybe*, but there's a far easier way.'

Thorne watched the smile growing on his friend's face and felt something tickle at the nape of his neck. He had learned from experience to take notice when those two things happened one after the other. 'So, tell me.'

'You harvest them from another body.'

'What?'

'You let another corpse decompose naturally. You wait for the flies to come, to feed and lay their eggs, for the beetles to pitch up and feed on the maggots. You wait for all that stuff to happen and when you've got enough, you just transfer them from the old body to the new one.' Hendricks shook his head, grinning. '*Course* that's how he did it. It's bloody genius.'

'There's another body?'

Hendricks leaned forward. 'Doesn't have to be human, though, does it?'

'Listen, I don't know what's in those sausages—'

'It's the sausages I'm on about, you dozy cock.' Hendricks pulled apart what was left of his sandwich, picked up a chunk of sausage and held it towards Thorne. 'The skin of a pig is so similar to human skin that they use it to train people like me. Right? They use pigskin to train medics learning how to treat battlefield

289

trauma, to test new surgical techniques, all sorts. It's a bit easier to come by now they've made grave-robbing illegal.' He nodded at Thorne and popped the piece of sausage into his mouth. 'You don't have a human body, you use the next best thing.'

'You telling me he used a dead pig to grow his bugs? That he killed a pig?'

'Wouldn't have to be a full-grown pig.' Hendricks shrugged. 'A piglet would do the trick. You can get a *lot* of bugs on a very small corpse.'

'Shit!' Thorne sat back hard. Hendricks looked at him. 'There was a local farmer in the pub, banging on about having one of his piglets stolen.'

'No need to thank me,' Hendricks said. 'I wouldn't mind one of those beers you mentioned though.'

Thorne rose slowly from his chair, still processing the information.

'And while you're up, I don't suppose you noticed any ketchup in those cupboards.'

# FIFTY-ONE

'You lot took your bloody time.'

'Yes, well, I'm sure you understand. With everything that's been going on.'

Bob Patterson looked like he didn't understand at all. As though a missing piglet was every bit as important as a missing girl. The farmer leaned out through the small gap he'd left between door and frame to peer at the warrant card Thorne was holding up. 'Well, at least they've sent a detective and not one of those useless articles in pointed hats.'

Thorne said, 'Right,' and turned to look again at the farmer's collie, racing back and forth along the fence of the nearest field. The dog had not stopped barking from the moment Thorne and Hendricks had pulled up.

'She's fine with people she knows,' Patterson said. He shouted at the dog to be quiet, but the animal carried on barking. Patterson stepped back and opened the door. 'Come on then ...'

The farm was five or six miles south of Polesford, on high ground the other side of Dorbrook. Driving along the rutted track, having turned off a road that was only slightly kinder on

291

his tyres, Thorne had seen that the farm was a small-scale operation. He had no idea how much of the visible land belonged to Patterson, but there was only a modest farmhouse, a barn and a couple of small outbuildings. To the left of the track, he had been able to see the metal pig shelters dotted across the pasture; rusted arches, moated with mud.

'I like pigs,' Hendricks had said, staring at the pens, the animals lying down or snuffling in front of them.

'I could see that last night,' Thorne said. 'The way you polished off those sausages.'

'They're a damn sight cleaner than people think, did you know that? If you say that someone's living like a pig, that's actually an insult to the pig.' He wound down the window, made grunting noises.

'Doesn't smell that clean,' Thorne said.

'Cleverer than dogs, as well.'

'I've never seen a pig fetch a stick.'

'Only because they can't be bothered,' Hendricks said. 'Chimps, dolphins, elephants, then pigs, they reckon. The cleverest animals.'

'Then way down the list there's a couple of the blokes you've been out with.'

'Yep.' Hendricks put the window up. 'Fit as fuck and thick as mince,' he said. 'That's how I like 'em . . . '

Now, Patterson showed Thorne and Hendricks into a kitchen that might have been spacious had not almost every inch of floor and work surface been taken up. There were piles of newspaper bundled up with twine, rows of bulging bin-bags, cardboard boxes stuffed with magazines and industrial-sized tin cans filled with nuts and bolts, old cutlery, elastic bands.

Thorne glanced at Hendricks, who raised his eyebrows. Both knew someone with hoarding tendencies when they saw them. Hendricks had once performed a PM on a middle-aged woman who had died at home after years spent hoarding. It had taken police several hours to locate her body.

Patterson pointed them towards a table that was as much a workbench as anything else. It was covered in bits of wire, valves and circuit boards; the wooden casings of several old radios piled up at one end.

'My dad used to do this,' Thorne said. 'Take things apart and put them back together again.'

'It's relaxing,' Patterson said. 'Something to do.'

Only half of what Thorne had said was true. His father had developed this habit shortly after his Alzheimer's had begun to take hold. He would disassemble radios and TV sets with great enthusiasm, but they had tended to stay that way.

'You could have tea, but there's no milk.' Patterson was standing on one of the few visible patches of red and white chequered lino. It was heavily stained and torn, where it had not come away from the floor completely.

'No problem,' Thorne said.

Hendricks leaned close to him. 'He probably can't find the fridge.'

Patterson joined them at the table. He pushed a few of the radio parts to one side.

'Let's talk about your piglet,' Thorne said.

Patterson nodded. Said, 'You want a description?'

'I think I know what a piglet looks like,' Thorne said. He was aware of Hendricks looking away, giggles approaching fast.

'You know what a Tamworth looks like?' Patterson waited. 'Thought not.' He folded his arms. 'This isn't a big operation, not like those intensive places everywhere. Thousands of animals, sows in crates.'

'I think we passed one on the way here,' Thorne said. Row upon row of low pig-sheds, fifty feet long. Metal towers, a vast concrete slaughterhouse with a crane alongside.

Patterson huffed. 'I farm my pigs in pasture, which is better for them, better for the meat. Heritage breeds. Tamworth and Berkshire.'

'Right,' Thorne said. He had taken a notebook out, but the page remained blank.

'Only got a dozen sows to farrow, so I can't afford to be losing piglets right, left and centre.'

'So . . . this was a Tamworth piglet, was it?'

The farmer nodded. 'Light brown. Lovely little thing. I'll find you a picture, if you like.'

'That would be helpful.' Thorne could only presume it would be a generic picture and that Patterson did not take photographs of every single piglet. 'When did it go missing?'

'I can't remember the exact date . . . six weeks ago, maybe.'

Thorne glanced at Hendricks. Three weeks before Jessica Toms had gone missing. 'Taken overnight, was it?'

Patterson nodded. 'There last time I changed the feed. Gone the next morning.'

'You don't have electric fences, anything like that?' Hendricks asked.

'Small place, like I said.'

'Not just you though,' Thorne said.

Patterson looked at him.

'You don't run this place on your own, I presume.'

'A couple of local boys help out,' Patterson said. 'I manage.'

'Could it have been one of them?'

'Yeah, I did think about that, but they're good lads.'

'You sure? Your dog didn't bark,' Thorne said. 'You'd have woken up if she had.'

'Yeah, I thought about that an' all.'

Thorne put his notebook away. The page contained nothing but an atrocious doodle of a pig. 'In the pub, they were saying you'd been accusing all sorts.'

Patterson looked like he'd swallowed something very sour. 'Yeah, well, balls to the lot of them.'

'The landlord said you'd had a go at *him*. Told him you'd be keeping an eye on his menu or something.'

'Said the same in all the pubs round here. Kept an eye on that Indian place too. Someone pinches some fish, you try the fish and chip shop first, don't you? Stands to bloody reason, I would have thought.'

When Thorne and Hendricks stood up to leave, Patterson went digging in a few of the boxes until he found the photograph he was looking for. He handed it to Thorne. Half a dozen light brown piglets.

He pointed. 'That's the one that was stolen.'

Thorne looked at the picture out of politeness, then dropped one of his cards on to the table. He made the same speech he'd made a hundred times before. If you think of anything that might help, don't hesitate, blah blah blah.

'I don't get it,' Hendricks said. 'You're obviously fond of them, so doesn't that make it harder when it comes to having them slaughtered?'

The farmer looked at Hendricks as though he was an idiot. 'They're money, is all. I'm fond of money too. You take one of my animals, you might just as well be mugging me in the street and taking my wallet.'

Driving back down the track, the dog still barking, Hendricks said, 'I'm sure I'm right, about the piglet.' He looked at the photograph of the pigs that Thorne had placed on the dashboard. 'But something still doesn't make sense.'

Thorne slowed, rattled across an animal grid.

'Why did he go to all the trouble?'

'To implicate Bates,' Thorne said.

'Yeah, but however old the body had looked, there's no reason

Bates couldn't have done it. Everyone would presume Bates was responsible, so why make it look older than it was?'

Thorne had asked himself this question already. The answer was hardly comforting.

'You'd have a point, if he was only planning on doing it once.'

Hendricks understood. 'This was like a dry run.'

'Now, everyone believes Bates is the killer, which is exactly what the real killer wants. But he can't get away with killing a second time, not with Bates in custody. Not unless the body fits in with that timescale.'

Thorne stopped at the end of the track, checked traffic, then pulled out fast on to the road. The photograph of Patterson's pigs slid along the dashboard.

'You reckon he's got more bugs lined up then?'

Thorne nodded. 'And I think Poppy Johnston's still alive.'

# FIFTY-TWO

She's stopped screaming, because now she knows there's little point and because she has no voice left. Her throat is raw and it hurts to swallow, to slurp at the inch or two of water on the floor all around her. By the end, the sound of her screams bouncing off the walls in the dark had been making her head thump, but for a while at least she thought it might have been worth it. She knows that if the rats can get in, then somewhere there must be a way out. A missing brick, a hole in the floor somewhere. She had thought that perhaps her voice might carry through the rat-lines and up and out into the open air, but now she imagines her cries buried somewhere above her in the soft earth or lost in a tangle of tree roots. Perhaps if someone walking around up there were to dig down, one of her screams would come bubbling up and whoosh out like gas or something. Like those hot springs or whatever they are that she's seen on TV documentaries, places in Iceland and America she used to talk about going to one day.

She thinks about the one exotic place she's visited; a school trip to France the year before.

She thinks about the boy she had been going to meet that

night, who was a bit of an idiot, if she was being honest. And another boy, two years above her, who seemed nice. She'd heard from various other girls that he liked her and she'd seen him looking.

She thinks about the girl at her school who had a kid at fourteen. She'd thought the girl was a silly slag, same as everyone else, that she'd chucked her life away, but now she's eaten up with envy and there's a pain where she's never felt one before.

Mental, some of the things she thinks about . . .

Could I eat a rat?

I hope the police are using a nice photo.

Will my wrist get skinny enough to slip out of this shackle before I die of starvation?

And her mum and dad in bits, because they were bad enough when the dog died. And her horrible, lovely brother, and his boat. And the smell in the kitchen when she came home, and music and getting into bed and laughing and watching rubbish on the telly and her mates and all of it, and how stupid she is, and how sorry.

How stupid.

*Have a drink now, if you like . . .*

More than anything, she wishes that she had drunk a lot more of whatever he had put in that bottle. She imagines discovering that for some reason he has left loads of the stuff down here with her, gallons of cheap, warm vodka spiked with enough drugs to knock out an elephant.

So she could down it all, bottle after bottle, until she became part of the blackness.

So she could *choose*.

# PART THREE

# STILL, LIKE YOU'RE DEAD

# FIFTY-THREE

From the edge of the bed, Charli watched her brother looking at himself in the mirror. He gently touched a finger to the almost perfect half-moon, purple beneath his right eye, traced it slowly down to the swollen bottom lip, dabbed at it. There was a hint of a smile as he squared his shoulders.

'I still don't know why you went,' Charli said.

Danny continued to study himself. 'Told you, I needed to get some books.'

'I know what you said.'

'So. Be quiet then.'

'Since when do you give a shit about schoolwork?'

'Nothing else to do, is there?'

Charli went back to work with tweezers, plucking at the small hairs on her shins. There was music coming from outside. Some idiot with a radio. The crowd was not as large as it had been, but looking out earlier she'd recognised faces and it was clear that some people were coming back day after day. She wondered if they were now on some kind of tourist map. See the historic abbey then come and gawp at the house where the monster's family was staying. Some people had been sitting on folding chairs in hats and coats, drinking tea and eating sandwiches and when she'd been online she'd seen the selfies people had posted that they'd taken outside the house. Thumbs up, grinning like morons. There were stupid jokes and some people had made comments about the 'Bates motel', which she didn't understand.

'I think you were showing off,' she said.

Danny turned round. 'What you talking about?'

'Going to the school.'

'You're mental.'

'Like you're enjoying being famous or something.'

'Yeah, because I really wanted to get punched.'

Charli switched legs, carried on plucking. 'You were smiling, before. Looking at yourself.'

Danny turned back to the mirror. 'Just thinking about what I'm going to do to that dick when I'm back at school.'

'I told you,' Charli said. 'We won't be going back to school.'

'Doesn't matter. Wherever we go, I'll be coming back to sort him out. I know exactly who he is and I know where he lives. See how hard he is without his mates around.'

Charli laughed. 'You had two coppers with you.'

'They were nowhere near me.' Danny glared at her in the mirror. 'He came up from behind when I wasn't looking, didn't he? Anyway, you weren't even there, so you don't know what you're talking about.'

Charli knew who the kid was, too. Whatever the reason for her brother going up to the school, the boy who had attacked him was now the one doing all the showing-off. She had seen the pictures he had posted on Instagram. Posing like a victorious boxer, mates holding his arms aloft. A comment left underneath:

not the first time danny bates has been given a good fisting!

Charli leaned across to put the tweezers down on the bedside

302

table. She brushed the tiny hairs from the duvet. It was probably just one of the lame gay jokes kids like Danny made without thinking. But all the same she wondered if it might actually be what they thought; if they believed that because Steve had done what everyone said he'd done, then he must have been doing the same things at home.

To Danny and to her.

She knew that Danny had seen the picture too, had gone looking for it as soon as he was back in the house. He hadn't mentioned it.

For a few minutes they said nothing, listened to the voices from the bedroom next door. Charli flicked through a magazine and Danny sat at the foot of the bed, staring at the door.

'She's supposed to be an old friend of Mum's, but she wasn't even at the wedding, was she? When Mum married Steve, I mean.'

'So?'

'So, how come they're spending all this time together, having these secret conversations like they're BFFs?'

Charli glanced up from her magazine. 'Ask Mum.'

Danny swept a hand back and forth across the grimy carpet, sending dust and tiny fragments of grit jumping. 'Come on, do you trust her?'

'Haven't really thought about it.'

'End of the day, she's a fed like the rest of them.'

'You didn't hear what she said to that bitch Carson and the others.' Charli laid the magazine down. 'When her and Mum got back from the hospital and found out about what happened at the school. Gave them all a proper bollocking.'

Danny shrugged, unconvinced. 'I think she knows something about Mum,' he said. 'From when they were at school.'

'Like what?'

'I don't know. Like she's got something on her. Has to be some reason she's here all the time. Spending the night. Why else

303

would Mum be so matey with her all of a sudden?'

Charli said, 'Maybe you've got it the wrong way round.'

Danny turned, brushing the dust from his hands.

'Maybe Mum's got something on her.'

Linda looked genuinely happy for the first time in days. She had been clutching the piece of paper as though it were a winning lottery ticket, since snatching it from the manila envelope a few hours before. She unfolded it again, nodded and smiled, then held it out so that Helen could see.

'Come on, this proves it, surely.'

Helen pretended to look. She had been shown the piece of paper several times already and had known what it was straight away. The visiting order from Hewell prison had arrived at the Bates family home that morning and been delivered to the house shortly afterwards – along with a final reminder from an electricity company and several pieces of junk mail – by a police officer who had not looked entirely pleased at having to play postman.

'He filled this in a couple of days ago, right?' Linda pointed at the date on the form. 'So why would he do that and then try to kill himself? *Really* try, I mean.' She folded the visiting order again, held it against her chest. 'It was obviously just a cry for help or whatever they call it. You don't make plans, organise something like this and then try and top yourself. Stands to reason.'

'Not necessarily,' Helen said.

Linda looked at her, pressed her palm against the paper a little harder.

'I'm just saying that when people commit suicide ... when they *try* to ... they're usually not thinking very clearly. Things like that don't cross their mind.'

Linda nodded, her smile soured. 'Well, thanks for that. Stupid, really, thinking you might be on my side.'

'I'm not saying you're wrong.' Helen stifled a yawn. 'But I've

304

had to deal with suicides where they'd got holidays booked, train tickets in their pockets, all sorts. When you're that down . . . you know? Those things don't matter.'

'Yeah, well I'm not going to let you piss on my chips, however much you might want to.'

'Why would I want to?'

'Steve just needs help, that's all.'

'You're probably right,' Helen said. She stretched out a hand to touch Linda's arm. 'Sorry . . . I wasn't trying to be negative.'

'It's OK.'

'And I am on your side,' Helen said. 'I'm just tired.'

She and Linda had shared a bed the night before, top to tail as they had done countless times when they were teenagers. Helen had barely slept, had been up early to pull on the same clothes she had been wearing the previous day. She felt washed out and grubby, unable to focus on much beyond a hot bath and her own bed. A few hours alone with Alfie.

'When are you going?'

Linda brightened again. 'Tomorrow.' She stood up and walked across to the full-length mirror on the side of the wardrobe. 'Shit, I wish I could get my hair done. Not much chance of that though, is there?'

'Not really.'

'I can imagine the conversation in the hairdresser's.' Linda laughed. '"Going anywhere nice on your holidays? Your old man killed any young girls lately?"'

'I could always try and do something.'

Linda leaned closer to the mirror, tugged at her hair. 'The state of me.'

'You look fine.' The lying had been getting easier and easier since she'd come back.

'You think I should take the kids?'

'Up to you,' Helen said.

'They'd love to see him.'

'Maybe next time?'

'Yeah.' Linda sucked in a deep breath. 'God, I'm nervous already.' She walked back across to the bed and sat down. 'It feels like it's been ages.'

'He'll be pleased to see you.'

Linda nodded. 'It'll be fantastic. You think I'll be able to touch him? I mean, will there be one of those screens?'

'I really don't know,' Helen said. 'I shouldn't think you'll be able to get very touchy-feely though.'

'I just want to see him. I just want to show him that someone believes he's innocent.' Linda looked at Helen. 'You know?'

Helen was still not ready to tell her friend that someone else believed it too. Not quite. She was thinking about a conversation she'd had the day before at the hospital. A chance encounter; things that had been overheard and passed on. Chinese whispers could make the most mundane exchange sound bizarre, she was well aware of that, but this one did not sound quite so strange when you knew the people who had been doing the talking.

No more than a casual chat, for those two.

Helen needed to sit down and talk to Tom.

# FIFTY-FOUR

'Consulting with the police is never going to pay the mortgage,' Hendricks explained. 'It's a pretty specialised area, after all, so he's teaching most days.'

Dr Liam Southworth had agreed to meet Thorne and Hendricks between lectures, and on the forty-minute drive south to the Warwick University campus, they discussed the best way to make their approach. Hendricks thought he knew exactly how to play it, but Thorne was not convinced.

'He's a scientist,' Thorne said. 'We should make it all about the science.'

'That's one way.'

'Tell him he'll be helping an innocent man.'

Hendricks looked dubious. 'At the end of the day, we're asking him a favour. And we need this done quickly, don't we? I reckon I know which buttons to push.'

Thorne pulled out and accelerated past a van doing sixty in the middle lane. 'You were wrong about that bloke in the pub, remember? The first night.'

'Twenty quid says I'm not wrong about the bug man.'

'Fair enough . . .'

The science block was not easy to find, but they had arrived in good time and, after asking several students for directions, they finally knocked on Liam Southworth's door a little after three o'clock.

He showed them into a small office with a view across a narrow strip of lawn to several other modern blocks. Rain was beginning to streak the window. Thorne and Hendricks dragged two uncomfortable-looking chairs from against the wall as Southworth sat down behind a cluttered desk, tapped at his keyboard for a few seconds.

'Won't be a minute,' he said.

'No rush, Liam,' Hendricks said.

One wall was lined with books and the other was taken up by framed certificates dotted among a collection of insects in glass cases. Beetles, moths, enough spiders to give an arachnophobe heart failure. Thorne stared at a black and yellow beetle the size of his hand and decided that if he were ever to come across one inside a body, it would definitely be the main suspect.

Southworth looked up, followed Thorne's gaze. 'It's an elephant beetle.' The Dublin accent was straight out of a Guinness commercial. 'Mainly found in Central and South America.'

'Thank God for that,' Thorne said.

The entomologist looked at Hendricks. 'Nice to see you again.'

Hendricks said, 'You too.' He casually slipped off his leather jacket to reveal a tight white T-shirt underneath and nodded towards Thorne. 'This is Tom.' He rubbed a hand along one tattooed forearm. 'I told you about him.'

The man behind the desk eyed Thorne for a little longer than might have been expected. 'Right. Hello.'

Thorne nodded.

'Strong, silent type,' Hendricks said.

Southworth reddened a little. He was on the short side and stocky, with collar-length fair hair and a babyish face. He reminded Thorne of that actor who had died of a heroin overdose, though Thorne could not remember the name. Southworth was wearing khaki trousers and a blue button-down shirt, but did not seem altogether comfortable; like someone who was trying a little too hard to look like an American college professor.

'So, something interesting, you said.' Southworth looked at Hendricks again. 'When you called.'

'It's not something you'll have heard before,' Hendricks said. 'Put it that way.'

'Right, well I'm all yours.'

Something something Hoffman, Thorne thought. That actor.

Hendricks kicked things off. He talked about their suspicions about the time of Jessica Toms' death, his theory about the killer's judicious use of entomological evidence, and finally their visit to Bob Patterson's farm. Thorne enjoyed watching Southworth's reaction as Hendricks talked. It became clear very quickly that, whatever else might happen, they certainly had his attention.

'Couldn't think of anyone better to come to,' Hendricks said, when he'd told the story. 'I told Tom that you were just the man we needed.'

Southworth reddened again. He took off his wire-rimmed glasses, wiped them on his shirt, put them on again. He said, 'Blimey.'

'You keep some of the specimens,' Thorne said. 'Right?' He nodded towards the insects on the wall.

'Not here,' Southworth said.

'No, but you do keep them. Several examples of each insect taken from the body.'

'Of course. Some are kept for use as evidence later on and some we hold on to just . . . out of interest. Can't bear to throw them away sometimes. I'm talking about the more interesting ones, obviously.' Southworth smiled. 'It's not like I've got an enormous maggot collection or anything.'

'So, what we're talking about is possible then?'

'Certainly a first.'

'Possible, though?'

Southworth sat back. Behind him, the rain was a little heavier against the window. 'Yeah, sure, theoretically. If you're right and the insects removed from the body had initially invaded the body of a pig, fed on it, then that animal's DNA should still be present within the insects themselves.' He nodded to himself, puffed out his cheeks. 'It's actually the sort of thing people publish papers about.'

'There you are then,' Hendricks said. 'One more good reason to help us out.'

'Well, it wouldn't really be me,' Southworth said. 'This is a bit out of my area. I think I'd need to ask someone at the lab to do it. Can't imagine too many of them have ever done a post-mortem on a beetle though.'

Hendricks laughed. 'Just need to find someone who likes a challenge.'

'I think I know who to ask first,' Southworth said. 'She's usually up to her eyeballs, but you never know. She's a mate and all that.'

'Anything you can do,' Thorne said.

Southworth looked at him. 'This *is* within the parameters of the inquiry, is it?'

Thorne and Hendricks exchanged a look. This was always going to be the trickiest part.

'I mean you're with the Met and Dr Hendricks is . . . well, I'm not quite sure where Dr Hendricks comes into it.'

'It depends on how you define your parameters,' Thorne said.

Southworth said, 'Ah . . . '

'For now, we'd prefer to keep it between us. If that's OK.'

'Well, it does put a rather different complexion on things.'
Southworth suddenly looked a little awkward. 'This isn't the first
case I've worked on with the police and I'd rather it wasn't my
last, you know? I'm not sure I should really get involved in anything they might not approve of.'

Thorne exchanged another look with Hendricks. Things had
been going so well.

'I'm sure you understand,' Southworth said. He looked at
Hendricks, blinking hard behind his glasses. 'Don't get me
wrong, it certainly sounds interesting, but I'd have to think very
hard about anything unofficial.'

There was a knock on the door and, at the summons from
Southworth, a nervous-looking student put his head around. He
asked if he could have a quick word and Southworth told his visitors that they would have to excuse him for five minutes.

When Southworth had stepped outside, Thorne said, 'So, not
the only gay in the village, then?'

'You're cramping my style,' Hendricks said. 'You do know
that?'

'Sorry.'

'I'm pretty sure I can persuade him.'

'Hardly your type, I would have thought.'

'No?'

'I know you think his accent's sexy, but I wouldn't have said he
was that fit.'

'He's cuddly.'

'And he's obviously not thick.'

'We need this doing, don't we?'

'You're telling me you're prepared to make the sacrifice, are
you?'

Hendricks shrugged. 'A shag's a shag. Besides which, that
sofa's seriously uncomfortable.'

When Southworth came back, Thorne told him that a call

had just come through and that he needed to be elsewhere fairly urgently. Southworth looked a little disappointed, until it became clear that Hendricks did not have to go anywhere.

'Thanks for sparing the time,' Thorne said, getting up.

'Well, it was every bit as interesting as Phil said it would be.'

'And thanks for thinking about it.'

'I'll call you later,' Hendricks told Thorne.

Thorne was only halfway back to Polesford when Hendricks called.

'Piece of piss.'

'Really?'

'Pick me up in the morning,' Hendricks said. 'You can bring the twenty quid with you.'

# FIFTY-FIVE

Having decided once again to forgo the specialised dining area, they ordered food and took a small table at the end of the bar. The young girl who brought their meals over was clearly used to people making the same decision.

'Shelley's tried telling them, but they know best.' She lowered her voice. 'Trevor and his wife. It always stinks of bleach and it's too near the toilets. Puts everyone off, doesn't it?' She smiled. 'Enjoy your dinner . . . '

Thorne got stuck into ham, egg and chips, while Helen picked somewhat less enthusiastically at scampi and salad. Thorne asked how things had been going with Linda. Helen told him about the visiting order arriving, the visit Linda would be making to Steve Bates in Hewell prison the next day.

'Nice to see her a bit happier,' she said.

Thorne nodded, sipped at his pint. 'Well, with any luck, I reckon we'll be able to make her even happier pretty soon.'

Helen folded her arms. 'Oh yeah, when exactly *were* you planning to tell me about the bugs?'

'Sorry?'

'You and Phil working out that they were actually put into the body. That they'd come from somewhere else.'

'I haven't seen you, have I?'

Helen reached for her phone, held it up. 'You heard of these?'

Thorne tried hard not to show his irritation. What about those things Helen had chosen not to share with him? He had only found out about those kids spitting at her because Linda had mentioned it. He felt sure there was plenty else besides.

He took another drink. Said, 'How did you find out?'

'I ran into Paula at the hospital yesterday.'

'How the hell did *she* know?'

'She came down from her ward because she'd heard what was going on, that Bates had been brought in. She told me her mate who runs the café had overheard you and Phil talking about it. Bugs and bodies.'

'Jesus, this place.'

'I had to pretend I knew what she was talking about.'

'I hope you told her to keep it to herself.'

'I think it might be a bit late for that,' Helen said.

The waitress stopped at their table as she collected glasses and asked if everything was all right. Thorne told her it was and nodded across at Trevor Hare who stopped pulling a pint to wave at them. The place was busy enough, but there was plenty of room at the bar and several empty tables. Thorne wondered if there was a search party out looking for Poppy Johnston tonight.

'I didn't tell you about it because there wasn't anything to tell. It was just a theory of Phil's, that's all.'

Helen leaned towards him. 'It's a bit more than that now though, isn't it? I could tell by how pleased with yourself you were looking.'

314

While they finished eating, Thorne told her exactly where Hendricks thought the bugs had come from and about that morning's visit to the pig farm. He told her where they had spent the afternoon and why Hendricks would not be coming home.

Helen was excited, the snippiness of a few minutes earlier gone. 'So we can prove it.'

'I think so,' Thorne said. 'You know how persuasive Phil can be.'

'That's fantastic.' Helen downed the last of her wine. 'I can't wait to give Linda some good news.'

Thorne looked at her.

'What?'

'You didn't seem very interested before,' Thorne said. 'When I told you I thought Bates wasn't the killer.'

'I didn't want to give her any false hope, that's all.'

'"Pissing in the wind." I think that was how you put it.' Thorne conjured half a smile to let her know he wasn't being altogether serious. '"Poking around in misery."'

'Sorry,' Helen said. She reached for Thorne's hand. 'And sorry about having a go at you just now.'

'Bloody hell, I'd really hate to be across the table from you in an interview room.'

'You've no idea,' Helen said.

Thorne went to the bar to get more drinks. When he came back to the table, Helen said, 'Thanks for doing this, all right?'

'It's only a glass of wine.'

'Seriously.'

'I'm counting on a fair few brownie points.'

'Lots.'

Thorne smiled. 'And I didn't even need to go antique shopping ... '

Helen had called her father after leaving Linda's and, for a few

315

minutes, she talked about their conversation, every bit as awkward as it had been the first time they'd spoken after the pictures had appeared in the newspaper. She was telling Thorne about the much more enjoyable chat she'd had with Alfie, when she looked up to see a figure approaching from the kitchen.

She sat back. 'Twat incoming.'

Thorne turned to see Shelley, the poetry-writing chef, striding to the table.

'All good?'

Thorne said that it was.

'You didn't finish.' The chef pointed to the remains on Helen's plate.

'Sorry,' Helen said. 'Is there a fine or something?'

Shelley laughed rather too hard and tugged at his beard. He shook the bracelets back down on to his wrist. 'Long as you enjoyed it.'

'Ham and eggs was good,' Thorne said.

Shelley bowed his head in thanks for the compliment, but insisted that he could not take much credit. 'Local ham's very good.'

'Long as it didn't come from a stolen piglet.'

Shelley laughed again. 'You've been talking to Farmer Bob then, have you? Thinks we're all thieves.'

'Not sure that particular pig would be very fresh now anyway.'

The chef stared down at the table. 'So, you done, then?' When Thorne said that they were, Shelley shouted the young waitress across and told her to take the plates away. He stepped aside as she reached a little awkwardly for them. Said, 'Can't get the staff.' He watched her walk away towards the kitchen then turned back to Thorne. 'Just wanted to say that I'm finished in an hour or so if you fancy a drink later on. I enjoyed our conversation the other evening.'

'I don't know how long we'll be staying,' Helen said.

Shelley nodded. 'Well, the offer's there. I'll be out in the garden probably, if you fancy one after hours.' He nodded towards the bar. 'Can't see his nibs firing me for that, not with the boxes of knocked-off whisky he's got piled up in the cellar.'

As the chef walked away, Helen muttered, 'Wanker.'

'He's certainly full of himself.'

'I saw him the other day with that girl. The waitress. Coming out of one of those buildings in the garden.'

'That's where he stays,' Thorne said.

'She's only a kid.'

'He's not that old himself.'

'Probably got her into bed by writing her some shit poem.' Helen looked disgusted. 'Look at him.'

Thorne turned and saw that Shelley was standing in the doorway, surveying the crowd proprietorially. He followed the chef's gaze and saw a young girl who had just come in and was walking a little nervously towards the bar. She was eighteen or thereabouts, hair tied back into a tight ponytail, and from where they were sitting, Thorne and Helen could hear snippets of the conversation when she arrived at the bar.

'What you having, Rory?' Trevor Hare seemed pleased to see her. 'Coke, is it? Or do you fancy going mad? Have a shandy if you want, I shan't tell anyone.'

'Coke's fine,' the girl said.

As Hare worked the drinks gun, he asked the girl something about her grandfather. She said that he was fine. 'Well, not fine, but you know.' She said, 'Those places are awful though.'

'Tell him I said hello,' Hare said, 'when you see him.'

The girl sipped her drink for a while, raising her head to cast a glance towards Thorne and Helen's table every few minutes.

'You know her?' Thorne asked.

'Never seen her before,' Helen said.

317

Once she had finished her drink, the girl stepped away from the bar and walked towards them. She looked as though she was heading for the Ladies, but cut across to their table at the last moment.

'I saw your picture in the papers,' she said.

'OK,' Helen said.

'You're a friend of Linda Bates.'

Helen nodded.

'Can I sit down?'

Thorne stood up and the girl squeezed in between them. She was slight, with legs like matchsticks in skinny jeans and a short, silver Puffa jacket. Close up, she was pretty, though the heavy make-up was working hard to disguise the fact. She had looked a little severe from a distance and it was hard to know if that was what she wanted or not.

'This is a bit of a nightmare, actually,' the girl said. 'You being a friend of his wife's. But I'm hoping it means you'll help me.'

'Help you how?' Helen asked.

'Help me prove Steve didn't kill anyone.'

The girl looked at Helen and then at Thorne. She was making a fair attempt at hiding her nerves. Eventually, Thorne said, 'Why don't you think he killed anyone?'

'Because the night everyone reckons he took Jessica Toms, he was with me. It was me he was meeting in that pub.'

Helen looked past the girl at Thorne. He gave the smallest of nods, happy to let Helen take the lead.

'You and Steve were together?' Helen asked. 'That's what you're saying?'

The girl nodded. 'Yeah, it was all crap, that stuff about getting a quote or whatever. He'd used the same excuse a couple of times before. We had to meet in places that were a bit out of the way, obviously.'

'Right,' Helen said.

318

'So, I can give him an alibi, can't I?'

'Sounds like it.'

The girl smiled then let out a deep breath. 'So, what do we do? I need you to tell me the best way to do things, you know?'

'OK, let's take it one step at a time,' Helen said. The girl could easily have passed for eighteen, but Thorne and Helen had both overheard the conversation at the bar. What the landlord had said to her about drinking. 'How old are you?'

'Sixteen,' the girl said. 'Seventeen in a few months. In six months.'

'And how long have you and Steve been seeing each other?'

The girl sat back and shook her head. 'Yeah, I knew you'd ask that.'

'So, you know why I'm asking.'

'We started going out a while ago, but we didn't *do* anything until I was sixteen, all right? I swear.'

'OK.'

'Steve didn't want to. He's not like that.'

'There's no need to get upset,' Helen said. 'We just need to get the facts straight.'

The girl reached into an oversized handbag and took out a compact. She checked her face then laid the mirror on the table. 'You're both coppers, right?'

'Not round here though,' Helen said.

'Will you come with me?' The girl looked at Thorne. 'When I go to the police?'

'I don't think that's a very good idea,' Thorne said. He looked around, recognised the faces of several local officers, though none seemed to be paying him any attention. He exchanged another nod with Trevor Hare, then turned back to the girl. 'But we'll tell you exactly what to say.'

'Promise? Because I'm shitting myself.'

'Just tell the truth,' Helen said.

'I am telling the truth.'

'I know you are.'

'We'll do everything we can,' Thorne said. He took out his phone. 'Give me your number and I'll give you mine. You can call any time, OK?'

The girl took her own phone from her bag, clearly comfortable with this familiar exchange of information. Her hands flew across the keypad as Thorne told her his phone number.

'Now call me,' he said. As soon as his phone rang he ended the call. 'Now, I've got your number. What's your name?'

'Oh, God.'

'I heard Trevor call you Rory?'

She rolled her eyes. 'Short for Aurora.' She clocked Thorne's look of surprise. 'Blame my mum. Latin for dawn, apparently. She found it in some book. Could have been worse, I suppose. I could have been called Dawn.'

'It's a nice name,' Helen said.

'You reckon?'

'Aurora . . . ?'

'Harley,' the girl said. 'Like the motorbike.'

Thorne added the name to his contacts list. 'Right, first thing is, you need to get across to the Police Control Unit. Tell them you've got important information and they'll take it from there.'

'That easy?'

'To start with, yeah,' Thorne said. He looked at the girl's small hands as her fingers drummed against the edge of the table. The chipped pink nail polish. 'Listen, it's brave of you to come forward.'

The girl shrugged. 'Had to, didn't I?'

'Not everybody would have done.'

'Up to them, isn't it?'

'Still.'

'I love Steve and he says he loves me.'

Thorne caught Helen's pained expression. He guessed she was thinking about Linda. 'I'm just saying, knowing this place. It might not *end up* being very easy.'

'I know what they're like.' The girl looked around. 'It was hard enough just coming over and talking to you two. I could have done with some vodka in that Coke, I tell you.'

'Well, we're on your side.' Thorne looked at Helen. 'Right?'

Helen was already pushing her chair back, getting to her feet. 'Excuse me . . . '

They watched Helen walk quickly away towards the toilets. 'She your girlfriend?' the girl asked.

Thorne nodded.

'Well you know then.'

'What?'

'What it's like when you care about someone.' She picked up her compact again, checked her make-up. 'Being brave doesn't come into it.'


Helen dropped hard on to her knees in front of the toilet bowl and grabbed the edge of the seat with only a few seconds to spare. She retched once, twice, then heaved up the food that the chef had been so proud of, the taste not much better coming up than it had been going down. She carried on retching, her stomach in spasm until there was nothing left. She spat and wiped away the gloopy brown strings then climbed, a little unsteadily to her feet.

She flushed, then stepped out of the cubicle and across to the dirty sink. She threw cold water on to her face and ran wet fingers through her hair.

She didn't look quite as bad as she felt.

When she came back into the bar a few minutes later, she could see that Thorne and the girl were no longer at the table. She found them on the pavement in front of the pub.

'I need to go and see Linda,' she said. 'Now.'

Thorne nodded.

The girl was looking at her feet.

Helen walked across and wrapped her arms around the girl. Even with a thick jacket, there was nothing of her. She said, 'Don't be scared.' She pulled the girl closer and held on. 'There's no need to be scared.'

# FIFTY-SIX

'She's lying,' Linda said. 'Course she is. Polesford's full of little bitches like that.'

'I don't think so.'

'And you'd know, would you?'

'I talked to her,' Helen said. 'She's just trying to help Steve.'

'Oh, is she?'

'So are we ... Tom and me. We think we can get proof that he didn't do it and this girl's statement alongside that—'

'Fuck her statement and fuck her help.'

They were standing in the kitchen and Linda did not seem too concerned about their conversation being overheard. She had been in bed when Helen arrived and the officer watching TV in the next room had looked as though he was ready to turn in himself when he'd let Helen in.

'I know this can't be easy to hear,' Helen said.

'That what makes you such a good copper, is it? Your sensitivity.' Linda tightened the cord of her dressing gown and stared until Helen looked away. 'Whose side are you on, anyway?'

'I told you, yours and Steve's.'

'And how do you think things are going to be between me and Steve after this?'

'Isn't proving he's innocent more important?'

'Right this minute, no it isn't,' Linda said. 'Right this minute, I couldn't care less.'

'Shall I make some tea?'

Linda looked at her, barked out a laugh. 'You are joking, right?' She pushed past Helen to the fridge, took out a half-empty wine bottle then reached up to the cupboard and grabbed a glass. She poured, drank. She said, 'Can you prove Steve didn't do it, or can't you?'

'Tom thinks he can.'

'Good.'

'It's all about when that girl was killed. The insects on the body—'

Linda raised a hand to shut Helen up. She clearly had no need of further detail when there was a more basic reason for asking. 'So why does anyone need to know anything about this girl?'

'It can't hurt to establish an alibi,' Helen said.

'Can't hurt *you*.'

At that moment, Helen understood that this pain was something Linda was familiar with. That it was not the first time she had reached for a bottle late at night; eaten up by rage and self-pity and railing against one of those 'little bitches' Polesford was apparently so full of.

It was almost certainly the first time she had shared it.

'I should let you get some sleep,' Helen said.

'Sleep? You think?'

'Sorry.' Helen was struggling for words that did not sound pat or pathetic. The truth was that she wanted to be out of the house, out of the firing line. Every snap and sneer was adding weight to the guilt and the shame.

324

Her throat burned and she could still taste the sick in her mouth.

The copper next door was watching football. A roar went up, a goal or a bad tackle.

'I feel so stupid,' Linda said.

Helen said nothing. For trusting him? For choosing to believe that he wouldn't do this again?

'What am I supposed to tell the kids?'

'I don't know.'

'How can I tell Charli that we know her stepdad's innocent because he was with a girl younger than she is?' The wine had gone and now the fight was quickly going out of Linda too. She closed her eyes and leaned back against the worktop.

'What can I do?' Helen asked.

Linda said, 'Tell me what she's like.' She folded her arms and smiled grimly, as though relishing Helen's discomfort. 'Is she pretty?'

'She wears too much make-up.'

Linda rolled her eyes. 'Short? Tall? Has she got nice firm tits?'

'How is this going to help?' Helen asked.

'Know your enemy,' Linda said. 'We learned that a long time ago, right, Hel?' She plucked casually at a loose thread on her dressing gown, pulled it out. 'So, what's her name?'

There was another roar from the adjacent room. The copper shouted something at the television.

Helen said, 'I don't know.'

It appeared that even the most committed of gawpers needed to sleep sometimes. Outside, there was only a group of kids smoking and drinking cans of cider under a streetlamp. They didn't give Helen a second look. A pair of uniformed officers were talking at the end of the drive.

'How did that go?' Thorne asked as they drove away.

'How do you think?'

Helen could only hope that the conversation would begin and end there. As of now, she had no wish to talk about how painful it had been in that house, for Linda and for her. She did not want to discuss the things that had been said or why others had remained unsaid.

The reasons for the lies.

'Can't have been easy.'

'No,' Helen said.

It was only a five-minute drive back to Paula's at this time of night. They drove in silence through the town centre, deserted save for a few people carrying kebabs who had presumably been drinking somewhere after hours or simply didn't know any better.

The streetlighting stopped as the road narrowed just past the final parade of shops, and within a few seconds of Thorne flicking on his main beam they drove past three teenagers walking back towards the centre of town. They held up their hands against the dazzle. Gestures were made.

'Cheeky bastards.'

'Turn round,' Helen said.

'Where?'

'Reverse then.'

'What's the matter?'

'Those boys . . . '

Thorne understood and did as he was told. Mercifully the road was straight with no traffic to be seen and, within thirty seconds, Thorne had slammed on the brakes and Helen was getting out of the car.

The boy with the dirty blond hair grinned when he saw Helen walking towards him, but the smile disappeared when he saw Thorne; the look on his face. The Asian kid and his mate took a step back, moved behind the blond boy, the biggest of the three.

'Good move,' Thorne said. 'Not such ballsy little gangstas now, are you?'

'What d'you want?' The blond kid shrugged, put his shoulders back.

'I don't want to piss about.' Thorne stepped close to him. 'Now, I could just do you with assaulting a police officer, but I'm guessing you don't really want a criminal record, not if you want that special job in KFC, right?'

'It's her word against ours,' the boy said.

'And I don't fancy all the paperwork, if I'm honest.'

The boy looked at him, squared up. The others had stepped even further back into the shadows.

'So, say sorry nicely, I'll just give you a slap and we can forget all about it. Fair enough?'

'Let me,' Helen said.

The boy raised his hands to protect his face as Helen pushed in front of Thorne and came at him, but it wasn't his face she was aiming at.

Her knee came up hard and she stepped smartly back to give the boy room to go down.

The Asian kid said, 'Fuck . . . '

The boy dropped to his knees and then rolled on to his side on the grass verge, moaning and cursing, cradling his balls. Thorne walked back to the car as Helen moved to put one foot on either side of the writhing figure on the ground, leaned over and spat.

# FIFTY-SEVEN

Thorne was about to set off for Warwick, to collect Phil Hendricks, when he got a call from Aurora Harley.

'Can I see you?' she asked. 'I went to the police, like you said, and they were horrible. I don't know what to do.'

Helen was spending the morning at Paula's. She said she would wait until Linda got back from visiting Steve. She said she would go and see her then, presuming Linda wanted her to and was up to it. She didn't say any more about what had happened the night before; the late-night visit to tell Linda about Aurora, the incident with the boys at the side of the road.

Thorne had never seen Helen as angry, had been shocked by the violence. Her eyes, flat as she had meted it out. There was no doubt that the kid had deserved everything he had got, but Thorne could not help but suspect he was paying for something he had nothing to do with.

It had been coming since Helen had first set foot back in Polesford.

They met outside the abbey. The girl was wearing the same thick jacket she'd had on the night before and it was certainly

328

cold enough for it. Thankfully, the rain had kept away again. The local newspaper Thorne had flicked through before he'd left Paula's said that the floodwater had subsided still further, but that those areas affected by it were not out of the woods yet.

'So, what happened?'

They walked through the archway into the graveyard. There was a couple at the noticeboard, a man walking slowly along one of the narrow paths, studying the gravestones.

'I went to the control unit place like you told me to and a copper took all my details, then they sent a car for me crack of dawn this morning, drove me to Nuneaton.' She shook her head. 'Waste of time. Should have had a lie-in.'

'Why?'

'They didn't believe me, that's why.'

'They said that?'

'Didn't have to. Bloke looked at me like I was five years old or something. I was only in there fifteen minutes.'

'What was his name?'

She shrugged. 'Some dick with one of those stupid electronic cigarettes. Thanked me for coming in, nodded a lot and asked a few questions, then told me they'd be in touch. Made it pretty obvious that nothing I'd told him made a blind bit of difference.'

They had reached the part of the graveyard that Thorne and Helen had visited a few days earlier. Thorne looked along the line of headstones, identified Sandra Weeks' grave. The flowers Helen had laid were nowhere to be seen.

'What kind of questions did he ask?'

'Stuff about the pub,' she said. 'That night I met Steve. Wanted to know which football match was on the TV or something.'

'Did you tell him?'

'I don't know the first thing about football and it wasn't like we were there for very long anyway. It was where we'd arranged to meet, that's all. We had one drink then got in the car and left because we had better things to do.'

'Right.'

She looked at him, a trace of a smile. She had clearly made an effort for her early-morning visit to the police station and was wearing almost as much make-up as she had the previous evening. 'We had sex in Steve's car.'

'I know what you meant,' Thorne said.

They stopped at the entrance to the abbey and looked up. The gargoyles leered, stuck their tongues out. There was almost no wind and the flag was limp above the turrets.

'You want to go in?'

'If you like.'

She nodded. 'Freezing my tits off.'

If anything it was colder inside, and certainly quieter. Their footsteps were unnaturally loud against the stone and instinctively their voices dropped to a whisper. The man Thorne had seen outside was at the far end, where steps led up to the high altar, bending to read an inscription on the font.

'You believe in any of this?' Aurora asked.

Thorne shook his head.

'Me neither. Stupid. Just something to make people feel better when things turn to shit. What d'you call it? A crutch.'

'For some people, I suppose.'

'Nice though.' She walked forward, staring up at the windows, motes of dust dancing in the streams of coloured light. 'Peaceful.'

'You never been in here before?'

'You been to the Tower of London? Buckingham Palace?'

'Not since I was a kid.'

'There you go then. You never appreciate what's on your own doorstep.' She walked further on past the rows of wooden pews, stopped to look at a Norman tomb; a knight carved in stone, arms folded across the sword on his chest. She waited for Thorne to join her. Said, 'So what do I do now?'

'You could try talking to a different copper.'

She shook her head. 'Been there, done that. I want people to know. The whole town's talking about Steve like he's some kind of monster, like a paedo or something. I want them to know it's not true.'

Thorne waited, let the man who had been at the front of the abbey walk past them, back towards the entrance. 'There's plenty of reporters around. I'm sure they'd be interested in your story. Probably pay a fair bit, too.'

'How much?'

'A lot, I should think.'

The girl appeared to like the sound of that.

'You got a job?'

She looked at him like he was stupid. 'I'm doing A/S levels, aren't I? English, French and drama.'

'What do you want to do?' Thorne asked. 'After.'

'Get out as fast as possible,' she said. 'Maybe Birmingham or somewhere.'

'What about a job?'

'I'd rather work in Burger King there than have a decent job here.' She smiled. 'Steve said he'd come with me.'

'What about university?'

She pushed her hands into her pockets. 'Steve said it's a waste of time. We want to get a place together, start enjoying ourselves.'

Thorne said nothing. He'd never clapped eyes on Stephen Bates, but guessed he was the sort to say anything that might get someone like Aurora Harley into bed. That cocky chef was another one, the sort who couldn't keep it in his pants. Making fools out of young girls with his bullshit and his books.

He watched her running a hand across the effigy, fingers

tracing the smooth edges of the sandstone. She didn't seem the sort to be impressed by the likes of Shelley or Steve Bates without good reason. Perhaps she was just a bad judge of character. Maybe she was just smart in all the ways except the one that really mattered.

'So, you reckon I should talk to one of those journalists, then?'

'Up to you,' Thorne said. 'They can twist things though.'

A shrug. 'No more so than anyone else round here.' She took cigarettes from her pocket and they began walking back towards the door. 'Was all that stuff about you twisted? In the paper?'

'Some of it,' Thorne said.

She was flicking her lighter on and off as they walked. 'You seem all right to me.'

Thorne thought: *Terrible* judge of character.

# FIFTY-EIGHT

It wasn't like too many people arrived at these places full of the joys of spring, Linda thought, but the whole process seemed designed to make a bad mood a damn sight worse. The queuing to get through that first reception area for a start; dumped on a chair and stared at, nobody in any real hurry to help, however polite you were being. Not a lot of people skills, the officers, especially the women. By the time you'd filled in the umpteenth form and had your picture taken you'd already lost the will to live, and that was before the metal detectors and these unsmiling arseholes going through your stuff and taking everything off you. Like your mobile might explode at any minute and your fags were laced with heroin or something.

Wasn't it getting *out* that was supposed to be impossible?

Linda understood why it was necessary, she wasn't stupid, but something about the way it was all done made her feel grimy and unwelcome. Like the very act of coming to see a prisoner made you one notch above a scumbag yourself. She tried telling herself that she needed to toughen up and get used to it. It was the way she'd been made to feel ever since that first knock on the door and maybe she'd been naïve thinking it wouldn't be the same coming here.

They knew who she was, didn't they?

The visiting area was smaller than she'd expected. A rubberised floor and four or five tables and chairs. Maybe there was somewhere else for the general prison population, those who weren't on remand, the ones who weren't vulnerable. A vending machine stood in one corner, a prison officer sitting alongside with a magazine. There were more officers around than prisoners, only two when Linda sat down to wait. A man in his early twenties opposite a woman who was probably his mother and one who was much older, maybe seventy. Linda knew that there were all sorts in a vulnerable prisoners' unit, not just sex offenders. Ex-coppers, lawyers, whatever, but looking at the two already sitting there, it was impossible not to wonder.

Was the old man a judge or a kiddie-fiddler? Maybe both. The way she saw it, there were far too many child abusers getting sent down for less time than somebody who'd nicked a shirt during a riot.

When Steve was led in, she felt her heart start to race.

A thrill, for those first few seconds, same as that first time she'd seen him. Her and a girlfriend on the piss in that pub in Dorden, him and his mate buying them drinks all night, giving it all the chat. He was funny and full of himself, his shirt was open a long way down, and he was just what she needed.

Today, he was wearing grey tracksuit bottoms and a sweatshirt with a bib over it. Red for the vulnerable prisoners. He looked even thinner than he had done in court, and paler. His hair was all over the shop.

He sat down and smiled and said, 'Hello, gorgeous.'

When she'd had that conversation with Helen about what it would be like, this was the moment that Linda had been imagining. Hands reaching across the table, squeezing and stroking.

334

It was lucky for him that the rules prevented it. She could have happily reached across and taken one of his eyes out.

'How are the kids?' he said.

'They're OK.'

He nodded. 'Listen, I'm sorry about the other day, I don't know what I was thinking. They told me you came down to the hospital.'

Linda noticed the frayed edge of the bandage poking from the sleeve of his sweatshirt. 'You must have been feeling awful,' she said.

'I was all over the place,' he said. 'You've no idea what it's like in here.'

'Bad, is it?'

'Worse than I imagined. Worst bit is missing you and the kids, you know?'

'I know.'

He sat back. 'Sorry, love. You didn't come here to listen to me moaning.' He smiled; same smile as that night at the pub in Dorden. *They reckon when a woman goes for a night out she's usually got a friend who's not quite as attractive as she is. But it's obviously rubbish, because me and my mate have been staring at you two all night and we can't decide* which *one of you is the tastiest.* 'Glad you did come though. Couldn't sleep last night, thinking about it.'

'Tell me about the girl,' Linda said.

It was hard to read his expression. Shock, anger, and, by the time he finally spoke, something that looked like genuine disappointment. 'Oh for Christ's sake, I thought at least you'd believe I didn't do anything. How could you think I'd done those things? You know me better than anyone.'

'I don't mean the girl they think you killed. I mean the girl I know you've been shagging. The sixteen-year-old girl?' She watched his face change again, his Adam's apple bobbing as he swallowed, and wondered where his chat was now. He blinked

335

quickly and she could almost hear his mind working as he struggled to find whatever words might help him. 'It's why you couldn't look at me in court, isn't it? If that's what guilty looks like, you'd better try and avoid it next time you're standing in the dock.'

'I met her a few times,' he said. 'That's all.'

'Don't lie to me.' She leaned forward, just enough to remind him what she was capable of, 'no touching' rule or not. 'Don't even try to lie to me.'

'I swear.'

'So, what exactly was it you were thinking, those times you were "meeting" her brains out?'

'Please, love—'

'Same thing you were thinking the last time, or the time before that? Not that they were quite as young as this one, were they? Not still doing homework, as far as I can remember. Were you thinking: *Look at me, I've still got it?* Sad old twat who normally has to sit and toss himself off in front of the computer and look what I can still pull? Were you thinking how great you were, was it making you feel like you were twenty-one again? Looking up at some kid bouncing up and down on top of you and thinking, how great is that arse and look at those tits and thinking how much nicer they were than what you had at home? What you were stuck with?' She shook her head and stared for a few moments, enjoying it. 'No, definitely not that. Because the only thing I'm certain about is that you were not thinking about me. While you were lying and sneaking off and shagging that little slag, you did not spend one second thinking about me or about my kids.'

She leaned back again, looked around. The prison officer by the vending machine dropped his eyes quickly back to his magazine. The woman visiting the younger of the other prisoners turned back to him.

'I don't know what to say to you,' Steve said.

Linda was thinking much the same thing. She could, for example, tell her husband that the young girl they had been discussing was determined to give him an alibi. She could mention that a pair of high-ranking police officers from London believed he was innocent, that they and a forensic expert were working hard to prove it.

For the time being though, she decided to keep those things to herself.

# FIFTY-NINE

They didn't even get as far as Cornish's office. After ten minutes making small talk to a desk officer, he came down to greet them, showed them through to what was basically a waiting room just off the main reception area. He seemed cheerful enough, puffing happily on his e-cigarette as he talked, like he was happy to be taking a break from proper police work.

Thorne said, 'You saw Aurora Harley this morning.'

'Yeah, she told me she'd spoken to you.' Cornish looked at his watch. It was just after eleven thirty. 'You don't waste a lot of time, do you?'

'She said you didn't take her seriously.'

Cornish shook his head. 'Not true. Kids like to exaggerate, don't they?' He was sitting on a plastic chair. He hooked a second one with his boot and pulled it into line so that he could put his feet up. 'Look, I did exactly what anyone else would have done. What you would have done, I'm sure. The girl was interviewed, a statement was taken and we're in the process of passing every-thing on to the CPS, but in all honesty it's not like we're holding the front page. I can't see anything she told us changing the focus of this investigation or of the forthcoming prosecution.' He took another hit of his e-cig, hummed with pleasure as the tip glowed blue. 'You know you can get these in different flavours, right?' He held it up. 'This is cappuccino. You get a fag and a cup of coffee at the same time.'

'Why doesn't it change anything?'

'Sorry?'

'What she told you.'

'She was all over the place for a start,' Cornish said. 'She couldn't give us any real details. She couldn't remember what was on TV in the pub that night, couldn't even remember the name of the pub.'

'I was in some pub a couple of days ago,' Thorne said. 'Had lunch there. Couldn't tell you what the place was called, but I'm sure you're not going to call me a liar.'

'Listen, I'm perfectly willing to believe that Bates was giving her one, but if that's the case, she'd say anything to get him off, wouldn't she?'

'No, I don't believe she would.'

'You telling me you've never questioned an alibi from a loved one? Most of the time they're no better than prison confessions.'

'So why didn't she come forward straight away?'

'God knows.' He smiled, tapped the end of his e-cig against his teeth. 'Maybe she was busy with exams or something.'

'I reckon it took her that long to pluck up the courage,' Thorne said. 'It took a lot of guts.'

'And I'm grateful that she did come forward.'

Thorne looked at him.

'I mean, it confirms that Bates likes teenage girls, doesn't it? If anything, it makes the case against him stronger, so I suppose I should thank you for pointing her in our direction.'

Hendricks had said nothing, sitting there looking at his phone as though he was paying little attention to the exchange. Now, he said, 'Just so you know, when we prove that Bates didn't kill Jessica Toms, that he didn't abduct anybody, we won't be making a song and dance about it. When your mug is all over the front of the paper because you're the copper that got it wrong and there are lawsuits flying about faster than shit off a shiny shovel, we won't bother marching back in here to tell you what a bollocks you made of the whole investigation. Fair enough?' He smiled. 'We're happy to leave that to somebody else.'

Cornish blinked. He had clearly felt on safe ground jousting with Thorne, but something about Hendricks – his manner perhaps, the threat in his appearance and in that nice friendly smile – seemed to disconcert him for a moment or two. 'Prove it, how?' he said.

'Whoever killed Jessica Toms disguised the time of death,' Hendricks said. 'He planted insects on the body to make it look like she'd died a lot earlier than she actually had. Like Bates had killed her as soon as she'd been taken.' Cornish raised a hand, trying to get in, but Hendricks wouldn't let him. 'It's why the body was partially burned. Just enough to open the skin, give the bugs something to feed on. All so it would look like Bates, so it'll *still* look like it was Bates when he kills the next girl.'

Cornish shook his head, as though this was one piece of foolishness he simply could not allow to stand. 'Poppy Johnston is dead, we all know that.'

'So, why haven't you found her?' Thorne did not bother waiting for an answer. 'Same reason you didn't find Jessica, not until the man who killed her wanted you to. Because she isn't there to find. Not yet.'

'And when she is, you're telling me she'll be crawling with these bugs that actually came from somewhere else.'

'We might be able to prevent that,' Thorne said. 'If you'd stop being a smartarse and listen to what we're telling you.'

340

Cornish took a drag, hissed out coffee-flavoured smoke and thought about it. 'Where did all these incriminating insects come from?'

Thorne looked at Hendricks. *Do you want to tell him, or shall I?*

Hendricks told him.

'Christ, I think I've heard it all now.'

'So, easy enough to prove, see? Just a question of extracting some nice porky DNA from one of those bugs.'

'Right, and who's doing that for you?'

'I've got one or two contacts,' Hendricks said. He and Thorne had talked about this on the way there. If Cornish went for it, they would happily hand everything over, make the job Liam Southworth was doing every bit as official as he wanted. If not, they weren't going to volunteer anything, let Cornish think Hendricks had a fully equipped mobile DNA unit parked in a lay-by somewhere.

Cornish tucked his e-cigarette into his top pocket and swung his legs to the floor. 'Let's go mad for a minute, shall we, and assume all that stuff happened ... the dead pig and the bugs being planted on Jessica Toms' body. I still don't see why it couldn't have been Bates that did it?'

'What?' Thorne had been unprepared for this.

'Why not?'

'Give me one good reason why he'd do any of that.'

'I don't need one,' Cornish said. 'We're talking about someone who abducts young girls, does whatever horrible things he does, then murders them and dumps their bodies. These are not ordinary people, Tom, you know that as well as I do.' He let that hang for a few seconds while he got to his feet. 'They don't do things for "good" reasons.'

'Even you must know how lame that sounds,' Thorne said. 'How convenient.'

Cornish shook his head. 'They're twisted, simple as that, and

341

the day I start to understand why they do anything is the day I start looking for another job.'

Now Thorne stood up too, and walked across to put himself between Cornish and the door.

'Don't be a knob.' Cornish sighed, fastened his jacket and looked from Thorne to Hendricks. 'First you show up, then your tattooed mate ... honestly, it's like the bloody circus has come to town. Clowns and freaks. Round here, we're just ordinary coppers doing a decent job and whatever you think, that means trying to prove someone's innocent every bit as much as trying to prove they're guilty. Like it or not, this time we got the job done.' He stared at Thorne, waiting for him to move.

Hendricks walked quickly across and dropped a hand on to Thorne's shoulder, all smiles. 'Now, I've got thick skin,' he said. 'Thick, *freaky* skin, so I don't take offence easily. But my mate here ... well, why don't I just move him out of your way, before he kicks your teeth in with those big clown shoes of his?'

Thorne stepped aside and watched Cornish move quickly past him towards the door. 'You didn't do the job properly,' he said.

Hendricks asked Thorne to drive him back to Polesford. He was going to collect his stuff from Paula's, pick up his car, then drive straight back to Liam Southworth's place in Warwick.

'He gave me a key,' Hendricks told him, beaming. 'I mean, it's probably best if I'm on the spot when his mate in the lab comes through for us. Plus, he's got a massive flat-screen TV ...'

In slow traffic on the M42, Thorne said, 'Do you think we rattled him?'

'Cornish? Oh, yeah, I reckon so.' Hendricks looked across, saw Thorne's expression. 'You *wanted* him to give us the bum's rush, didn't you?'

'We've made a better job of it than he has so far, haven't we?'

'Not bad for a clown and a freak,' Hendricks said.

342

'A freak with thick skin, remember.' Thorne glanced at his friend and smiled. He knew better than anyone how thin that elaborately decorated skin really was. 'How badly did you want to punch him?'

'I wanted to shove that stupid pretend fag up his arse.' Hendricks turned to look out of the window for a few seconds, then put his head back. 'That stuff about people who were not "ordinary" and you knowing that as well as he did. That was about Bardsey, wasn't it?'

'He brought it up first time I met him,' Thorne said. 'Wanted me to know he'd done his homework.'

Hendricks nodded. Said, 'That thing's going up his arse sideways.'

Thorne grinned, but he had no way of knowing what DI Tim Cornish would do with the information they'd given him, how long he would wait before trying to take over or shut them down. Thorne could only hope they got what they needed in the time they had left.

Hendricks began to sing quietly, murdering 'Send In The Clowns' as they inched forward and waited for the traffic to clear.

# SIXTY

'The kids wrote letters to take in to him,' Linda said. 'Spent ages on them.'

'What did you do with them?'

'They're in a drawer in the bedroom.'

They were sitting in the small back garden in overcoats. Linda had made coffee, though Helen had smelled the wine on her breath when she'd arrived. Charli and Danny were upstairs, while the coppers on the afternoon shift mooched about or watched TV in the living room. Carson was in the kitchen, trying not to make it obvious that she was keeping an eye on them through the window. She had not been at the house for a couple of days and Helen had begun to wonder if something had happened in the wake of the incident at Danny's school. She was friendlier than she had been before, presumably because she was worried that if there were to be any complaint about what had happened to Danny, it was likely to come from Helen.

'I'm not going to say that him lying was the worst part of it.' Linda pulled a biscuit from the packet on the table and dunked it. 'I mean, obviously him screwing around was way worse, but denying it didn't help. Like he could be unfaithful *and* play me for a mug.'

'What about once he'd admitted it?'

'I didn't really give him chance to say anything.' She tried to look pleased with herself. 'Just told him what I thought of him.'

'Which is?' Helen looked at her.

'That he's ruined my life and ruined the kids' lives and I can't forgive him for that.' She saw Helen's reaction. 'What?'

'It's happened before though, hasn't it?'

Linda picked up her mug and cradled it. 'Yeah, he's got drunk, been stupid a few times.'

'And you stayed together.'

'Not the same,' Linda said.

'So why is this time any different?'

'She's sixteen.' Linda shook her head, as though her reasoning were obvious. 'Jesus, how do you think that makes me feel?'

'Like shit,' Helen said.

'Like I'm no good for anything. Like in a few years when the kids have both buggered off, and I haven't got them and I haven't got a bloke, there'll be no point to me at all.' She stared at the fence. 'Sixteen, for God's sake. Yeah, he wants something younger ... firmer, it's not like I don't understand that, but when she's still at school you start to wonder about things you really don't want to be thinking about, you know?'

Helen nodded.

'I hate him for that as much as for doing it in the first place. For those ... thoughts.'

Helen nodded again, and smiled to suggest that what she was about to say was not altogether serious. 'So, you won't be in any rush to take him back this time, then.'

Linda seemed confused. 'Not really an issue, is it? He's going to prison.'

'Right,' Helen said. 'But I mean, if he wasn't.'

345

'I don't need to think about it, do I?'

Helen glanced back towards the kitchen and saw Sophie Carson turn casually away, as though she'd been checking on the weather. She looked back to Linda. 'Are you going to tell the kids?'

'About him and that little slag?' She shook her head. 'What's the point in upsetting them? He goes down and they're probably never going to see him again, are they? I mean, yeah, they might ask about going to visit, but I'll just tell them he doesn't want them to come.'

It sounded like bravado, Helen thought. Linda was getting very good at it. 'Probably sensible,' she said.

Linda took a sip of coffee, then grimaced and leaned across to tip what was left into a ceramic pot, the plant long dead. 'I hate the bits of soggy biscuit at the bottom,' she said.

They heard a small cheer from the crowd at the front of the house. The kind of thing usually reserved for a copper losing his helmet, or someone managing to get a picture taken beyond the cordon. Such moments had become part and parcel of a fun, family day out at the Bates place and the noise had become commonplace now, unremarkable.

'Stupid thing is that, despite everything, I still think he's innocent.' Linda shrugged and sat back on the garden chair. 'I know when he's lying, I've always known.'

Helen nodded. It was all a question of which lies you could live with and which ones ate you up.

'You telling me you don't know when Tom's telling you porkies?'

'I think so,' Helen said. 'Not really been together long enough.'

'Don't get me wrong, I want him to suffer for what he's done to me. I wouldn't be losing too much sleep if some big bastard knocked him about a bit in the shower, but he still doesn't deserve to spend the rest of his life in prison. Not when he didn't do anything.'

Helen looked away. She had spoken to Thorne who had told her exactly how the conversation had gone with Cornish. All manner of cats had come tumbling out of bags and it was time to let Linda know about them. Though she might not have been as thrilled now to hear it, Linda deserved to know that she'd been right all along about her husband being innocent. But there was something else Helen needed to come clean about first.

'I wasn't telling the truth yesterday,' Helen said. Her voice sounded weak, so she cleared her throat. 'When I told you I didn't know who the girl was.'

'I'm not with you,' Linda said.

'Her name's Aurora Harley.'

# SIXTY-ONE

Thorne felt oddly disappointed that it had taken so long for the call to come. Could it be that taking him down a peg or two had become so routine that it was no longer a priority? He'd have put money on the hammer falling within half an hour of his leaving Nuneaton station, but as it turned out he had been back in Polesford over an hour before Brigstocke rang.

It was probably just down to a glitch in the chain of command. It would have taken three or four conversations before any complaint had even got to Russell Brigstocke. There must have been a hold-up, Thorne decided, that was all, an unanswered call or an email diverted to a spam folder. Perhaps Cornish's chief superintendent had been busy getting his hat altered.

Something important, had to have been.

Walking through the market square, Thorne had stared at Brigstocke's name pulsing on the screen and imagined his boss getting increasingly irritated. He had let the mobile ring a few times before he'd dropped the call. He knew there would have been some impressively creative swearing.

He hoped the inevitable call back would not come in the next few minutes, as he was planning on using the phone.

He sat in Cupz, at a table near the counter. Tea and a toasted sandwich, same as last time, the local paper he had glanced at first thing that morning laid out in front of him. The front page was dominated by the continuing search for Poppy Johnston, though the tone of the reporting had subtly changed. As far as finding Poppy alive went, there was talk of 'hope fading' and the 'desperate efforts' of those still looking. Though it was never made explicit, it was clear that those writing the stories believed, as the police themselves did, that they were looking for a body.

Inside, there were more Stephen Bates stories: a suggestion that the suicide attempt had been an effort to escape attacks in prison; a 'reliable source' inside HMP Hewell describing Bates' outrageous demands for fillet steak and the latest games console; an interview with a woman he'd worked with ten years earlier who said he was 'moody' and 'secretive' and that he'd always taken a 'strange interest' in her fifteen-year-old daughter. The important adjectives were emboldened and there was a picture of the woman looking suitably horrified, pressing an old photo of her young daughter to her bosom.

It was a highly professional exercise in barrel-scraping.

Thorne looked across at the woman working behind the counter – Donna, was that her name? – and they exchanged a smile. He turned away and took another bite of his sandwich, then he reached for his phone.

He stabbed at the numbers, then waited.

'It's me ... yeah, I went in to see him this morning.' He listened for a few seconds. 'Yeah, right, it's like we thought. The case against Bates is falling apart bit by bit.' He said nothing for a while. He held the handset between his chin and shoulder to take a mouthful of tea. He nodded, hummed assent. 'Don't worry, I'll keep you up to speed, but right now the CPS are having kittens because what looked like evidence has turned out to be useless. I know . . . well, they're already talking about being sued for wrongful arrest.' He laughed. 'Yeah . . . I'll let you know as soon as I hear any more. Call me later if you want to.'

When he'd put the phone away, he looked across at the woman behind the counter again. He asked for more tea and she told him it was coming right up. The colour in her face told him she'd heard every word he'd said, which was exactly what he wanted.

Thorne had not been speaking to anyone.

He went back to the paper. The other big story was still the flooding, specifically the clean-up operation, which had begun in areas where the floodwater had subsided sufficiently. There were reports of dead livestock and other animals being taken away, their bodies revealed as the water level had fallen. On the letters page there was a good deal of ghoulish speculation as to whether Poppy Johnston's body might soon be discovered in the same way.

The woman brought Thorne's tea across. She glanced down at the paper and said, 'Horrible, isn't it?'

Thorne nodded and turned the page.

Nothing had shaken his conviction that Poppy Johnston was still alive. The business with the phone was no more than a punt, mischief as much as anything else, but Thorne hoped that a few loose tongues might go some way towards bringing a killer to the surface.

When Charli heard the door slam downstairs, she went to the window and pulled the curtain back. She watched Helen Weeks walk quickly down the path, cameras flashing all the way as she fell in between two uniformed officers.

'It's her,' she said. 'Mum's friend.'

'About bloody time.' Danny was lying on the bed, playing *Donkey Kong* on an old Nintendo Gameboy that Gallagher had given him. 'Just trying to buy me off,' he'd said to Charli. 'So I don't sue her fat arse for getting punched or whatever.'

Charli heard Helen's name being shouted by reporters as she was escorted to a waiting BMW.

'Why the hell are they still so interested in her, anyway?' She watched as the car drove off. 'That's her boyfriend in there,' she said, pointing. 'The other copper, the one who was on the front of the paper.'

'What?'

'Her boyfriend's a copper as well.'

Danny sucked his teeth and threw the Gameboy to the end of the bed. 'That thing is *so* shit. It's like, steam-powered or something.'

'Better than nothing,' Charli said.

Danny turned and punched the pillow behind him until he was comfortable. He touched the bruise beneath his eye, which had blackened still further. 'Better off together, I reckon,' he said. 'Feds. Who the hell else is going to stand them? Can't smell anything when you both stink.'

Charli walked across and dropped on to the bed.

They sat in silence for a while, then Danny said, 'I was thinking . . . I bet Steve's already the top G in that prison.' He nodded, smiled. 'He'll be bossing the place already, for sure.'

'You think?'

He sat up. 'I *know*, man.'

Danny was suddenly brighter than Charli had seen him in a few days, chattier. Part of her wanted to tell him to shut up, that he was talking like a little pretend gangsta twat again, but it was nice to see him excited about something. She said, 'Yeah?'

'Yeah . . . I know how it works in them places. You have to bust a few heads to begin with, just to show everyone who's the baddest, but then you're number one and nobody can touch you. You're living like a G, anything you want. *Literally.*'

'That's just in films.'

'For real,' Danny said. 'You wait until he gets out. I bet he'll have the *best* stories.'

There was a soft knock on the door and their mother walked in. Charli shifted along to make room for her to sit down.

'All right, Mum?'

'Just tired.'

'Not seen you since you got back,' Charli said. 'You haven't told us what it was like when you went to see Steve.'

'Did you give him my letter?' Danny asked.

Linda nodded. 'He was pleased.'

'I was just saying how he was going to be all right in there, how he was going to end up bossing the place and everything. I bet he had people running around doing whatever he wanted, didn't he?'

Linda said, 'Do us a favour love. Go down to the kitchen and get me a glass of wine.'

Danny looked horrified, pushed at Charli with his foot. 'Why can't she go and get it?'

'Mum asked you,' Charli said.

'Please, love.'

'Can I have one?'

'You can have a Coke or something, and there's crisps in the cupboard.'

Grumbling, Danny swung his legs off the bed, and sloped to the door. He said, 'Taking the piss,' before he slammed it behind him.

Linda turned to Charli immediately. 'There's something I need to ask you before your brother comes back.'

'What? Has something happened—?'

'Just let me say it, OK?'

Charli nodded, waited. The wine her mother had sent Danny to get was obviously not going to be her first.

'Did Steve ever . . . touch you?'

'*What?*'

'Please, baby, you've got no idea how hard this is. You know what I'm talking about.' Linda took a deep breath and said it again quickly. 'Did he touch you?'

Charli stared at her mother.

# SIXTY-TWO

It's like being high.

She's moved beyond the pain now, beyond the fear. The agony has become numbness and she no longer feels as though her arms and legs belong to her, will do what she wants them to do. The terror has given way to a strange kind of excitement; an exhilaration that feels familiar. Her and her friends out in the fields with cider and cigarettes, screaming their heads off then laughing like lunatics.

It's not being chilled out, nothing like that, not like she gets on weed when she can afford it. It's more like that time she was persuaded to try MDMA at a party. The only time she's ever done it.

Everything intensified; louder, brighter, lovelier.

She laughs, remembering how that night was and where she is now.

It's funny, she thinks, how the darkness stops being dark after a while, becomes just a different kind of light. It shifts; blooms and withers. It has moods. Maybe it changes when her moods change. Thickens, gets gritty, comes closer.

Sounds bizarre, but she doesn't even know if she's thinking straight.

She does know that it's a very different kind of dark when she shuts her eyes. Black velvet behind the lids, with a blanket of speckles, like stars that glow and dart and three bright spots which are always fixed. Close together.

Her mother, her father, her brother.

Any time she wants them, there they are.

The smell, which at any other time would have her chucking up her chips, has become one she is used to, something she breathes in easily now, something she tastes, and the rustlings and scratchings are nearly drowned out by the low drone, which is sometimes in her head and sometimes coming from deep in her throat.

She remembers the night she took that little blue tablet, the warnings from her mates. Enjoy it while you can, because afterwards it's not so great.

Didn't stop her, of course.

Now, she drifts high above the pain and the fear. The knowledge that there is a man who did this and who might come back to finish what he started. The thought that when he does, she will probably be dead, if she isn't already. She smiles, and her dry lips crack, but she doesn't feel it.

Being dead would certainly explain a lot.

Poppy closes her eyes and seeks out those three bright pinpricks.

Waiting for the comedown.

# SIXTY-THREE

It was oddly disconcerting, as though Thorne and Helen were invisible. Sitting there, drinking in Paula's front room; heavy metal providing the unlikely background music while Paula and her boyfriend discussed the Bates case as if they were alone.

'I'm not saying I don't think he did it, but maybe the police should be looking at alternatives. That's all I'm saying.'

'Sounds like they've got enough evidence.' Jason Sweeney nodded his head to the music for a few seconds. 'You don't charge someone unless you think you can put them away.'

'Something still not right though.' Paula cast the latest in a series of hopeful glances at Thorne and Helen. Thorne wondered if she'd heard something already, if her friend Donna had been on the phone. 'I mean, obviously we don't *know* because we're not close to it.' Another glance, desperate for Thorne or Helen to chip in.

'Closer than most.' Sweeney pointed his beer can at Thorne and Helen. 'Not everyone in town's got coppers as houseguests, have they?'

'Horse's mouth.' Paula narrowed her eyes at Thorne. 'Not that the horse is saying a lot.'

'What are we listening to?' Thorne asked.

'Slayer.' Sweeney closed his eyes and nodded some more. 'It's a compilation I put together. Helps clear my head a bit at the end of the day. Blow some of the shit out.'

'So, your mate Phil gone then?' Paula sipped her wine casually.

'Yeah, he's out of your hair.'

'Working on the case somewhere else, is he?'

Thorne could not help but admire the woman's determination, her attempt to come at things from a different angle.

'He found a cosier bed,' Thorne said.

Paula shook her head, smiling. She knew they were playing a game and was quickly learning that it was one she was not going to win. She growled in mock frustration. 'Well, because *somebody* needs to learn to keep their voice down, we know it's all to do with bugs. Creepy-crawlies or what have you.'

Sweeney drained his beer. 'Insects on a body.' He belched softly. 'A very accurate way to determine the time of death if there's significant decomposition.'

Paula rolled her eyes. 'Bloody hell, listen to him.' She looked at Thorne. 'It *is* something to do with that though, isn't it? Whatever you're secretly working on, your line of inquiry, whatever.'

Thorne cocked his head as though considering how much to reveal, teasing. 'Can't say.'

'Why not? You said yourself you were only here on holiday, that you weren't really involved.'

She was trying hard not to show it, but Thorne could see that the woman was growing irritated at her failure to elicit any information. It was as though she felt entitled to something because she had provided him and Helen with a bed for a few nights. Or perhaps it was because Helen had not let her play hopscotch twenty-five years earlier. 'We don't want rumours spreading,' he said. 'There's still a girl missing.'

Paula nodded, but she looked disappointed.

'I suppose it's like that thing doctors have to swear to,' Sweeney said. 'It applies whether they're working on something or not.'

'Hippocratic oath,' Paula said.

'Right.'

'Yeah, well that's bollocks for a start.' Paula dug an elbow into her boyfriend's ribs. 'This one went to a doctor once with piles, next day all his mates in the pub were pissing themselves and asking if he wanted a cushion.'

'I need to go to bed,' Helen said.

Thorne turned to look at her. She had been quick enough to accept the offer of a drink when she and Thorne had got back, but had sat in silence ever since.

'I'll come up with you,' he said. When Helen made no objection, he laid the can, still half full, down on the coffee table. 'Thanks . . .'

Paula nodded towards the stereo and nudged Sweeney again. She said, 'We'll turn it down a bit.'

Thorne came out of the bathroom and walked into the bedroom to find Helen crying. She was not making much noise, but the effort involved in staying relatively quiet as she wept contorted her face between the strangled sobs.

He asked what the matter was, whispered it. He wasn't even sure that she'd heard him come in, that she knew he was there.

After a minute or so, he thought that she did, but perhaps she hadn't heard him speak. The music was still loud enough downstairs.

He had no idea what to do.

She would not look at him.

He lay down next to her and waited. He watched her chest heaving, stared at the heels of her hands when she pressed them to her eyes. It was several minutes before her breathing returned to something like normal and she was ready to say anything.

'I was abused.' She looked at him for a second or two then went back to staring at the far wall. 'Here, when I was twelve. Thirteen, too. It went on for a couple of years, I suppose ...'

She folded her arms across her chest, lay still for a minute or so.

'He was a friend of my dad's, someone he'd worked with for a while. He said that if I told anyone then he'd go to my dad and say I'd been asking him to do it, that I was just a little slut, and he convinced me that my dad would believe him and not me. He said it was all my fault, that I'd made him do it, and it took a long time before I started to believe that it wasn't. That I hadn't encouraged him in some way. It wasn't just me. It's what he said to Linda as well ... how he stopped her from saying anything.' She glanced at Thorne. 'We talked about it ... not at first, but after it had been going on for a while. From then on we tried to look after each other, to stay together whenever we could, to avoid the situations where he could get us on our own. There was a place he took us to, where it first happened, I mean, but afterwards there were times he would come to the house ... he'd just turn up and pretend to be surprised when my dad wasn't in. When it was just me and Jenny. He'd help himself to a beer, sit down next to me and talk like he was just waiting for Dad to get home. Sometimes he'd be touching me when Jenny was in the same room ...

'I swore that I'd never let him get near her, but I don't know for sure. I couldn't be with her all day, every day. There might have been times, you know? I knew he was looking at her and once, when he caught me, he said that I'd better keep loving him or he'd have to try somebody else and I knew he was talking about my sister. "Loving" him. That's how he described it. Like loving means bleeding. Lying still like you're dead and throwing your guts up afterwards.

'Jenny never said anything, but she was so cold with me after I left and I've always wondered. The way she judges me sometimes. I've always thought that I must have let her down ... that she thinks maybe I didn't do enough to protect her.

'Same with Linda. I think it's why I wanted to come back when I found out she was in trouble.' She shook her head. 'I *know* that's why. I needed to be here for her now, because I'd left so suddenly back then. I never even told her I was going ... and we were supposed to be a team. He'd already stopped by then, because we were too old for him, I suppose, but talking about what he did made it so much easier for both of us afterwards and once I'd left she had nobody. She had to cope with it all on her own. Bumping into him in the pub or in the street, him looking at her, making sure her own daughter stayed well away from him. I can't imagine what that must have been like. Jesus ... Steve screwing around, everything that's going on ... it isn't the only reason she puts a bottle away before lunchtime every day.'

Thorne inched towards her. He reached across until his hand found hers, but she did not return its pressure.

*Lying still, like you're dead.*

He swallowed and mentally worded a question, but there was no need to ask it.

'He's not here any more ... there's no way I would have come back if he'd still been here. My dad still mentions him sometimes though. They stayed in touch after Mum died and Dad moved down south and I lived in dread of him coming to visit or something. Dad rang me up a year or so back, told me how sad it was that his old mate had gone downhill so fast, that he'd had to go into care. A residential home, somewhere the other side of Tamworth, I think. Sometimes I'd imagine going to visit him in there ... just so I could see him shrunk and helpless, so then maybe that would be the memory I'd have of him and not the one I've had every day for twenty-five years. Saying he was

360

sorry ... still sweating while he tucked his shirt back in. I'd go to that place, so I could enjoy watching him sit there, weak as a baby and stinking of shit and not able to do anything.'

Now, Thorne felt his hand being squeezed hard.

'Just so I could watch him.'

She turned her head to look at Thorne. 'His name was Peter Harley, and that girl we met in the pub is his granddaughter. That girl with a thing for older men.'

Thorne remembered Helen disappearing soon after Aurora Harley had introduced herself. The way she had been afterwards. Her face grey, ashen, but something smouldering as she clutched at a skinny girl's silver jacket.

*There's no need to be scared ...*

His thoughts reeled like drunks, lurched and tumbled over one another; scraps and screams and images he would never be able to unsee. Plenty of pictures, but only one word able to find its way into his mouth.

Just Helen's name.

From downstairs, the shriek of a guitar and a bass like a punch to the heart, and, in their bed, only the ragged gulp and moan and the catch in the chest as Helen began to cry again.

# SIXTY-FOUR

He hears things.

It's that kind of place, after all, one of the things he likes best about being here. In a big city, people never get to know what anyone else is up to, not really, never get to *care*; minding their own business and suspicious about anyone who might be interested in theirs. They casually raise their newspaper or turn their music up while someone is getting attacked in the same train carriage. They slink away, mortified, when others start to argue or laugh too loudly.

They don't want to get involved.

Admittedly, the business that gets talked about here is not always earth-shattering. Who's shagging who, who's fallen out, who got pissed and punched someone. Still, it helps you feel part of something. He also knows that what he's hearing is rarely the unvarnished truth. That's the nature of rumours when you get down to it. Things get exaggerated, the facts get twisted the more a story is repeated. A stupid row can become an impending divorce within the space of three conversations and a harmless bit of flirting in the pub yesterday is likely to become full-on sex in a toilet cubicle by the same time tomorrow.

He likes to hear it, all the same, to feel like he's monitoring the heartbeat of the town. He doesn't like what he's been hearing about that policeman, though.

Thorne.

Even allowing for the exaggeration, it's clear that the copper from London has been making a far better job of things than the coppers who are being paid for it. They all did exactly what he'd wanted them to do, went for all that lovely evidence like ferrets down a rathole, thank you very much. How the hell did Thorne and his skinhead boyfriend see something that the rest of those idiots couldn't?

Good luck, bad luck. Whichever shade of it you were on the receiving end of, he'd always known that luck was something you could never guard against. He'd had his fair share of the good sort, after all.

Having someone like Bates around had been the biggest slice of it he could ever ask for.

He'd known what they were up to for a few days already. There had been some chatter about insects being important and then talk about the visit to Bob Patterson's farm, so it was pretty obvious that they'd put a lot of it together. But thank God, he was also hearing how nobody else was very interested, telling Thorne and his mate they should mind their own business, which was pretty ironic, all things considered.

He'd told himself there was no need to panic just yet. He had to carry on as normal, that was all, sit tight and keep his ears open.

Now though, there were whispers that the case against Bates wasn't quite as solid as anyone had thought. Now, so he'd heard more than once, people who actually mattered were starting to sit up and ask questions.

Cornish and his boss, the CPS, for heaven's sake . . .

The plan had always been to let things die down a bit. To bide his time until there were a few less coppers knocking about, then go back to see Poppy and celebrate in style. He'd thought things would ease off a little once Bates had been arrested, that they might at least scale down the search and give him a chance to have some fun. The flooding hadn't made things any easier.

He hadn't thought things would get *quite* as stupid as they did, and it wasn't like the police could be seen to ease off now, was it? Not with film crews everywhere you looked and half the country's reporters still hanging around to watch. Hard as it was, he'd resigned himself to the terrible fact that by the time the coast was well and truly clear, there might not be a great deal of his lovely Poppy left to enjoy.

The very idea that she might not be there for him when all this was over enraged him. Just considering the unfairness of it for more than a few seconds left him feeling scalded, almost breathless. He'd put so much effort into it, so much thought.

Any more talk about arresting the wrong man though, he might have to take a risk by going back to make sure.

# SIXTY-FIVE

Thorne's phone rang just after six thirty am and he scrabbled for it, a reflex. Were he not on holiday, a call this early would almost certainly mean that he'd caught a murder.

It was not a number he recognised.

'Woke you, did I?'

'Yeah.' Thorne shifted to the edge of the bed and dropped his voice, hoping that Helen had not been woken up too. Neither of them had got a lot of sleep. 'Who's this?'

'It's Bob Patterson.'

It took Thorne a few seconds to place the name. 'It's very early.'

'For you, maybe. I've been up since five.'

'Well done.'

'So anyway … I've been thinking about whoever stole my piglet.'

'Right,' Thorne said. Helen turned towards him, groaning softly. He reached out to touch her shoulder. Her skin felt cold, so he pulled the sheet up.

'Reckoned you might be interested,' Patterson said. 'That's all. You said, if I thought of anything that might help.'

'Who is it?' Helen asked.

Thorne shook his head and sat up. 'I'm listening, Mr Patterson.'

'I've not got time to tell you now, have I?' The farmer sounded exasperated. 'I've still got animals to feed. I'll be having my breakfast in an hour or so though . . .'

While the farmer gave him instructions, Thorne watched the first thin fingers of light from outside reaching through the gap in the floral curtains. When the call had finished, he tossed his phone on to the bed and sat there as, unbidden, a conversation with his father came into his mind.

It was more than just the memory of those old springs and speakers on Bob Patterson's kitchen table. It had been an attempt to understand why his father had felt the need to get up at stupid o'clock every morning, the time getting progressively earlier in inverse proportion to the number of things the old man actually needed to do.

'I can get up when I want, can't I?' Jim Thorne had begun to sound irritated, the fuse getting shorter as the Alzheimer's took hold. 'Free country last time I checked.'

'I'm only thinking of you,' Thorne had said. 'You got up every day to go to work and now, when you've got the chance . . .'

'Why would I want to stay in bed? Festering.' The old man had been walking quickly from room to room, checking each one out but refusing to say what he was looking for. Now, he stopped and looked at Thorne, an increasingly rare moment of clarity. He said, 'You get to my age you have to grab hold of every second by the throat. Sleeping it all away would be like giving up.'

'I know that, but most of the time you end up falling asleep again anyway, sitting in front of the telly.'

'It's a question of making an *effort*.'

Paula was working an early shift so Thorne guessed that the

central heating had already kicked in, but it had not quite taken the chill off the room yet. He slipped quickly back beneath the covers.

'What did he want?' Helen asked.

'Something about the pig he had stolen. Says he wants to meet me.'

'Right.' Helen's eyes were still closed and she spoke softly, as if she were not quite ready to wake up, to engage.

'Are you going to Linda's?'

'Don't know yet.'

Thorne could hear Paula moving around downstairs. The chink of crockery and the scrape of a chair, a radio being switched on. He tried to place the song, but couldn't. 'So, is that all right?'

Now, Helen opened her eyes. 'Why wouldn't it be?'

'I don't know. Just ... if you wanted to talk some more.'

'I think I've probably said everything.'

Thorne nodded. Helen's words had been mumbled, deadened by the pillow, but still there had seemed an odd emphasis to them. Was there a suggestion there was more she was waiting for *him* to say? Had he not said enough the night before?

Had he not said the *right* things?

'I'll call you when I've spoken to the farmer.'

Helen turned over slowly. She said, 'I'm not ill, Tom.'

'Tell you what he said about the pig, I mean.'

Helen watched him struggle to get dressed in the semi-dark. Moving as quietly as he could, digging for clean socks and underwear in the suitcase he had still not bothered to unpack.

She was happy for him to go, keen to spend some time alone.

She had not meant to be sharp with him, but it felt as if the filters that modified her reactions were no longer working, as though they had been slowly eaten away from the moment she had set foot back in Polesford. It was obvious that he had been worried for a while, that her behaviour had seemed strange, but there had been no way to control it. It felt like the circuits in her brain had been rewired by a lunatic; the connections to her heart misfiring or burned out completely. She had been ready to kill that teenager for gobbing at her, that journalist for doing her job. She craved affection and support and yet she had no idea what to do with them when they were offered.

There was no more than a crumb of comfort in knowing that she was not alone, that Linda Bates probably felt the same way.

She had told Helen that she would call, but Helen was not expecting her to. She wondered if they would ever see one another again. Their conversation about Aurora Harley, about the things the girl's grandfather had done, had been no more ... cathartic than the one with Thorne.

Tears, but a strange reluctance to touch, to make any kind of physical contact, and when it was over it felt as though they were all but unknown to each other again.

So many times at work she had told strangers how much better they would feel once they had told this or that terrible story. It was important to share these things, she would blithely tell them, to get it off their chests so that they could move on.

A weight off their shoulders.

It had not felt like that telling Tom, did not feel like it now. He had held her for a long time afterwards, said all those things anyone with an ounce of empathy or compassion would say, but she had felt something hardening with each overly gentle touch and promise, every whispered assurance.

The weight had moved somewhere else, that was all.

Now, she lay still, knowing that he was dressed and ready to leave but that he was standing at the end of the bed, watching her. Eventually, she heard the door open, the slow drag back across the carpet and the soft snick as he closed it behind him

368

with as little noise as possible. She pulled the bedclothes close around her neck and shoulders, hoped that she might be able to get back to sleep for a while.

It wasn't Tom she had needed to tell.

Hendricks woke to the sound of self-satisfied babble on Radio 4 and the sight of Liam Southworth's fingers crawling across his chest. They stopped to tease a nipple for a while, then began to move down. Hendricks turned his head and saw the grin he'd quickly come to recognise as meaning it was time to get naughty.

That was how Liam described it. 'Getting naughty'.

'Sleep well?'

Hendricks nodded. 'Knackered.'

Liam's grin widened. 'Me too.'

'Haven't you got a lecture first thing?'

'I set the alarm early.'

'Come here.' Hendricks reached across and drew Liam to him, stretched his arms wide across the pillows as Liam laid his head on his shoulder. 'That's nice.'

'Yeah, it is,' Liam said.

Hendricks meant it. He felt as relaxed as he had in a long time, having finally come to terms with his surprise at not feeling the urge to bolt once he'd got Liam Southworth into bed. He looked at Liam's fingers, now moving through the sparse tufts of hair on his chest. Liam's own chest was almost hairless, something else Hendricks liked. His last few boyfriends ... partners, whatever ... had been very much on the hirsute side – certainly far hairier than Liam was at any rate – and although he had found it sexy up to a point, there was no denying that a frenzied bout of tongue-thrashing was a lot more fun without the inevitable stubble-rash.

Recently, the other stuff had been that bit less gentle too, and both he and the men involved would have certainly described what they'd been up to in bed – or more memorably in the toilets at several clubs – in rather more graphic terms than Liam. That had been fine with Hendricks at the time. It had been what he had wanted, needed. This though, the last couple of nights, had been something else altogether, something he hadn't done for a long time. Yeah . . . this was all right.

Nothing wrong with getting naughty.

'Might be getting some news today from my pal in the lab,' Liam said.

'That would be good.' Hendricks was thinking that Thorne would be pleased and that Liam's accent really was the sexiest thing he'd ever heard.

'She's done us quite a favour, you know?'

'Yeah, I know.'

'And she's still asking questions about who's going to pay for it. I mean you know how much all this stuff costs, right? The extraction of the sample, the front-end analysis, the bio-chemical procedures.'

'Can't you just buy her a box of chocolates or something?'

'I mean just the use of the electrophoresic laser, you know . . . '

'Bloody hell,' Hendricks said. 'You seriously need to work on your pillow talk.'

'Just telling you.'

'I'm kidding.' Hendricks was surprised at feeling the need to qualify his remark, to be sure that Liam did not feel bad.

'One thing though.' Liam's fingers stopped moving against Hendricks' chest. 'I got a call from Tim Cornish.'

'Right.'

'Not best pleased, as you can imagine.'

'Oh, I can.'

'Once he'd finished shouting the odds, he made it pretty clear that he was the first person I should call. You know, if we got a result.'

'Wanker made out like he wasn't interested.'

'Yeah, well I can promise you, he is.'

'What's he going to do with the information when he gets it, anyway?'

'What's your mate Tom going to do with it?'

Hendricks sat up a little. 'Is this going to be a problem for you? I mean with all the consulting jobs?'

Liam was shaking his head.

'You're not going to lose any work over it, right?'

'Long as I tell Cornish first, it'll be fine.'

'Sure?'

'I was worried you'd be pissed off,' Liam said. 'That's all.'

'It is what it is.' Hendricks shrugged. 'Not sure Tom's going to be too chuffed, but what can you do?'

'Sorry.'

'It's fine.'

'Let me make it up to you . . . '

'There's no need, honest.' Then Hendricks saw that welcome grin again and watched Liam raise the duvet above his head and duck down beneath it.

Hendricks lay back and said, 'I've forgotten about it already.'

# SIXTY-SIX

It was a greasy spoon Thorne had not come across so far, tucked away between a builder's yard and a dental surgery, a couple of streets behind the market square. It didn't appear to have a name, but probably because it didn't need one. In the steamed-up windows were laminated pictures of the delights available within that almost certainly fell foul of the Trade Descriptions Act, but only someone without a sense of smell would need the help.

Whenever people talked about favourite smells, it was usually something airy-fairy like freshly cut grass or sea air. *New books*, for pity's sake . . .

Thorne had started slavering when he was still a street away.

It was small, no more than half a dozen tables which were all taken, and Thorne spotted Bob Patterson straight away. He recognised the occupant of the adjacent table too; the chef-cum-poet from the Magpie's Nest, with whom the farmer seemed to be chatting happily. Patterson still had a plateful, but it looked as though Shelley was about done. He reached for his jacket and tossed a few scraps of bacon rind to Patterson's dog, which was lying beneath the farmer's table.

They both nodded at Thorne as he passed on his way to the counter. He ordered the full English and took a mug of strong tea back to Patterson's table, taking care not to kick the dog as he sat down.

'Surprised she's allowed in,' Thorne said.

'They all know her in here.' Patterson dropped a morsel of his own and nodded towards the man behind the counter who was watching, seemingly unconcerned. 'Me and the owner have a good relationship.'

'You supply the bacon?'

Patterson looked horrified. 'I hope you're joking. This is mass-produced, factory shit.' He pushed a piece of it into his mouth. 'I've got a mate who gets them cheap eggs.'

Shelley stood up. He said, 'I'm just off, but ...'

'Checking out the competition?' Thorne looked around. 'I mean, I presume they're open for lunch.'

Shelley scoffed. 'Hardly.'

'Had you down as the muesli type.'

'Yeah?'

'Fruit, maybe.'

The chef smiled thinly and lifted up a shoulder bag; battered, brown leather. Thorne guessed there was a notebook full of meaningless poetry in there, maybe a novel he could take out at an opportune moment. 'Decent bit of grease doesn't hurt once in a while though, does it? Oh ...' He reached for the tabloid next to his empty plate and held it towards Thorne. 'You seen this?'

Thorne looked at the picture, the headline. They were enough for the time being. He went back to his tea.

'Talk about putting the cat among the pigeons,' Shelley said. When it became clear that Thorne had no intention of responding, he dropped the paper on to Patterson's table, then leaned down one final time to scratch the dog's ears before he left.

'Arrogant arsehole,' Patterson said.

Thorne glanced up from his tea. 'Looked like you were best mates when I came in.'

'Just making conversation.'

'You don't still think he nicked your pig, do you?'

Patterson stared at him, a triangle of fried bread dripping from his fork. 'Course I bloody don't.' He popped the bread into his mouth and carried on. 'Because whoever took that pig had no intention of eating it, did they?'

Thorne's food arrived and he got stuck in. He had put half of it away, almost managing to catch up with Patterson, before either of them spoke again.

'He had a point though, didn't he?'

'Who?'

'*Him*. Cut-price bloody Shakespeare.' The farmer waved his fork in the direction of the door and then stabbed at the news-paper. 'Changes things a bit, don't you think?'

'I've no idea,' Thorne said.

'Course you have. We're not all stupid round here, you know?'

'Never thought you were.'

'You're involved.' The farmer looked towards the paper again. 'With that girl, with all of it.'

Glancing around, Thorne could see that several other cus-tomers were reading the same newspaper. He thought about the Harleys; another set of parents whose lives had suddenly been turned upside down. And he thought about a different girl and the things she had endured to protect her little sister.

'I never intended to be,' he said.

Patterson smiled, showing yellowing teeth, a sliver of tomato caught on the bottom set. 'You get caught up, don't you? When it's your job. Something about pigs, I'm interested, I can't help myself. Same for someone like you, I'm guessing. With murder.'

Hungry as he was, Thorne pushed the black pudding to one side. 'You said you had some information.'

'Well, let's just say I've been putting things together.' Patterson tapped the side of his head. 'Not very difficult, not once people started hearing things and talking about them. That's how I found out my pig wasn't stolen to make bacon sandwiches.'

Thorne grunted, ate.

'The pig's important, I know that much.' The farmer leaned forward. 'Important to whoever it was took those girls. Killed one of them.'

'Like you said, I'm involved.' Thorne was trying to hide his impatience. 'Bearing that in mind, I'm sorry to say that so far, none of this was exactly worth getting out of bed for.'

Patterson's shrug suggested that he didn't really care, that he had better to come. 'So, obviously you know that this fella Bates is not the one, right? That the police have ballsed it up and the real killer's still knocking around somewhere.'

Thorne nodded again. That was always going to be the problem with deliberately leaking bits of information in the hope it would spread. Eventually you would be the one being told things you already knew. 'You said you had something to tell me about the man who stole your pig.' Thorne dropped his voice. 'The real killer.'

Patterson laid his knife and fork down and wiped the back of his hand across his mouth. 'Well, I know he was on foot, for a start.' He waited for a reaction then nodded down at his dog. 'She barks at people she doesn't know ... well you've seen, haven't you? But she's not psychic, is she? She makes the din of the bloody devil if there's *any* car coming towards the place, and she didn't make a squeak that night. So, I reckon he parked up somewhere and walked the rest of the way. Probably stuck the piglet in a sack, something like that, then carried it back to the car.' He nodded, pleased with himself. 'Oh yeah, he certainly planned it all out.' There was a hint of 'you're welcome' in the look he gave Thorne before he went back to his breakfast. 'So . . . do with that what you will.'

Thorne watched the farmer mop up what was left on his plate with a limp slice of toast and controlled the urge to tell him that his dog had probably worked as much out weeks ago. 'Thanks,' he said.

'Right, well I can't hang around here gassing all day.' Patterson pushed back his chair. 'Things to do.' He stood and nodded to the man behind the counter, then turned for the door without saying goodbye, the dog at his heels.

Behind him, Thorne could hear the owner shouting orders through to the kitchen. He watched the farmer leave, thinking that even if being busy meant filling cardboard boxes with yellowing magazines, at least the old man had plans. Thorne had left the house with the distinct impression that Helen was happy to be left alone, and he had no idea what he was going to do with himself.

*I'm not ill, Tom . . .*

He remembered the expression on Helen's face; one that he had never seen before, that perhaps she would not recognise herself. Her mouth twisted in pain, or rage, or determination. Perhaps a mixture of all three. Her eyes wide and bloodshot, fixed on a spot somewhere on the far wall of that bedroom, as someone on an unsteady boat might focus on the horizon to avoid being sick.

Now, Helen needed time and space and he would give her as much of both as was necessary.

He looked at his watch. It was still only ten past eight.

Thorne ordered more tea and reached for the paper.

# SIXTY-SEVEN

Helen pulled a spare dressing gown of Paula's over knickers and an old T-shirt and went downstairs. The house was a lot warmer than it had been when Tom had left, but it wasn't doing her any favours. She had managed to get another couple of hours' sleep, but she still felt listless and heavy; deadened, as though she was moving underwater.

She picked up the newspaper from the front door and carried it into the kitchen.

She made herself coffee; two spoonfuls from the jar and only a dash of milk. She needed it, needed *something* before she felt able to read beyond the front page. She briefly considered searching through the kitchen cupboards for spirits, then thought about Linda and changed her mind.

MURDER SUSPECT'S TEEN GIRLFRIEND. A picture of Aurora Harley in school uniform.

She felt suddenly sick looking at the picture again. A memory, triggered. The coffee kept the nausea at bay and energised her, though that might just as easily have been the anger that began to crackle through her as she read the story.

It was clear that Aurora Harley had spoken to the newspaper, might even have supplied the photograph, but she was not the one telling the story. Quotes had been carefully selected and placed to suit the angle being vigorously pushed. Helen was hardly surprised, but that didn't keep the anger in check. It didn't stop her wishing she'd smacked that journalist in the pub when she'd had the chance.

That same smug face staring out above this morning's byline.

Helen could imagine the woman's reaction when Aurora Harley had come bowling along in her squishy, silver jacket. Eyes wide and a fat smudge of crimson blusher beneath those delicate cheekbones.

*I just think she deserves a chance to tell her side of the story ...*

The bitch would not have been able to write the cheque quickly enough.

While keeping on just the right side of the law, the paper had clearly decided that continued pandering to the lynch mob was good for business and that Stephen Bates was guilty as charged. It stood to reason that, whatever his teenage girlfriend might have to say, she was living proof that he was the scumbag most right-minded people thought him to be. Surely, her very existence was only going to be one more weapon in the prosecution's already well-stocked armoury.

The glee was just about disguised, even as those doing the reporting revelled in their disgust.

*'It's stupid,' says the petite teen. 'How could he have kidnapped anybody when he was with me?' Aurora Harley shakes her head and holds her hands out in an effort to look genuinely bewildered. Perhaps it is a gesture she has learned from one of her parents. Her mother is currently claiming disability benefit and her father is a labourer who, at thirty-nine, is only a few years older than the man his daughter now claims to have been sleeping with.*

On the next page, Linda's ex-husband was keen to get in on the act and give his reaction to the Aurora Harley revelations. This time, Wayne Smart was pictured with his children as toddlers; Charli with front teeth missing and Danny grinning on Smart's shoulders. The perfect father.

*'Even if Bates didn't do it, this news makes me even more determined that he shouldn't be allowed near my kids ever again, my daughter especially.'*

Even if Bates didn't do it. It was the first time Helen had seen even the smallest degree of doubt expressed in print. Perhaps it was a good sign.

She pushed the paper away, turned it over so she wouldn't have to look at that front page again. She stared out across the fields and downed the rest of her coffee.

In her school uniform, for God's sake . . .

'Morning.'

Helen jumped, then turned. She laughed nervously and apologised. She had not heard Jason Sweeney come in.

'No, *I'm* sorry.' Sweeney held up his hands. 'Didn't mean to—'

'I didn't think there was anyone else in the house,' Helen said.

He walked across and flicked the kettle on. 'Not working until tonight.'

'Oh, right. Don't you usually sleep in if you're working late?'

'Yeah, usually.' Sweeney was wearing the same ratty dressing gown Helen had seen before. It was sprouting loose threads and one of the belt-loops had come away. She found herself wondering if he was wearing anything underneath. 'Just woke up for some reason and couldn't get off again.'

'Sorry, I hope that wasn't me.' When Sweeney turned to get milk from the fridge, Helen quickly drew her own dressing gown tighter across her chest, despite having a T-shirt underneath.

'Why don't I do us some breakfast?' Sweeney asked.

'It's OK, thanks. I'm fine with coffee.'

379

'I do a mean scrambled eggs. Got some tomatoes somewhere as well.' He bent and began rummaging in the compartment at the bottom of the fridge.

'I don't normally bother with breakfast,' Helen said.

Sweeney laid the box of eggs on the worktop, the tomatoes he'd managed to locate. 'You've got to have *breakfast*.'

'I don't see why.'

'It sets you up for the day, doesn't it?'

'Like I say—'

'What are you doing with yourself today, anyway?'

'I'm not really sure.'

'Thought you'd be over at Linda Bates' by now.'

'I'll probably go later.'

'I can give you a lift if you like.'

'Right. I'll let you know.'

'Tom already gone out, has he?'

'Yeah.'

'Early bird then, like Paula . . .'

Helen was thrilled to hear her mobile buzzing in the pocket of her dressing gown. She was already standing as she took it out and saw who was calling. She gestured with the phone, excusing herself as she walked towards the door, and Sweeney shrugged his understanding. She waited until she was out in the hall before she answered it.

'I didn't wake you, did I?' Thorne asked.

'No, I've been up a while.'

'Did you get back to sleep?'

'For a bit.'

'Everything OK?'

'Tell me about the farmer,' Helen said.

'Waste of time,' Thorne said. There was a pause. 'Decent fry-up though.'

'That's a shame.'

Another pause, longer this time. 'Did you see the paper?'

'I was just reading it.'

'Not a surprise.'

Helen said, 'We threw her to the wolves.'

'Well ... *you* didn't do anything,' Thorne said. 'I was the one who told her she could talk to the press.'

'It doesn't matter who said it.'

Helen waited. She could hear Sweeney moving around in the kitchen, humming to himself. 'So, what are you going to do now?'

'She knew what she was getting into. I did tell her.'

'She's a kid.'

'She was fine with it,' Thorne said. 'I told her what they were like. She was keen on the money.'

'So, what are you going to do?'

'I'm sure I can amuse myself.'

'OK ... '

'I'll call you in a bit.'

'You don't have to, honestly.'

'Or you call me. When you're ... ready or whatever.'

'It's fine, Tom. Call if you want to.'

There was just the crackle on the line for a few seconds. Then Thorne said, 'Right, I'll leave you to it.'

Helen ended the call and turned to find Sweeney watching her from the kitchen doorway.

'Everything OK?'

Helen slipped the phone back into her pocket and stepped towards the stairs. 'I'm just going to go up. Have a shower and get dressed.'

'What about your breakfast?'

'Like I said, I'm not really hungry.'

Sweeney said, 'I've already started making you some.'

# SIXTY-EIGHT

'How come you and Mum aren't talking to each other?'

Charli looked at her brother. 'What?'

'You had a row or something?'

'I don't know what you're talking about,' Charli said.

They were downstairs in the sitting room. Danny was sprawled in the armchair and Charli had her legs pulled up beneath her on the sofa, a small brown cushion hugged close to her chest. Danny scowled at the TV remote as though its failure to get more than the basic channels on the television was an unforgivable act of betrayal. With limited choice in the matter, he sat watching *Bargain Hunt*, shaking his head and sucking his teeth.

'Like just now,' Danny said. 'Outside the bathroom.'

'What?'

'You and Mum. All those funny looks and not saying anything.'

'Can't you find anything else to watch?' Charli asked. 'This is shit.'

382

'You said you didn't care what was on.'

'Yeah, but it's like I can feel my brain cells dying off.' Her chin dropped on to the cushion and she let out a theatrical snore. 'Old people buying rubbish then trying to sell it to other old people.'

'It's since yesterday.' Danny flicked through the channels. 'Whatever's going on with you and Mum. After she sent me down here to get her wine or whatever.'

'I don't remember.'

'Yeah, you do. I knew something was going on. Like she was trying to get rid of me or something.'

'Why would she be doing that?'

'You must think I'm stupid.'

'No, but I think you're a dick who can't find anything decent to watch on telly.'

'It was something about Steve, wasn't it?'

'What was?'

'The row you and Mum had.'

Charli sighed as though her brother was simply being too ridiculous to engage with any further. The same way she did whenever he tried to talk to her about music or how slaggy her friends were, or when he commented on what she was wearing. She waited for him to turn back to the television, then shouted, 'Oi!' When he turned round, she laughed and threw the cushion at him, but he raised an arm to swat it away, in no mood to mess around.

Charli said, 'What's up with you?'

'What's up with *me*?'

They said nothing for a while. It was a lot quieter outside the house than they had become used to and there was no need to turn the volume up on the television to drown out the shouts. Danny tuned back into *Bargain Hunt*, ignoring the tutting from the sofa, the comments about how lame the programme was, how lame *he* was. He watched for another few minutes, then threw down the remote and stood up.

'This is such bollocks.'

'So find something else,' Charli said.

'No, *you*, I mean. You're being such a bitch and I'm completely sick of it.'

'Calm down. Jesus . . .'

'We've got to be honest with each other, you said.' Danny began kicking at the base of the armchair. He would not look at her. 'Always tell the truth. No bullshit, you said.' He was kicking harder, the chair inching across the carpet. 'No bullshit.' He turned to look at her, shaking his head. His mouth was tight as though he were about to spit or burst into tears. 'And what's so funny is that you're full of it.'

Charli watched her brother march out. She winced as the door slammed behind him and hugged the cushion that little bit tighter.

He had every right to be angry with her, because now she wasn't telling him things and she had promised that she would, and he was anything but stupid. That's how families worked, wasn't it? You could pick up on any little thing, a falling-out or whatever. The smallest change in the atmosphere, like a draught coming from somewhere.

Usually, anyway.

The day before, upstairs, with Danny out of the way, she had been so angry. How on earth could her mum have asked her something like that? Where the hell had it come from?

Easy to understand now, of course. Charli had seen all the stuff on her Facebook page, the links to the story in the paper, the things that girl had said about Steve. Danny had seen it all too, the stupid comments and the photos posted by trolls with nothing better to do. He knew just as well as Charli did why there weren't quite so many people outside the house any more. Now, a lot of the reporters were outside that girl's house. Now, *she'd* know what it was like to be shouted at and studied like you were one of those sad white mice in the school biology lab.

Maybe it was exactly what the girl deserved.

*Maybe,* because actually Charli couldn't tell what the truth was any more. Not even when she was telling things to herself. She wanted to make it all better with her mum, but wasn't sure how. She probably just needed to leave it be for a while, let everything settle down a bit.

She rubbed at the small dark spot on the shitty brown cushion; watched the next one form and the next, then lifted it to her face to press the tears away.

She knew why her mum was being the way she was. Why she was angry with herself as much as anybody else. Why she felt guilty and couldn't look at anyone and was floating around the place like a ghost who'd died with a bottle in her hand.

Her mum had asked her a question and Charli had answered it.

And her mum thought she had lied.

Linda had been talking for a while.

She sat at the kitchen table, sometimes staring down at the scarred laminate and sometimes looking to the two police officers for a reaction. She talked, while Carson and Gallagher listened. Or rather they did a good job of looking as though they were listening. Both were well used to scenarios such as this; to nodding or smiling or shaking their heads at the right moments and they both felt strongly that being able to . . . 'tune out' when necessary did not make them any less caring or empathetic. Carson had spent a good deal of the previous half-hour thinking about what to do when her mother was no longer able to look after herself, while Gallagher had been trying to decide whether to sleep with a married firearms officer who had made it pretty clear that he was bang up for it.

'You've got to admit, this makes a hell of a difference, right?' Linda leaned too hard on the newspaper, which tore as she pushed it across the table towards the officers. Both had read the story already, but Carson stepped forward, pretended to look at the front page again. 'Yeah, I know ... well she *would* say that, blahdy-blah ... but there's got to be enough to make them think about it, surely. Make them ... reconsider a bit. Your boss, I'm talking about. The powers that be. The ... *senior investigating officer.*' She put on a bizarre sing-song accent as she carefully enunciated the words; like she was announcing a visiting dignitary from some exotic country. 'Maybe not enough to get the charges dropped, but, I don't know, enough to get them ... *lowered.*' She laughed and looked to Carson and Gallagher for a reaction.

'Look, Linda, I couldn't say even if I did know something,' Carson said. 'But I can promise you that I don't.'

'Oh, it's "Linda" now, is it? *Linda.* That's nice, makes me feel all warm and tingly. Maybe we should have a group hug or something.'

'Would you prefer I didn't use your first name any more?'

'Yes, matter of fact I would.' Linda sat back and folded her arms. 'I'd like you to call me Mrs Bates ... no, wait, bollocks to that ... I'd like you to call me *madam.*'

Carson said, 'Whatever you want.'

Linda cocked her head and peered at the photograph of Aurora Harley. 'I wonder if he touched her too, the old bastard. Wouldn't mind betting his own family wasn't off limits.'

Carson looked at Gallagher who shrugged, equally confused.

'Anyway,' Linda said, 'this business with the alibi isn't going to make much difference one way or another, because there's going to be proof. Oh yeah ... proper *forensic* proof, so it's all going to change and you'll have to say "duh ... we got it wrong" and let him go.'

Carson and Gallagher waited.

'What?' Linda leaned across the table. '*What?* Bloody hell, look at you two ... pair of ugly fucking bookends. An ice-queen and a shortarse Jock ...'

'Shall I make us some coffee?' Gallagher asked.

Linda laughed. 'You can have whatever you fancy, but I certainly don't want coffee. What is it with you lot and fucking hot drinks? I don't want coffee or tea or ... hot chocolate.'

'OK.'

'Or fucking *Horlicks*. Christ's sake.' She sat breathing heavily for half a minute. She rolled her head around slowly, then looked up and pointed at the two officers. 'Anyway, you won't be around for much longer, because there's real proof coming and your case is going to collapse like a shit sandcastle or whatever and everyone's going to know you've all been wasting your time. You hear me? Real proof.'

Carson sniffed. 'You said that already, madam.'

'That's better.' Linda nodded, pleased. 'A bit of respect, for a change.'

'So, what's going to happen, Linda? When this amazing bit of proof comes along and knocks our sandcastle down.' Though it had clearly been wine doing the talking, Carson had finally run out of patience and was eager to get a dig in. She pushed the tattered newspaper back towards Linda; the picture of the girl who had been sleeping with her husband. 'You going to welcome him back with open arms?'

'Oh, I don't want the fucker *back*,' Linda said. 'I know what he didn't do and I know damn well what he *did* do, and whatever happens when he gets out he's not coming back to me and my kids. He's not coming back to Charli.' She shook her head. 'We'll be fine as we are, thank you very much, just like we were before

I ever met him.' She held up her left hand, stared at the mark where her wedding ring used to be. 'What, you seriously think I'd take him back?'

She rubbed at the small dark spot on the newspaper; watched the next one form and the next . . .

# SIXTY-NINE

'Nice,' Thorne said. Nodding approvingly, he followed Hendricks along a carpeted hallway lined with framed black and white photographs into a smart, modern kitchen. Every inch of bleached wood and stainless steel was spotless. 'Looks like you landed on your feet.'

'Oh, yeah.' Hendricks was barefoot, wearing a black vest and tracksuit bottoms. He padded across the tiles and loaded a capsule into a shiny Nespresso machine. 'Not that I've spent a great deal of time on my feet.' He flashed Thorne a grin. 'On my knees, mostly.'

'I don't need the details.'

'Don't forget I'm doing all this for you.'

'Course you are,' Thorne said.

They took their coffees into an equally smart and tidy sitting room. Wooden floors and cowhide rugs, chrome and soft leather, floor-to-ceiling shelves crammed with books, high-end magazines and CDs which Thorne immediately began to peruse.

'I told you I'd call,' Hendricks said.

'Sorry?'

'When I heard anything from the lab.'

Thorne took out an album and examined it. He hadn't heard of the band, but was impressed that the collection was in alphabetical order. 'I know, but I thought I might as well come and keep you company in the meantime.'

'Oh yeah?'

Thorne found an Emmylou Harris CD and waved it at Hendricks. The album she'd made with Daniel Lanois. 'He's got good taste in music, anyway.'

'Mostly.'

'How's he afford all this on a lecturer's salary and a bit of consulting work?' Liam Southworth's flat was on the top floor of a portered block a few miles from the Warwick University campus. Thorne had seen signs for the gym on the way in, the entrance to a private parking garage.

'He is a *senior* lecturer.'

'Still.' Thorne put the CD back in its place and began poking around the room, touching things. He picked up a small, marble sculpture from the top of a cupboard. He had no idea what it was supposed to be, but it looked expensive. 'Is there some kind of black market in dead beetles?'

'I think he inherited some money,' Hendricks said. 'Not really talked about it.'

Thorne wandered back and sat down next to Hendricks on a sofa which looked a lot more comfortable than it felt. Hendricks passed him a wooden coaster for his cup which Thorne dutifully set down gently on the glass table next to him.

He smirked. 'Look at you. Coasters.'

'Not my place, is it?'

'You weren't wrong about the TV.' Thorne nodded at the huge screen mounted on the wall, a built-in shelf lined with DVDs.

'The sound's incredible,' Hendricks said.

'I bet.' Thorne had already clocked the sub-woofer, the Bose speakers high up in the corners of the room.

'So, what you been doing with yourself?' Hendricks sat back and sipped his latte. 'Apart from turning up here to keep me company.'

'I met up with Patterson, the pig farmer. Complete waste of time. After that, I went for a walk in the woods.'

Hendricks stared. If he had been at home and less concerned with not making a mess, he would probably have spat out his coffee for comic effect.

Thorne shrugged. 'Yeah, I went back to the spot where Jessica's body was found, hung about there for a bit. Then I just . . . walked around. You know, nice enough day.'

Now, it was Hendricks' turn to smirk. 'Look at *you*. Walking.'

'No law against it.'

'No, but you *are* normally someone who thinks there should be.'

Thorne did not want Hendricks to know that trudging through the woods for almost two hours had simply been about killing time; that although he was now enjoying himself considerably more, he was still trying to kill it.

He had no desire to talk about why.

'So, what's Helen up to?'

Hendricks knew him far too bloody well. Thorne guessed that his friend had known something was up from the moment Thorne had arrived out of the blue.

'She's just kicking around at Paula's, I think.'

'Sounds good.'

'I think she wants to be on her own for a bit.'

'Right . . .'

Hendricks was asking the question.

'You were . . . bang on,' Thorne said, eventually. 'Remember you said something about home and bad memories? Turns out that town's got some pretty bad ones for her. So . . .' Thorne did not want to say any more. He knew that Helen would tell Hendricks what those bad memories were if and when she was ready; they were close enough. Seeing the look on his face now though, Thorne found himself wondering if Hendricks already knew. Or perhaps he had guessed. 'Thing is, I don't know what to say to her. I don't know if the things I did say were the right things.'

Hendricks put his drink down. 'Not sure there's ever any *right* things. You know . . . depends on the situation, obviously, but whatever it is . . . you just say what you're feeling and you can't go far wrong.'

'I wanted her to feel better,' Thorne said.

'Course you did, mate. I'm sure you told her what she needed to hear.'

'I hope so, Phil.'

'I mean, you're not a complete twat, are you?' Hendricks smiled. 'Not all the time.'

Hendricks phoned out for pizza and they ate from the boxes, in front of the TV. They talked about music and football for a while and Thorne asked a few more questions about Liam. When Brigstocke called again and Thorne dropped the call, they both enjoyed listening to the irate message the DCI left. Reading the text message that arrived from him a few minutes later, saying much the same thing.

FFS!! Maybe u should have quit after Bardsey. You'll be lucky to end up back on the beat. Saw a vacancy for a lollipop man but that's probably out of your league . . .

'I think I'm getting addicted to daytime TV,' Hendricks said. Thorne had been enjoying his friend's running commentary

392

on *Doctors*, *Win It, Cook It* and especially *Cash in the Attic*. 'That's serious.'

'I know and as far as I'm aware there isn't a single support group, there's no rehab centres.'

'It's disgusting,' Thorne said.

They watched and took the piss, the pin-sharp images and surround-sound heightening each unintentionally comic gem and profoundly undramatic moment.

'We could do this,' Hendricks said.

'What?'

'Knock up a reality show.'

'You reckon?'

'Piece of piss. We just use what we know, right? How hard can it be? People love a bit of murder and forensics, don't they? *Ice 'Em, Slice 'Em*, what about that?'

Thorne laughed, as he usually did. These sessions with Hendricks had often been the only time he was able to relax during some of the tougher investigations they had worked on together. A way to decompress, to forget, if only for a few hours. But there was no way he could forget what Helen had told him. The pain in the telling and the deeper pain of those events she was recalling, still eating her up after almost thirty years.

Despite Hendricks' best efforts, Thorne was craving the simple distraction of the Bates case.

The case he was not supposed to be involved in . . .

When Liam Southworth called, Thorne enjoyed seeing his friend's face change, *soften*. He watched Hendricks turn away and lower his voice and Thorne decided it might be a good time to check out the toilet.

When he came back, Hendricks held up the phone and said, 'We're in business, mate. We've got Percy Pig in our bugs. A hundred per cent match for porky DNA. Good news, right?'

Thorne nodded, his mind already racing, but unable to go anywhere.

'One thing, though.' Hendricks told him that Cornish had already been informed, that Liam had been given no choice in the matter.

'Doesn't make any difference,' Thorne said. 'I won't be holding my breath for an apology, or a "thank you".'

'So, what's next?'

'I haven't got a fucking clue,' Thorne said.

They sat around for another ten or fifteen minutes, but Thorne was unable to settle. When Hendricks got up to carry the pizza boxes into the kitchen, Thorne announced that he was heading back to Polesford.

'You want me to come with you?' Hendricks asked.

'It's fine,' Thorne said. 'I'll call and tell you what's happening.'

'Let me know how Helen's doing, will you?'

Thorne pulled on his jacket and said that he would. As he was walking to the door, Hendricks shouted through from the kitchen.

'What about *Corpse in the Attic*? Come on, mate, you *know* that's a winner.'

# SEVENTY

Jason Sweeney knocked on the bedroom door and walked in without being invited. Helen was lying on the bed. She had picked up a book but been unable to focus and had read the same sentence several times without understanding it, before finally giving up.

She swung her legs off the bed, tugged down the polo shirt she was wearing over jeans.

'Sorry.' Sweeney was still wearing his dressing gown.

You should have waited until I asked you to come in, then, Helen thought. 'It's OK, I was just reading,' she said.

'Just thought you might want to know ... there's stuff on the TV. That schoolgirl Bates was supposedly banging.' He saw Helen's reaction. 'Sorry. Having a relationship with.'

'I'm not really interested, to be honest.'

'Oh.' Sweeney looked a little crestfallen. He shifted his weight from one slippered foot to the other. 'I thought you would be.'

'I saw the paper,' Helen said. 'There won't be anything new on the TV.'

'You're Linda's mate though, aren't you?'

'Yes, I am.'

Sweeney nodded slowly. 'A bit of a turn-up, don't you think?' He leaned against the door jamb. 'This girl, I mean.'

Helen looked at him. The dressing gown was gaping at the top. Black hairs curled against the pale fat of his chest. 'I'll come down,' she said.

She left it ten minutes and, as she'd hoped, by the time she walked into the sitting room, the news channel had moved on to a report about flood clean-up operations. The damage had been far worse in the south-west and parts of Wales than it had been locally.

Sweeney was in his armchair, a can of beer nestled in his lap.

'Aren't you supposed to be working later?' Helen asked.

'It's only the one can.'

She could smell the fags on him from several feet away. 'It's one can too much when you drive for a living.'

He laughed. 'It's like I said last night. You lot are never off duty.'

'I'm off duty right now,' Helen said. 'It's just friendly advice.' She sat down on the sofa and concentrated on the television. Now it was a sports round-up, but she pretended to be engrossed. She was wondering what Thorne was doing.

'You think they'll release him now?' Sweeney asked. 'Bates.'

'Not because of the girl.'

'No?'

'Alibis from spouses, partners, whatever. They really need to be checked out and even then ...'

'Some other reason, then?'

'Sorry?'

'"Not because of the girl", you said. Sounds like there might be another reason.'

'Not that I'm aware of,' Helen said.

Sweeney smiled and swigged. 'I reckon you're not as off duty as you say you are.'

'You can reckon all you like.'

Another smile, another swig. 'I noticed you were keeping very quiet last night,' Sweeney said. 'When Paula was talking about the bugs and all that, how it was important. You just sat there like a shop dummy, never made a peep.' He was watching her. She kept her eyes on the screen. 'I mean it was obvious you knew something.'

Helen's mobile buzzed. She looked and saw a text from Thorne.

on my way back to polesford hope you're feeling ok.

'Didn't want to say anything with your other half around, that it?'

Helen typed a reply while Sweeney talked.

Come and pick me up . . .

'Maybe he wouldn't have liked it if you'd let something slip, given you what for later on. Don't worry, I get it.'

. . . We can go for a drink or something . . .

'Some couples are like that, aren't they?'

. . . Get an early dinner x

Sweeney leaned forward. 'He's not here now though, is he?'

# SEVENTY-ONE

Thorne put his foot down.

He had felt a rush of excitement on receiving the message from Helen, at having a good reason for going back. It had not been exaggeration when he had told Hendricks he had no idea where this new DNA evidence would lead. Other than straight into a brick wall, of course.

Now, Thorne knew beyond reasonable doubt that Stephen Bates was not the man they were looking for, but in truth he was no closer to identifying the man actually responsible for the murder of Jessica Toms. He knew who the killer *wasn't*, but that wouldn't cut much ice with the likes of Tim Cornish and it wouldn't help save Poppy Johnston.

If she was still alive to save.

His desire to get back to Polesford – and Helen – as quickly as possible, was soon compromised by Friday afternoon traffic on the M42. To compound his frustration, it seemed to be moving fast enough in the other direction. Perhaps somebody was trying to tell him something.

He put a CD on, a compilation he'd made. Johnny singing

about the darkness he saw, then Hank sounding like there was something even blacker inside him. The traffic crawled past a junction while Thorne tried and failed to decide if he'd be better coming off the motorway; tried and failed to gain any comfort from the fact that those *officially* working on the inquiry would be feeling every bit as frustrated as he was.

Despite the fact that they had misread the evidence, and in Cornish's case refused to accept the possibility that they might have done so, Thorne knew they had gone about things the same way that any other team would have done.

They had simply run out of options.

In a town the size of Polesford, an obvious step would have been to take DNA samples from every man of a suitable age, but without anything to match those samples to, it was a pointless exercise. In burning the body of Jessica Toms, eliminating any traces of his own DNA had not been the killer's main objective, but it had certainly been a very useful side-effect. It had become clear that they were looking for someone with at least a basic knowledge of forensic procedure. That, whatever was driving him, the man who had taken Jessica and Poppy was far from stupid. Unless – like so many Thorne had come across – he made a careless mistake, he would remain free to kill again; in Polesford, or more likely somewhere else, once the investigation had run out of steam and the media circus had upped sticks and moved on.

Thorne asked himself if he would be satisfied, knowing that he had at the very least proved a man's innocence. It sounded as though Helen's relationship with Linda Bates had about run its course, and if that was the case, he and Helen would probably be leaving sooner rather than later. Would getting Stephen Bates off the hook be enough?

Thorne knew very well that it would not.

For all the killers he had put away, it was the ones he had

failed to catch who kept sleep at bay now and again or nudged him awake in the early hours. Then there were those he had caught and failed to hold on to.

He thought about a man called Stuart Nicklin. Wherever he was and whatever he was calling himself now, Thorne knew their paths would cross again, that Nicklin would make sure of it. It was something no sane individual would look forward to.

After forty minutes of stop-start, the traffic finally began to move a little more freely. If it stayed that way, he could be back with Helen before the CD had finished.

He put his foot down again.

Driving through Polesford on his way to collect Helen, Thorne saw a small group of teenagers gathered in the semi-dark outside a shop. They were banging on the window, shouting at someone inside. He slowed, then when the driver behind began sounding his horn, he pulled on to the pavement and flicked on his hazards. He had wondered if the boys he and Helen had confronted the previous night were among those doing the shouting, but quickly saw that they weren't. If anything, these kids were even younger, boys and girls. Watching one of them kicking at the door, Thorne realised they were standing outside the milkshake bar he had walked past on his first day in town.

He watched as a young woman came out of the shop to confront them. He lowered his window and heard her tell them to piss off, that she would call the police if they didn't. After hurling a few final insults, the group wandered away, exchanging back-slaps and high-fives, and as the woman walked back into the milkshake bar, Thorne could finally see who it was they had been abusing; the solitary customer, her back to the window, hunched over a table near the counter.

Thorne parked on a side street and walked back.

When he knocked on the lighted window, the woman behind

the counter pointed to the CLOSED sign. He shook his head and banged again, gestured towards the figure at the table. Aurora Harley turned to look at him and said something to the owner. Though she looked far from happy about it, the woman walked across and let Thorne in.

'Any trouble, I'm calling the police,' she said.

Thorne sat down, but Aurora Harley did not look at him. He stared at her hands, the bracelets around the thin wrists, the chipped nail polish. He thought about reaching across to take one, but decided against it. He nodded towards the woman who had reluctantly let him in. 'She doesn't look like someone you'd want to mess with,' he said.

'Friend of my mum's.' She finally looked up at him. Her eyes were red, blotted liner snaking down one cheek. She hunched her shoulders still further, her chin disappearing inside the silver jacket Thorne had recognised from across the road. 'Probably the only one they've got left.'

'I'm sorry,' Thorne said.

She shrugged. 'It's not like you didn't warn me what it might be like.'

'I should never have suggested it.'

She looked up again, attempted a smile. 'Well, I got a bit of dosh, like you said. I mean, probably won't be enough so we can all move or anything.'

'It won't come to that,' Thorne said.

'You reckon?'

'There'll be another story, a bigger story. There always is.'

The smile had been clinging on, but now it slipped completely and the tears came again. She said, 'They put dog shit through my mum and dad's letterbox this morning.'

Thorne became aware that they were being watched by the woman behind the counter. He looked across, gave a small nod that he hoped would suggest empathy and understanding but got only a look of contempt in return. Even if she didn't know it had been Thorne's suggestion that had led to all this, the woman had clearly decided he was responsible.

*We threw her to the wolves.*

Thorne fished a serviette from the chrome dispenser and passed it across. Aurora pressed it to her face, then added it to the small collection of used ones scattered around her half-drunk milkshake. She summoned a smile again and shook her head. 'All I did was tell the truth. How can people hate you so much for telling the truth?'

'They don't hate you,' Thorne said. 'They just need a target, that's all. A scapegoat makes them feel better about their own shit lives. They need a witch to burn.'

'Bloody hell, I hope it doesn't come to that.' The girl laughed, and Thorne laughed with her. He glanced across again. The woman at the counter was still scowling. She finally looked away from him to switch on another lamp near the till, the daylight all but gone.

'It will get better,' he said. 'You just need to keep your head down.'

'What about Steve?' she asked. 'Are they going to let him go?'

'I hope so. I mean they should, but ...'

'What's so unfair is that nobody seems to care that I'm upset too. I'm grieving about Jess as much as anyone.'

'I didn't know you knew her,' Thorne said.

'She was one of my best mates.'

'Oh. I'm sorry.' Thorne did not know why he was surprised. Why it had never occurred to him that, being the same age, the girls might have known one another.

'We went through primary school together, got chucked out of girl guides at the same time.' Finally the smile looked settled. 'We got our tattoos done together, the same design and everything. A dolphin ...'

402

Thorne could not recall any mention of a tattoo in the postmortem report he had seen on Jessica Toms. Then again, there had been precious little skin left. 'Where did you have them done?'

'A place in Tamworth.'

'No, I meant *where*.'

Aurora giggled, reddening, and leaned towards the straw in her milkshake. 'Well, nowhere I can show you, put it that way.'

She slurped at her shake, and Thorne blinked . . .

. . . and it was as quick and simple as remembering where he had left his keys.

He knew who had killed Jessica Toms.

'You all right?'

He must have said something to Aurora Harley after that. Goodbye or take care or whatever.

I need to go . . . .

But thinking back later on, those moments remained missing, and Thorne could remember nothing but the sound of his feet against the pavement and the rattle in his chest as he ran.

# SEVENTY-TWO

If there had been a piano playing when Thorne rushed into the bar of the Magpie's Nest, it would certainly have stopped. That's how it felt as the small group of regulars in there turned to look at him, for those few long seconds before they went back to their drinks and conversations.

Some old Roxy Music song on the jukebox.

Trevor Hare grinned at him from behind the bar. He said, 'Someone looks like they need a drink? Pint, is it?'

Thorne stared, still trying to decide the best way to play it. There was one more thing he wanted to check. He said, 'Pint would be great,' then turned and wandered across to the back wall.

He walked up to a table, and, ignoring the complaints of the couple sitting there, leaned right across it to get a good look at one particular stuffed fish. The carp, caught at Pretty Pigs Pool. He checked the date on the plaque; the same one he had seen several times in a file at Nuneaton police station.

When he turned round again, Trevor Hare had gone.

Thorne rushed to the bar, just as Hare's wife appeared behind it, wiping her hands. 'What can I get you?'

'Where's he gone?'

'Sorry?'

'Your husband.' Thorne moved quickly to the hatch in the bar and lifted the flap. Hare's wife moved to block his way.

'You can't—'

Thorne pushed her aside and ran through into the storeroom. There were boxes of glasses and bar snacks piled floor to ceiling, barrels, bottles and cleaning equipment. He tore through into a narrow hallway, then quickly up a carpeted stairway that he presumed led to the living area above the pub. It only took a matter of seconds to ascertain that all the rooms were empty.

He took the stairs back down three at a time and burst out through the back door into a delivery area. Breathless, *helpless*, he stood and looked up and down the unlit alleyway. It was deserted. He could hear Trevor Hare's wife shouting somewhere behind him, and above that, the noise of a car accelerating away from somewhere nearby.

He reached for his phone.

Ignoring the stares of the customers, the swearing from the landlord's wife, Thorne ran back through the bar and out of the front door. He was already dialling by the time he reached the pavement.

'Where are you?' Helen asked. 'I thought you were coming—'

'It's Trevor Hare,' Thorne said. He was watching every car that passed, leaning down to stare at each driver. 'The landlord of the Magpie's Nest. He's the killer.'

'*What?*'

'He's gone, that's the important thing.' Thorne was still breathing heavily, struggling to get it all out quickly. 'He knows I've sussed him and so he's gone. He took a car ...'

'OK, calm down. We'll find out the reg and they'll get him.'

'That's no good.' Thorne was shouting. 'Look, I've got nothing, not really, it's all circumstantial. I know it's him, and I can explain why, but right now there's nothing that's going to put him away. There's only one person who can do that . . . she's the only real evidence.' A motorbike roared past. Thorne waited for the noise to die down. 'He's gone for Poppy.'

Helen said nothing for a few seconds, then Thorne heard her breath catch.

'What?'

'He knew Peter Harley,' she said.

'Hare?'

'Remember him talking to Aurora in the pub? He was asking after her grandfather, telling her to say hello to him.'

Thorne remembered. Hare smiling, pouring the girl a drink.

'Maybe they were more than friends,' Helen said. 'Maybe they . . . compared notes.'

'What are you thinking?'

'The place Harley took us,' Helen said. Another sharp intake of breath. 'Jesus, Hare actually *mentioned* it, the first night we were here.'

'Where is it?'

'It's a disused pumping station.' Her voice was barely above a whisper and Thorne strained to listen. 'Rubble, more or less. But there's a room underneath, what's left of the underground workings.'

'How far, Helen?'

'It's on the edge of the woods, just beyond that fishing pool we went to.'

'Pretty Pigs Pool?'

'Yes . . .'

Thorne knew that Helen was right. He began running towards his car. 'I think I can find it.'

'No, I know the quickest way,' Helen said. 'Wait there and I'll come and get you.'

'He's got a good start on us.'

Thorne heard Helen talking to someone, but could not make out what was being said over the sound of his own ragged breaths.

'We can take Jason's four-by-four,' she said.

# SEVENTY-THREE

She's not Poppy any more.

Poppy has never felt any of these things; the pain, the howling hunger, the strange and simple desire to be gone for ever. Never screamed until she thought her guts would burst or kicked out at things that were trying to feed on her. Poppy Johnston has never felt as if she were floating above her own body, never imagined damp to be silk or darkness to be sunshine, and never laughed because she believed she was going to die.

Now, she's somebody else.

She's not sure who or what she's become, but then again she's finding it hard enough to remember who the girl called Poppy was. The one they were presumably still looking for. That girl was like someone she'd seen in a film or read about. A friend of a friend.

Stupid name, anyway . . .

Her nan had *never* liked it, had always given her mum a hard time. It's a flower, for God's sake, her nan would say and whenever her mum pointed out that plenty of girl's names were the same as flowers, I mean Rose and Daisy for a start, her nan would sit there huffing and puffing for a while, saying the name

'Poppy' over and over like she was sucking a lemon or something. Then she'd say, 'It's a bloody dog's name.'

No, not a dog, she thinks now, because dogs are way smarter than she is, than she'd *been*.

Poppy. Poppy. POPPEE . . .

She says the name over and over again, like her nan had done, until it begins to sound every bit as stupid as her nan thought it was. Saying it and saying it to remind herself that this is who she used to be. Now, it's just a name to be scratched on to a stone in the abbey or scribbled on a card, left with some flowers. The name of a girl who was probably dippy and forgot where she'd left things and lost expensive phones. Who thought life was pretty great and that bad things didn't happen to people who didn't deserve them.

That girl's shadowy now, faded.

She shuffles through the water until she is pressed hard against the metal pipe, and lets her head fall back against the brick. It's a dull thud that she can feel down through her shoulders and each day she has begun to do it harder and faster; daring herself, wondering how long it will be before she feels something crack.

She can't really remember the girl she was and is only just beginning to understand the one that she's become. She doesn't know if it's a good thing or a bad thing, but she has come to realise that – were it ever to happen – her parents would not be getting back the same child they had lost.

She lets her head fall back again and again, enjoying it.

She doesn't know who she is, or where she is, or how long she's been there.

She knows only that, whatever is coming, she's ready for the end.

She freezes when she hears something metal rattling above her, and, when the hatch opens, and torchlight dances across the water that's running down the stone steps, Poppy doesn't know whether she's screaming in terror or relief.

# SEVENTY-FOUR

'Hare knew about Jessica's tattoo,' Thorne said. 'He mentioned it one night when I was in the pub ... the big "mein host" act, telling me what a lovely girl she was. The tattoo wasn't in a place he could possibly have known about unless ...' He stopped and reached out to steady himself against the dash as the Land Rover accelerated into a tight corner. In the absence of blues and twos, Helen was improvising; hazards flashing, lights on full beam and the horn blaring any time she approached a bend.

'He could have heard about it from almost anyone,' Helen said. 'The girl's tattoo.'

'*What?*'

'Come on, you know what this place is like for gossip.' She glanced at him. 'Look, I know you're right, OK? I'm just making the points any decent defence counsel's going to make.'

Thorne nodded, happy enough to reel off the other reasons he was convinced that Trevor Hare was the man they were looking for. 'He's an ex-copper, so he knows all about DNA and how to hide it. He knows about bugs and time of death, he knows the conclusions that Cornish and his team are going to jump to. He was as good as involved in this case from the kick-off, getting info from all the coppers in the pub, feeding them stuff when it suited him. He went to *them* at the very beginning to admit that those girls' DNA would be all over his car.'

'Hiding in plain sight,' Helen said.

They drew close behind a car whose driver seemed unimpressed with the flashing lights behind him. Cursing, Helen leaned on the horn then swerved to accelerate past.

'More than that,' Thorne said. 'Like he was flaunting it. The alibi he'd given himself for the day Jessica Toms was taken, sitting up there on the wall of his pub. Easy enough to get any old fish stuffed and mounted and any date you fancy inscribed on it. Easy enough for him to get that fag-end as well. Steve Bates smoking in the pub garden, Hare empties the ashtray out at the end of the night, piece of cake. Oh, and let's not forget that Patterson's dog knew him well, so not a problem for Hare to go to the farm and steal that piglet.'

'He knew *Bates*,' Helen said. 'That's the most important thing.'

'Yeah, he knew exactly who to set up. Innocent or not, Bates has certainly got the right ... tastes.'

They were driving north, roaring through the same small villages they had passed five days earlier, and finally on to narrow unlit roads; darkness beyond the treeline and a layer of dirty pink on the horizon. This time there was no diversion to add unwelcome time to the journey. 'Another ten minutes,' Helen said. 'Maybe less ... then depending on how far off-road we can take the car, maybe another five on foot.'

'That's OK,' Thorne said. He was shifting in his seat, growing increasingly agitated. 'We don't want him to hear us coming anyway.'

There was still water on the road, the Land Rover's wheels spraying the hedges and dry-stone walls. A lone dog-walker with

411

a torch waved and shouted as the car sped in her direction, turning at the last moment to try to avoid the deluge.

'Shit,' Thorne said. 'Torch.'

'There might be one in the boot.'

'This is half-arsed.' Thorne shook his head. '*I'm* half-arsed. I'm half-arsed and I'm an idiot.' Helen jumped a little next to him as he slammed his hand on the dash. 'Doesn't matter that I know it's Hare, because there's no more evidence on him than there is on Bates, and he knows that. Less, if anything. So of *course* he has to kill the girl.' He slammed his hand down again. '*Idiot* . . .'

'You said that, Tom.'

'Why the hell didn't I try and take him the right way? Why didn't I call for back-up and wait? Go in there mob-handed, job done.'

'We're not far away—'

'Why didn't I at least just march in there and pull him straight over the bar?' Helen slowed, then braked hard and reversed quickly until the Land Rover's headlamps lit up a decent-sized gap in the wall. 'Because the sad truth is I wanted to . . . enjoy it.'

Helen pointed and talked fast. 'The road swings all the way around, right? It's another five miles or so, but if we go across country I reckon we can take a few minutes off. It's what the car's for.'

She had put the car into gear before Thorne had finished nodding.

Hare closed the hatch quickly behind him, shushing her as he came carefully down the steps. They were steep and running with the water that had come pouring in while the hatch was open. He kept the torch pointed at his feet until he was safely down.

Then he turned it on the girl.

Still screaming, Poppy pressed herself back against the wall as he got closer.

He said, 'Yes, I should have thought about the tape coming off, shouldn't I? Got wet, did it?' He nodded in answer to his own question. 'Now, I bet it's been a lot nicer not having that stuck over your mouth, hasn't it?' He winced at the screaming, waited until she paused to take a breath. 'I can easily put it back on, so it's up to you. You stop making that terrible noise and we can leave things as they are. Or I have to put the tape over your mouth again and I really don't want to do that.'

He waited, cocked his head one way and then the other; will you, won't you? He smiled when it became clear that she was not going to scream any more.

He stepped closer and crouched down next to her, watching her eyes screw tightly shut when he shone the torch in her face. He looked at her for a while, then reached out. She flinched when he touched her hair, her head cracking against the brick.

'I know,' he said. 'I'd be angry too, and I'm sorry, but I couldn't get here any sooner. I wanted to, I promise. God, you've got *no* idea how much I wanted to come and see you, but things were a bit tricky and it was impossible to get away. Did you feel abandoned? Did you think I didn't want to be with you any more? Oh, Pops, that's so silly ... '

He stood up and took off his jacket. He used the torch to locate the nail he'd banged into the wall months before, and hung it up. He crouched down again and shivered theatrically.

'Look, I know that on a magic island, you and me would be in a nice hotel somewhere. There'd be a lovely soft bed and we'd have an expensive meal and some nice wine, which I would have been more than happy to shell out for, by the way. But beggars can't be choosers, can they, so we'll just have to make the best out of a bad lot.' He reached out again and this time, when he laid his fingers against her cheek, she turned her head quickly and tried

413

to bite him, the hand that was not shackled reaching up to try and scratch.

He pulled back fast and stood up. He walked back to where his jacket was hanging.

'Oh, that's fine, too,' he said. 'Yeah, we can do it like that, if you prefer. Like you don't actually want it and I'm making you. Like you don't really love me.' He nodded and reached into one of the jacket pockets. In the darkness behind him, he could hear her kicking her feet and thrashing at the chain. 'It'll be like a fantasy kind of thing, like a game.'

He turned. 'It'll be fun.'

She began to scream again as soon as she saw the knife.

They left the Land Rover at the edge of Pretty Pigs Pool and walked.

There was no torch to be found in the car, but a sliver of moon helped and as they made their way through the waterlogged field that sloped away towards the woods, they used the light from their phones whenever it began to feel treacherous underfoot.

Helen led the way, pointing and hissing instructions. Their feet were sinking with each step; an inch or two one moment, a foot or more the next, water soaking their jeans up beyond the knees.

'You OK?' Thorne asked.

Ahead of him, Helen nodded and pressed on towards the trees below as quickly as she was able. Thorne could not remember seeing her so determined, so focused. A drive so at odds with how he knew she must be feeling about the place they were trying to find.

'It's not far,' she said. 'This is the worst bit.'

A few minutes later they had reached the treeline, and though there were a few more inches of water underfoot, the ground itself was firmer and progress was quicker.

414

Helen moved through the woods as though she had made the journey every day of her life. She stepped easily around the dark trees and chose paths without thinking. Struggling a little to keep up, Thorne could not help but imagine her coming here as a young teenager.

Being *led* here.

*Saying he was sorry . . . still sweating while he tucked his shirt back in . . .*

Like Thorne wasn't fired up enough already . . .

After a few minutes, Helen stopped and waited for Thorne to catch up. She pointed to a clearing a hundred yards or so away. Thorne could see nothing at first, only the absence of trees, then as they stepped slowly closer, he could make out the stumps of brick columns, like uneven teeth. The footprint of a small building.

'Why the hell didn't they search here?' Helen whispered.

'It was probably under a foot of water,' Thorne said. 'Anyway, from what you've told me, you'd never know there was anything here. Anything underneath, I mean.'

'*I* knew,' Helen said. 'I should have thought, I should have said something.'

Thorne took hold of her wrist as they drew closer. 'Listen. You've got nothing to blame yourself for, not a thing. If Poppy Johnston's dead, only one of us is responsible, and it's not you.'

In silence they covered the last few feet and stepped across the ragged stone perimeter on to what was left of the concrete floor. There was virtually no water gathered now, though a few puddles in uneven parts of the floor and scattered lumps of sodden timber made it clear that there had been up until very recently. Thorne turned on his phone, switched on the flashlight app and looked around.

He saw the trapdoor straight away. The metal hasp was pulled back and a large padlock had been tossed to one side. Several sheets of corrugated iron and heavy beams that had presumably been used to disguise its existence were lying nearby.

He raised the phone and passed the light across Helen's face.

She nodded and took a step closer, her chest rising and falling fast beneath her jacket.

Thorne felt the first spatter of rain on his face as he crouched down. Dry-mouthed, he licked at a drop, but it could not wash away the taste of metal in his mouth.

He opened the trapdoor quickly and got to his feet, shone the light from his phone into the blackness. Helen moved across to join him and both of them peered down, their hands over noses and mouths to block the sickening stench that rose from below. There were only steps, cobwebs, water dripping from the edges of the hatch.

Then the voice of Trevor Hare from somewhere in the dark.

'That'll be Tom, I presume. Got your mate with you, I'm guessing.' A figure stepped across to the bottom of the steps and Thorne was immediately dazzled by a torch rather more powerful than his own. 'Oh, no, I'm wrong, you've brought your better half.'

A scream filled the pause. 'I'm here. I'm *down here*.'

Hare said, 'Why don't the pair of you come down and join the party?'

# SEVENTY-FIVE

As soon as they had begun to descend, Hare told them to close the hatch behind them, then used the torch to guide Thorne and Helen down the steps. Once they were down, he made very sure that they got a good look at the knife and its proximity to the face of the girl who was kneeling next to him, her wrist shackled to something and her back against a wall. He ordered Helen to stay where she was at the bottom of the steps and waved Thorne away from her and into the far corner.

'Right then,' he said.

It was hard to say how big the room was by the light of a moving torch, but Thorne guessed it was no more than twelve feet square. As the light flashed across the scarred brick walls and bare stone underfoot, he glimpsed rusted pipework and what remained of an electric motor mounted on high girders that appeared to have been sheared off. Perished rubber drive-belts lay tangled in pools of water, like dead snakes on the pitted floor. Thorne did not need to have seen it to know exactly where the sweet, meaty stink was coming from.

Hare shone the torch at Helen. She raised her hands to shield her eyes from the glare. He said, 'So, I've got to ask. How the hell did you know about this place?'

'Lucky guess,' Thorne said.

Hare ignored him, kept the light on Helen. 'I know you didn't follow me.'

Helen said nothing. She sensed that Trevor Hare knew the answer already and even if it was only a suspicion, she was certainly not going to give him the satisfaction of confirming it.

'Been here before, maybe?'

'Listen.' Thorne took a step and Hare immediately swung the torch around.

'Steady.' He moved the knife towards Poppy, who began to whimper and tug at the chain.

Thorne raised his hands. 'OK, just ... look, I don't really think you've got a great many options here, Trevor.'

'*I've* not got options?'

'We don't want anything to happen to Poppy and I don't think you want to go to prison.'

'All makes sense so far.'

'So, strikes me the easiest thing is if you just walk out of here.'

Helen gasped as something scuttled past her nearby. She kicked out at the darkness.

'You get used to them,' Hare said. He reached out to lay a hand on Poppy's head. 'Didn't do you any harm, did they, Pops?'

'Come on,' Thorne said. 'Just leave her alone and get out of here.'

'Right, and how long before I'm picked up, d'you reckon? A day? An hour?'

'You get a chance,' Helen said. 'There isn't a good way for this to end otherwise, not for you.'

'I think there's an option you haven't considered,' Hare said. 'We'll stick with the idea of me going and obviously that means you two staying here.'

'Fair enough,' Thorne said.

'But I'm afraid I'll have to take Poppy with me.' He leaned down to snake an arm around Poppy, who immediately began to scream again and pull at the chain. 'I've got some more of that vodka you like in the car,' he said. 'You get that down your neck and when you wake up, we'll be miles and miles away.'

Poppy pulled harder. She said, 'I'm not *fucking* going anywhere with you.'

Hare stood up and shook his head. 'It's a game we play. I'm somehow forcing her and she doesn't like it.'

'That's not going to happen,' Thorne said. 'You know we can't let you go anywhere with her.'

'Well, of course, and I can imagine that back when I was doing what you two do, and kidding myself I was making a difference, I would have said exactly the same thing. Problem is, problem for *you*, I mean, is I'm the one that's got the girl and got the knife. So really, I'm the one that decides who goes and who stays down here to have fun with Roland Rat and all his mates.' Hare brought the torch slowly up towards his face, to make sure they could both see the smile, the steel in it. 'How's that sound?'

'Sounds like hot air to me,' Helen said.

Hare swung the torch to her. 'Like what?'

'Empty threats.'

'You saw the other girl's body, did you?'

'You love Poppy, I can see that. Anyone can. I don't believe for one second that you'd hurt her.'

'Well, yes of course I love her, though I've had precious little chance to show it, what with one thing and another.'

'I know.' Helen was keen to keep Hare's focus on her. With the light in her eyes she could no longer see anything of Thorne, but she was hoping he was taking the chance to move a little closer to Hare and the girl.

'Of course I love her and I want to spend some time with her,

I mean what else do you think this has been about, but I need to take care of myself, don't I?' He sniffed. 'If it came down to it, I'd carve her up as easy as I did that pig.'

'I don't believe that.'

'Up to you,' Hare said. 'Take a gamble. You'll be the one who has to live with it. Something else to keep you awake at night.'

Helen did not need torchlight to tell her that Hare was grinning.

'So, here's what's happening.' Hare moved the torch beam slowly back and forth between Helen and Thorne. When the light fell on Thorne, Helen could see that he was looking at her. It was never there long enough for her to ascertain his intentions, any message he might be trying to send. 'You pair need to keep very still while I get this chain unlocked.' Poppy began to squeal again and this time Hare leaned down quickly and laid the blade of the knife against her cheek. 'Shush. You really need to keep it down, Pops. Giving me a headache . . .'

'*Please*,' Helen said. 'Just leave her alone and leave. Lock us all in here and by the time anybody finds us you'll be long gone.'

'Well, you've got part of that right.' He snapped his fingers. 'Let's start by getting shot of your phones. Just take them out slowly and chuck them on the floor nice and hard.'

Helen went first, then Hare moved the beam across to Thorne and watched him do the same. Helen winced at the crack as his phone smashed on the stone floor.

'Very good,' Hare said. 'Now, you just need to keep still while I get this done, and we'll be out of your way.'

From opposite corners, Thorne and Helen watched as Hare stepped across to where a jacket was hanging on the wall. Using the torch to monitor them every step of the way, he reached first into one pocket and then another, until he found what he was looking for. He held the small key up to the light so they could both see it, then leaned down slowly.

420

'Right, now this'll be a bit easier if you ... here you go.' He gently manoeuvred Poppy from her knees on to her backside. She was crying steadily and put up no resistance, struggling to catch her breath between sobs. 'Soon have this thing off you, love.'

Thorne watched and waited for the right moment. He knew instinctively that Helen would be thinking the same as he was. If they allowed Hare to take Poppy out of here, then she was dead anyway.

They both knew what Hare had done to Jessica Toms the moment he was done with 'loving' her.

His back against the wall, Hare struggled to get the key into the shackle around Poppy's wrist. He said, 'Bloody thing,' and tutted as though he was struggling to thread a needle, then when he tried, somewhat clumsily, to move the knife to the same hand that was holding the torch, Poppy lashed out.

There was a dull crack as her boot connected hard with Hare's lower leg and then a crash as both torch and knife fell to the floor.

Thorne and Helen both moved quickly, but so did Hare.

'He's over here,' Poppy shouted. 'He's *here* ... '

Helen made for where she thought the knife might have fallen and as she scrabbled for it in the water, she was aware that Thorne and Hare were already struggling. She could hear blows being landed, breath being punched out. It was long seconds before her fingers finally closed around the handle of the knife and she stood and moved back to the bottom of the steps at the same time as she heard bodies go crashing into the far corner.

There were a few moments of silence.

'Where is he?' Poppy shrieked.

'Tom?' Helen heard moaning and then saw a figure rising from the far corner. She moved back, felt the bottom step hard against her heel. 'Tom, that you?'

Thorne's voice came from somewhere closer to the floor; pained, winded. 'Don't let him leave ...'

She heard a grunt of anger that she knew had not come from Thorne, a second before the figure ran at her.

She tightened her grip on the knife, held on tight even as she felt the push, before the blade slipped easily into flesh.

Hare – and Helen prayed that it *was* him – sighed as he stepped away and off the knife, and, in that moment when Helen froze, realising what she had done, he was charging at her again, pushing her aside and clambering up the steps.

Thorne shouted Helen's name.

She spun round and watched Hare crash out through the hatch. 'Tom?'

A second later there was torchlight dancing across the steps and turning to see where it was coming from, Helen saw Poppy climbing unsteadily to her feet. The girl's hands were trembling so much that she could barely hold the torch steady.

Helen lifted the knife, looked at the blood.

Then Thorne was moving slowly towards her, panting and holding his side.

'He ran on to it,' she said.

Thorne nodded and knelt, reached to pick up the two halves of Helen's handset, the battery. He wiped everything down on his shirt, snapped it all back into place and tried to switch it on. 'Nothing,' he said.

As Helen watched Thorne climbing the steps and heading out into the darkness after Trevor Hare, she heard Poppy's voice behind her.

'I'll tell them it was me ... tell them *I* did it.'

Helen turned and walked across, arms outstretched.

'I wish it had been me,' Poppy said.

# LONDON

# SEVENTY-SIX

Helen kept on smiling as she walked towards reception, used her pass to go through the security door and took the stairs to the second floor. She returned each nod of recognition, said 'fine' and 'thanks' every time she was stopped and asked how she was doing. She did her best not to react to the looks of surprise and the whispered conversations that began almost as soon as she had walked past.

It was like being back in Polesford.

Three weeks since she had left her hometown for what she guessed would be the final time; four since she had last been in this place.

It felt like a lot longer.

She spotted her DCI moving between desks in the incident room. She hung back until she had caught his eye and watched him try to hide his irritation when he saw her. He nodded towards his office and she followed, another 'fine', another 'thanks' or two along the way.

DCI Adam Bonner sat back and sighed. He leaned forward

again and straightened some papers. 'You're not supposed to be here, Helen.'

'I know that.'

'So, why make it more difficult than it has to be?'

'I'm not trying to make it difficult.'

'It's just routine, you know that. It'll all get sorted in a couple more weeks and you can get back to work. But until then ...'

Helen had been suspended on full pay, pending a full investigation into the events leading up to the death of Trevor Hare. The evidence of Poppy Johnston looked more than likely to clear Helen completely, but until the Professional Standards Directorate had finished looking into it all, there was still a ... shadow.

Thorne had told her not to worry. He had lost count of his run-ins with the Rubberheelers. Bonner had said the same and did so again now.

'You've just got to sit it out,' he said. 'Have a holiday or something. I mean your last one wasn't exactly relaxing, was it?'

Hare had been found floating face down in Pretty Pigs Pool at first light the following day. Wedged against the bank, as ducks, lily-pads and empty cans floated nearby. The post-mortem had determined drowning to be the cause of death. Trevor Hare was a reasonably fit fifty-five-year-old and, according to his widow, a strong swimmer. In his comments, the pathologist had noted that heavy blood loss due to the knife wound – though not life-threatening in itself – might have contributed to the victim's inability to get himself out of the freezing water.

It was unclear, and likely to remain so, how Hare had ended up in the water to begin with. He knew the area well, but it was dark and he was wounded, disoriented perhaps. He could easily have slipped. The ground was treacherous.

'Don't know,' Thorne had said. 'Don't care.'

426

'What about it?' Bonner asked now. 'There's some good last-minute deals to be had in Greece this time of year.'

'I'm here to report a case of historic child abuse,' Helen said.

Bonner looked at her.

'It's what we do, isn't it? Well, it was last time I was here.'

The DCI lifted a notepad from the other side of the desk. 'How historic are we talking about?'

'Twenty-five years.'

Bonner gently laid his pen down. 'Helen, you know as well as anyone what a nightmare these old cases are. You sure?'

'I'm sure,' Helen said. 'And I know what a nightmare it's going to be.'

The DCI picked up his pen again. 'You got a name for the perpetrator?'

Helen gave him the name. 'He's in a care home near Tamworth. I'll need to check the exact address.'

'A care home?'

Helen was already shaking her head. 'I don't care if he's old, Adam. I don't care if he's bedridden and living on mashed potato and pissing through a tube. I want him done for this.'

Bonner had learned over several years of having Helen on his team that there was little point in arguing when she was this fired-up about a case. 'Fair enough,' he said. 'We'll start the preliminaries, but you know you won't be able to work it, don't you? With this Standards thing still going on.'

'I can't work it anyway.'

Bonner looked at her again, a flicker of confusion. He went back to his notebook. 'Right, what's the victim's name?'

'It's me,' Helen said. 'I'm the victim.'

She stopped in the car park and leaned against a wall, keen to get some air and to let her breathing return to normal. A squad car pulled in and parked up and she watched two uniformed officers that she recognised step out. One of them clocked her and looked set to come over, so she stared down at her phone until he had gone inside.

There were some difficult conversations to be had before she could think about talking shop.

With her father. With Linda . . .

They had not seen one another since the events at Pretty Pigs Pool and, until now, Helen had been content to leave the ball in Linda's court. She had left her number, but Linda had not called. Helen remembered their last conversation, the night they had talked about Aurora Harley, then, finally about her grandfather.

*It must have been hard coming back.*

*Harder staying.*

*Home, wasn't it? Never had a way out.*

*Did you ever see him?*

*A few times. I wanted Wayne or Steve to kill him, almost told them about it once or twice. He* smiled *at me in the street . . .*

Helen had been told that Linda's house was on the market, but knew little of her plans beyond that, assuming that she and the kids would be looking to start a new life far away from Polesford and from her husband, charges against whom had been quickly dropped and whose whereabouts had not been released to the press.

Until a photograph had appeared a few days before of Bates and Linda strolling through a Tamworth shopping centre. Now there was speculation about the size of the wrongful arrest settlement.

There was talk of a book deal . . .

Helen would need to tell Linda what she was doing and that she had already passed on her name to those who would soon be arresting Peter Harley. It might well put another zero on to that rumoured contract for a book, but Helen did not know how happy Linda would be about it.

428

The same went for Aurora Harley, of course, but having made her decision, Helen could not afford to dwell on that. There were those much closer that she needed to consider.

She walked to the car, got inside and sat for a few minutes thinking about how best to broach the subject, that there was little point in going round the houses. Worrying that she was thinking way too much. Her thumb moved across the screen of her phone and she rubbed at a smudge with the edge of her shirt.

Then she dialled her sister's number.

# SEVENTY-SEVEN

When the call had ended, Thorne came out of the bedroom. Hendricks lowered the volume on the TV and turned round. 'How did it go?'

'Pretty good, I think,' Thorne said. 'She sounded ... *up*. Her sister's going round later on.'

'Yeah, well let's see how long she stays "up" for.'

'Didn't go too badly on the phone apparently.' Thorne was trying to be optimistic for Helen's sake, but he knew what Hendricks meant, how difficult Helen's sister could be. It was inconceivable that things would be the same between them after tonight and he could only hope it was a change for the better.

'You not going over later then?'

Thorne shook his head. Since coming back from Polesford, he had spent more than the usual number of nights alone at his own flat in Kentish Town, and he had enjoyed them. Hendricks had been travelling to and from Warwick a fair deal and this was their first chance to catch up in a while.

'Just you and me then, big boy.'

Thorne went into the kitchen to collect beers. When he came back, Hendricks said, 'You think she's doing the right thing?'

'Seeing her sister?'

'All of it.'

Thorne passed a bottle across and sat down. Having seen how painful it had been for Helen to tell him what had happened all those years before, the thought of her having to going through it again in detail – in interview rooms, from a witness box – was terrible. But that had been her choice and there was nobody else qualified to make it. 'Right thing for her,' he said.

'She say anything about the suspension?'

'Still ongoing.' Thorne took a swig. 'A good few weeks yet, I reckon.'

'Should have accepted the girl's offer. To say that she'd been the one holding the knife.' Hendricks looked as though he had more to say, but then his phone rang and he went into the kitchen to take the call, closed the door behind him.

Thorne knew that his friend was only half joking. There weren't too many people mourning the death of Trevor Hare and even though Thorne knew the internal investigation would work out in her favour, it seemed hugely unfair that a good officer like Helen had to spend weeks on suspension for unintentionally sticking a knife in him.

'Helen gets suspended and you come out smelling of roses,' Hendricks had said back then. 'You, with an entire drawer in the DPS filing cabinet. I did *not* see that coming.'

It was not an outcome anyone with any sense would have bet on. Several days' worth of very positive press. The letters of thanks from the parents of Poppy Johnston and Jessica Toms.

Even Russell Brigstocke had forgiven him.

Once she'd been checked over and released from hospital, Poppy Johnston's evidence had helped them piece things together a bit more, but with no killer to question, the picture was still largely reliant on best guesses. Poppy had been able to confirm that Stephen Bates had given her a lift on the night she was taken. He had been flirty with her in the car, she told them, made certain suggestions, so she had asked him to drop her off at the bus stop. She had only been there a couple of minutes when Trevor Hare had driven up.

Whether or not Hare had taken Jessica Toms the same night Bates had given her a lift would never be known, but it was obvious he had been watching Bates for a while and knew very well that he was over-fond of young girls. He knew that Bates had already picked up Jessica and that her DNA was there to be found in his car. He knew that he was safe to target her and then Poppy, now that a ready-made suspect had unwittingly lined himself up.

It was just a question of providing a little more evidence.

The cigarette end had been ideal and easy enough to get hold of. The fact that Bates lied to the police could only have been a bonus and the material found on his computer must have been a very pleasant surprise, if Hare hadn't known about it already.

Thorne still believed that Jessica Toms had been killed no more than a day or two before Poppy had been taken. It was his suggestion that her body had been kept in the boot of Hare's car between then and the time he chose to bury it in the woods after Bates had been arrested. Forensic tests on the vehicle found parked near Pretty Pigs Pool confirmed Thorne's theory, though there was still nothing close to a 'thank you' from DI Tim Cornish. Poppy herself had been convinced that Jessica's body had been down there with her in Hare's improvised dungeon the whole time, but it turned out, of course, to have been the seriously decomposed body of Patterson's missing piglet. What the rats had left of it. By the time it was finally examined, the stinking corpse was still alive with plenty of those useful bugs and beetles that Hare had been planning to use on the body of Poppy herself.

'Your Liam would have had a field day,' Thorne had said.

'He's not *my* Liam,' Hendricks had said.

Now, that appeared to have changed, too.

Hendricks wandered back in and picked up the beer bottle he'd neglected to take with him. 'That was Liam on the phone,' he said.

Thorne had never thought it was anyone else. 'He well?'

'Yeah ...'

It was clear that there was more and that Hendricks wanted to be asked what it was. 'And?'

'He's thinking of applying for another job.'

'What kind of job?'

'Not so much what as *where*,' Hendricks said.

Now, Thorne understood. 'London?' Hendricks nodded. 'How do you feel about that?'

'Well, he might not get it.'

'So, how would you feel if he did?'

'Actually, I think I'd be ... OK with it.'

Hendricks looked more than OK, and Thorne pulled a suitably shocked face. 'Bloody hell, you're full of surprises.'

'Well, one of us has got to be.'

'Meaning?'

'Meaning you can't always follow the same path. Well you can, but eventually you get hit by a car.'

'Sorry?' Then Thorne realised that Helen must have told him about the badgers, and more specifically, who was like one. 'Oh, right, me being predictable. That's such crap, Phil.'

'Scared of change, then.'

'Are we going to order food, or what?'

'Fine with me.'

'Bengal Lancer?' He saw Hendricks grin. 'Because their food's the best.'

Hendricks wandered into the kitchen. 'I'll sort the plates out ...'

433

Thorne had the number for the Indian restaurant programmed into his phone. They immediately recognised the incoming number and called up the delivery address. 'The usual order, Mr Thorne?'

'Yeah, the usual order.'

The waiter said something else, but it was hard to hear above the noise of Hendricks laughing from the kitchen.

# ACKNOWLEDGEMENTS

I am hugely grateful, as ever, to a great many people for helping to drag this one across the finish line. Without them, it still would be suffering from stitch on the first bend while everyone else had changed and gone home ...

Thanks to Elizabeth Orcutt for advice on newspaper print deadlines and to John Manlove PhD for his help with the rather more esoteric business of extracting porcine DNA. Wendy Lee was brilliant as always and I remain extremely fortunate to have benefited from the copy-editing skills of Deborah Adams. Both have stopped me from looking foolish on *many* occasions.

For the umpteenth time, I am in the debt of Professor Lorna Dawson from the Environmental and Biochemical Sciences Group at the James Hutton Institute. Not only was her professional expertise invaluable, she possesses a darkly twisted imagination that would put a great many crime writers to shame and a wicked sense of humour. As evidence of this, I need only point out that the subject line of one of her emails, in which she was casually discussing insect infestation on the charred body of a pig, was *Smoky Bacon*. Thanks, Lorna, and the pork scratchings are on me.

Thanks to Michael Weston King and Lou Dalgleish. The songs of My Darling Clementine have been with me throughout the writing of this book and working with them on *The Other Half* has been an unalloyed pleasure. Long may the heartache continue.

'Thank you' in neon letters fifty feet high to David Shelley and Sarah Lutyens for being the best in the business. And above all, as always, thanks to Claire. Unlike those unfortunate enough to come up against Tom Thorne, I continue to get away with murder.

Did you enjoy *Time of Death*?
Turn over now for your
free short story,
*Stroke of Luck.*

# STROKE OF LUCK

So many things that could have been different.

An almost infinite number of them: the flight of the ball; the angle of the bat; the movement of his feet as he skipped down the pitch. The weather, the time, the day of the week, the whatever.

The smallest variance in any one of these things, or in the way that each connected to the other at the crucial moment, and nothing would have happened as it did. An inch another way, or a second, or a step and it would have been a very different story.

Of course, it's *always* a different story; but it isn't always a story with bodies . . .

He wasn't even a good batsman – a tail-ender for heaven's sake – but this once, he got everything right. The footwork and the swing were spot on. The ball flew from the meat of the bat, high above the heads of the fielders into the long grass at the edge of the woodland that fringed the pitch on two sides.

Alan and another player had been looking for a minute or so, using hands and feet to move aside the long grass at the base of an oak tree, when she stepped from behind it as if she'd been waiting for them.

'Don't you have any spare ones?'

Alan looked at her for a few, long seconds before answering. She was tall, five seven or eight, with short dark hair. Her legs were bare beneath a cream-coloured skirt and her breasts looked a good size under a sleeveless top. She looked Mediterranean, Alan thought. Sophisticated . . .

'I suppose we must have, somewhere,' he said.

'So why waste time looking? Are they expensive?'

Alan laughed. 'We're only a bunch of medics. It costs a small fortune just to hire the pitch.'

'You're a doctor?'

'A neurologist. A consultant neurologist . . .'

She didn't look as impressed as he'd hoped.

'Got it.'

Alan turned to see his team-mate brandishing the ball, heard the cheers from those on the pitch as it was thrown across.

He turned back. The woman was holding a hand up to shield her eyes from the sun.

'Will you be here long?' Alan said. She looked hesitant. He pointed back towards the pitch. 'We've only got a couple of wickets left to take.'

She dropped her hand, smiled without looking at him. 'You'd better get on with it then.'

'Listen, we usually go and have a couple of drinks afterwards, in the Woodman up by the tube. D'you fancy coming along? Just for one maybe?'

She looked at her watch. Too quickly, Alan thought, to have even seen what time it read.

'I don't have a lot of time.'

He nodded, stepping backwards towards the pitch. 'Well, you know where we are.'

The Woodman was only a small place, and the dozen or so players – some from either team – took up most of the back room.

'I'm Rachel, by the way,' she said.

'Alan.'

'Did you win, Alan?'

'Yes, but no thanks to me. The other team weren't very good.'

'You're all doctors, right?'

He nodded. 'Doctors, student doctors, friends of doctors. Anybody who's available if we're short. It's as much a social thing as anything else.'

'Plus the sandwiches you get at half-time.'

Alan put on a posh voice. 'We call it the tea interval,' he said.

Rachel eked out a dry white wine and was introduced. She met Phil Hendricks, a pathologist who did a lot of work with the police and told her a succession of grisly stories. She met a dull cardiologist whose name she instantly forgot, a male nurse called Sandy who was at great pains to point out that not all male nurses were gay, and a slimy anaesthetist whose breath would surely have done the trick were he ever to run short of gas.

While Rachel was in the *Ladies*, a bumptious paediatrician Alan didn't like a whole lot dropped a fat hand on to his shoulder.

'Sodding typical. You do fuck all with the bat and then score *after* the game!'

The others enjoyed the joke. Alan glanced round and saw that Rachel was just coming out of the toilet. He hoped that she hadn't seen them all laughing.

'Do you want another one of those?' Alan pointed at her half-empty glass before downing what was left of his lager.

She didn't, but followed him to the bar anyway. Alan leaned in close to her and they talked while he repeatedly failed to attract the attention of the surly Irish barmaid.

'I don't really know a lot of them, to tell you the truth. There's only a couple I ever see outside of the games.'

'There's always tossers in any group,' she said. 'It's the price you pay for company.'

'What do you do, Rachel?'

She barked out a dry laugh. 'Not a great deal. I studied.'

It sounded like the end of a conversation, and for a while they said nothing. Alan guessed that they were about the same age. She was definitely in her early thirties, which meant that she had to have graduated at least ten years before. She had to have done something, had to do something. Unless of course she'd been a mature student. It seemed a little too early to pry.

'What do you do to relax? Do you see mates, or . . . ?'

She nodded towards the bar and he followed her gaze to the barmaid who stood, finally ready to take the order. Alan reeled off a long list of drinks and they watched while the tray that was placed on the bar began to fill up with glasses. Alan turned and opened his mouth to speak, but she beat him to it.

'I'd better be getting off.'

'Right. I don't suppose I could have your phone number?'

She gave a non-committal hum as she swallowed what was left of her wine. Alan handed a twenty pound note across the bar, grinned at her.

'Mobile?'

'I never have it switched on.'

'I could leave messages.'

She took out a pen and scribbled the number on the back of a dog-eared beermat.

Alan picked up the tray of drinks just as the barmaid proffered him his fifty pence change. Unable to take it, Alan nodded to Rachel. She leaned forward and grabbed the coin.

'Stick it in the machine on your way out,' he said.

Alan had just put the tray down on the table when he heard the repetitive chug and clink of the fruit machine paying out its jackpot. He strode across to where Rachel was scooping out a handful of ten pence pieces.

'You jammy sod,' he said. 'I've been putting money into that thing for weeks.'

Then she turned, and Alan saw that her face had reddened. 'You have it,' she said. She thrust the handful of coins at him, then, as several dropped to the floor, she spun round flustered and tipped the whole lot back into the payout tray.

'I can't . . . I haven't got anywhere to put them all . . .'

She'd gone by the time Alan had finished picking coins off the carpet.

It didn't take too long for Rachel to calm down. She marched down the hill towards the tube station, her control returning with every step.

She'd been angry with herself for behaving as she had in the pub, but what else could she do? There was no way she could take all that loose change home with her, was there?

As she walked on she realised that actually, there had been things she could have done, and she chided herself for being so stupid. She could have asked the woman behind the bar to change the coins into notes. Those were more easily hidden. She could have grabbed the coins, left with a smile and made some beggar's day.

She needed to remember. It was important to be careful, but she always had options.

She reached into her handbag for the mints. Popped one into her mouth to mask the smell of the wine. The taste of it.

As she walked down the steps to Highgate station she dropped a hand into her pocket, groping around until she could feel her wedding ring hot against the palm of her hand. There was always that delicious, terrifying second or two, as her fingers moved against the lining of her pocket, when she thought she might have lost it, but it was always there, waiting for her.

She stood on the platform, the ring tight in her fist until the train came in. Then, just as she always did, she slipped the ring, inch by dreadful inch, back on to her finger.

Lee pushed his chicken Madras round the plate until it was cold. He'd lost his appetite anyway. He'd ordered the food before the row and now he didn't feel like it, so that was another thing that was Rachel's fault.

She'd be in the bedroom by now, crying.

She never cried when it was actually happening. He knew it was because she didn't want to give him the satisfaction, or some such crap. That only proved what a stupid cow she was, because he couldn't stand to see her cry, to see *any* woman cry, and maybe if she *did* cry once in a while he might ease off a bit.

No, she saved it up for afterwards and he could hear it now, coming through the ceiling and putting him off his dinner.

The row had been about the same thing they were all about. Her, taking the piss.

He'd backed down on this afternoon walking business, on her

going out to the woods of an afternoon on her own. He'd given in to her, and today she'd been gone nearly six hours. Half the fucking day and no word of an apology when she'd eventually come strolling through the front door.

So, it had kicked off.

Lee was bright, always had been. He knew damn well that it wasn't just about her staying out of the house too long. He knew it all came down to the pills.

There'd been a lot more rowing, a lot more crying in the bedroom since he'd found that little packet tucked behind her panties at the back of a drawer. He was clever enough to see the irony in that as well. Contraceptive pills, hidden among the sexy knickers he'd bought for her.

He'd gone mental when he'd found them, obviously. Hadn't they agreed that they were going to start trying for a kid? That everything would be better once they were a family? He was furious at the deceit, at the fool she'd made of him, at the time and effort he'd wasted in shafting her all those weeks beforehand.

There'd been a lot more rowing since.

Christ, he loved her though. She wouldn't get to him so much if it wasn't for that, wouldn't wind him up like she did. He could feel it surging through him as he lost his temper and it caused his whole body to shake when it was finished, and she crawled away to cry where he couldn't see her.

He hoped she knew it – now, with her face buried in a sopping pillow – he hoped she knew how much he loved her.

Lee dropped his fork and slid his hand beneath the plate, wiggling his fingers until it sat balanced on his palm. He jerked his forearm and sent the plate fast across the kitchen.

Watched his dinner run down the wall.

He watched them.

He lay on the grass, just another sun-worshipper, and with his arm folded across his head he spied on them through a fringed curtain of underarm hair. He watched them from his favourite bench. His face hidden behind a newspaper, his back straight against the small, metal plaque.

*For Eric and Muriel, who loved these woods . . .*

He watched them, and he waited.

He watched *her* of course at other times too. He'd followed her home that very first day and now he would spend hours outside the house in Barnet, imagining her inside in the dark.

He couldn't say why he'd chosen her; couldn't really say why he'd chosen any of them. Something just clicked. It was all pretty random at the end of the day, just luck – good or bad depending on which way you looked at it.

When he was caught, and odds on he would be, he would tell them that and nothing else.

It all came down to chance.

They'd begun to spend their afternoons together. They walked every inch of Highgate Woods, ate picnics by the tree where they'd first met, and one day they held hands across a weathered, wooden table outside the cafeteria.

'Why can't I see you in the evenings?' Alan said.

She winced. 'This is nice, isn't it? Don't rush things.'

'I changed my shifts around so we could see each other during the day. So that we could spend time together.'

'I never asked you to.'

'There's things I want, Rachel.'

She leered. 'I bet there are.'

'Yes, *that*. Obviously that, but other things. I want to take you places and meet your friends. I want to come to where you live. I want you to come where *I* live.'

'It's complicated. I told you.'

'You never tell me anything.'

'I'm married, Alan.'

He drew his hand away from hers. He tried, and failed to make light of it. 'Well, that explains a lot.'

'I suppose it changes everything, doesn't it?'

He looked at her as if she were mad. 'Just a *bit*.'

'I don't see why.'

'For fuck's sake, Rachel.'

'Tell me.'

'I don't ... I wouldn't like it if I was the one married to you, put it that way.'

She looked at the table.

'Don't cry.'

'I'm not crying.'

Alan put a laugh into his voice. 'Besides, he might decide to beat me up ...'

Then there were tears, and she told him the rest. The babies she didn't want and the bruises you couldn't see, and when it was over Alan reached for her hand and squeezed, and looked at her hard.

'If he touches you again, I'll kill him.'

She appreciated the gesture but knew it was really no more than that, and she was sad at the hurt she saw in Alan's eyes when she laughed.

Afterwards, Rachel leaned down to pull the sheet back over them. A little shyness had returned, but it was not uncomfortable, or awkward.

'I *would* tell you how great that was,' she said. 'But I don't want you to get complacent.' She turned on her side to face him, and grinned.

'I was lucky to meet you,' he said. 'That day, looking for the ball.'

'Or *un*lucky.'

He shook his head, ran the back of his hand along her ribcage.

'Did you know that a smile can change the world?' she said. 'Do you know about that idea?'

'Sounds like one of those awful self-help things.'

'No, it's just a philosophy really, based around the randomness of everything. How every action has consequences, you know? How it's *connected*.' She closed her eyes. 'You smile at someone at the bus stop and maybe that person's mood changes. They're reminded of a friend they haven't spoken to in a long time and they decide to ring them. This third person, on the other side of the world, answers his mobile phone doing ninety miles an hour on the motorway. He's so thrilled to hear from his old friend that he loses concentration and ploughs into the car in front, killing a man who was on his way to plant a bomb that would have killed a thousand people.'

Alan puffed out his cheeks, let the air out slowly. 'What would have happened if I'd scowled at the bloke at the bus stop?'

Rachel opened her eyes. 'Something else would have happened.'

'Right, like I'd've got punched.'

She laughed, but Alan looked away, his mind quickly elsewhere. 'I want to talk to you later,' he said. 'I want to talk to you tonight.'

She sighed. 'I've told you, it's not possible.'

'After what you told me earlier, I want to call you. I want to know you're OK. There must be a way. I'll call at seven o'clock. Rachel? At exactly seven . . .'

She closed her eyes again, then, fifteen seconds later she nodded slowly.

It was a minute before Alan spoke again. 'Only trouble is, you smile at anyone at a bus stop in London, they think you're a nutter.'

This time they both laughed, then rolled together. Then made love again.

Afterwards they talked about all manner of stuff. Films and football and music.

Nothing that mattered.

Alan lay in bed after Rachel had left and thought about all the things that had been said and done that day. He wanted so much to do something to help her, to make her feel better, but for all his bravado, for all his heroic notions, the best that he could come up with was a present.

He knew straight away what he could give her, and where to find it.

It was in a shoebox at the back of a cupboard stuffed with bundles of letters, a bag of old tools and other odds and sods that he'd collected from his father's place after the old man had died.

Alan hadn't looked at the bracelet in a couple of years, had forgotten the weight of it. It was gold, or so he presumed, and heavy with charms. He remembered the feel of Rachel's body against his fingers – her shoulder-blades and hips – as he ran them around the smooth body of the tiger, the edges of the key, the rims of the tiny train wheels that turned.

After his father's death, Alan had spoken to his mother about the bracelet. He asked her if she knew where it had come from. The skin around her jaw had tightened as she'd said she hardly remembered it, then in the next breath that she wanted nothing to do with the bloody thing.

Alan put two and two together and realised how stupid he'd been. He knew about his father's affairs and guessed that, years before, the bracelet had been a failed peace offering of some sort. It might even have been something that he'd originally bought for one of his mistresses. His father had been a forensic pathologist and Alan was amazed at how a man who exercised such professional skill could be so clumsy when it came to the rest of his life.

It wasn't surprising that his mother had reacted as she had, that she'd wanted no part of the charm bracelet. It had become tainted.

Alan was not superstitious. He sensed that Rachel would like it. He wouldn't give it to her as it was though. He would make it truly hers before he gave it.

He knew exactly what charm he wanted to add.

From Muswell Hill it was a five minute bus ride to Highgate tube. Rachel leaned back against the side of the shelter. Her hair was still wet from the shower she'd taken at Alan's flat.

She'd thought so often about how she might feel afterwards. It had been a vital part of the fantasy, not just with Alan but with other men she'd seen, but never spoken to. The sex had been easy to imagine of course. It had been gentler than she was used to and had lasted longer, but the mechanics were more or less the same. Where she'd been wrong was in imagining the feelings that would come when she'd actually done it. She'd been certain that she'd feel frightened, but she didn't. Fear was familiar to her, and its absence was unmistakable. Heady.

She waited a couple of minutes before giving up on the bus and heading for the station on foot. Had there been anybody else at the bus stop, she might well have smiled at them.

Lee didn't think that he asked too much. Not after a long day talking mortgages to morons and assuring mousey newlyweds that damp was easily sorted. At the end of it, all he wanted was his dinner and some comfort.

He couldn't stand her so fucking cheerful.

Taking off his jacket and tie, opening a beer and asking just what she was so bloody chirpy about . . .

Had she been up to those sodding woods again?

*Yes.*

Who with?

*Don't be silly,* Lee.

Sucking off tramps in the bushes, I'll bet.

Then she'd laughed at him. No outrage like there should have been. No anger at his filthy suggestions, at the stupid suspicions that he'd only half tarted up as a joke.

A jab to the belly and another to the tits had shut her up and put her down on the floor. Now, he straddled her chest, knees pressed down on to her arms, his hands pulling at his own hair in frustration.

'We were going to do the business later on. I was well up for it and tonight could have been the night we did something special. Made a new life.'

'Lee, please . . .'

'You. Fucking. Spoiled. It.'

'We can still do it, Lee. Let's go upstairs now. I'm really horny, Lee.'

He shook his head, disgusted, gathering the spit into his mouth. She knew what was coming, he could see it in her eyes and he waited for her to try and turn her head away as he leaned down and pushed the saliva between his teeth. Instead, she just closed her eyes, and he thought he saw something like a smile as he let a thick string of beery spittle drop slowly down on to her face.

As soon as the seven o'clock news had begun, Alan reached for the phone and dialled the number.

It was answered almost immediately, but nobody spoke.

Alan whispered, realised as soon as he had that he was being stupid. He wasn't the one who needed to be secretive.

'Rachel, it's me . . .'

Suddenly, there was a noise, above the hiss and crackle on the line. It was a guttural sound, that echoed. That took him a few moments to identify. An animal sound; a gulp and a grind, a splutter and a swallow. It was the sound of someone sobbing uncontrollably but trying with every ounce of strength to assert control. Trying desperately not to be heard.

Alan sat up straight, pressed the phone hard to his ear.

'Rachel, I'm here, OK? I'm not going anywhere.'

He watched the comings and goings with something like amusement.

For a fortnight he watched her leave the house in Barnet midmorning, then come home again by late-afternoon. He stayed with her most of the day when he could, saw her meet him in the woods or sometimes go straight to his flat when they couldn't be arsed with preliminaries.

When they wanted to get straight down to it.

He watched her leave the flat, eyes bright and hair wet. The smell of one man scrubbed away before she went home to another.

He wondered if the man he saw climbing into the silver sports car every morning knew that he was a cuckold. On a couple of occasions he thought about popping a note under his windscreen to let him know. Just to stir things up a bit.

He hadn't done because he didn't want to do anything that might disturb the routine. Not now that he was ready to take her. Besides, mischief for its own sake was not his thing at all.

Still, he couldn't help but marvel at the things people got up to.

On the day Alan had hoped to give Rachel the bracelet, his mother tripped on the stairs.

*So many things that could have been different . . .*

Two weeks before, the jeweller had shown him a catalogue. There had been charms that would have carried more or less the same meaning but Alan knew what he wanted. He'd ordered one specially made. He'd decided against the diamond spots and gone for the enamel, but still, it wasn't cheap. He'd thought of it as a dozen decent sessions with one of his private patients. He always thought in those terms whenever he wanted to splash out on something.

A fortnight later, half an hour before he was due to meet Rachel in the woods, he walked out onto Bond Street with the bracelet. Then, his mother called.

'Don't worry, Alan. It's just my ankle, it's nothing.'

A message that said *'come and see me now, if you give a shit . . .'*

He phoned Rachel and left a message of his own. She was probably on her way already, was almost certainly somewhere on the Northern line. He made for the underground himself, steeling himself for the trip to his mother's warden-controlled flat in Swiss Cottage.

As he walked, he realised that his mother would see the bag. It was purple with white cord handles and the name of the jeweller in gold lettering. He couldn't show her the bracelet for obvious reasons.

He decided that if she asked, he'd tell her he'd bought himself a new watch.

Lee wasn't stupid – God, it would all have been a lot easier if he were – but it couldn't be very much longer before he noticed how often she was going to the toilet or taking a shower just before seven o'clock.

She collected her bag on the way upstairs, then, once she'd locked the bathroom door she switched the phone on, set it to *vibrate only*, and waited.

Tonight she was desperate, had been since Alan had failed to meet her at lunchtime. She'd waited in the woods for twenty minutes before she'd got a signal, before the alert had come through. She'd listened to his message once then erased it as always. Walked back towards the tube, unravelling.

Sitting with her back against the side of the bath, she thought there was every chance that he might not ring at all. His excuse for not turning up had sounded very much *like* an excuse. Not that she could blame him for wanting to call a halt to things. She knew how hard it was for him in so many ways.

She almost dropped the phone when it jumped in her hand.

'Where were you?'

'Didn't you get the message? I was at my bloody mother's.'

'I thought you might have made it up.'

'Jesus, Rachel.'

'Sorry . . .'

A sigh. Half a minute of sniffs and swallows.

'God, I wish I could see you,' he said. 'Now, I mean. I've got something for you. I wanted to give it to you this afternoon.'

'I'd like to see you too.'

'Can you?'

The hope in his voice clutched at her. 'There might be a way.'

'By the tree in half an hour. The woods don't shut until eight.'

'I'll try . . .'

When she'd hung up she dialled another number. She spoke urgently for a minute, then hung up again. When she heard the land-line ringing a few moments later she flushed the toilet and stepped out of the bathroom.

Lee was holding the phone out for her when she walked into the lounge. She took it and spoke, hoped he could hear the shock and concern in her voice despite the fact that he hadn't bothered to turn the television down.

'That was Sue,' she said afterwards. 'Her brother's been in a car accident. Some idiot talking on his mobile phone, ploughed into the back of him on the motorway. I said I'd go round.'

Lee's team had been awarded a penalty. Without turning round to her, he waved his consent.

He was astonished to see her leave the house alone at night. The husband did of course, jumped in his sports car every so often to collect a takeaway or shoot down to the off license, but never *her*.

He'd been planning to do it during the day; he knew the quiet places now, the dead spots en route where he could take her with very little risk, but he wasn't a man to look a gift horse in the mouth.

This was perfect, and he was as ready as he'd ever be.

He presumed she'd be heading for the tube at High Barnet. He got out of his car and followed her.

It took Alan ten minutes to get to the woods. By half past seven he'd got everything arranged.

He hadn't wanted to just give her the bracelet. He'd wanted her to come across it, to find it as if by some piece of good fortune. Luck had played such a big part in their coming together after all, which is why he'd chosen the charm that he had. There was only really one place that he could leave it.

The light was fading fast. The few people he saw were all moving towards one or other of the various exits. He dialled her number.

'It's me. You're probably still on the tube. Listen, come to the tree but don't worry if you can't see me. I'll be nearby, but there's something I want you to find first. Stand where the ball was found, then look up. OK? I'll see you soon . . .'

He moved away from the tree so that he could watch from a distance when she discovered the bracelet. It worried him that it would soon be too dark to see the expression on her face when she found it. He sat down, leaned back against a stump to wait.

It was the away leg of a big European tie and one-up at half time was a very decent result.

Lee was at the fridge, digging out snacks for the rest of the game when the car alarm went off. That fucking Saab across the road again – he'd told the tosser to get it looked at once. The wailing stopped after a couple of minutes, but started up again almost immediately and Lee knew that uninterrupted enjoyment of the second half had gone out of the window.

He picked up his keys and stormed out of the front door. The pratt was out by the looks of it, but Lee fancied giving his motor a kick or two anyway. He might come back afterwards, grab some paper and stick a non-too subtle note through the wanker's letterbox. Maybe a piece of dogshit for good measure.

Rachel's phone was lying on the tarmac half way down the drive.

Lee picked it up and switched it on. The leather case had protected it and the screen lit up immediately.

He entered the security code and waited.

There was a message.

Rachel had realised her phone was missing as soon as she came out of the station. She knew Alan would be worried that she'd taken so long and had reached for the phone to see if he'd left a message. A balloon of sickness had risen up rapidly from her guts, and she'd begun running, silently cursing the selfish idiot who'd thrown himself on to the line at East Finchley, then feeling bad about it.

A few minutes into the woods and still a few more from where Alan would be waiting. It was almost dark and she hadn't seen anyone since she left the road. She looked at her watch – the exits would close in ten minutes. She knew that people climbed over fences to get in – morons who lit bonfires and played 'chase me' with the keepers – so it wouldn't be impossible to get out, but she still didn't fancy being inside after the woods were locked up.

She thought about shouting Alan's name out; it was so quiet that the sound would probably carry. She was being stupid.

Still out of breath, she picked up her pace again, looking up at the noise of feet falling heavily on the path ahead, and seeing the jogger coming towards her.

Alan rang again, hung up as soon as he heard her voice on the answering machine.

He looked at his watch, leaned his head back against the bark. He could hear the distant drone of the traffic and, closer, the shrill peep of the bats that had begun to emerge from their boxes to feed. Moving above him like scraps of burnt paper on the breeze.

He slowed as he passed her, jogged on a stride or two then backed quickly up to draw level with her again. She froze, and he could see the fear in her face.

'Rachel?' he said.

She stared at him, still wary but with curiosity getting the better of her.

'I met you a few weeks ago in the pub,' he said. 'With Alan.' Her eyes didn't move from his. 'Graham. The cardiologist?'

'Oh, God. Graham ... right, of course.'

She laughed and her shoulders sagged as the tension vanished.

He laughed too, and reached around to the belt he wore beneath the jogging bottoms. Felt for the knife.

'Sorry,' she said. 'I think my brain's going. I'm a bit bloody jumpy to tell you the truth.'

He nodded but he wasn't really listening. He span slowly around, hand on hip. catching his breath. Checking that there was no-one else around.

'Well . . .' she said.

He'd have her in the bushes in seconds, the knife pressed to her throat before she had a chance to open her mouth.

He saw her check her watch.

It's time, he thought.

'Rachel!'

He looked up and saw the shape of a big man moving fast towards them. She looked at the shape, then back to him, her mouth open and something unreadable in her eyes.

He dug out a smile. 'Nice to see you again,' he said.

With the blade of the knife flat against his wrist, he turned and jogged away along the path that ran at right-angles to the one they'd been on.

'Was that him? Was that him?'

'He was a jogger. He just—'

Lee's hand squeezed her neck, choked off the end of the sentence. He raised his other hand slowly, held the phone aloft in triumph. 'I know all about it,' he said. 'So don't try and lie to me.'

There were distant voices coming from somewhere. People leaving. Laughter. Words that were impossible to make out and quickly faded to silence.

Lee tossed the phone to the ground and the free hand reached up to claw at her chest. Thick fingers pushed aside material, found a nipple and squeezed.

She couldn't make a sound. The tears ran down her face and neck and on to the back of his hand as she beat at it, as she snatched in breaths through her nose. Just as she felt her legs go, he released her neck and breast and raised both hands up to the side of her neck.

'Lee, nothing happened. Lee . . .'

He pressed the heels of his hands against her ears and leaned in close as though he might kiss, or bite her.

'What's his name?'

She tried to shake her head but he held it hard.

'Or so help me I'll dig a hole for you with my bare hands. I'll leave your carcass here for the foxes.'

So she told him, and he let her go, and he shouted over his shoulder to her as he walked further into the woods.

'Now, run home . . .'

Alan had given it one more minute ten minutes ago, but it was clear to him now that she wasn't coming. She'd sounded like she was really going to try, so he decided that she hadn't been able to get away.

He hoped it was only fear that had restrained her.

He stood up, pressed the redial button on his phone one last time. Got her message again.

There were no more than a couple of minutes before the exits were sealed. He just had time to retrieve the bracelet, to reach up and unhook it from the branch on which it hung.

He'd give it to her another day.

Standing alone in the dark, wondering how she was, he decided that he might not draw her attention to the newest charm on the bracelet. A pair of dice had seemed so right, so appropriate in light of what had happened, of everything they'd talked about. Suddenly he felt every bit as clumsy as his father. It seemed tasteless.

Luck was something they were pushing.

He stepped out on to the path, turned when he heard a man's voice say his name . . .

*The footwork and the swing were spot on.*

The first blow smashed Alan's phone into a dozen or more pieces, the second did much the same to his skull and those that came after were about nothing so much as exercise.

It took half a minute for the growl to die in Lee's throat.

The blood on the branch, on the grass to either side of the path, on his training shoes, looked black in the near total darkness.

Lee bent down and picked up the dead man's arm. He wondered if his team had managed to hold on to their one goal lead as he began dragging the body into the undergrowth.

\*

Graham had run until he felt his lungs about to give up the ghost. He was no fitter than many of those he treated. Those whose hearts were marbled with creamy lines of fat, like cheap off-cuts.

He dropped down on to a bench to recover, to reflect on what had happened in the woods. To consider his rotten luck. If that man hadn't come along when he had . . .

A young woman with Mediterranean features was waiting to cross the road a few feet from where he was sitting. She was taking keys from her bag, probably heading towards the flats opposite.

She glanced in his direction and he dropped his elbows to his knees almost immediately. Looked at the pavement. Made sure she didn't get a good look at his face.

The next High Barnet train was still eight minutes away.

Rachel stood on the platform, her legs still shaking, the burning in her breast a little less fierce with every minute that passed. The pain had been good. It had stopped her thinking too much; stopped her wondering. She sought a little more of it, thrusting her hand into her pocket until she found her wedding ring, then driving the edge of it hard against the fingernail until she felt it split.

Alan had thought it odd that she still took the ring off even after she'd told him the truth, but it made perfect sense to her. Its removal had always been more about freedom than deceit.

An old woman standing next to her nudged her arm and nodded toward the electronic display.

*Correction. High Barnet. 1 min . . .*

'There's a stroke of luck,' the woman said.

Rachel looked at the floor. She didn't raise her head again until she heard the train coming.

New from **Mark Billingham**
and My Darling Clementine

Available on CD and download
from 21 May 2015